Praise for *Winter's Myths*

WOW is Greenwood's approach original. I love what *Winter's Myths* had to say... about the necessity of story-telling... about the pitfalls of being afraid of the world at large... about what it means to define yourself as human or otherwise. It's so rare that I read something that feels special to me... and *Winter's Myths* felt special.

— JONATHAN EDWARD DURHAM, AWARD WINNING AUTHOR OF *WINTERSET HOLLOW*

Greenwood's post-apocalyptic cast inhabits a world of wonders, where what is commonplace to the reader becomes dark, magical, treacherous... and miraculous. He leavens terror with whimsy. His work is visionary, one of the most original voices in the genre in this new century.

— S.P. SOMTOW, WORLD FANTASY AWARD WINNING AUTHOR OF *THE BIRD CATCHER*

Winter's Myths forces you to abandon your expectations and run with the weirdness, and you'll want to... It's wound with a thread of terror and mystery that keeps you scouring the story for answers, characters that will keep you coming back, and rich descriptions that unnerve, endear, and terrify.

— JUSTINE MANZANO, AUTHOR OF *THE ORDER OF THE KEY*

Greenwood has masterfully woven a tale ripe with suspense, quirky WTF moments, and dystopian despair that will keep your jaw dropped to the floor so much that you'll end up with a linoleum imprint on your chin…Action, suspense, loss, love, and characters that will live in your head long after the words pass by your eyes. Do NOT miss this.

— JAE MAZER, AWARD WINNING AUTHOR OF
MR. PICKET BLACKMAW

Winter's Myths dances through genres at breakneck speeds, inundates you with unbridled comedic and fantastic absurdities one moment, and reverts to a grounded tale of survival by the next breath… Greenwood nails it all down into a streamlined, cohesive masterpiece, packed to the brim with philosophical soundness, rock solid dialogue, and heartfelt thematic power. I'm in love with this story.

— ANDREW L. HICKS, AUTHOR OF *THE ART OF BEING HUMAN*

Winter's Myths

SEASON ONE

GAGE GREENWOOD

TANNER'S SWITCH PUBLISHING

Gage Greenwood

Contents

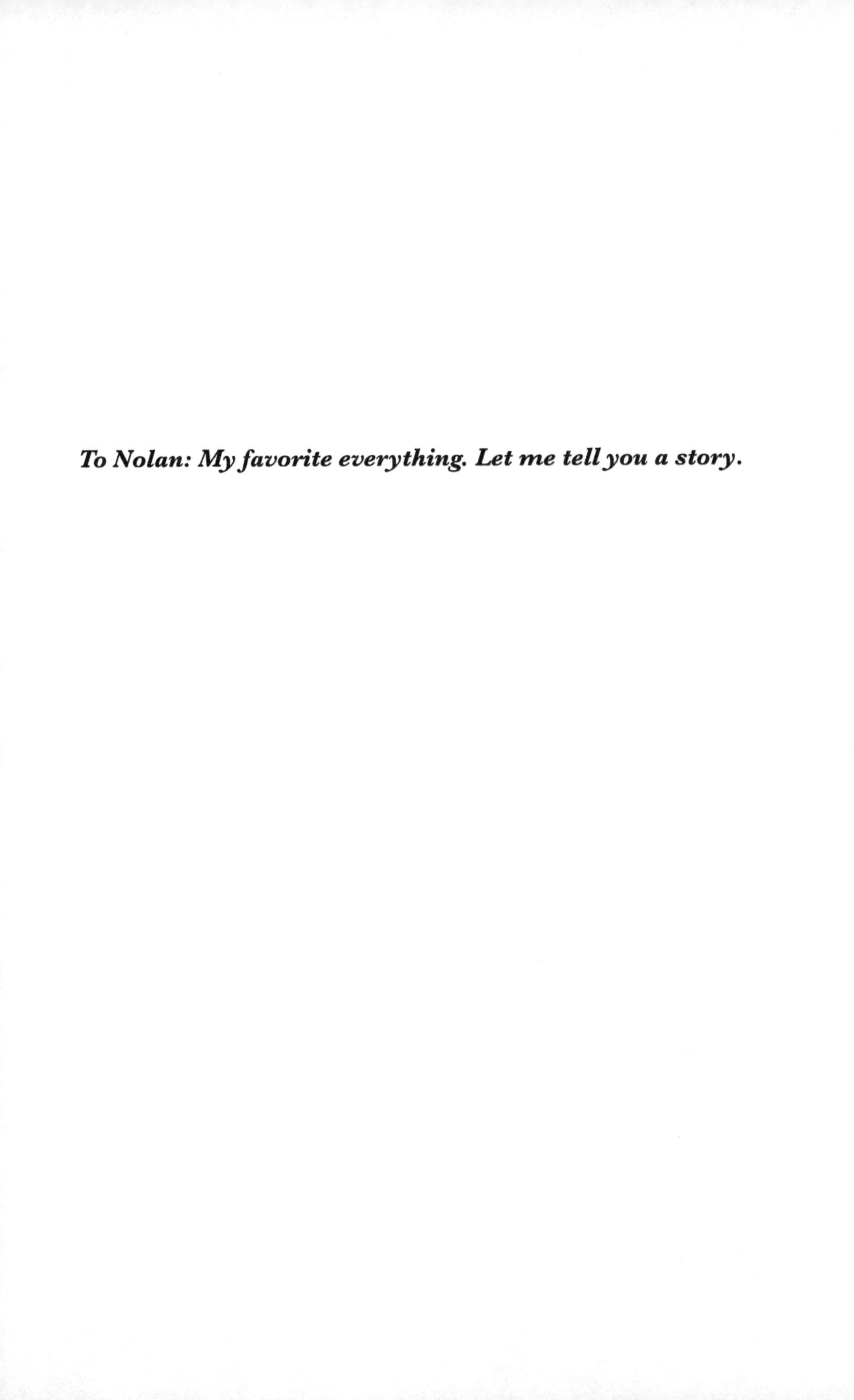

To Nolan: My favorite everything. Let me tell you a story.

CHAPTER 1
In the Beginning

In the beginning, darkness.

A big bang.

Winter's shoulder slammed into the concrete slab once more and, with a low crunch, the slab separated from the wall.

"Run!" his mother had said.

Winter's daughters, Violin and Candlestick, caught their breath behind him; uneven, shivery breaths.

Winter gripped the concrete, jamming his fingers into divots wherever he could find them, pulling, grunting. His shoulder throbbed. His heart punched.

Run. Run to where? What existed outside their world other than death?

He dug his feet into the soft gravel, heaved, and the concrete moaned as it opened its mouth.

A raging, tumbling noise like an eternal thunder pushed through the narrow opening, and the whiteness pouring in swallowed everything. He held a scream as it bleached his eyes.

On the first day, light.

CHAPTER 2

The Belly of a New World

It blinded them. Brutal light. Winter dropped his bag and put one hand over his eyes. With his other hand, he slashed around himself, searching for his daughters.

He gripped an arm. Candlestick's. He knew by the small size.

He rattled his fingertips against her skin, speaking in rapid taps. They called it the language of fear, used when silence was necessary. Usually, they communicated this way by tapping their fingers against their own hips, the receiver of the conversation reading the taps from a distance. But now, blinded, Winter tapped roughly against Candlestick's flesh, ensuring she knew what he was saying.

"Use both hands. One on sister. One on me. Do not let go. Do not let go. Do not let go." He tapped the last sentence, repeatedly, until she responded.

Pinky, long tap. Pinky, long tap. "Okay. Okay."

The rough, thunderous noise continued to roar in front of him and without sight, he could only presume what caused it. All the horror stories he'd been told as a child came flooding back into his mind.

At seven years old, Winter had snuck to the forbidden hall leading to the cement slab and just as he reached it, his mother grabbed him, brought him into her arms, and squeezed him into her chest. "Do not go near here. Everything outside of that door is pain, or worse. The only thing the upper world does is kill."

Winter separated his fingers, allowing the light to hit his eyes. He needed them to adjust quickly. Who knew what threats approached, masked by fiery light and belching thunder?

He stepped forward and back again, unwilling to exit without his senses. Slowly, the surroundings outside the slab took form, blurring into shapes and outlines. Jutting stones. His feet left the safety of their home, the only place they'd ever known, and entered the world above. The place of demons.

Earth.

He pressed his palms against the wall of stones, using it as a guide. Violin's hands left his shirt, and then Candlestick's hands released, too.

"Violin!" He tapped against his hip, fingertips cracking from the force.

The noise surrounded him, powerful crashes. He'd never heard such a loud sound, so deep and angry it hurt his brain. He forgot the taps and screamed, "Violin! Candlestick!"

"Daddy. Here," Violin yelled.

Her voice came from the same place as the volatile sound. He turned toward it, still unable to make it out, but he saw his daughters, their silhouettes bent low, examining something.

"Daddy!" she yelled louder.

"Do not talk out loud," he shouted with the same weight in his voice that she had used.

His eyes continued to adjust as he approached them, their outlines turning into colorful blobs, which grew more defined the closer he came.

Water. The loudness came from water, and so much of it. He'd been told of a place where water raged. It was where they got their electricity, his uncle had told him, but he could never picture it. If they used water for electricity, there didn't seem to be much for them otherwise. In the underworld, it trickled in from old pipes, sometimes taking twenty minutes to fill a tub.

Here, enough water to drown their entire community gushed down a stone wall every second. It never ended, never weakened, never slowed. It just poured and crashed down the bank.

Violin and Candlestick leaned toward it, cupping their hands into it as it flowed past them.

Violin grabbed Winter's forearm and tapped. "Have you seen water so big?"

"No." One soft tap with his index finger.

"It's so fast."

Candlestick reached in and took a handful, slapping it against her face and laughing. *Amazing*, he thought, *that children can find wonder during grief. How, after seeing death and horror, could they smile?*

"Careful," he said, pulling her back away from the edge.

When she turned to him, a smile grew across her face. He hadn't seen her smile like that in a long time.

"It's water, Dad." She spoke out loud, but softly, gently. "Just water."

He bent down, knees cracking, and put his hands out, letting the water skim the bottoms of his fingers. His heart raced.

"It's just water," Candlestick repeated.

"It's forceful. It's dangerous."

"It's just water."

"Nothing is *just* up here. It's always dangerous."

"It's fun," she said, her voice sinking as her face deflated.

He wanted to relax, to let her play, to give her ten minutes to forget they had just lost everything they knew and loved. As far as he knew, it was just water, but it terrified him. "It's too much."

He stood, realizing he had let the water take his mind off everything else around them. Humans could be here. Threats from all angles.

As he scanned his surroundings, the overbearing fear left him and replaced itself with a deep panic, the kind that rattled in his chest and squeezed his lungs. The fear was good, productive even. This new panic threatened to shut him down entirely. He had fantasized about this world, feared it, dreamed of touching its danger, but now that he stepped into it, and danger hadn't presented itself, all he felt was dread.

A forest of trees loomed across the waterway, more still above the cliffs behind them and from the walls where the water fell. Trees everywhere. He knew of trees, had listened intently as his mother talked about them. Nature had been one of the few upper world things she would discuss, but even that required prying. Knowing of trees meant nothing now that he saw them lined around him like humongous fingers. He and his daughters sat in a palm; any minute, the Earth could make a fist and crush them.

The colors! All over, the colors so much deeper than anything he'd ever seen.

Bright blue hovering over them, a red and orange forest floor, sprinkles of green on some of the tree branches, even the drab ochre dirt had more vibrancy than anything underground. And that disc. The bright, blinding disc in the sky. *What was it?*

Candlestick noticed him staring at it, and she asked, "What is it?"

"It's a fire in the sky. It keeps us warm."

Violin and Candlestick moved to his side, and with him, looked around at the open landscape.

"Stay close to me," Winter said as he turned toward the hole they'd just exited. A small protrusion peeked from the cliff, ending with the stone slab, now removed by Winter's hands. Their home. Strange to see from the outside, so unassuming. Just a hole, hollow and dark.

He walked back to it, touched the hole's frame, and rubbed his hand down the stone. An empty cavern now. Violin and Candlestick whispered behind him. Empty indeed.

"Let's move," he said as he picked up his bag.

He asked the children to latch onto his shirt. They followed the water until their home was out of view and they were swallowed whole into the belly of a new world.

CHAPTER 3

Everything Will Eat You

They walked until the cliff lowered and opened into a sprawling field of dirt and yellow grass. In the underworld, they had exercised by training for multiple hours a day in self-defense, evasion, and silent maneuvering, but their bodies were ill prepared for hours of walking and the monotonous motions in the leg muscles. Nagging blisters formed on Winter's Achilles Tendon. His daughters started their trek by marching their legs in big, exaggerated steps, but now, their feet dragged against the ground and their shoulders slumped.

In the field, they paused, Winter giving the children time to play in the grass. "Quietly," he said. As Violin and Candlestick plucked blades of grass from the ground, Winter took in everything around him, studying the details, looking for traps, threats, expecting all of it to grow teeth.

Violin and Candlestick had lost their giggles, but Winter still awed at their steel emotions. Eventually, he knew they'd cry, they'd breakdown, but now they focused on adapting. *Did fear cage their other emotions, or was the tragedy too massive for them to comprehend?*

The grass left red welts on the kids' legs, and he wondered if even that could be harmful. It was too chilly for them to be wearing their dresses anyway.

He plopped his bag down and as he fished through it for their pants, something moved along the trees that fenced in the field. A large, black thing.

Winter stood slowly but tapped rapidly. "Do not move!"

Violin and Candlestick went still.

The lump moved closer but stuck to the tree line. This was the first living creature he'd seen on Earth and it did not disappoint in both its beauty and its ability to strike him with panic. His mother had warned him that the creatures on Earth were bigger than any he saw in the underworld—the rats, raccoons, and squirrels—but she did not express how massive, did not prepare him for monsters larger than even him.

It lumbered closer and Winter made out its form. Its fat, furry body swayed as the creature stepped forward. It stuck its snout into the grass, searching and smelling.

"What is it?" Violin asked.

Winter put his finger to his lip and with the other hand tapped, "Danger."

During training, they sometimes had to stand still for hours at a time, practicing the art of silence and, as his uncle called it, 'turning into a wall.' The tapping language, the stillness lessons, these skills were drilled into Winter his entire life, and to his daughters after him, but only now did they come into practice. It was easy to stand still in the face of imaginary danger, another thing entirely to see a threat's bulbous body moving toward them.

The creature turned to look at them, only fifteen feet away now, and Winter stiffened. Violin and Candlestick's breathing intensified but they followed their lessons well, keeping still, quieting even the fastest of breaths.

Time slowed as the beast stared at them. Every muscle tensed and tightened in Winter's body. And then, the creature yawned and moved along, uninterested in them.

They remained still until the monster had moved a great distance away.

"We are too skinny," Winter tapped. "No meat."

Candlestick giggled, and he regretted instigating noise, but the creature didn't turn back. It had made up its mind and Winter was thankful for it.

Violin tapped at her side and pointed to the sky. "What is that?"

A glowing orb hovered behind the naked tree branches, blurry like a lightbulb behind a shade. He turned toward the other disc, which now faded behind the horizon.

Violin followed his stare. "Look. It's going away and it's getting colder. You were right, Papa."

"Yes."

"What will happen when it's gone?"

"I don't know," he said, trying to hide his concern.

"Will it ever come back? Is it leaving forever?"

"I don't know."

"And if that one gives us heat, what does the other one do?" Violin turned back to the blurry, glowing orb.

"I will tell you later. We must keep moving."

He tossed them both a pair of pants. As they dressed, he thought of his mother hemming the fuzzy pants a few months ago. She had worried about using too much electricity during the winter months, so she prepared for the cold season by making bundles of warm clothes, unknowing how little any of it would matter.

He didn't know what they were moving toward. They had no destination, no plan, no idea what type of shelter might exist on Earth. This was a world they never expected to step on, let alone live on, so for all their preparing and training, they were ill-equipped to navigate it. Their lives were built and fine-tuned to withstand invasion, not to invade. They were born sentries with nothing left to guard.

Winter grabbed his children's hands and guided them toward the woods. The area scared him. He didn't like the shrouded nature of it, but he also worried about being out in the open. Yes, something could hide amongst all those trees, but amongst those trees, his family could hide, too.

They walked until the glowing orb rose further, nearing the tops of the trees. Winter began to understand the orbs. One for daytime, and one for sleep time. They were notifications.

Every time they heard rustling or movement, they panicked, ducked, hid. It slowed them down and frayed their already weary minds.

Besides the giant black beast in the field, they'd only encountered smaller creatures, furry little things, skittish and fragile, but as far as Winter knew, *the only thing the upper world did was kill.* Who knew if these little animals had poisonous bites?

They kept moving. The blinding disc all but disappeared beyond the horizon, and with it, not only warmth, but light. The new disc didn't provide either. Winter clutched his children's hands as they walked, creating a human rope. "Do not let go. I can't see you well, so I need to feel you. I need to know you're here."

The darkness grew relentless and the rustling grew louder. The nighttime creatures were bigger than their daytime counterparts. Even in the darkness, he caught glimpses of them. One had frail legs, but massive, evil horns. As startling as the creature was, Winter and the kids refrained from screaming, another thing to thank their training for, but Candlestick's fingernails sunk deeper into her father's palm. The beast may have been bigger than the daytime things, but it was equally skittish. When Winter's foot slipped off a tree root and made loud, crunching noises in a pile of leaves, the horned thing ran with speed Winter would have never guessed possible.

Candlestick pointed out small dots in the sky. She asked about them but Winter dismissed her questions, too concerned about where they were going, what dangers lurked around them, and what they would do next.

"They make shapes if you connect them," Candlestick said. "Those look like Mamma."

A pang landed in Winter's throat, tears forming in his eyes. He gulped and shook away the memory of blood dripping from his wife's mouth.

Eventually, the path led them to a long wooden barricade, but a poorly designed one. The wood pieces were skinny, and there were sizable gaps between them.

"What was this made to block?" Winter tapped.

He peeked through the cracks.

"What do you see Papa?"

"Hard to say." He pushed his daughters closer. "I think it might be a shelter."

"Can we stay there?"

"I don't know. What if something already does?"

CHAPTER 4

The Water Thief

Winter cracked a board and ripped it off the barrier. He crawled through into a square area of impossibly green grass that practically glowed against the charcoal air around it. In front of him, a big shelter made of stones and wood loomed. The structure had windows, but Winter couldn't see through them. It was too dark on both sides.

He instructed Violin and Candlestick to hide in the wooden barricade's corner while he approached the door.

Peeking in, Winter saw nothing. He put his hand on the knob, took a deep breath, and turned.

The door groaned and Winter retreated, backing off about five feet. He waited for a response, but none came.

After a moment, he entered.

It *was* a home, he decided, but the oddest objects filled it.

A rectangular black box perched on top of a shelving unit. Under it, smaller black boxes sat on shelves. They had wires traveling to the bigger box, to each other, and to the wall. Winter noted the strange words on the objects: Sony on the frame of the black rectangle, Roku on a small object wired to it.

Winter knew electricity, understood it on a fundamental level, but this setup made no sense. He had read many books on the subject. In fact, the only books he had ever read were children's books or ones about electricity. His mother had noticed his desire to understand it when he was just a child when she caught him fiddling with his uncle's generators.

"Your uncle will train you to make those machines function. Would you like that?"

He nodded. "I like the way it rumbles."

And so began his destiny as the electrician of their community. He had built hundreds of small generators, repaired old ones, and handed them off to his uncle, who left the community to place them where they needed to go. Thinking of his uncle and mother brought a bubble of grief into his throat. He released it with a sigh and moved on.

Books. Furniture. A weird, cushioned thing that looked like a chair, but was longer than a bed. *For sitting or sleeping?*

Still no sign of life.

He made his way up a flight of stairs, cringing every time his silent movements met creaky wood. In the bedroom, he peeked out the window to check on the kids. They hung in the corner, Candlestick touching everything in reach, Violin studying the environment.

He kept searching.

One room in the middle of the hall caught his attention. The floor, the walls, and the objects were all white. It had pipes and a hard chair, also white. The chair opened, and inside was a bowl of water.

He had no time to figure out the purpose of these things. He left the room and moved on to clear the rest of the rooms before waving the girls in.

Outside the front window, the house had a square section of more bright, green grass. The green ended where a cement path sliced one side of houses with another side. Houses everywhere. Shelters. *Could humans live in any of them?* He wanted to believe they'd gone extinct. His mother said billions of them lived on this planet, but he hadn't seen one. They must be gone, right?

Directly across from his new shelter, a small section of woods separated two houses. This little segment of forest, shadowy and thick, sent a chill down Winter's spine. So close, so ripe with opportunity for threats. A million eyes watching, and Winter wouldn't have a clue.

On his signal, the girls ran in. He yelled at them to be careful and not to touch anything, but they didn't listen. Instead, they found light switches in each room, and clicked them up and down. None of them worked.

Violin charged upstairs, Candlestick following close behind. Meanwhile, Winter checked boxes under the large thing called Sony. He followed the wires and tried to figure out the point of their connection, what they could have done.

The girls screamed. Winter ran, his heart gunning.

He found them in the white room, Candlestick giggling.

"Don't scream if you don't mean it. Don't scream unless you need help." He wasn't tapping and he wasn't whispering.

"Sorry, but look." Candlestick shook her hand at her sister, telling her to do something.

Violin pushed down on a lever attached to the white chair. The water inside the bowl swirled around and drained down.

"It steals the water," Violin whispered.

"No," Winter said. "We need water."

Water trickled back into the bowl, and now Winter laughed with surprise.

"What is this thing?"

He pressed the button, and the water swirled down, but this time it didn't come back. "Did I break it? Shit."

After they experimented with objects in the house, they all gathered in the room with the rectangle box. A stone column in the room had burnt wood clustered in the bottom, and Winter figured it was a place to light a fire and warm the house, so he broke pieces from the outside barricade and piled them in the room. After he made a fire, he and the girls cuddled on the long chair thing.

"What's that?" Violin asked, while she reached toward a shelf and grabbed a small box. It looked like a book, but smaller. Winter took it and tried to open it, but it didn't open like a book. After some finagling, it popped open. A series of discs dropped out. They were strange things, silver, but when moved, a rainbow streaked across them.

Rainbows. Another thing his mother had told him about. After she mentioned streaks of color in the sky, Winter cried, wishing he could see them. His mother said, "A rainbow can be anywhere." She took a series of drab colored clothing and placed them next to each other. "See," she said. He pretended to be impressed with the line of grays and browns.

Here, seeing the bright colors glide across the disc, his eyes watered all over again.

The pictures on the front of the discs showed the same man in different disguises. In one, he was wearing a giant white suit with a goofy bubbled helmet. In another, he wore tight clothing while in mid-dance. In some, he was young, others old, but always different. Different hair, facial hair, glasses, no glasses. But always the same man. Yet not the same at all.

The front cover read: The Kevin Bacon Collection.

"Who is that?" Candlestick asked.

Winter sighed, examining the pictures, flipping through the discs, noting the man and his various disguises.

"Who is it?" She repeated.

"This is Kevin Bacon, the demigod. I will tell you a good night story." Winter pulled them closer. Before he began, he gave one last glance out the window toward the dark, wooded area.

CHAPTER 5

Kevin Bacon: Demigod

Three gods watched over the Earth. Azerka, the goddess of darkness, she who monitored the shadows. Beelza, goddess of light, she who monitored the currents. Orelon, he who served the two goddesses and punished as they saw fit.

The gods created the humans, gave them all they needed to survive, and cherished hovering above them as their weak mortal bodies toiled and suffered. There was glory in omniscient sight when such vision couldn't be returned.

The power of the gods was vast. A finger here, gently pressed to the wind, and an entire population could disappear. A whistle for a flood, a wink for an earthquake. Watch them grow, those puny little humans, and tear the growth asunder, broken down until nothing but a morsel remained. Still, always, the humans rebuilt. It was their nature to suffer, to build, always aiming for an unnamed goal, for something that didn't exist, but that they assured themselves did. Oh, the goddesses watched in wonder at the spectacular hope that man survived on. They drank it, swallowed it, slept in it. The goddesses wondered how many times they could wipe it from the humans' faces. Always, it returned. Always.

And for this, the goddesses loved humans. For their endless

enjoyment of human hope. Hope was a noose, a gift given to the goddesses by humankind. "Here, I give you my life, and allow you to strangle at your will."

Without hope, the goddesses wielded only one weapon: murder. And what fun would that be?

Orelon loved the humans for a different reason. While he was often the one to deliver punishment, he found no joy in it. He hated their resilience, and wished they were more breakable, less... pliable.

What he loved, however, was their scent. They made the most noxious odors from their bodies, their mouths, from deep within their pores. They stunk. The heavens smelled like fruits, and that was nice for a while, but once a cloud of human filth enveloped him, the nastiness of putrid funk left the fruit smells wanting.

He snuck to the world whenever he could, floating around unaware humans, smelling them.

One day, he lingered around a farmhouse, looking for scents. Farms were notorious for offensive odors.

A man stood in front of a pile of lumber. He held two discs in his hands and spun them with absurd speed.

Orelon smirked. "Well well, human. Where did you find those skills?" He whispered.

The man drove a spinning disc through the wood, chopping off clean, even pieces. Flecks of wood pieces poured through the air.

"How are you doing this?"

The man turned and released a disc. It shot out of his hands and blazed by Orelon's head, driving straight through a large oak tree. Orelon stiffened, startled into a frozen shell. He shrieked as the disc flew past his face yet again and back into the man's grasp.

Orelon's heart raced, and for once, boredom escaped his body.

"What are you doing here?" The man asked. "Get off my property."

Orelon mumbled and shook his head, as if he could rattle the shock out of his brain. "You can see me?"

"Of course I can see you. What are you doing here? Who are you?"

"What is your name?" Orelon asked with a dry throat.

"You're on my property. I asked you first."

Orelon smiled, remembering himself. Yes, this man had talents beyond any mortal Orelon had ever witnessed, but he still confronted a god.

So, Orelon vanished and reappeared behind the man, hoping to send a chill up the unlucky fellow's spine. "You asked first, but I answer to no one."

The man spun and threw a disc. Orelon disappeared again, but not before the blade touched his cheek, making a small cut.

When he emerged behind the man a second time, he learned, too late, the man had predicted Orelon's movements. The strange human had already thrown the second disc, which slashed Orelon's ear on its way back to the human's hand. Blood trickled from his cheek on one side, and his ear on the other. Pain! Glorious pain. He'd forgotten how wonderful it felt.

They were warning shots, he understood. The man toyed with him. As a god, a little pain brought joy, but taunting? Well, that enraged him.

"Are you a demon?' The man asked.

"Are you a god?" Orelon asked in return.

"Yes. Now answer me."

"Then, it's about time you discovered gods and demons are the same."

"Who are you?"

"I am everything."

"And I am Kevin Bacon, and you will submit to me."

Orelon put his hands up playfully, mockingly. "You win, mortal. But you must tell me how you gained such extraordinary skills."

"I told you, I am a god."

Orelon laughed. "Talented, sure. Quicker than any human I have ever seen, but gods create life and death. They give you the light and the darkness. You are no god."

Kevin Bacon launched his disc into the sky. It flew away from them, but instead of shrinking with distance, it grew until it landed in the heavens. He flicked his wrist, and the disc caught fire.

"There, now I have created light. We won't be needing yours anymore."

"Impossible."

Kevin Bacon swiped his arm down and the disc disappeared beyond the horizon. "And now, I give my people darkness."

Orelon lost his curiosity to the spirit of competition and threw his own arms up, flailing them above his head. A rainbow appeared. "And I give you colors."

Kevin Bacon threw the second disc into the sky, and it captured the rainbow before landing back in his hands. "And I steal them."

Orelon snapped his fingers. "You like your orbs in the sky?" A white, glowing ball appeared in the darkness above. "Mine will watch you. It is my sight, and it will remind you every night that I am here, keeping track of you. It is my eye."

Kevin Bacon frowned. He waved his hand. The sky gained thousands of tiny dots. "And these are all my eyes. Always watching you, everywhere."

"A human can't do these things. Not unless..."

"Unless he isn't a human at all. I learned that when I was a child. When I listened to you up in the heavens whispering about us. When I felt you landing on our world to cause pain and destruction. I know who you are. I've always known. But you? Do you know who Saria Gray is?"

"No. I don't waste my time learning the names of mortals."

"Saria was a friend of mine as a child. We walked together to school. She was an artist who made the most amazing paintings of our village. She knew of my skills, and instead of judgement only offered me praise. And then she died from a tree falling. A tree falling! Can you believe that?"

Orelon shrugged, boredom working its way back into his bones.

"I thought these were the ways of the Earth until I heard you discussing it with your sisters in the sky. Your whispers were always rattling in my skull, driving me nuts. I blocked them out whenever I could, lest I go insane. But that night, I listened, hoping to hear you bring her name to your lips, needing to know why you would take an innocent nine-year-old girl from the world. And what did I find out?"

Orelon put up a hand, showing his palm. "I don't know. You discovered how unimportant you are to me?"

"Yes. And that Saria's death brought you joy. You and your sick siblings killed her for a laugh. Gods? No, you are demons, no matter what you call yourselves." Kevin Bacon cracked his knuckles. "You focused too much on the girl, though. Your attention needed to be on me, because from that moment forward, I planned for the day I could kill you." He snapped his finger, and a new disc appeared in his hand. "That day is here."

Azerka and Beelza appeared behind Kevin Bacon.

"What is happening to our sky?" Beelza asked.

"Friendly competition." Kevin Bacon let a smile crawl up one cheek.

"Between whom?" Azerka stepped forward.

"Between he, a god, and me, a mere mortal."

The two women laughed and Azerka asked what the mortal did to compete with a god.

Orelon straightened, unsure how best to proceed. The conversation moved closer to revelations that would cause him immense pain and punishment.

"No competition at all. Let us leave this man." He stepped forward, ushering the goddesses to follow.

"You think we don't notice that the man sees us, Orelon?" Azerka had too much calm in her voice.

No turning back now.

"I am no man, ma'am. I am a god." Kevin Bacon lifted his hands and twisted his finger until all the dots in the sky shifted, moving into the outlines of pictures, warriors, and animals, flailing through the abyss.

Both women stared in awe. Azerka shot a glare at her brother, and with a clenched jaw, marched toward him. "How is this possible, Orelon? What did you do?"

Orelon floated backwards. "You don't understand. She was wonderful. She smelled so human."

Azerka grabbed his wrist. "You will suffer for this, brother."

"Wait a minute. Are you my father?" Kevin Bacon chimed in.

"Ah, I see you have the brains of a god, too, dummy. How'd you piece that puzzle together?" Orelon smirked.

"Well, once you mentioned the smell, I knew who you were talking about."

Orelon waved his arm at Kevin Bacon while looking at the goddesses: *See?*

The goddesses grabbed him. "We are leaving."

"Wait, don't you think I should join you guys? I am a god, after all. We've established that, correct?"

Beelza sighed and grabbed Kevin Bacon's arm. "Fine, let's go."

They flew to the heavens, where war would soon begin.

CHAPTER 6

An Awful Taste

Winter searched for food while the children slept. Violin and Candlestick knew the rules; if they woke and their father wasn't there, their job was to stay put. Leaving them alone scared him, but taking them out into the open while he searched for food frightened him more. Besides, he stayed close.

He searched the woods. They had a few things left in his bag, but the supplies ran low. Down below, they didn't hunt for food. They farmed and grew what they wanted to eat. Here, he found no crops, no cricket farms in jars. His family always told him food was easier to grow on Earth. If it were so easy, why weren't there crops everywhere?

He contemplated gathering mushrooms, leaves, whatever looked somewhat close to the foods they cultivated, but worried some might be poisonous, and he wouldn't know what.

He had seeds, but their food supply wouldn't last until the crops grew. Besides, crops were temperamental and the weather, soil, and atmosphere on Earth remained a mystery.

He left the forest and wandered down the cement lane. With his feet planted on cement, memories of home rushed to his brain. The icy walls and hard floors, cement all around them. He missed the drafts, the constant chill. An image of his wife wrapped in an old afghan, cuddled in their bed, crossed his mind and he pushed the thought away. Emotions would take away his alertness. For his daughter's sake, Winter's mourning needed to wait.

Large metal machines sat on turnoffs in front of the houses, or next to them. No wires traveled in or out of these machines, so they weren't generators. He noted the wheels, much like the ones on the wagon his mother gave him as a child, but larger. Could these machines possibly be for moving? Some were bigger than others and they ranged in color. Similar to the small boxes in the house, these wheeled machines had strange words on them. Subaru, Ford, Nissan. Despite their differences, each had a white plate on the front and back with letter and number combinations. Nonsense, he thought.

Panic set in. How would he feed Violin and Candlestick in such a bizarre world?

At the end of the cement lane, a giant house loomed, long, rectangular, made of beige brick. The front was clear glass. Above the glass, big letters spelled: TANNER'S SWITCH SUPERMARKET.

Food?

He snuck toward the building, hyper-vigilant, and on the lookout for people or animals. He saw nothing. Heard nothing.

He peered into the glass and saw a shelf of brightly colored bags and red boxes.

Food! He pushed on the door, but it didn't open.

He found a bunch of metal baskets on wheels strewn about in front. He grabbed one and ran it through the door. The glass shattered. He ran away from the sound, fearful that it would arouse some sort of trouble.

When he felt confident nothing was coming, he entered through the hole he'd created in the glass. He grabbed a bag and ripped it open. Crunchy, oval objects fell to the floor, some of them breaking as they hit the ground. They crunched under his feet.

He picked one from the bag and licked it. It tasted awful.

He moved into the main part of the building. An awful smell

assaulted his nose. He held in a gag and searched the shelves. The shelves were filled with stuff, but none of it familiar. Bags, cups, boxes, tins, but not an ounce of recognizable food. Flies swarmed around rotten mounds of mold. More flies crowded the building's back shelves, where wads of green decay were wrapped in pink baskets.

In one section, he found metallic cylinders with pictures of food on it. Corn. Beans. He grabbed them and smashed them against the shelves, but they only dented.

Down another aisle, he found knives. He used one to cut into the cylinders. As the picture promised, the container oozed out corn kernels mixed in goopy water. He picked some up with his hands and tasted it. His eyes watered. It tasted better than any corn he'd ever had. He'd been told the food grown on Earth was larger, and the crops bigger than even him, but he didn't know they tasted sweeter, too.

Before leaving, he grabbed the metal basket on wheels and filled it with corn, beans, peas, beets, and carrots. He found containers of water and put them in the basket, too. Containers! Imagine that.

After he pushed the wheeled basket through the shattered glass, he ran. He'd left the children alone too long. The basket roared down the cement and his spine tingled as he worried about what kinds of predators the noise might alert, but none came.

He ran into the house, and his heart ached. Violin and Candlestick weren't on the cushion thing. He yelled for them and heard a thumping above him. He ran up the stairs, heart pounding.

"Dad." Violin said from behind him.

He turned. "Where's your sister?"

"I don't know. We're playing. She's hiding."

He rested his head against the wall and took a deep breath. "Get her." He tapped against the wall.

Violin nodded and called for Candlestick. As they waited for her, Violin whispered to her father, "I am trying to keep her entertained, to keep her from thinking about Mom."

Winter listed his head. "Why?"

Violin's eyes grew wide. "It wouldn't be good for us."

Before Winter could respond, Candlestick ran in.

"I found food and water," he said.

In the kitchen, Winter used a knife to carve open a container. Beans poured out onto the counter, and they scooped them up and ate them, giggling with excitement.

"I found food and water," he said again.

The food store should offer them enough meals to last until the crops grew. In the meantime, he'd dig a ditch to collect rainwater and develop a new electricity route for the house so they could boil water and figure out what some of the weird things in the house did.

They spent the day snacking and relaxing. With his energy depleted, he refused to start a new project, and while the day went smoothly, he wanted the kids to enjoy the peace before life grew more difficult.

Candlestick and Violin played hide and seek and fiddled with the various items they'd found in the house, seeing what they did, or imagining what they could do. Violin's eyes betrayed the faux smile she carried with her. A heavy sadness stretched red branches toward her pupils.

Winter almost drifted off; his body desperate for a full rest.

"Dad." Violin shook him from the soupy world between reality and dreams.

He sat up, startled, but saw the calm on her face, and settled down. "What is it?"

"Look at this." She lifted a book.

The cover said *National Monuments: A Guide.*

He flipped through the pages, pictures of mountains and buildings, beautiful and awe-inspiring.

"Very nice." He handed the book back to Violin.

He peered out the window, sensing something. Across the lane, the oak and pine branches shook, and the leaves rustled. A shiver wormed up his spine. Something watched him. He could feel it in the marrow of his bones.

"What's this?" Violin flipped to a page and showed him.

A giant man, all grayish, sat on a chair. His arms rested on the sides of the seat. His thin frame and beard did nothing to mask the eeriness of his massive size next to the humans standing in front of him.

Under the picture it said: *Abraham Lincoln, the 16th President, honored by millions of observers every year at the Lincoln Memorial.*

Winter gave one more peek out the window and convinced himself he imagined the movements. A combination of sleep deprivation and high stress. No one watched them because, apparently, no one existed on Earth anymore.

"Get your sister. It is time for another story."

CHAPTER 7

Abraham Lincoln: Ice Giant

Abraham Lincoln climbed the mountain, his long lanky legs wrapping around the cliffs as he shimmied his way to the top.

His wife and sons waited for him outside the house: a giant wooden structure—made from large tree trunks—situated atop the highest peak. "You're home," the family shouted.

"I brought dinner," he said as he emptied his backpack. Small trees flopped out and scattered onto the ground. His children began to munch on the roots while his wife hugged him.

They all surrounded the trees and ripped off branches, gulping limbs down whole.

"Delicious," his wife said.

"How was your trip, Dad?"

Abraham Lincoln sat down next to his family. "They are getting more daring."

"Why won't they leave you alone?" His wife, Tanner, put her hands on his shoulders.

"They think us a threat, and can you blame them? I could inhale a village of them if I wanted."

His sons laughed at that.

"But you never have! All you've ever done is gone down to get us food. Trees! Shrubs! Not people. Not houses!"

"I know, darling. But they don't. They hear rumors. They hear bad things."

"They hear bad things because they make up bad things. You even knocked down trees and built them a dam when the rain threatened to flood them out."

"Settle down. I know this. We all know this. But they will never understand."

"What did they do, Dad?" His oldest son asked with his fists clenched.

Abraham patted his son's head. "Calm down. They just hid in the bushes and followed me to the mountain side."

His youngest son's eyes grew wide.

Abraham laughed. "Don't fear, Cornfield. They could never climb this high. We are safe."

Cornfield looked around the edges of the cliff, not believing his father.

Abraham kissed Cornfield on the top of his head. "I promise you. And does your father ever lie?"

"No, Papa."

"Thank you. Now let us all settle in by the fire and sleep."

As they all cuddled in, Tanner whispered in his ear, "I have an idea, a way to make the humans revere you as your family does."

He turned his face to hers, scrubbing her cheek with his beard. "How's that, my love?"

"Build them a storage facility for food. You can run around gathering all the wild animals much faster than they ever could. You could chop down their crops and deliver them to this storage place, and the people could go there and gather their food without having to hunt or grow their own. Think of the time you'll save them. Think of the mouths you'll feed. They'll love you for it, Abraham."

He kissed her cheek. "You think such hopeful thoughts, my dear. A store for food. A place to get everything you need. A super storage. I like it. Maybe I will try that."

He drifted off, enjoying the warmth of the fire.

Tanner woke him up in the middle of the night, shaking him violently. "The children are screaming!"

Abraham jumped from bed and ran to them. Both boys cuddled, shivering in the corner of the house.

"What is it boys?"

"You said no people could get up here, but we saw one."

"Where?" Abraham grabbed his hammer.

"Out there." Cornfield pointed toward the front.

Abraham crashed through the front door. "If you're out there, I suggest you run."

Footsteps crunched in the leaves behind the rocky cliffs surrounding his property.

"I'll give you one last warning."

A man appeared through an opening in the wall. "No need for threats, friend," the man said.

"We ain't friends. How did you get up here?"

"Long story." As the man walked closer, Abraham saw how disheveled he was. Cuts sprawled across his face, blood dripping down his cheeks. His clothes were tattered and torn.

"I have time. Tell it."

"I'd rather cut right to the chase. I need your help."

"My help? Why? Who are you?"

"The name is Kevin Bacon, and I kind of started a war with some Gods."

CHAPTER 8

Someone Else

They ate peas for dinner and sat in the yard while the moon came up. Violin joked, "Orelon's watching."

After dark, they cuddled on the cushions and lit a fire. Candlestick begged for more stories, but Winter asked to enjoy the silence for a while, so the girls flipped through books, pretending they could read them, and even trying to learn how. They rummaged through the upper rooms, always finding something new: a piece of cloth too thin, and small, to keep anything warm, weird art hanging on walls, crude drawings, waxy sticks.

Winter drifted off a few times but worry always returned him from sleep.

And then something scratched at the door.

Winter grabbed Violin and Candlestick and pulled them toward the back door.

"Stay here," he tapped.

He bent down low and headed toward the front window to explore. The scratching continued, and with it, an accompanying whine increased in volume. Winter could make out the back portions of an animal. Two legs moving back and forth. The front two were hitting the door. The animal had a tail that wagged rapidly.

The size of the animal gave Winter some relief. He could handle it if it managed to get in. He debated on opening the front door and letting it inside, if nothing else to shut it up before it alerted any unknown dangers, but also because the girls might enjoy meeting an animal up close. *But what if it wasn't as harmless as it looked? What if it bit with poisonous teeth?*

After a moment of consideration, his decision was made for him when something whistled from the darkness. A loud, authoritarian whistle. Demanding, and fierce. It came from the same area of woods where Winter had believed someone watched him the previous night.

Winter's chest caved in. He bent down, barely exposing his head in the window. Something was out there. Something that owned the animal.

The animal obeyed and ran toward the whistle. Winter kept watch from his corner of the window, praying whatever he saw could not see him in return, but he guessed with the fire blazing behind him, his presence would be easy to detect.

The animal ran toward the whistling, and a shadow appeared behind the shrubbery. It patted the animal on the head and said something Winter couldn't make out.

The figure was human.

Winter's heart sped up. The world spun around him. He was just starting to convince himself that the humans were all gone, that he and his children had the place to themselves, all of it. But if humans still existed, where were they? And what did this one want?

Did he send the animal to the door? Was he a threat?

People will always try to harm you, even the ones who pretend to love you. It's what they do. It's the only way they know how to live. Remember that, Winter. If you ever see a human from up there, run or kill it.

But the figure by the trees turned and left with the animal. The human had to have seen the fire going, had to know someone was here.

Winter grabbed the girls and told them to sit on the cushions while he paced around the room.

"What's wrong Papa?"

"What was out there?"

His legs shook, threatened to give way.

"What are we going to do?"

"Was it scary?"

If you ever see a human from up there, run or kill it.

"Do we have to leave?"

"Papa?"

Where would they go? What could they take? Is it safe out there at night? Would there be more people? Should they wait until morning?

Or should they run right now?

CHAPTER 9
Elijah and the Game

Bryce tossed his pack on the ground and rummaged through it for his pocketknife. The woods were rife with squirrels, and plenty of other small critters, worth killing and cooking. He tried to pawn the killing off on the other scouts, but sometimes they made him do it, just because they knew it affected him.

As he dug through his sack, a shadow formed around him.

"What the hell are you doing, Metalhead Bryce?"

Bryce looked up at Snake Charmer Elijah's silhouette shrouding the sun.

"Tryin' to find my knife. Lots of small game out here."

"Good thinking, but you have to keep up with the troop. You should have thought about the knife earlier."

Bryce sighed. *Fucking Elijah.*

"Yeah, I'll search for it while I walk."

They walked in silence. Bryce enjoyed the leaves crunching under his feet. They caught up with the rest of the pack, and he still hadn't found his damned knife.

"What's that?" Bryce asked. Elijah stepped to Bryce's side, examining the ground in front of them.

"Shit."

"Those are big fucking tracks."

Elijah stepped on them, his foot a fraction of the size. "Bear?"

"Hell no. More like a friggin' dinosaur."

Elijah shrugged and kept moving. Bryce sighed and joined him.

The troop walked single file; Small Danny in the rear, and Scout Leader Ferris in the front. Elijah slowed his steps when they neared the group and put his hand on Bryce's shoulder, letting him know he should slow down, too.

He leaned into Bryce's space and whispered, "Do you ever get sick of the small game shit? I want something bigger than rodents."

"Maybe we'll find a deer again soon." He tossed his backpack over his shoulder, giving up the search for his weapon.

"Mmmm. I would love some deer right about now. Hell, I'd be happy to cross another human. I'd eat a friggin' person, I don't give a shit."

Bryce laughed, hoping it was meant to be a joke. With Elijah, you never knew.

Scout Leader Ferris stopped, and the twelve scouts behind him gathered around. Bryce and Elijah joined them.

"Alright, let's take a short break and eat some jerky, drink some water. There should be a ton of little critters around these woods, but I'm not seeing shit. To be fair, we haven't exactly been stealthy." Ferris dropped his sack and knelt in front of a tree. He pulled out sticks of jerky and passed them around.

Bryce bit down and ripped a piece off. He hated jerky, especially with the minimal amount of floss in his possession. It made his teeth feel like shit. He chewed at it while Scout Leader Ferris talked to the group.

"There's a neighborhood up ahead. I know, because it's the one Scout Master Corey and I grew up in. We will be there by night-time. That's where Scout Master Corey and Loudmouth Scoundrel went. They ran ahead and are scouting the area to make sure it's all clear, but even after they clear it, when we get there, I want y'all to stay back while I scout the area a second time. If the coast is still clear, I'll give the signal and y'all gonna move quickly, raiding the pantries, bathrooms, closets, grab whatever we can carry that you think we might need."

Elijah raised his hand. "Can I have one of the guns?"

Ferris tore into some jerky. "Scout Master Corey and I will have one, and I'll give one to you, Bryce, and Sniper Liam."

Small Danny groaned. "I want to have a gun."

"I'm sure you all do, but for now I am only training those who are old enough to qualify for a driver's license."

Elijah slapped the ground. "Oh my God, I could be driving right now. I hadn't even thought about it, but thanks for opening that wound, SLF, super appreciate it."

Bryce thought about it often, wondering what he'd be doing if the world hadn't changed. He imagined himself driving, with Julia, to the beach and spending the day at the breachway. He'd given himself a whole other life, envisioning the universe where Julia still existed, where things like school dances and video games still mattered. He tried to remember the trivial bullshit that affected him before the vanishing and infuse those minor conundrums into his visions of what life could have been. It made it more visceral. Yeah, a nice date is fun to imagine, but add a little jealousy over a glance Julia gave to some dude with his shirt off at the shoreline, and suddenly the dream is palpable. Happiness was what a person wished for, but discomfort is what made that person alive.

He brought himself back to the present where the troop clamored about something he had zoned out on. Elijah was on his feet, creeping forward, and the rest of them were giggling, even Scout Leader Ferris.

Elijah craned his head and put his finger to his lip. "Shhhhhhh." He added his own giggle to the chorus and moved around some shrubs. He paused, frozen. Bryce wondered if he were even breathing. And then, flick.

A knife shot out of his hand and slapped into a tree about fifteen feet away. Bryce tilted his body to get a better view. The knife pinned a squirrel to the trunk. The little critter's body hung limply under the blade.

While the other scouts, and even Scout Leader Ferris applauded,

Bryce slowly pushed his way around the group and around the shrubs. He tailed Elijah as the shithead closed in on his kill.

Elijah ripped the knife from the tree and as the squirrel's body flopped to the ground, Bryce grabbed Elijah's wrist.

"How did you get my knife?"

Elijah turned to him and smiled. "Better protect your shit a little better, Metalhead Bryce."

He twisted Elijah's hand and took the knife. "Don't ever do that again."

As Bryce walked away, the troop laughed at something happening behind him. He told himself not to look, not to feed into Elijah's bullshit, but he had to do it.

Elijah stood in front of the tree with the squirrel in his mouth. He shook his head back and forth, letting the squirrel slap against his cheeks. He looked like a dog playing tug-of-war. He looked insane.

He *was* insane. Was Bryce the only one who saw it?

Scout Master Corey showed up amidst the *Lord of Flies* laughing and manic squirrel assault. Everyone turned to him, quieted, ready for the all-clear.

"We got a problem," he said, and Bryce sank within himself.

He understood this moment was a turning point. They were changing. Civilization leaving their blood cells every time they breathed out. Soon, they'd all be gnawing on raw squirrels, and swimming in blood.

CHAPTER 10

No Time to Mourn

Winter chose to stay, to keep them there in the house until he had reason to flee, but he planned for a quick escape. He put some cans of food and bottles of water in his bag and kept it by the back door. He opened the back barrier more, to create an easy run through if they had to move fast. The wooded area at night should provide them with a shrouded escape. Winter, Violin, and Candlestick had a lifetime of practice for silence. He wouldn't get any sleep, but staying awake would dull his senses, and he'd be less capable of protecting his children.

Part of him wished for the strength to stomp his feet down and declare this new shelter their home, but with his wife dead and his family gone, homes no longer mattered. His children did, but homes, he learned, die.

He questioned every decision, fearing there could be more humans no matter where he went. He could find himself running from one human, who showed no interest in interfering with him, only to walk into a greater, and more prominent, threat outside.

He pushed a table between the front door and the stairwell, using it as a barricade. The windows were fragile and he had no way to block all of them off.

Violin and Candlestick sensed his fear, and as if it were catching, they grew paranoid of every creak and sound. They played quietly and talked to each other in nothing but taps. Violin checked the windows with compulsion. Winter felt sorry for them, wished he masked his fear better, but he was also glad they took their own safety seriously.

On occasion, Winter went out the back door, snuck around the house and carefully reviewed the scenes around him, not just to look out for people, but to learn every inch of the landscape, to plan multiple escape routes, and to prepare for any necessary changes to their plans.

During the glow disc's peak, Violin ran to him, tapping frantically that she heard thumps upstairs. Upon inspection, Winter found a raccoon in one of the rooms eating mushrooms growing in the closet. Winter smiled, not just at the relief of finding a small creature instead of danger, but because of the familiarity. Raccoons occasionally snuck into the underworld and during harvest season they often had to set traps to keep them at bay. Winter always volunteered for the release mission because he enjoyed spending time with the creatures before shooing them into the shallow underground tunnels, away from the community.

When he went back downstairs, Violin and Candlestick stood at the bottom of the steps, leaning on the table barrier, staring at him, waiting for answers.

"Raccoon," he tapped, and the girls smiled.

"Can I show it to Candlestick?" Violin asked.

"Sure, just stay a little away. They can bite."

The girls darted up the staircase, whispering. For a moment, Winter accepted peace in his mind.

He sat on the cushions and stared out the window, alert to every rustle, breath of wind, and steady noise.

Violin and Candlestick came down the stairs. They sat on the floor in front of the cushions and looked up at him. He smiled at them.

"You're both beautiful." He tapped.

"Thanks Dad," Violin said.

"We wanted to tell you we love you and we are thankful for you," Candlestick added.

His eyes welled up. "You are my fire. Both of you."

"Will you tell us a story now?"

"I am proud of you both, for your resilience and how well you have applied your lessons to our journey. I am scared, though. You have played, you have giggled, you have worked hard, and been brave, but I have not seen either of you mourn, not once. You lost everything too. It is okay to feel pain."

Violin nodded. "No. Not now. We keep moving forward. There will be time for fear and sadness later. For now, emotion is weakness."

Winter smiled, then frowned. "You sound like your great-uncle, and your grandmother. No matter how much you trained like machines, you are not machines. You have feelings and should feel them whenever you need."

Candlestick sat by his side. "And you?"

He brushed the hair from her face and tucked it behind her ear. "And me what?"

"When will you mourn?"

Water welled in his eyes. "I have not stopped since they all died. I carry it in my chest."

Violin stood in front of him and took his hand. "We do, too."

He put his hands on her shoulders. "You wanted a story?"

She nodded, and Candlestick scooted closer.

"Then listen up; I have a good one."

A loud howl came from the woods across the street. Winter spun. The animal from the front door was back. He had a rope attached to him, and something used it to hold him back from charging at the house.

A shape emerged from the woods, a man. No, not *a* man. Three of them.

Winter stood up and pulled Candlestick up by her arms. "Both of you, go. Now! To the back door."

CHAPTER 11
Screwdriver

"Hide."

The girls ran to the backdoor and tucked themselves into a corner, as he had trained them to do.

Winter kept an eye on the window for a moment, waiting to see what the humans would do before making any choices.

Two of them ducked back into the woods. They were trying to be stealthy, but he caught shadows moving in both directions. They were going to flank the house. The man who stayed slowly moved forward toward the front of the house. He carried the rope holding the animal in one hand, and something black in the other. A weapon of some sort, Winter guessed.

Training kicked in. Winter dug into his bag and took out the only tool he brought with him, a screwdriver. From the kitchen, he grabbed the knife they used to open the vegetable cans.

He ran past his daughters by the back door. "Do not move," he tapped as he opened the door and slid into the yard.

He moved silently, keeping himself as close to the frame of the house as he could. He peeked around the side of the house, the same side with the giant metal wagon called 'Traverse LE.' A line of bushes stretched along the side wall. He could hide in them but might make a lot of noise in the process. The shrubs tended to be loud things, as he learned from his trek through the woods.

Something scratched at the front of the house. Following it, a series of knocks. The man and the animal were making their presence known.

Tic. Tic. Tic. Tic. Something moved down the cement area on the side of the house. It crept behind the Traverse.

Winter crouched and quickly moved to the front of the wagon. He pressed his toes into the cement, planning to lunge. As a tall, lanky man came around the side of the wagon, Winter leapt.

He tackled the man, but twisted during the fall, so he hit the ground on his back and held the man on top of him.

The wind left his body, but Winter's arm gripped tightly around the man's arms, keeping them in place, and with his other hand, Winter covered the man's mouth.

"Why are you here?" He whispered.

The man fumbled for something in his pockets with the little range of motion Winter had provided his hands. He pulled something out, but Winter couldn't see it.

It fired.

The shock caused Winter to release his grip. The loudness. The brutal, volatile loudness. The window in the kitchen shattered. Winter's ears rang. His heart lost its rhythm.

The man pushed himself off Winter and turned the boom weapon, placing it directly in Winter's face.

Winter swatted, and the boom weapon fired again, blasted the cement around his head, and created a shower of gravel that splashed against his face. The ringing in his ear intensified, and the world went otherwise silent.

Blood splattered on his face.

He felt it before he even realized he'd driven the screwdriver into the man's neck. A reaction to a threat.

"Never hesitate," his uncle had yelled during every training session. "Kill. Kill. Kill."

"If you have to kill, do it," his mother had told him. "Cry later if you must, but never hesitate to choose your own life over a human's."

As the man's body flopped down, Winter rolled over, avoiding the crash. Tears formed in his eyes. He knew he'd kill to protect his children but doing so didn't bring him joy. The practice of murder did nothing to prepare him for the actual event. The way the screwdriver pulled out of the human's skin, the way the blood splattered, the way life floated out of the man's blue eyes. Training never covered those realities.

He regained his hearing enough to hear the crunching of footsteps on cement.

"Did you kill the fucker?" A voice said, coming from the front of the house.

Winter grabbed the boom weapon and tried to figure out how to make it go boom but decided he didn't have the time for guesses and fumbling.

He sat up and leaned against the side of the wagon. *Let your heart rate slow. Take meaningful, deep, but silent breaths. Slow your enemy down by bringing peace into your mind.*

He ignored the slight ringing and honed in on the quietest of noises. Jingling. Crunching. The steps drew nearer. A foot came into view, crossing from behind the car. Winter lunged again.

He drove the knife into the man's neck and chest, over and over. There was no joy in murdering, but he'd do whatever it took to protect his kids.

The man dropped his weapon, another boom weapon from the looks of it.

As Winter pulled the blade from the man's chest, the animal jumped on him and bit into his arm.

He fell over with the creature still attached and dropped his knife. The animal dug in deeper, grinding its teeth into Winter's flesh. He glanced toward the knife he had dropped, and the boom weapon. He considered his options but liked none of them.

Instead, he relaxed his body, rested his head on the earth, and breathed deep as the animal continued to chew into his arm, deeper and deeper.

He put his free hand on top of the creature, rubbing its fur. "Will you be our friend?"

The animal kept gnawing.

"Please. Be our friend." He rubbed behind its ears.

"Please. Be a friend."

The grip from its jaw loosened.

"Good friend. Be a good friend."

It whimpered. Winter sat up and wiped the blood from his eyes with his shirt. The man's body lay on the ground, rivers of blood still running from his neck and chest. The creature stepped backward, slowly edging itself away. When it moved far enough, it turned and ran.

Winter stood, clutching his torn open arm. He hobbled around the yard, worried for his daughters and the location of the third person.

He crashed through the door.

"We must go now," he said to an empty corner.

"Girls?"

They did not respond.

CHAPTER 12

The Decoy

He ran through the house, but the girls were not there. Not in any of the rooms. Not in the yard. He clenched his teeth. He had trained them for this, to stay put, not to run, even when things were intense. The only time they were permitted to leave their designated spot was if he died—or they had strong reason to believe he had—or if they caught sight of a threat in their immediate area.

Maybe the third man had gotten to them. Maybe the boom shot scared them away, or the crashing of the kitchen window.

He ran into the woods, unconcerned about staying silent, yelling for them.

"Candlestick."

He ran, losing track of where he was.

"Violin."

Let the third man hear him. Let him come. He would kill him, too. Especially if he hurt his children.

His panic made him sloppy. He wasn't even sure he'd be able to find his way back to the house.

Leaves scrambled around him, flanking from both sides. He stopped and listened but the noise stopped with him.

In front of Winter, just a few feet, something darted from behind a bush.

He moved toward it, ready to kill. While the movement in front distracted him, something ran from a tree behind him, jumped on his back, and wrapped a hand over his mouth.

"Shhhhhh, Dad."

Tears formed in his eyes. He tapped, "Violin?"

"Yes. Shhhhh."

Candlestick appeared from behind the bush in front of him.

"Decoy in front. Attack from behind." He tapped.

"We are trained," Candlestick tapped with a smile on her face.

"We have to go. Don't speak." Violin whispered.

He followed them to a giant pool of water. They crouched down, suspicious, alert. He understood they had something to fear, something to tell him, but he couldn't help but smile with pride at how smart his children were, how prepared.

"Your arm." Candlestick tapped.

Violin covered her mouth at the sight.

"I am fine. Tell me what you need to say."

"There are many of them." Violin tapped. She took a stick and made lines in the dirt. "Eight of them, maybe more."

"Some of them were Violin's age, some a little older." Candlestick chimed in.

"Eight of them? Are you sure?" Winter asked.

"That's all we saw. They were running behind the house laughing. Then, there were some loud booms and they all changed."

"Changed?"

"Scrambled, acted mad. Some of them were grabbing sticks and getting ready to go out front, but an older one came from the side of the house and told them all to be quiet. He grabbed them, pushing and shushing them, telling them to go into the woods."

"Do you know what happened to me out front?" Winter tapped.

"Yes, I sent Candlestick to check through the window while I kept an eye on the kids out back. She said she saw you petting an animal and that there were dead men."

"Yes. Do you think the children were with those men?"

"Definitely. They were all wearing the same clothes. Brown pants and shirts with patches on them."

"Do you know why I killed them?"

"They were a threat."

"Yes. So, why did you end up in these woods?"

"We were careful."

"That's not what I asked."

"We followed them. We thought it would be smart to assess the threat, see where they lived, how many more of them there were. We hoped to hear from them why they were here, what they planned to do next, that kind of thing."

He couldn't help but smile. "And?"

"We lost them."

"You did good." He tapped.

"They probably heard you yelling for us. That's why we took you here, away from the path back to the house."

"Smart. Let's go back, but we must be careful. Keep aware of all our surroundings. Look out for them, make sure they aren't following. I have an idea."

The girls nodded, and followed him back onto the path, and eventually to the house.

"Grab everything we need to survive and leave anything we don't. Quickly, before they come back."

Winter found a giant bag stuffed with clothes in the white room. He poured the clothes onto the floor, and filled the bag with the water jugs, as many food cans as he thought he could carry, the boom weapons, and some knives. He put some more food cans in the bag he had brought with him, and still more in a smaller bag he found in the kitchen.

"I will carry this heavy one. Violin, you get my bag and Candlestick, please take this smaller one."

"Where are we going?" Candlestick tapped.

"Not far."

His back cracked as he heaved the heavy bag over his shoulder, using the arm that didn't have giant bite marks in it. Still, it hurt all the way into his gnawed arm.

The girls followed as he charged out of the house, moving fast, but quietly, peering left and right, hyper-aware of his surroundings. He ran into the same woods where the men had come from, across the street, and darted left, toward another house. This house had no barrier, so they moved into the back yard.

Winter placed his bag down, and the girls mimicked him. He tried the handle on the back door, but it was locked.

"Shit," he tapped.

Violin pointed to the house next door. "Let's try that one."

"No, this one." He crashed his elbow into the door's window. He cringed at the sound it made as shattered pieces fell to the floor inside. He reached in, unlocked the door, grabbed his bag, and went down a flight of stairs. The girls followed him into the darkness.

He looked around and found two metal machines with doors. He opened them and put some of the food and water from his bag into them.

"What are you doing?" Violin asked.

"Come on. We must go."

He unlocked a small window above the metal machines and slid his bag with the remainder of their goods through the opening.

"Your turn," he said to Candlestick.

He put his hands out and lifted her on top of the machine so she could crawl out. His injured arm burned as Candlestick's weight pressed against it. After she made her way out, he helped Violin up, and then crawled out himself.

He led them to the house Violin had pointed to earlier, and he tried the back door. This one opened without needing to smash the window. He repeated the same process at this house, and then brought the girls to yet another house, this one surrounded by a tall barrier.

"We have to climb, but do it fast," he tapped. He helped them over the wooden barricade, then hoisted himself up, biting back a scream from the pain in his injured arm as he climbed over.

As they entered the house, the girls headed down the stairs and Winter stopped them. "No. We are staying here."

"Why did we go to the other houses first?" Candlestick asked.

Violin stepped forward. "Because they could be watching us. We had to sneak between houses to make it confusing for them. And in case they do find us, Dad left food in the other two places so our stuff would be scattered, and we could try to come back and save what we can."

Winter smiled. "Exactly."

He glanced around the house, searching for weak points in their defenses, considering how to fortify it.

They had to be more cautious now. They couldn't light a fire and had to keep quiet. For now, they had to live like they did in the underworld. The stress and horrible sight of bloodshed put pressure on his brain and he couldn't stay still. Pacing. Tapping. Rubbing his hair. The sadness he noticed earlier in Violin returned, and he knew she neared a breakdown. He worried for the timing of it. Candlestick still seemed rather aloof to everything that had happened, and even toward the immediate threats.

"Now, I owe you a story." He hoped it would quell his own nerves as much as theirs.

CHAPTER 13

Furry Fury

Dance celebrated her 11th birthday by spending time with her crops. She did that every day, but why should her birthday be any different? The crops were her friends, after all, and they were good company; some of them even gifted her presents. Sure, corn and barley stalks were strange friends to have, but Dance created them herself, raised them, and nurtured them.

She named each one, watched them grow larger than nearby houses, and helped them learn to speak. Every morning, she sat in her rocking chair in the yard, sewing, reading, and chatting with her friends about the happenings in the woods around them.

She never ate the corn or barley. *Oh no!* The crops meant too much to her for eating, but she did let the forest animals nibble on them a little, and her crop friends encouraged it.

"What's a little soreness when we can feed the whole forest?" Gorblin the Great Corn said.

Dance laughed at that, because she knew once the animals munched on the corn or barley, she could repair the crops with her love. A jostle and a whistle, and the stalks were back to one hundred percent.

Dance created magic in the fields, but not just with the crops. She also possessed an uncanny ability to sew metal. She took large swaths of tin, iron, copper, and with nothing more than a needle and string, she pushed through the hard surfaces like they were cloth and weaved together magnificent machinations. Weapons of death.

Surrounding her corn crops, Dance lined the fields with her wagons of doom, large metal monstrosities on wheels. These powerful machines could crush an enemy with ease.

Today, she weaved boom weapons. She already had many, but a person could never have too many boom weapons. Besides, Hippock and Roder, the barley stalks, had given her the slender black metal for her birthday. If she didn't create something special with it, what kind of gracious friend would she be? She sewed together the long black arm and pried open a hole at the end where fire and death would pour out in a tumbling rage.

How she smiled when she examined the finished product.

At the edge of the field, along the forest line, Dance caught two squirrels leaving a pile for her.

The animals of the forest recognized the sacrifices made by Dance and her stalks to provide them with food, and they insisted on making payments. The problem was that animals had little to offer humans or corn stalks, which Dance and the stalks insisted was fine, but which the governing body of the woodland creatures insisted was not.

So, every morning, Dance woke to find a series of collected goods on her lawn. She and her crops had to pretend to be grateful, but the animals hardly understood human needs or wants. Old socks, moldy food, metal brackets. Well, sometimes those metal brackets came in handy.

"Excuse me," Dance called to the squirrels.

They turned to each other, unprepared for conversation. Eventually, they shrugged and darted toward her.

"Where do you get these gifts you leave for me?" She asked.

"The raccoons take 'em. We ain't allowed to go with them, so we can't be sure exactly. Would you like us to get a better answer for ya?" Filo asked.

"Yes, Filo. Would you mind?"

The squirrels ran off and Dance asked the stalks to tell her a story. They did, a long one about gods. Malicious gods. At one time, there were twelve but now, only three remained. They were hell bent on causing humans pain, which the stalks said would only lead to war with the humans. Humans would enjoy the spilling of blood for their freedoms, but that very freedom could be their curse. Without gods, humanity would only have itself and to govern oneself, humans must learn to self-reflect. The crops said humans were capable of greatness once they freed themselves from their shackles, but not without self-examination.

Always apocalyptic, those crops, Dance thought as she drifted off.

She awoke to a clattering at the edge of the field. She shot upright and dropped her half-finished boom weapon to the ground.

"Who is there?" She shouted.

"We apologize, ma'am." A raccoon stepped forward, three others behind him. "We were told you'd like to talk to us."

"I didn't realize you would show up here. I am sorry to inconvenience you. I told the squirrels to ask a question for me."

"And they did, ma'am, but it was a question we felt best answered in person. We assume it will lead to a larger conversation."

"Well then," she sat forward. "I look forward to mingling."

They ran to her, and while they certainly moved with the feral nature of raccoons, they had a uniform pattern to them, making it appear almost military in style. When they reached her, they stood on their hind legs and the raccoon who had spoken to her reached out a paw.

"The name is Rapture, ma'am. Pleasure to meet you."

She touched his paw with two fingers, just enough to shake his leg without rattling his brains. "Pleasure is mine. The name's..."

"Dance. We know. We appreciate all you do for the woodland creatures."

"And I appreciate your need to reciprocate, even though I insist it's unnecessary. But, I must know, where do you get those gifts?"

"You're not going to like the answer."

"I believe I already know."

"Do you? Then why did you ask?"

"Well, I just want to hear it from you."

"We take them from the dead."

Dance shifted in her seat. "That was not the answer I expected."

Rapture tilted his head. "What did you expect?"

"Honestly, the garbage."

"Well, yes. We take them from the garbage of the dead."

She thought about it for a moment. "Well, I suppose I have no problem with that. It's not really theft if the people are dead."

Rapture jolted back. "Heavens, no! You thought we stole them? Nay. We are not thieves. We murder humans and take their belongs once they are dead. We have never considered stealing from a living human."

Rapture's friends snickered at Dance's appalled face.

"You're kidding. Playing games with me?"

"I told you you weren't gonna like the answer."

She took a long inhale. "You murder people? And you expect me to be okay with that?"

He shrugged. "We don't really consider you when we do it."

"Why do you kill humans?"

"Only bad ones. The real mean bastards. A lot of the woodland community likes to eat them. Not me personally, but I do what's best for the group."

She cupped her hand over her face. "Who determines whether a human is good or bad?"

The raccoons looked at each other, confused by the question. "The council of woodland creatures, of course."

"What's the criteria?"

"I don't know, ma'am. I'm a man of action, not politics."

The corn crops waved in the breeze. They were talking to Dance, letting her know these new revelations made them uneasy. Dance agreed.

"I assume you think I'm not a bad human solely because I offer you my crops? Is that the reason I am alive and not animal food?"

The raccoons all laughed. "Come on. Look at ya. You wouldn't exactly be a big score."

She feigned a smile, trying her hardest to keep things polite. "I see."

"Besides, I gotta admit, these giant crop guys scare the crap out of us. We wanna stay on their good side."

"Mmmhhh. That's probably a good idea." She said. "But you're more than just not killing me. You offer me these kind gifts and seem so thankful for the food I provide. If anything were to happen to me, who would care for these crops?"

"We are very thankful, ma'am, and very much know your value to our community. But not every creature in the woods eats your food. Some like things a bit more..."

"Gamey?" She asked.

"That's as good a word as any. Me, though, I love the corn. But I also eat trash. One time, I had a nice pile of banana peels for ya, but I just like that junk so much, I ate the whole pile."

One of the raccoons in the back lifted his paw. "I can attest. I was so mad he didn't save any for me."

Dance clapped her hands. "You've all been wonderful to me, and I appreciate what you do, but I don't think I can accept gifts that come from people you murdered. I'm a girl who likes to keep to herself, so I'm not going to judge your actions or tell anyone else about them, but I also can't be accepting the gifts."

All the playfulness left Rapture's face. "Are you ending our agreement, then?"

"You all can come and eat your corn as you always do." She leaned back, trying to portray her desire to end the conversation there.

"Now, listen here. We cannot accept the food for nothing. We work for our food, one way or another, and we pride ourselves on that. We have to give back, and if you ain't accepting our gifts, then you ain't accepting the terms of our trade deal, and thus, you're shutting us out." The last three words left his mouth with a growl.

She straightened her back, trying to showcase how much larger she was. "I have offered you my food. That part of the deal remains. I cannot accept what you have been giving me, so I guess that part of our deal ends today. You'll have to find something else to bring me, if you insist on bringing anything at all. If not, you could always work for me, do a few odd jobs to pay your end."

"I'll have to bring this up with the council and see what they think of all this nonsense." He scrunched his face.

"You do that." She rubbed her hands together, wiping herself from the conversation. "Until then, we are done here."

As the raccoons left, she overheard one of them say, "She's making a mistake." And she, very much, thought she might be.

Even with all her machines and her crop guards, she wondered how much destruction would come from a battle between her and the animals. Still, she knew she must stick to her morals, and thus, if war was what they chose, then so be it. She better stay up late tonight making more weapons. Happy birthday, indeed.

She noticed the raccoons speaking to something amidst the trees outside her field and it made her hairs stand on end. She stood, trying to get a better view. She had to be mistaken. No, she could see now. The raccoons were speaking to a human. They gathered around him, waving their arms frantically and pointing in her direction, clearly telling this man about the conversation they just had. Who was he? What did he have to do with this? Were the animals working with certain humans? It only made sense. They worked with her for years, hadn't they? They probably had other human allies. But this felt different. He wasn't an ally. He looked like their leader.

The woodland creatures worried her, but if they were, indeed, being guided by a human, her worry turned to terror. Despite being one, Dance knew humans were terrible monsters.

As she thought about all of this, it began to pour fire from the sky.

CHAPTER 14

Ready for War

"That story was weird," Candlestick said.

"I suppose so," Winter said, peering out the window.

The house was pitch dark so he knew no one could see in, but he worried about it anyway. His heart still raced from earlier.

"I wanted another story about Kevin Bacon."

Violin leaned back on the floor, using her hands to prop her upper body up. "Yeah, why didn't this story connect with the others?"

He scratched his arm, a nervous tic. "It did, my dears. All stories come together in the end. Don't you fret."

He opened a can of beans with a knife and passed it to the girls, and then opened another can for himself. They gulped water from the bottles. They had plenty of food for a while, but not indefinitely. He knew he could no longer return to the store. This place wasn't safe anymore, not for wandering.

After they ate, Winter cleaned his wounded arm with some water, and wrapped it in some clothes he found in the basement.

He would need to move them somewhere new, somewhere he could grow crops and set up electricity stations. Too many questions crammed into his brain. *Where? How would they get there? Would it be more dangerous somewhere else? Were humans everywhere, or just here?* Every danger was scary, but the prospect that even bigger dangers loomed in the darkness made him want to stay put.

Violin had told him she saw children; children her age or just a little older. Those children seemed to be aligned with the men Winter killed. Maybe the men were the children's father and uncle and they, like Winter, were trying to survive with their children. Maybe they would have succeeded if not for their aggressive actions. If that were the case, though, the threat had mostly been diminished. Without their father and uncle, the children would most likely not be a threat, and may even flee to somewhere new, leaving this land to Winter.

He groaned. Too many maybes in every solution. Always too many maybes.

Violin and Candlestick asked to check out the upstairs. They wanted to see if it were the same as the last house.

"You can, but you move slowly and quietly. Do not press on anything you don't understand. Do not touch anything that looks strange, and nothing that could attract attention."

Something had changed in Violin since the incident. He could see it already. She examined things longer, kept scanning her environments. It wasn't fear, or a product of trauma. Just the opposite. It was a newfound curiosity. Even the way she spoke to Candlestick changed. Less big sister, more motherly.

He feared for their lives. He knew the road would only get tougher, and their chances of survival were scary, at best. But he saw a power growing in his daughter, and with it, a hope he wished not to dismantle. For her, he would fill his blood with hope, too.

But still, that sadness remained burning in her pupils.

He sat on this house's long cushion thing. Apparently, every house had one. He found a floppy book, this one much thinner, and with weaker paper. He flipped through it, staring at the bizarre photos. Everyone wore such weird clothing. Some of the clothes hardly covered any surfaces, and he wondered why they bothered wearing anything at all. In the underworld, you only wore clothes when you were cold.

Eventually, Violin and Candlestick rejoined him, sleepiness growing in their eyes.

"I can keep watch if you want to rest," Violin said to Winter.

"Thank you, but I'll be fine for a while. I will wake you up in a few hours to take my place."

She smiled, nearly jumped with excitement. "Okay."

"What do we do from here?" Candlestick asked while peering through the window.

"We just keep going and see what happens," he said in his calmest voice possible.

"That's not enough," Violin said.

He turned to her. "No, it is not. But for now, it is what I have."

She seemingly accepted his answer and took Candlestick's hand. "Come on. Let's get you to bed. I'll cuddle with you to fall asleep."

She ran back upstairs and brought down some blankets. After setting them up neatly on the living room floor, she and Candlestick tucked in and wrapped around each other, their heads touching like two plants growing into one another. It reminded him of his sister seeds, crops that protected each other as they grew, twisting around one another, wholly separate beings, entwining with the mutual goal of climbing toward the light.

Winter kept watch, considering what Violin had said. She was right, of course, it wasn't enough, but he had no ability to plan ahead. With every scenario he considered what could go wrong but struggled to see where things could go right. He supposed that was the curse of living on Earth. It was a place of doom, so doom was all there was to imagine.

The girls were shivering, and Violin's teeth chattered.

"You're still awake?" He asked.

"It's too cold, Daddy," Candlestick said. "I wish we could light a fire."

He touched the fireplace. "Maybe we can."

Violin shook her head. "We can't. We have to become a wall."

"What if we do the opposite? We make noise, but we make noise everywhere. We hide in the loudness."

"I don't get it," Violin said, but her eyes sparkled with curiosity.

"I may have been overly dramatic. Violin, you keep watch, protect your sister. I will go back to the old house and light a fire. Then I will go to the other houses and light one, too. I will get a fire going at every house we have been to. If someone notices the fires, we will see them trying to figure it out before they get to us. We will catch them in a state of confusion, and maybe even fear, wondering if our numbers have grown larger than theirs."

Violin jumped up and crashed into the couch. "Okay. I'll protect her, I promise."

He patted her head. "I know you will." As he walked to the back door, he stopped and turned back to his daughters, smiling. He pressed his pinky and thumb together and tapped them against his hip three times. "I love you."

They repeated the action back to him.

"Wait," Violin whispered.

He stopped, waiting for her to elaborate.

She pointed to the window. "Someone is out there."

He ran to the window but didn't see anything.

"There," she pointed to the side of a house across the way.

A young man crept around a blue metal wagon. He wore the same uniform as the men Winter had killed.

"They aren't fleeing, which means they are looking for us. Are you ready for war?" Winter asked.

Violin smiled. "Very ready."

CHAPTER 15

Elijah Rising

Metalhead Bryce counted the children, making sure they were all there. Two were missing. The kids all fidgeted, bit their nails, breathed heavily. These dumbasses wanted to go gung-ho into war and murder, and now they were seeing the result of it. They learned their lesson the hard way, but hopefully it stuck with them.

They could survive without murdering people.

Something crunched in the woods around him, and his heart skipped a beat. Elijah.

"Well, what the fuck was that all about?" Elijah said, waving his arms in the air.

"It was about us being a bunch of idiots who went charging into a neighborhood with shitty intel."

Elijah got right into Bryce's face. "A man just killed our two leaders, and you gave the order to..." Elijah put his hand on his chin in dramatic fashion. "Was it kill the man? Oh no, you gave the fucking order to run. To run? There's a lot of us, and there was one dude, and you had us run? You goddamned coward."

Bryce used his forearm to push Elijah back an inch. "There wasn't just one man. This is my problem. I saw at least two other people darting through the bushes. Scout Master Corey and his dog went there for like an hour and came back saying it was one dude. Scout Leader Ferris said when Corey came back, he would go scout the area out more, but as soon as we heard someone was there, you all got bloodlust in your eyes and we charged in without gathering more information. We were stupid. This shit isn't a game. Now we have dead people because we didn't play it smart."

Elijah stepped back and nodded. "Okay. Okay. Fair enough." He put his arms behind his back and inhaled deeply, then turned to the kids. "So, when do we go back and gather more..." He looked to the sky. "What did Bryce call it? Oh yeah, intel."

Bryce got in Elijah's face this time. "We don't. We move on. We find somewhere safe to stay for a while. It was one stupid neighborhood; there are dozens more around it."

"Is that what all of you want to do?" Elijah put his hands out to the group. "Do you all want to flee? After that man killed the two friends who kept us alive for so long? We just let that man keep on breathing?"

All the kids spoke at once, shouting different things, but Bryce knew that within the cacophony was an overwhelming desire to find and kill that man.

"This isn't a democracy," he said.

Elijah laughed. "It isn't? So, are you going to force everyone to follow you?"

"I am in charge. That was the hierarchy created by Scout Master Corey and Scout Leader Ferris."

"True, it is, but they're both dead, so I think this is up for debate."

Bryce pushed Elijah. "It's not. I'm taking care of this group now and I will protect us. If you don't like it, you can leave. Go have your revenge."

"The group can do as they see fit. They oversee themselves. If they want to come with me, where I'll go and kill that man and take over the whole neighborhood, then they have the freedom to do so. Besides, it looks like we left Liam. Are you just going to leave one of ours to die?"

"I won't let you put them in danger on a fool's mission. There was more than one man. We'll circle the area to find Liam and then we get the hell out of here."

"Ah yes. Your imaginary ghosts. Did anyone else see these others? Bryce keeps saying he saw two others but did any of you see them? Out of everyone here, wouldn't one of you have seen these mysterious people?"

Small Danny kicked some dirt in front of him. "I didn't see anything, man. Sorry Bryce."

Bryce scoffed. "So, you think I made it up? You think I just lied to you all?"

"It's not that, man. It was intense, and we were all running everywhere. Plus, Loudmouth Scoundrel was out there and he probably ran off when Corey got killed." Danny talked low, not wanting to argue with Bryce.

"The dog? You think I mistook a dog for two humans?"

"No. I think you got confused by the intense situation, your adrenaline was messing with you, and you mistook something for something else."

Bryce ground his teeth. "I can't believe this. You're all going to listen to Elijah and not me? You know his nickname is Snake Charmer, right?"

Elijah stepped forward. "Are you calling them snakes?"

"You've got to be kidding me. You think we call you Snake Charmer because you can charm snakes? You dumbass. We call you that because you charm people, but you're a snake. Get it? Snake Charmer. You can't be this stupid."

"Ah. Well." Elijah clapped. "Very clever nickname. So, who wants to go kill some asshole?"

"No, you don't get it. It doesn't matter if it was clever or not. Corey and Ferris gave you that nickname because they thought you were a piece of shit. They didn't trust you and would never put you in charge of anything. Frankly, I was shocked they gave you a gun."

Elijah took the gun from his belt. "But they did. And unlike you, I'm going to use it to save our friend who is missing and kill the man who may very well be out here looking to kill us."

He walked away, back toward the neighborhood, then stopped and turned back. "Who's coming with me?"

The kids all marched forward. Not even one stayed put. Bryce knew this was how things worked. When one kid is willing to do something dangerous, the rest must follow suit or risk looking like a coward, and to a kid, nothing is worse. Most of them kept their heads down when they passed Bryce which, he knew, meant they were ashamed to betray him, but that didn't make him feel better.

Small Danny at least looked him in the eyes and gave him a tap on the arm. "Sorry, man. I have to do this."

Bryce watched the group walk away, and there he was, the last kid standing, not wanting to look like the coward.

"Fine, we're doing this, but we do it my way."

The group stopped.

"We keep a distance. We monitor the area. We make sure we get an accurate count on how many of them there are. Once we're sure, you all can get your stupid revenge. Deal?"

Elijah chuckled. "Sure, Bryce. You're in charge. You're the big boss man. Thank you for your wisdom."

The group marched on to battle.

CHAPTER 16

Raining Bullets

The tall boy snuck around to the front of the house. He didn't see Winter and didn't appear to be looking. He was sneaking, clearly trying to stay hidden, so he wasn't hunting.

He crept around the house foolishly, oblivious to the eyes on him.

"Should we kill him now, while he doesn't expect it?" Violin asked. The eagerness in her voice sent a chill up Winter's spine.

"I wondered that, too, but this could be a trap. The others could be right nearby, waiting for us to come out. No one can be as stupid as this guy, right? Must be a trick."

Violin smirked. "You're probably right. He is dumb."

"I want to kill a human," Candlestick said.

"No, you don't," Winter replied.

Something crunched on the side of the house.

"Stay here, keep eyes on him," Winter said, as he ducked and ran to the other window.

A boy in the same uniform snuck behind the wooden barricade, his body disappearing and reappearing around the posts. He held one of the black boom weapons. More boys appeared behind the first, these ones smaller and bunched together.

Winter tapped to Candlestick. "Tell your sister many more on side of house."

She ran to Violin, shook her, and tapped the message.

Violin nodded and tapped back. Winter couldn't read her message. Candlestick dashed toward him, tapping. "The other one is crossing the road."

Winter's heart raced. He tapped, "Go get my bag and fill it with cans. Take my knife out, and that boom weapon. Place the bag by the back door. We must be ready to flee. Are you ready to run?"

She nodded and took off. He heard her messing with his bag in the kitchen, doing as she was told.

The leader of the pack on the side of the house whispered, ineffectively. Winter heard him clearly. "Pssst, Liam. Over here."

Violin shifted to the side window with Winter. She tapped on his arm so he could keep his concentration out the window. "The boy is coming here."

A second later, the boy appeared. Once he regrouped with the rest of the boys, everyone spoke at the same time. Winter could still hear their whispers, in fact, they only rose in volume, but because they all spoke at once, he couldn't decipher what they were saying.

One of them broke through the chatter and spoke loudly and confidently. "Listen, we split into groups of two and we check out every house."

"No, I told you, I'm in charge. We can't let the little kids go door to fucking door without a gun toward a man who just killed two of our leaders who did have guns. That's insane."

"Maybe you should let me finish, dickhead. Meanwhile, Liam, me, and Bryce, if he's not being a coward, will march up and down the center of the road with our guns ready, on patrol. If any of you see anything, you shout. Clear?"

"I fucking told you we are just assessing."

"CLEAR!" He shouted, and pushed two of the smaller boys, who ran out into the road. Then he pushed two more, and they did the same. After he pushed all the smaller boys out, he and the Liam kid marched out into the road, holding their boom weapons. The one who had argued with the leader boy made a fist and punched the fence.

Winter ran to the window out front, Violin right behind, and watched their movements. Just as the kid had described, the smaller children were going door to door, starting down the road, near the house they had originally stayed at. Liam marched back and forth right in front of the house they stood in now. The authoritative kid stood in the center of the road with his arms behind his back, smiling. He scanned the road and shouted, "Come out, come out, wherever you are!"

The argumentative kid ran to him and pushed him. "Why would you alert them to our presence? You're terrible at this."

The two boys continued to bicker while Winter turned to Violin and grabbed her by the shoulders. "I have an idea, but you must listen good. That boy is correct. They are terrible at this."

She tapped, "Talk in taps. We need silence."

He didn't listen. "They're going door to door from the same side of the road, and they are going in from the front. See?" He pointed down the road where two boys finagled with some tools at a door until it popped open.

"So, when they get to the house next to us, we sneak out back and wait. When they come here, we hop the wooden barrier and run over to the house they just checked, where some of our stuff is. We can grab some more food. Put everything in bags and hang out until they leave. Then, we leave too."

She shook her head. "What about the kids in the road? They'll see us running across to the other house."

"They are pacing. We will have to time it carefully."

"Okay. I am ready to fight if we get caught."

"Be ready to run first. Fight second."

Winter brought his attention back to the kids. Liam stared down the road at the rest of the boys, not even paying attention to what happened around him.

Winter tapped, "Go tell your sister the plan."

Violin took off.

The leader boy in the middle of the road yelled, "Hey, why are you all working on the same side of the street. Switch it up. Some of you come down this way."

Shit.

Two of the kids ran toward the house they were in. Winter fell back, out of view. He lost his breath.

He ran from the window to the kitchen where Violin talked to Candlestick.

"Now. We go now." Winter lifted Candlestick up and threw the bag over his shoulder. His arm throbbed and ached.

The doorknob rattled. The kids had some fancy tools for unlocking doors. They'd be in the house in seconds.

He and his daughters ran out the back and crept along the back wall. The kids inside the house talked loudly enough so Winter could make out where their muffled voices. They must be in the kitchen already.

He peered through the gaps in the barrier, around the side of the house, where the Liam kid paced. As soon as Liam disappeared in front of the house, Winter tapped, "Go."

He threw his bag on top of the barrier, using the strap to keep it in place, not wanting it to land on the ground with a loud thump. He helped Violin over first, praying the children inside the house weren't looking out the window, and that Liam gave them enough time to clear the space between houses.

Violin, in a swift motion, unhooked Winter's bag from the barrier as she landed. Then, she dashed behind the next house over, carrying the heavy sack with her.

As he lifted Candlestick, Liam came back into view, and Winter pulled his daughter back into his chest and fell to the ground. His pulse throbbed in his temples as he peered from Liam to the back door, terrified it would open. The wait was unbearable. Everything tensed, and his mauled arm shot waves of hot pain into his brain.

Liam finally returned to the front of the house, and Winter launched his daughter over the barrier, before hopping over it himself.

He charged for the back door of the new house. Easy entrance since he left it unlocked.

They ran in to the bottom floor and Winter pulled a bottle of water from the machine thing. He guzzled a little and handed it off. "Drink up. We have lots of running to do."

The girls took turns taking sips.

"When the boys leave the house we were just in, we can try to sneak back there and hopefully hide out until they are all gone. Come upstairs. I will monitor the windows."

They ran up the stairs and as they neared the front window, the door handle rattled. The boys were here. Too soon. The leader kid must have sent more this way.

He didn't have time to get them all out of the house before that door opened.

"Run," he said to the girls, and they listened, fleeing for the back door.

Winter ripped one of the cord straps from his bag and straightened himself against the wall by the front door.

The door opened and a boy walked in. Winter kicked the door shut before the second kid could enter, slammed himself against it to block it from opening, and wrapped the bag strap around the inside boy's neck. He used all his force. The kid's feet lifted off the ground and a choking noise slipped from his throat. The pain in Winter's arm intensified, but he ignored it. Outside, the door banged. "Hey, dude, let me in. Stop being funny. We aren't supposed to be messing around."

The kid's face grew red and purple.

Another voice: "Small Danny, don't fuck around. Let Turtle in." It was the tall kid's voice. Liam.

Small Danny slashed at his neck, trying to free himself from the cord. The knocking at the door stopped, and the front window smashed to pieces. A rock crashed onto the floor, and it startled Winter so much, he loosened his grip.

Small Danny found some breathing room and pushed forward, knocking him and Winter to the floor. Winter tightened again, with Small Danny now on top of him. The kid he had blocked from coming in (Turtle?), now climbed through the window, but with the front door unblocked, Liam, with his boom weapon, opened it.

"What the fuck is going on?" Liam said. He saw his friend flailing on the ground atop Winter.

Liam lifted the boom weapon. "Let him go."

"You yell for your friends, and I will kill him. You promise to let me leave, and I will let him go and you'll never see me again."

Liam closed one eye and straightened the boom weapon.

"Do we have a deal?" Winter tightened the rope.

Liam moved the weapon around, trying to find a way to boom Winter without booming his friend.

Turtle was in now, standing in the room. He looked scared, unsure what to do. His eyes darted from Liam to Winter, clearly hoping Liam would resolve the situation.

"Your friend will be dead in seconds. Make a choice."

"Deal," Liam said.

Boom.

Liam's chest exploded, raining red over the entire room.

Turtle Boy screamed and jumped back out the window. He shouted into the street. "They killed Liam! They killed Liam!"

Winter looked everywhere, trying to make sense of what happened while Small Danny slapped at the cord around his neck. Winter let go, and the kid flipped over, heaving for breath.

Violin stood in the kitchen, holding a boom weapon in her hand.

"I figured it out," she said before tears poured from her eyes at the bloody stage she'd created. "I'm sorry. I just wanted to protect you."

From outside, someone shouted, "They have guns, too!" A chorus of screaming chaos showered the street. Booms came from everywhere. Glass and pieces of wall splashed throughout the house.

Winter's eyes widened. "Run. Now." He reached down and took Liam's weapon, then jumped over Small Danny, charging toward Violin. She aimed her gun forward, ready to fire back, but Winter grabbed her arm, pulling her with him as they made their way to the back door.

The front door slammed open and loud footsteps, many of them, came through.

Winter pointed toward Violin's boom weapon. "How do I use it?" He asked as they flew through the back door.

Violin pulled against his running, stopping him. She touched a movable piece on the weapon. "This. You put your finger through here and pull that in."

Winter nodded. "Now, let's go. I'll use mine. Don't use yours unless they kill me."

They ran toward Candlestick, who stood along the forest line, waiting for them, her eyes darting at the sounds of war around her.

The back door slammed open. "Why is everyone running? I got this guy." A boom blasted from the yard into the woods near where Winter ran. He turned and fired his own boom weapon as Violin had instructed. It made its loud roar, but Winter had no idea if he managed to hit anything. The strength of it nearly knocked him over. He wondered how Violin managed to stay upright after using hers.

The authoritative kid yelled, "You better hope one of those shots hits me because I will never stop hunting you down."

They ran through the forest, thick brush scraping their legs. While they hadn't been trained in endurance, the children showed great ability to run for long periods, never slowing, never falling over. In fact, Winter tired before they did, but still, the rustling of someone following continued. More than one set of steps.

As they continued deeper into the woods, Winter turned and shot his boom wildly. Someone screamed. A few booms went off behind him and multiple voices began shouting at one another. Winter ignored the crackling and crunching below his feet and tried to focus only on the voices, hoping to learn their approximate location.

Eventually, the voices faded in volume as Winter, Violin, and Candlestick ran further and further into thick forest.

They were not in the clear yet, but a sense they could find relief eased Winter's heavy breathing. They crossed a small stream of water. The coldness ached against Winter's feet. The girls moaned a little, too, as they crossed.

Their breath became visible, thin clouds escaping their mouths.

Suddenly, water poured from the heavens, a deluge of it, and with it, loud booms. At first, Winter thought the kids were back, using the boom weapons. But no, this was from up above. Just like his story about Dance and the crops. The fire in the sky.

"What's happening?" Violin asked, shivering from the cold and rain. Her hair stuck to her face and her lips twitched. Still, she ran.

Winter stopped, couldn't run another inch without catching his breath. He spoke to them in quick bursts between deep inhales and exhales. "It is rain, and thunder. Your grandmother talked of it quite frequently. It was something she missed about the Earth. You may not remember, but we heard the rumblings sometimes in our home. Out here it's so much louder."

Violin grabbed his hand. "I know you are tired, but we must keep running."

Winter nodded. "I think they stopped. We can pause for a moment."

Candlestick wrapped her arms around her torso. "Why would Grandma like this? It's horrible."

"I have no idea. She was a strange woman."

A brilliant light streaked across the thick darkness of sky, and a loud boom followed.

Winter jumped with fright. "This is terrible. We need shelter."

"What is it? The *thundra*?"

"Thunder. I will tell you another time."

The three of them turned left and right. They were in the middle of a deep forest and Winter had no idea how far they were from another place to stay. Murderous children were somewhere behind them, thick brush and trees all around. Winter hugged his daughters. They were worse off than when they had started. Cold. Wet. Tired. Winter's arm throbbed and bled through the dressing.

Something crunched in the brush beside them.

TANNER'S SWITCH
SUPERMARKET

CHAPTER 17

A Lion Attacking a Horse

"Aim your boomer," Winter yelled to Violin.

Together, they pointed their weapons toward the brush where the noise came from. In his peripheral, Winter noticed Violin's steady hand trained on its target with a steel foundation. Winter's own hand trembled. He was unused to holding his arm up with weight on it, especially with some of his flesh torn out.

The movement paused, then increased. The bushes opened, and a creature broke through: the animal who tore into Winter's arm.

"I'll kill it," Violin said, crying again. She closed her eyes and aimed.

Winter put his hand on top of her boom weapon and gently pulled her arm down. "No."

The rain continued to fall, but it had lessened in intensity. The animal's coat looked thinner and sleeker now that it was wet.

Winter dropped to his knees and extended his hands. "Did you come to be our friend?"

The animal moved forward, hesitant and slow.

"What are we doing? We have to keep moving, and that thing tried to eat you. Let's kill it and get going." Violin raised the weapon again.

"No," Winter said with more force.

The animal put its head down, but peeked his eyes up, like a shy child.

Candlestick stepped forward, putting her hands on her dad's shoulders. "He's cute."

"He's deadly," Violin added still crying, as if she wanted this kill to help her remove the remorse from her first.

"He is us," Winter said.

Violin whimpered. "I'm sorry I killed that boy. I just wanted to protect you."

The animal reached Winter's hands, and Winter slowly brought them around the thing's mouth until his hands touched the top of the creature's skull. He pressed down on the fur, down the animal's back, and the creature responded with a flailing tail.

"And he just wanted to protect his people."

"But his people were bad people," Violin said, her voice steadying.

"And he learned that, as did you, which is why you did what you did."

Candlestick came around Winter's side and added her own pats to the animal. "Can we keep him?"

"I'm afraid not," Winter said, still rubbing the creature's wet fur. "I can't feed another mouth."

Winter stood, and the animal followed him with its eyes.

As Violin cried, Winter embraced her with a hug. While he squeezed her and talked to her, she kept her gun aimed. "You did what you were trained to do. You're still young, so you never got the parts where they stripped the emotions from it."

"But maybe we can become his people, and then he will protect us," Candlestick said.

Winter pulled Candlestick off the animal. "A relationship must be beneficial to both parties. He won't protect us if we can't take care of him, and we can't."

Violin put her gun away. "Can we please keep moving? I'm cold. I don't want to be out here anymore."

Winter nodded. "Yes, let's move."

Candlestick sighed. "How far do we have to walk? I'm tired."

Violin wrapped her arm around her sister. "We keep moving until we don't have to anymore. We find a new place to live, far away from those people. We have weapons now. We will make a new home; one we are much more prepared to fight for."

She looked to Winter for approval, and he gave it with a slight nod. He'd tell her later how proud he was, but for now, he needed to think ahead to every possible scenario, to every possible outcome.

They marched on, slower now, walking on sore, cold feet. The rain had let up, but the soggy ground still smooshed cold muck onto their feet. The girls did not whine or complain. They just followed, and so did the animal.

They passed some footprints larger than any Earth animal Winter had seen, and it sent an icy shill up his spine. He didn't mention it to the girls; no need to add more dread to their already weary minds.

"I can't take care of you. Go your own way," Winter said to the smaller animal following them.

"Can we, at least, name it?" Candlestick turned, walking backwards, so she could examine the creature.

"Fine," Winter huffed.

"Let's call him Kevin Bacon," Candlestick giggled.

"No. He needs a better name."

The animal made a loud growl and ran into the thickness of night. Winter and his daughters froze. The creature dashed through the thick brush, hard and determined. In the distance, other creatures scattered. Those large horned creatures were certainly not the perpetrators of the tracks Winter had witnessed.

"He was watching out for us," Candlestick said. "He was protecting us."

Winter squinted his eyes. "It seems he was."

Violin smiled. "We should call him Lion."

Winter tilted his head. "Where did you get that word from? What does it mean?"

Violin pointed forward. "We should keep moving. I saw the

word in your book. *A Lion Attacking a Horse*. George Stubbs. We got our names from the book. So should he."

Winter grabbed Candlestick's hand and followed Violin. "You're getting too smart. How did you figure out how to use the weapon?"

"Kevin Bacon," she said without looking back at him.

He stopped moving, waiting for her to elaborate.

She finally stopped. "On the discs, there were pictures. One of them showed Kevin Bacon holding a weapon that looked just like ours. He had his finger around the bottom part. When you were in danger, I held it the same way, and felt that the button thing pressed in. So, I pressed. I wasn't sure it would do anything, but I had to try."

"Well, thank you." He leaned forward and scruffed her hair. "We are lucky it hit him."

She pushed his hand off her head. "I aimed it like we used to with the slingshots. Close one eye."

He nodded again. She always had answers. In so many ways, she was better than her father, She could think further ahead, clearer, could apply logic to situations where he couldn't. It made him both proud and insecure.

They walked for hours, Lion following the whole way. Eventually, the hot disc rose in the sky. The way it emerged among the tree lines awed them into stopping to appreciate it. Surrounding the disc, orange and gold splashed along the horizon.

"While we are stopped, let's open a can of corn." He pried a can open with his knife and they all scooped handfuls into their mouths while they sat on the dense forest floor, blanketed by wet leaves and slash. Lion hovered, whimpering and sticking his snout into their circle. Winter glared at Candlestick when she dropped a few kernels to the ground, letting the animal eat the tiny pieces.

"We cannot do that. We just don't have enough."

He pulled out a jar of dead crickets and gave it to his daughters. They took a few and ate them.

"We only have a few cans of beans left and the crickets are almost gone. We will need to find more protein."

Violin stared at the sky. "It looks like the fire disc forgot its job."

She was right. While the fire disc continued its ascent, the weather did not improve. Winter's fingers and toes throbbed and Candlestick shivered. Steam poured from their mouths.

"Maybe we need to get closer, where the colors are. It is grey above us. Bland, like home."

Violin chomped on a cricket. "Home wasn't bland. Earth is bland. Colors and murderers aren't flavor."

Back on their feet, they trekked on. Soon after, they approached a large section of cement with yellow lines running down it, splicing it into three sections. Metal wagons were everywhere. Some of them were smashed into barriers on the sides of the cement, and some of them were smashed into each other, entwined like Winter's daughters on cold nights.

The rain started again, but gently.

"Maybe we can get into one of these machines and cuddle until the rain stops," Winter said.

But no, it wasn't rain. As it continued, the droplets turned to white balls. Violin brought her sister into her chest.

"What is it?" She asked.

Winter smiled. He lifted his hand and let the flakes fall into his palms. He laughed and spun wildly.

Violin stared at him, cross. "What are you doing?"

"It's winter."

"It's you? You're talking mad."

He laughed harder. "Yes, it's me."

"Winter, you pick your own name. Remember that. You are winter because you chose it. You are winter because you felt connected to it. You are winter, and winter is you."

He handed his mother the book. "I like that page, Mama."

"It's beautiful, isn't it?"

"I wish I could see it."

"I wish you could, too. But some of the best things are guarded by the worst."

He put his head down. His mother waved the book in front of him.

"One day, you will have your own children and they, too, will pick their names from this book."

And then a newer memory crept into his brain. One less than a week old.

"You'll finally get to see it," his mother said as she gripped his hand. "You'll finally get to see it. Now take those beautiful children and run."

"I can't. I won't leave Sleeping Gypsy."

"Sleeping Gypsy is dead. I know you don't understand this, but she is dead, and if you see her, you will be dead, too. I can only hope the sickness is not already in you three. You must leave. I will be the last guardian of this place, just as I was the first. I will die with my creation here, but I won't let my most precious creation go with us. You and your daughters must go."

"I cannot leave her." Water burst from his eyes.

"Do you want your children to die?"

He shook his head.

"Then you will run."

He wept, loudly and bravely.

"This is no time to mourn. Run."

Run.

Run.

Run.

A loud rattling stole him from the memory. "Girls?"

He ran to the sound, behind a large metal wagon, bigger than all the rest, almost as big as the house they had stayed in, Violin and Candlestick stood, staring into a void. On the side of this monster machine, the words, "Tanner's Switch Supermarket" spread across in red lettering. He'd seen those words on the food store he'd raided, but this was no food store, just a large metal wagon.

He followed his girl's eyes. Inside the back of the giant thing were dozens of boxes, and plenty of empty space.

"I figured out how to open it. We can stay in here until the cold stuff stops falling." Violin shimmied up into the large space. She put her hands out to lift Candlestick. Lion jumped up and joined them. Winter stared.

"I have an idea. Stay put." He ran to the broken wagons and took pieces of metal where he could find them and tossed them into their new cabin. After he collected enough, he went into the woods lining the cement and grabbed leaves and sticks.

Once he gathered everything he needed, he used the metal pieces to build a makeshift box, a poorly made one, but it would suffice. He tossed in the sticks and leaves.

"Do you know how to close this thing?"

Violin walked to the opening, and reached up, she pushed down, and a new wall slid down, blanketing them in darkness.

He rubbed some sticks together until they caught and blew on the orange flakes until it blossomed into a fire.

"Okay, now open the wall."

"Won't the wind put the fire out?"

"The metal around it should protect it enough, but if we don't open the wall, the smoke will kill us."

She opened it. "Are you sure this is a good idea?"

"No, but I think so, and I have good ideas, don't I?"

She shrugged. "Most of the time, but your fireplace idea with those kids wasn't a very good one. I didn't have the heart to tell you."

He smiled. "No, I guess that idea was rather stupid, but I wanted to keep you both warm. I would do anything for you, even stupid things."

She hugged him. "I love you dad."

"I love you, too." He bent down to the fire. "Oh, would you look at this."

The girls crowded around him.

"The fire is melting the metal. The humans can even make metal weak and stupid."

Candlestick laughed. "It is warm, though."

"We will only be able to use it for a little while. If it starts melting through, it will reach the floor, and we will be trapped in flames. Plus, I need to make a funnel to push the smoke out, so the wind doesn't blow it in here and kill us."

Violin moved to the back of the space and rummaged through the boxes. "What is all this stuff?" She tossed bags and weird packages onto the floor.

Winter stood up and shouted. "It's food. It's food!"

He ran to it and examined the packaging. "I think so, anyway.

Open more."

She ripped boxes open, and sure enough, more cans with pictures of beans and corn and greens and things he'd never seen before.

They all smiled and laughed. "Food." Winter held some cans in the air. "Food." He knelt down and scrubbed Lion's head. "Even enough for you."

After they settled down, Winter knifed some cans open and they ate around the fire. Lion's snout got stuck in a can, so Winter scooped the contents onto the floor of their new cabin. Lion devoured it. Winter laughed and gave him more. The wind whipped outside, and the white winter gathered on the wagons and cement, forming immaculate white hills.

The sight horrified him, excited him, scared him, and delighted him.

"Now, I jumped ahead. I told you about Kevin Bacon and his meeting with Abraham Lincoln, but I never did explain what happened to him up in the heavens."

CHAPTER 18

Kevin Bacon and the Colorful Blobs of Everything

Kevin Bacon followed the three gods down a hall filled with plaster masks. He had so many questions, but since the gods seemed very unhappy right now, he thought it best to shut his mouth.

They turned a corner toward the end of the hall and walked into an open room. Stone pillars held the roof up, but otherwise the room showcased a spectacular view of vibrant floating colors, melding into each other, and gooping into glorious blobs.

"What am I seeing?" Kevin Bacon said, putting his hand out as if he could touch the colors.

"Everything." Azerka said.

"But what is it?"

Orelon laughed. "She wasn't being vague. It truly is everything. Imagine a farm, your farm for example. Puny, pathetic, in shambles. Now imagine it from high up in the sky. You could see the whole structure, all its edges and corners. The higher you get, the more you lose those features, until you are so high that you can't see your puny little farm at all." He waves his arms toward the floating colors. "This is everything, but we are so far away from it, examining it from such a distance, that it looks like what you are seeing."

"Everything?" He waved his arms around, wanting to absorb it all into himself.

"Even us. We are in there, too." Beelza chimed in.

"It's beautiful, but what do you get from it if you can't make anything out but these colors?"

"Not so much of a god after all, is he?" Azerka sat in a chair, sighing.

"I don't get it. Explain it to me."

"We will explain nothing to you. It is you who will explain things to us. But first, Orelon, we need some answers from you."

Orelon flopped down in a chair, intentionally over dramatic and petulant, but smirking all the way. "Fine. But I have already told you all you need to know. I slept with his mother."

Kevin Bacon raised his arms, ready to attack, but Beelza put her arm in front of him. "Relax."

He complied. "Fine. But continue to be so cavalier about my mother and I'll hurt you."

Orelon didn't respond to the threat, which somehow made it worse, made it feel weaker than if he mocked it, as expected.

"The first question I have is how a god who is supposed to be watching the humans managed to miss the one who was living with godly powers for... How old are you?" Azerka turned to Kevin Bacon, and he responded to her by holding up one hand with his fingers splayed. "Fifty years?"

Kevin nodded. "Yes, Ma'am"

She turned back to Orelon. "Fifty years?"

Orelon leaned forward, ready to answer. "Well, you know how I was just explaining to our young friend here about zooming out on his barn. That's sort of how I took my job with the humans. I watched over them from a distance. There are millions of them, you know. It would be awfully difficult for one god to see everything that happens all the time. And they are rather boring. If I did just watch them nonstop, I'd never watch them at all, because they'd put me to sleep."

"You think this is funny?" Beelza stomped her foot. "You think it is funny that you have managed to give our greatest threat powers as strong as ours? We ask you to watch them for this very reason, to ensure they never get stronger. Instead, you have managed to give them strength freely."

Azerka stood, moved in one swift motion until she was face to face with Orelon. "How many more of them are there?"

Orelon shrugged.

"How many more are possible?"

"If I had to guess."

"No, if you had to be one hundred percent sure."

"Ah, I see. That's much clearer. Twelve possible."

Beelza screamed, roared, and raged. Kevin Bacon covered his ears, felt the wrath in his brains.

"Write down the name of every single woman. We will find them ourselves."

Orelon, unfazed by the hostile show of his peers, gritted his teeth. "And of the ones I am sure of?"

Azerka grabbed Orelon's shoulders. "So, you did know. You knew you bore children with the humans, and you played naïve this whole time?"

"Oh, I wasn't playing. I did not know about him. I do know of three others."

"I'll kill you myself." Azerka slapped him.

Orelon waved his hands around. A piece of paper and a feathered pen appeared in front of him. He stuck his tongue out and bit down on it as he scribbled onto the paper. "Here is your list of every child I know to be mine, and the names of every woman who could have possibly bore others. Now, will you settle down?"

"So, I have brothers and sisters?"

They all turned to Kevin, silent and angry.

"That's good to know is all." He said.

"It is unimportant since they will all be dead by morning."

"What?" Before he could react, Beelza slashed her arm and a wind stole him, flinging him into the air. He crashed into a pillar. All three of them were swinging and flailing their arms, and he was flying across the room, smashing into chairs, pillars, and the hard floor. Pain coursed through every muscle, traveling through his bloodstream, into his heart, lungs, and brain.

"I kind of feel like a bad father." Orelon said and laughed.

Kevin Bacon, crashing into everything in sight, clenched his fist until a disc formed in his hands. He flung it as he sailed across the room. It sliced through a pillar, and then another, until all the pillars had been cut through. Then he did it again, and again, flinging his discs as the gods tossed him around the room, until the foundation of each pillar was ripped to dust, and one by one, they collapsed to the floor.

The ceiling rumbled; big fissures formed like lightning bolts.

"Well, dammit." Orelon looked up. The gods paused their assault and raised their arms, the three of them working in conjunction to repair the ceiling. The lightning bolts shrunk, and the ceiling glued itself back together.

While the collapsing ceiling took their attention, Kevin ran toward the paper with the list of Orelon's potential children on it. He snatched it, crumbled it into his pocket and dove into the colorful blobs of everything.

It really was everything. He flew through universes, and sparks of light, dust, and decay. He experienced every moment of joy, pain, hunger, and death. He screamed as it absorbed into him, too much of all. Humans yearn for knowledge, beg to have greater experiences than the human mind allows, but that barrier protects them from madness, from the insanity of truth, the overwhelming reality of how fragile and minuscule we are, and the dread of knowing it all fits into an orb of chaos, and horror, and pain. Every smile, every laugh all serves a purpose to a greater god: The God of Hunger, and he eats. Dear God, he eats.

Just when Kevin Bacon thought his brain would explode, the pressure released, and everything opened to let him in, let him see it all as a series of circuits, all wired into each other and processing life. A baby born in earthly waters connected to an explosion years away. A stream in the woods sent signals to a giant ball of gas in an unknown world. A speck of sand lit up his fire disc, powering it with microscopic beams.

He saw it all, felt it all, until he felt nothing. Because in the end, everything is nothing. Nothingness is not the absence of something, it is the epitome of it. We are nothing.

He landed, crashed, slammed into the earth. And he cried. He cried until the Earth filled with cold sky water. He bellowed angry rumbles, and streaks of bright light flew from his palms, dressing the sky with brilliant flashes.

CHAPTER 19

Fuel to the Fire

Bryce marched back to the meeting spot with Elijah right behind him. He'd gathered most of the kids from the street, but a few were missing. He knew they were safe because the man and his daughters fled in the other direction. The whole situation was such a clusterfuck and his nerves were frazzled, he worried what else could go wrong, not that the worst possible outcome hadn't already happened.

He bit back tears. He couldn't show that level of weakness right now. Poor Liam. And poor Maximum Jack. The kid was fucking 12 years old, wasn't even involved in the fight, probably didn't even want to be there, but felt pressured by Elijah. The man wouldn't have even shot Jack if Elijah hadn't chased him through the fucking woods like it was an action movie, forcing the man to fire back. It was just a wild bullet, unaimed.

Fuck.

He fucking warned everyone, but no one had listened. He'd feel redeemed if his friends' blood wasn't staining his shirt.

Elijah remained uncharacteristically quiet, which Bryce knew meant he would eventually make a spectacle. Elijah was planning his speech, thinking how to save face and put it all on Bryce. Good luck, asshole. Bryce did everything he could to prevent this.

When they landed back at the meeting spot, a few kids were already back and waiting. Good. They ran in the right direction. Smart kids. He did a quick head count. Everyone was there who wasn't dead.

Small Danny rubbed at the red line on his neck.

Some of the kids were shivering. The rain had ceased, leaving everyone cold and wet.

Bryce guessed fear and trauma played equal parts in their trembles.

He wasn't trembling, nor was he cold. In fact, the rage building inside him made him hot.

"Make a fire," he said to the kids.

"How?" Turtle responded.

"Figure it the fuck out." He dropped his pack on the ground and snatched his knife.

Some of the kids moved about with little enthusiasm, not really trying to figure it out at all, but unwilling to argue.

Turtle stayed put, as did Small Danny.

Bryce took his knife and marched to the tent area. Scout Leader Ferris' tent sagged in front of him and Bryce, once again, held in tears. He glared at Elijah before entering the tent. The rat bastard just stood there and watched everyone else do work. Nothing to say, he cowered like the loser he was. Bryce went into Ferris's tent and scrounged around, searching for the Altoids tin.

He found it in Ferris's pants pocket, and Bryce grimaced at his need to steal from the dead. "I'm literally picking his fucking pockets," he mumbled.

He put the Altoids tin in his backpack, kicked Ferris's clothes to one side of the tent, and then used his knife to cut out the floor. He pulled the tent floor from under the piles of stuff and tossed it outside, then cut the front off the tent as well. He then took the three remaining sides, and strung them to the trees nearby, creating a high canopy.

The other kids gathered around, watching him while they shivered and clutched their own torsos.

"Did any of you find any dry sticks, kindling of any kind?"

A few of the boys tossed some small sticks toward him, not enough to do much, but it would be a start. He scooped some dead pines and leaves that had lived under Ferris's tent and mixed them with the sticks. For good measure, he added a pair of Ferris's pants to the pile.

He stood up. "Find some bigger firewood, doesn't matter if it's wet. It'll do for now. Bring enough to last for a while."

The kids listened. Turtle joined the group, eager to help. Small Danny talked to Elijah, whispering. It irked Bryce, almost made him quake with fury, but for now, he decided to do nothing. Elijah would go his own way tomorrow. Bryce would demand it. He planned to remind the group why he deserved to lead them, a point worth drilling home, as if the bloodshed weren't enough.

The group made a hefty stack of wood, impressive for a five-minute search from traumatized kids. Bryce took some of the firewood and made a spaced stack with the kindling and Ferris's pants underneath it. He opened the Altoids tin and poured out the dry tinder inside it. His zippo got the tinder going, and he used a twig to push the fiery clump into the stack. Slowly, the flames caught.

"Take some of the other wood and bring it around the fire, try to get it drying out."

The group gathered around, and they all sat in silence for a while, soaking in the heat.

Eventually, Elijah and Small Danny joined them, too.

The younger kids whispered amongst themselves, until their voices rose, and then the choral mishmash of dumb, young boys blossomed into normal conversations. No one talked about what happened. They all just laughed and joked and pretended life was normal. Bryce embraced it, wanting them to move on, to forget the night and move forward with him.

Until Elijah ruined it.

"Does anyone want to talk about how Bryce's scary boogie men were two little girls?" He said playfully, as if he were just trying to be a jokester and not an antagonistic asshole, but Bryce knew better. He knew Elijah always had a plan.

Bryce cleared his throat and swallowed a piece of jerky. "Does anyone want to talk about how Elijah's plan was so stupid it got two of our friends killed by those little girls?" Sure, the girl only killed one of their friends, and the man killed the other, but most of the kids didn't know that.

Elijah raised his hands in the air, crossing his wrists, as if he were getting handcuffed by a cop. "Yeah, you're right, bud. I admit it, you're a smarter leader than me. I went in..." He put his hands to the side of his head and opened his fingers as he moved the hands away, mimicking an explosion. "...like a moron. I was angry and acted stupid. I should have listened to you."

"Thanks," Bryce said, still holding off from getting too confrontational. *In the morning*, he thought. *In the morning.*

Elijah chomped on some jerky. "But there's just one thing we all gotta talk about for real."

Everyone looked up.

"They were girls."

"And?" Bryce cracked his neck, releasing the tension built up in his shoulders.

"Girls, dude."

Bryce scrunched his forehead. "What the fuck are you getting at?"

"It's the end of the goddamned world, Bryce. We're like some of the last people in existence, and we are all dudes. We're a group of dudes. How do we repopulate the world with a group of dudes?"

Bryce threw his remaining jerky into the fire. "Jesus, man. They were friggin' kids. Like, children, you psycho."

Elijah shrugged. "It's the end of the world, dude."

Bryce slapped his forehead, couldn't even think of how to argue against such insanity. Some things are so asinine, it's hard to come up with a retort for them. You'd have to dig back to the very fundamentals of morality.

Elijah dropped it and the group reopened for normal conversation. Bryce noticed Elijah whispering to Small Danny on occasion, and his skin crawled anew.

"I think we should all get to sleep," Bryce said after a while.

He threw some more logs on the fire and the boys scattered to get their sleeping bags.

It took Bryce a long time to fall asleep. His body itched all over, something that happened to him during times of heavy stress. But eventually, he dropped into a deep sleep…

Until Small Danny screamed.

Bryce shot out of his sleeping bag. "What's wrong?"

He ran toward the screams. Some of the other kids woke up and followed him. A thin layer of white covered the forest floor. Bryce loved the snow, and wished he had a moment to enjoy it.

Small Danny lay twisted down a small crevasse, no deeper than ten feet down.

"What happened?"

"I was walking to take a piss and fell down here."

Bryce lay down and extended his hands into the crevasse. "Can you reach up to me?"

"I can't. I can't stand."

"Shit, alright."

Bryce jumped down and put his arm around Small Danny's back, trying to lift him, but Small Danny fought against it.

"It hurts too much. My leg is fucked."

Turtle hovered over the edge of the crevasse and Bryce pointed to him. "Get some of the other kids and tell them to get down here. If they go around that way," he pointed toward a downward slant in the crevasse wall, "they can get down here easier."

Turtle nodded and ran away.

A few minutes later, he came back with two other kids.

"Come help me lift him."

The three of them ran over and they all heaved to lift Small Danny. He moaned as they pulled him up.

Someone yelled from above. No, more than one person yelling.

"What's happening up there?"

One of the kids flailed off the edge and slammed into them,

knocking the group over. A few seconds later, another one flopped down.

Bryce pushed a kid off himself and stood just in time to see Small Danny running away from the group. Running.

"What the fuck?"

It was raining again, liquid slapping down against them. No. What was that smell? Oil. Bryce knew without looking where it came from.

Stupidly, Bryce's first thought was, "Where did Elijah get oil?" and he followed this dumb thought with a second, even dumber thought, "Why didn't he help me light the fire?" The third thought caught on to what was happening. "Oh shit," he said out loud as a bottle spun down toward them, shooting fire from its top, a pathetic little flickering flame.

"I'm sorry guys. I really am," Small Danny said with Elijah's arm around his shoulders.

Bryce stared in disbelief as they walked away. His body ignited into flames.

CHAPTER 20

A Proper Way to Die

The white built up, creating smooth mounds along the cement. It covered the bottoms of the metal wagons and streamed into their temporary home, where the fire melted it, and created slushy water at the entrance.

Lion slept, curled within himself by Winter's feet. Winter, Violin, and Candlestick also slept in short bursts, taking turns playing sentry. Winter made a funnel from broken metal pieces he found on the cement to keep them safe from smoke inhalation. Luckily, the cheap metal on the base of their stove kept the fire contained and Winter was able to keep the flames going.

For a moment, they had peace, but Winter knew it couldn't last. They had food, at least, some water, but not a lot, and a warm fire.

In its own way, peace made him uncomfortable. Everything on Earth had proven worthy of his fear, and he'd come to expect the worst. Peace? It was a lie. He'd rather see the threat in front of his face than imagine it around the corner.

As his daughters slept, Winter jumped down from the shelter. His boots crunched into the whiteness. It shocked his feet, icy, cold, and wet. He wiggled his toes and laughed. "The stuff Mother liked." He shook his head. Bursts of steam escaped his mouth as he scanned the environment. He knew the metal wagons were for traveling, but wished he knew *how* they moved. They could be helpful to use.

"It is all beautiful, though, isn't it?" Violin asked as she hopped down. Her eyes grew wide as her boots slapped into the frosty mounds. "Ahhhh! That's freezing."

Winter laughed. "I know. It's terrible and wonderful all at once. How did you sleep?"

She giggled. "Good. What do we do now?"

He sighed, long and hard. "I am torn. We should rest up and eat a lot of food. I hate to leave this place. We have warmth and so much to eat, but I don't trust it. Too many things in the way of my vision. I can't see what's coming."

Violin kicked some of the white and a universe of flecks danced through the air. "I agree. This seems to have most of what we need, but I feel unsafe. Maybe we are just still too close to where we were, not far enough away from the danger."

Winter nodded. "That may be the problem."

"Do you remember when Mom went through a period where she would only talk in funny voices?"

Winter laughed. "Yes, of course I do. I couldn't have a normal conversation with her without laughing."

"Yeah. Sometimes I just randomly start laughing thinking about it."

Winter made his voice raspy and throaty, "Winter, would you like me to sew you a new shirt?"

Violin cracked up, and that made Winter laugh harder, too. The cold made his throat raw, and he coughed within his laugh. It hurt and felt great.

Violin's face grew red as she cracked up. Tears formed in her eyes, but then her face turned, the smile drooped, and the tears built into pools. "I miss her so much, Dad. I can't take it."

He ran to her, squeezed her tightly against his chest. A clump of ache rose from his belly. "Me too. I have held it in to keep my mind straight, to focus on protecting you, but I hurt so much."

"She died alone, without us. We left her."

He openly wept now, soft, cold tears dripped on Violin's brown hair. "I know. I miss them all. I never knew it was possible to lose everything all at once."

"Can we go back there?"

"I don't think so. I don't think we can ever go back."

"Never?"

"I don't know."

Violin pushed herself off him. "I never got to say goodbye. I just accepted it all. I did what I always do. I followed you and did what I was told, but I don't want to do that anymore. I want to say 'no' to you. I want to tell you we can't leave Mama behind. We can't just run without saying goodbye. It's not right. I don't care if I died, too. I would have died proper, by doing what was right." Her voice increased in volume. It echoed in the vastness of their surroundings.

Part of him wanted to tell her to quiet down, worried she would alert trouble, but he loved her, and he knew she needed to scream.

"I know. I just tried to do what was my version of right. My life is all about protecting you."

"I am my own person. I should be allowed to choose my own death. If I wanted to die with my family, would that be a bad end to a good life? No. It would have been how it should be."

Winter put out his hand, letting her decide if she would take it. "But would you choose that death for your sister? Because if you chose to stay, so would we all, and Candlestick would be dead too. If you made the decision for yourself, you would have ended her life, too."

She slowly lifted her arm and touched his hand. Her pinky and index finger came together and tapped Winter's palm three times. "No. I would not have."

He took a step closer, and she mimicked him until they were back in an embrace.

He tapped on her back, repeating her statement to him.

"Sometimes, the best thing to do is also the worst."

She nodded, her head brushed up and down against his torso. Then, she mumbled something.

He pulled away.

"What?"

"Candlestick believes your stories."

He tilted his head. "What do you mean?"

"She thinks Kevin Bacon is real and really created the fire disc."

Winter smiled. "He did."

She wiped snot from her nose. "I know."

He put his hands on her cheeks and kissed her forehead. "This is what we have now. This is who we are. This is our world. This is our life."

"I know."

"Together."

"Always."

"Always."

"You, me, Candlestick, and Lion." She giggled.

Winter huffed. "Yes, I suppose we can't abandon him now. He will protect us and we will protect him."

"Kevin Bacon permitted."

They both chuckled.

He turned toward their shelter. "Come with me. I will tell you a tale that you can share with your sister when she wakes up. I also need your help planning what to do from here. I can't do it alone."

She wrapped her arm around his back. "You're never alone."

CHAPTER 21

Guts and Glory

Abraham Lincoln threw another log on the fire. The flames soared, and flecks of red ash spread between him and Kevin Bacon.

"Does it hurt?" Kevin Bacon asked.

"What?"

"Sitting by a fire when you're made of ice? Your chin is melting a little."

Abraham Lincoln laughed loudly, scaring three birds from a nearby tree. "No sir. It just reforms. Maybe like how you humans pour salty water from your skin."

Kevin Bacon narrowed his eyes. "How do you know it's salty?"

"Never mind. Would you like a log to eat? We have plenty for both the fire and for food."

Kevin Bacon waved his offer off and stood. He stared down at the village below. The lights from the houses, tiny little dots, represented lives. Lives he could irrevocably change for the better by taking the throne from the three gods. For Saria, the only friend who never judged him.

Abraham moved next to him; his arms tucked into his pits. "So, we are brothers, huh? And we have more siblings out there?"

"Indeed."

Abraham pointed toward the houses. "A man lives there with his two daughters. His sister lives..." He moved his hand up a few centimeters. "...there. His mistress is just down the hill. Sometimes I think we are all connected and related. It's as if only six degrees separate us all."

Kevin Bacon rolled his eyes. "That seems a little far-fetched, friend."

Abraham took in a big breath. "You may be right. What is the plan now?"

"We find our brothers and sisters before the gods kill them, and we have a big ole family reunion."

"I don't like the idea of leaving my family alone for so long."

Abraham Lincoln's wife ran out of the house, waving. "Abraham, when will you be leaving? Please tell me you'll both stay for dinner, at least."

Kevin Bacon nodded. "I'm not sure my teeth can handle trees, but since you so kindly dressed my wounds, I wouldn't think of driving your husband away without having a last dinner with his family."

"Last?" Abraham and his wife asked in unison.

"Poor choice of words. Sorry."

Kevin Bacon sat impatiently while Abraham Lincoln and his family devoured an entire tree. His feet tapped, and his fingers rattled against his knees. All he could imagine was the leaping head start the gods had on him. He had no chance against them without an army of siblings on his side. He must gather them fast.

Unfortunately, even with large gulps, a tree can take a while to eat.

After dinner, Kevin sat alone at the table while Abraham said his goodbyes. He hugged his two sons and his wife for long stretches and went back for seconds and thirds.

"I can't imagine being away from you for so long," Abraham said to his wife.

"I know. I will miss you, but you must do this. If Mr. Bacon is telling the truth, these gods want you dead, and that will keep you from me for much longer than this adventure."

Abraham hugged his wife and sons one more time, packed a bag, and lifted Kevin Bacon onto his shoulder while they climbed down the mountain.

"Which sibling do we find first, brother?" Abraham asked as they descended.

Kevin pulled out the list, now crumpled from the journey. He scanned it closely. "Ah. The top three are the ones Orelon was sure of. He listed the names of his children here. The rest are all just potentials. So, we should start with what we can be sure of. The top one on the list is two names. Actual siblings living together. Brother and sister. Let's start there, fluff up the army by two!"

"Double our size in one go. I like it."

"Their name's sound quaint."

"What are they?"

"AAAAHHHH and NNNNOOOO."

Abraham let out a giant roar. "Quaint, indeed."

They marched down the path, through the town of humans, not hiding from the townspeople who watched in terror as the giant lumbered by their fragile houses.

Abraham rubbed his furry chin. "Hmmmm. Where are we going?"

"It looks like this list has accompanying locations, but I can't make heads or tails of what the words mean. I think I can figure it out the same way I found you."

"How's that? I should have asked that a long time ago. How did you find me?"

Kevin Bacon grinned. "I closed my eyes and asked everything where to go."

"You asked what?"

"Everything. I am in tune with everything now."

"I don't understand."

Kevin pat Abraham's shoulder. "Me neither, friend. Just keep rolling forward and I'll tap into my nonsense."

Abraham shrugged, nearly knocking Kevin Bacon off his shoulder.

They marched on for miles, which moved remarkably fast thanks to the giant's massive gait. Eventually, Kevin Bacon stopped him.

"There. In those trees."

"Our siblings live amongst the trees?"

"I believe so. Maybe I should go in alone for now. Don't want to startle them."

Abraham nodded in agreement and Kevin jumped down.

Trees lined the sides of the dirt path they traveled. Kevin sighed, staring at the dark stretches in front of him. He slowly walked in and found himself, and his surroundings, shrouded in complete blackness.

He pulled a disc from his pocket and spun it in his hands until it lit on fire. The glow from the flames opened the area to his eyes. Trees. Shrubs. Nothing else.

"Hello? Is anyone there? I am looking for AAAAHHHH and NNNNOOOO. I am here peacefully. Just looking to chat."

The shrubs around him shook. Suddenly, two giant black creatures, furry and bulbous, flanked him from both sides. They smashed into him, crushing his body. He flopped to the ground.

"Listen here, animals. I am a god, and I would prefer to do things nicely. I am just looking for some long-lost siblings. I have no fight with you."

One of the blobbers growled and stood on its back legs. The other roared.

Kevin Bacon stood up and put his hands out. "We really don't have to do this. I don't want to battle you. I am fighting gods. Imagine what I could do to a forest animal. Huh?"

One of the blobber's eyes turned red, and the other's turned green.

"Ah, what the heck is this?"

Bright streaks of light shot from their eyes. The streaks blasted into Kevin Bacon, singeing his clothes and burning his flesh.

"AAAAHHHH" Kevin screamed.

"What?" The blobber with the red eyes said.

"What?" Kevin asked back.

"Huh?"

"What?"

"You said my name."

"Huh?"

"AAAAHHHH."

"What are you yelling in pain for? You're the one who burned me with your weird shooty eyes."

"I'm not yelling in pain. I am saying my name."

Kevin clutched the burned flesh on his stomach. It was literally smoking. "You're AAAAHHHH? So, Green shooty blob here must be NNNNOOOO."

They nodded. Kevin smiled. "Oh, so you are my brother and sister."

The trees above them peeled apart like a fruit skin, and Abraham Lincoln's large head came into view. "Everything all right in here?"

Kevin put his hand up. "Just fine. A little misunderstanding."

The green eyed blobber snarled. "Misunderstanding is right. This puny little booger thinks he's related to the mighty blobbers AAAAHHHH and NNNNOOOO."

Kevin Bacon huffed. He took his fire disc and tossed it into the air. It flew around the forest, knocking into tree branches, severing them from their trunks. Tree limbs rained down around them.

He formed another disc in his hands and flung it straight ahead. It flew ferociously, spinning through thick tree trunks. In a line, trees collapsed in chunks before the disc returned to Kevin Bacon's hand. "I may look like a human, but I am much more."

AAAAHHHH stood on his back legs. "I'm convinced."

NNNNOOOO shrugged her large front paws. "Works for me. Can we eat now?"

Kevin Bacon slapped his forehead. "Am I going to have to wait for every sibling I meet to eat a meal before we move on with this adventure?"

"Adventure, you say?" NNNNOOOO asked.

"Yes, sister. I need you to help me on an adventure."

The two blobbers looked to each other. Finally, AAAAHHHH said, "Tell us more."

Before Kevin Bacon could say more, AAAAHHHH's body exploded into large pieces of furry animal flesh and guts. A large hunk of innards slapped against Kevin Bacon's face.

Abraham Lincoln ripped trees away from his face to get a better view. NNNNOOOO screamed, "NNNNOOOO," and ran to her brother, or what was left of him, which was very little, other than streaks of red.

Kevin cleared the muck from his face with his sleeves.

Two women and a man came through the forest. The gods. Azerka, Beelza, and Orelon stood together, their hands on their hips, looking impossibly cool. Smoke poured from Orelon's hand. "Sorry I had to kill your brother. He is also my son, so you can imagine my regret." He giggled.

Kevin Bacon drew three discs and waved his hand, making them float in front of his face. "Abraham Lincoln, will you do me a favor and pound these three into the ground?"

"Not a problem," the ice giant shouted.

"No need." NNNNOOOO yelled. "I will kill them myself."

She charged at the gods.

"Not a good idea," Kevin cautioned. He tossed his discs, trying to distract the Gods before they could explode the other blobber. The gods jumped in different directions, dodging the discs. Abraham Lincoln pounded into the ground, slamming his fists into the dirt. He aimed for the gods, but they dipped, rolled, and spun away from him each time.

Paying too much attention to the ice giant, Azerka missed the green streak of light coming her way. It blasted into her, and her beautiful purple gown burst into flames. She screamed and tried to pat it out, but Kevin Bacon's disc sliced through her arm. Half her arm flopped to the ground.

"What the? My arm! It's gone!" she yelled.

Orelon stopped and stared at his suffering sister. Abraham Lincoln slammed his fist into his father's flimsy god body. When

Abraham's fist came up from the ground, Orelon was smooshed deep into the dirt.

Azerka grabbed her arm. "Okay, enough of this. Let's go."

She vanished, and her sister disappeared a second later. Orelon lifted himself from the dirt, dusting himself off. NNNNOOOO shot another green blast his way, but with a wave of his hand, the blast redirected and crashed into a tree, which tumbled toward NNNNOOOO and Kevin Bacon. They dipped out of the way as the large tree crashed to the forest floor.

"Don't get cocky, you fools." Orelon said through long breaths. "You caught us off guard and got a good jump on us, but you are not able to defeat us. We aren't fleeing. We just aren't wasting our time. We have more of your siblings to kill. See you soon, I'm sure." He bowed and vanished.

They all stared in disbelief. What the hell just happened?

Abraham looked down to his brother and sister. "That went pretty well."

NNNNOOOO growled at him. "Well? My brother is dead."

"Oh, yeah, I am sorry. I just meant, ya know. We just fought gods and kind of won."

Kevin Bacon collected his discs. "So, this adventure I was telling you about. It was to find the rest of our siblings and to kill those three."

NNNNOOOO hugged the spot where her brother exploded. "I don't understand any of this, but I must kill that man. If you're offering to help me do that, I am in."

"Welcome to the team, sister," Abraham hollered from above the trees. "Welcome to the team."

Kevin Bacon stopped moving. Something blinked behind one of the trees where the gods had stood. He moved toward it, slowly.

"Mr. Bacon, what is wrong?" Abraham asked.

"Can you see that blinking thing?" Kevin pointed toward it.

NNNNOOOO put her paw on his shoulder. "Don't go closer."

Abraham leaned his face down, trying to get a better look. His eyes grew three times the size of Kevin Bacon. "Run!"

CHAPTER 22

They Come Out at Night

Winter and Violin walked around the cement area, searching for anything useful, while they discussed what their next plan would be. Violin suggested they move on in a day, so they could have some time to rest and recuperate. Winter thought it a good idea but felt antsy to move on immediately. Maybe she had been right about them still being too close to the fight.

They figured out how to open the metal wagons and get inside them but found most of their search useless. After a few checks, Winter found some clothes in one of the wagons, a few warm shirts that would be good for the girls, and a thin shirt perfect for him to rip apart and use as dressing over his wound.

His pain wasn't getting better, and a weird heat radiated up his arm from the site of the bites. He'd never felt pain like it before, and he'd been electrocuted three times.

"Dad?"

Winter glanced up, alert. Candlestick jumped from the shelter with Lion right behind.

"Hello," he tapped. Thumb once. "Good morning," Thumb and

index finger. Pinky, index finger, followed by two taps with the middle and ring finger.

"What are you guys doing?" She asked as she approached him.

"Searching these wagons for supplies. Planning what to do next."

She put her head down. "I'm smart, too, you know."

He put his arm around her. "Yes, but you also sleep late."

They giggled.

"So, tell me, smart girl, what do we do next?"

She puckered her lips. "We keep moving, but not until we take a day to rest and eat a lot."

Winter looked to Violin, who smiled at him. "Looks like you are smart after all, and also like you and your sister should be leading me."

Violin closed the door on the metal wagon she had been searching. "You'll take our suggestion, then?"

Winter stretched his arms upward. "Yes, I will listen to you. Let's take the day to eat. I am hungry. Are you both hungry?"

They nodded. Lion wagged his tail.

"I know you are hungry, Lion. You are always hungry."

As the girls picked out cans of food, Winter finagled with the stove, checking it all functioned well. Once satisfied, he searched the forest for more wood and rekindled the fire.

They sat around the heat most of the day, eating, napping, telling stories, revisiting old memories. Violin retold Winter's tale about Kevin Bacon, filling Candlestick in on the latest adventure. The fire disc rose and descended. A strange glow of purple and orange highlighted the horizon as the fire disc faded behind the trees in the distance.

For a while, they had absolute silence. Even the wind had calmed and left the world quiet and peaceful.

"Dad," Violin said and stood.

"Let's enjoy the quiet." He said as he closed his eyes and rested his head against the wall.

"Dad!" Louder now.

He opened his eyes. "What's wrong?" He stood and moved to her.

She pointed down the long cement path.

A figure darted down the stretch of cement, zigzagging around the metal wagons.

"Get the boom weapons," Winter said.

Violin ran to his bag and searched.

As the figure came closer, Winter made out that it was human, and large. He lumbered, clunky, out of shape.

"Hurry," Winter said.

Candlestick came to his side. "What can I do?"

"For now, hide. Go to the boxes and stay back there."

As the man came closer, Lion's fur stood up on his back. He snarled and let out a low growl.

"Here," Violin handed Winter a boom weapon.

Winter jumped down from the shelter. "You two stay in there. Violin, get the other boom weapon and be prepared for anything. If anything goes wrong, close yourselves in there."

Winter trained the weapon on the man, who seemed unconcerned about the boomer. The man's eyes were wide, his face coated in panic.

"Hide. Run. Your gun ain't gonna do shit on them."

Lion made loud, protective noises, but stayed in the shelter with the girls.

Winter tightened his arms, the man closing in on him. "Stop. Don't move."

"Sorry dude. I'm much less afraid of you than them."

"Who?"

"You can't be out at night, man. They come out at night."

Who?" Winter shouted again.

The man whizzed past him, red in the face, clearly unused to this level of exercise. Winter almost shot him, but the man moved to the side of the shelter, not into it. He was running past them.

"Who?" Winter tried one more time.

The man turned, completely out of breath. He bent over, clutching his knees. Heaving. "The lampposts."

"*The what?*"

"The fucking monsters! Where have you been for the last three or four nights, man? Hide." He forced himself upright but fell sideways banging into the side of the shelter.

Winter kept the gun on him and slowly moved back into the shelter. Just as he hopped up, a loud thudding and crunching came from the woods around him.

"Fuck, they're here," the man said.

"Close it!" Winter shouted as he moved away from the shelter's opening.

Winter kicked their heating unit until the whole thing collapsed outside of the shelter with a loud clang.

"Wait! Let me in!" the man shouted from the side of the shelter.

Winter shook his head and Violin slammed the front wall shut. Winter grabbed both daughters, squeezing them into one solid shape. "Stay tight. Stay silent."

"Please, let me in," the man said. Winter noticed the sliding door jiggling, and he ran to it, holding his foot on the handle to keep it closed. The man tried to open it, but Winter fought against him.

A horrendous screeching came from outside. Inhuman. Chills ran up Winter's spine, and his hair stood on end.

Loud thudding on both sides of their shelter, so forceful the floor under Winter vibrated.

The man outside screamed.

Snapping, crunching, liquidy squelching. Then, the screams stopped.

Lion's low growl turned into a yipping howl.

"Stop him," Winter tapped.

Candlestick knelt next to him, petting his fur. "Shhhhhh," she said in a soft tone.

The monster screeched right outside the wall.

Bang. The shelter shook, and a large dent popped in the side wall.

Lion's roaring intensified.

Bang. Bang. Bang.

Violin covered her mouth, holding in the scream building in her chest. Winter nodded, letting her know she was doing well.

He ran to Lion, wrapped his arm around the animal's head and forcefully pressed its mouth shut.

Bang. Bang. Bang. Dents grew all over the side of the shelter.

The whole enclosure shook, tilted to the side, ready to fall.

It stopped. Winter held his finger up, letting the girls know it wasn't over yet, to stay quiet. With his other hand, he continued to hold Lion's mouth shut. The animal still made a grumble through his shut teeth, but it was the best Winter could do.

Candlestick tapped, "Do you think they are gone?"

Bang.

Bang.

Bang.

The dents in the side of their new home closed inward, deeper, more dramatic.

Bang.

The floor shifted under them, and they all tumbled onto their backs as the entire shelter fell to its side.

CHAPTER 23

What's Necessary to Survive

Small Danny knew he would land in Hell for what he had allowed to happen. *Allowed*, he stressed to himself. *Allowed*. He didn't actually kill anyone. He just, you know, let it happen. Put pieces in the correct places.

Cowardly? Sure. He wouldn't pretend otherwise. He knew what he was, and that's why he did what he did.

He liked Bryce much more than Elijah. In fact, Elijah disgusted him. But who would do better at keeping him alive? Bryce was smart but weak. Elijah was stupid but strong. He would prefer someone in the middle, but since no such person existed, he had to choose which one would keep him alive the longest.

He second-guessed his decision from time to time, as the two of them trekked through the woods, aiming to find the man and the girls. Elijah was the one who led them into a stupid battle they were unprepared for and caused multiple deaths because of his rash decisions. He was dead set on revenge, which probably meant he would make many more dumb choices. And without the rest of the gang, there weren't as many targets. But still, at any sign of danger, Small Danny thought Elijah would run out, guns blazing, and make himself the bigger target.

On top of that, when it came to gathering supplies, stealing, killing, doing what was necessary to survive, Elijah would welcome the immoral choices needed, where Bryce would have let them starve if it meant not harming another person.

"Do we know where we are going or are we just guessing?" Small Danny asked.

Elijah turned to him. "Kinda both. They ran this way, so we gotta watch out for signs of where they went. But don't worry, we will find them eventually."

"Do we need to? I mean, I'm all for killing them, but isn't surviving more important?"

"We can do both, bud." Elijah touched the gun in his belt. Small Danny hated the way he kept doing that, as if he needed to feel it to stay focused.

Small Danny tried to remember the way back to the camp, just in case they needed to get back fast. They were hours out, though. It must be three or so in the morning, if Danny had to guess, and they had fled the camp around midnight, grabbing the bare necessities to keep them alive for a few days. Yeah, he had a lot of doubts.

The ground shook, and a giant tree slammed into the forest floor a hundred feet in front of them.

"Jesus, that scared the shit out of me," Danny said.

Elijah laughed.

Boom! Boom! Loud crashes. Tree branches fell to the ground.

Elijah turned around, grabbed Danny, and shoved him behind a tree. They both leaned against the trunk.

"What the fuck is happening?" Danny asked.

"I don't know but shut the fuck up."

The booms continued. Entire trees timbered down. Danny peaked around a side, his heart pounding in his throat.

He couldn't see anything, just trees, but one of them looked odd. Thin and sleek black. Then it moved, bending in the middle, like it had a knee. Fuck, it had a knee.

Danny gulped down a scream. "What the hell is that?"

Elijah turned to look and stayed frozen on the sight as the giant limb thing moved.

It headed toward them, and Danny got a better sight. They were huge, over ten feet tall, long limbed, with arms stretching all the way down their bodies. The long, thin nails on the fingers scraped against the dead leaves and snow. Their necks curved in a U, so their heads hung down, and a bright, powerful glow saturated their faces. Molten liquid dribbled from their faces and sizzled against the icy forest floor.

Danny turned away from the sight and pressed his head against the tree trunk. "What the fuck is happening? Elijah! What the fuck is that thing?"

Elijah said nothing, just kept watching. His eyebrows bent down in the middle, deep in thought, but he otherwise remained impressively steady. Maybe Danny had made the correct decision.

He finally turned to Danny. "Listen. Whatever the hell that thing is, it isn't good. If it keeps coming this way, don't move. Maybe it will go right past us. Whatever you do, don't make a fucking sound. If it turns, I have an idea."

Danny nodded. Elijah's idea probably involved doing something stupid to piss the giant thing off, which might mean Danny could sneak away while Elijah did his idiotic plan. Sweat built up on his forehead, despite the cold. This was insane. The deep fear turned his stomach and rattled his skull, messing up his thinking. He couldn't concentrate. He just wanted to cry. Not just cry, but bawl his fucking eyes out.

"All right. It's coming to our left. Stay here, don't fucking move and don't make a noise. I'll be right back."

Danny nodded again, unable to do much else. His fingers gripped the bark so hard his nails cracked.

Elijah stepped slowly away to the tree on the right. The thing boomed with its giant steps to the left. It was getting closer, judging by the trembling in the ground beneath Danny.

He watched as Elijah crept to the next tree.

Elijah paused, looked toward the monster, and darted to another one. He did this again and again, until he was about thirty feet away. He dropped his sack and fumbled for something inside.

The monster was too close. Danny could hear it breathing now, a powerful, heavy breath.

A warm sensation ran down Danny's leg, and he didn't give a shit how embarrassing that was.

He felt the presence of the thing right next to the tree. He made himself turn back to Elijah just in time to see him throw something.

Whatever he threw dinged against the tree Danny leaned against.

The creature screeched. A claw reached around the tree, skimming the top of Danny's head. Elijah threw something else. It made another loud noise.

Danny understood. "You asshole!" He shouted as the monster turned around the trunk and dug its claw into Danny's belly. Blood dribbled from his mouth.

As the monster dug deeper into him, he stared at Elijah who was running away. He wished he could have stayed quiet so the monster would hear Elijah's footsteps, but he couldn't help but scream as the thing sunk its teeth into him.

CHAPTER 24

Frying the Destination

Winter's head slammed into the wall of the shelter, which was now the floor. Heavy boxes crashed beside them. They righted themselves against the new side of the structure. Candlestick clutched her father's arm. Violin breathed heavily and aimed her boom weapon toward the side the monster continued to slam into. The bottom of the shelter, where the wheels were, seemed harder for the creatures to dent, because as much as they slammed into it, it hadn't pushed in as the other side had.

Lion wriggled and fought against Winter's grip, trying to let out his warning cries, but somehow, Winter held tight to the animal's mouth.

Violin tapped Winter's arm. "What should we do? What's the plan?"

Winter shook his head, tears forming in his eyes. He couldn't tap back to her, because his hands were clutching Lion, trying to keep him silent. He moved his mouth, hoping she could read his words. "We do nothing but stay silent until this stops."

Every bang caused Winter's heart to leap. Candlestick dug her fingers into his arm. Violin's hands lost the steadiness they had

114

against the boys. Her fingers trembled as she moved the boom weapon around, aiming at walls.

The monster banged into the side again. The shelter shifted, not quite turning over again, but it slid against the cement below.

Then, something slammed into what was now the top of the shelter, where all the dents were from earlier. The monster was standing above them.

Slash marks drove through the metal, bits of it raining on top of them. Large black claws dug into the newly created holes. Winter whimpered at the sight. Violin trained her weapon toward them. She removed one hand from the boom weapon and tapped against her hip. "Do I fire? It will be loud. If I don't kill it, I might make things worse."

She seemed good with the weapon, but she was correct. Who knew how well these things could withstand the booms? If they stayed silent a little longer, the monster might give up and move on.

He waited for Violin to look at him directly and mouthed the word, "Wait."

She nodded, keeping the weapon on the target. With her other hand, she tapped, "Dad, I'm scared."

It slashed again, making the holes bigger. Something moved around the holes. It looked like the fire disc, but with teeth.

Candlestick removed her fingers from Winter's arm and covered her mouth with both hands, her eyes wide in panic.

Drips of hot flame dribbled from the creature's fire disc face. They leaked into the shelter, singeing the metal floor. A small fleck of it hit Lion and he squirmed with such force, he managed to free himself from Winter's grip.

He hollered and in return, the monster screeched, slashing and tearing through the wall like it was weak flesh. Winter shouted, "*NO!*" and flung himself forward, trying to grab the animal. The burning substance dripped onto him, melting his clothes and the flesh underneath. Tiny red burns grew on his back. He gritted his teeth and moaned.

Boom!

The monster screeched and dropped hard against the ceiling. Its face landed in one of the claw holes, and the fire disc in it dimmed to darkness.

Violin let out a huge breath. "Did I kill it?"

Lion continued to yelp. Winter stood, staring at the beast.

"I think you did."

He cried, letting the anxiety drip down his face. Candlestick ran to him and hugged him tight. "Come here," he told Violin, and she too came in for a hug.

"Oh my Kevin Bacon, that was the worst moment of my life."

They all cried, big cathartic tears.

A screech. One, then two, then many. Screeches from everywhere.

The thudding of large steps surrounded them.

A bang on one side, shoving the shelter and pushing Winter, Violin, Candlestick, and Lion across the room. A bang on the other side, and they fell backwards. The boxes shifted too. Some of them fell from their piles and slid across the floor.

The things kept smashing into the sides, pushing them all around. Winter's head spun. The girls tried to grab onto him but kept falling away.

Bang! Boxes everywhere. Lion roared and roared.

Bang!

Violin dropped her boom weapon and scrambled to pick it up.

The monsters screeched furiously.

Winter eyed the weapon and ran for it. As he bent down to grab it, the monsters slammed into the shelter again, and he fell forward, bashing his head against the wall.

Everything turned to black.

"WINTER, COME TO DINNER." Mama said.

"I'm working, Mama." Crouched by his machine, Winter tinkered with the circuits.

Mother shook her head. "The work can wait. You are doing wonderful things for us, for our people, but you can't do everything all the time."

"I can, and I will."

His mother bent low and extended her hand. He stared at it. She smiled, the kind that said: I am proud of you.

He took her hand and stood, leaving his invention to wait. He turned to it, giving it one last look before exiting the room.

His mother guided him to their kitchen table, past some of the other community members. Mona Lisa and her husband, Icarus. Guernica, Venus, Kiss, Arnolfini, Memory. Each person greeting him with a smile. The genius, the boy who would carry them into a new world with his inventions, his ability to communicate with electricity so well.

He sat with his mother and Uncle Café Terrace. Mother passed them plates of crickets and beets. His uncle dug right in.

With a mouthful, Café Terrace talked to Winter. "Tell us how the new generator is working."

Winter frowned. "I will get it working."

"I know that, boy. I am asking how it is currently going." His uncle chuckled. "Get it? Currently."

Winter pretended to laugh with him. "In truth, it is not going well. Something isn't right. Do not worry, but as for now, I need to figure something out."

"What exactly do you need to figure out?"

Winter stabbed some crickets with his fork. "When the water passes through, the generator functions correctly, but when the electricity reaches the destination..." He put his head down.

Café Terrace made a popping sound with his mouth.

"Yes, it fries the destination."

His uncle wiped his mouth with his sleeve. "Finish up your dinner and I will have a look."

Winter sighed and took a bite of cricket. He didn't want his uncle to help. He needed to figure it out on his own. As smart as his uncle was, he didn't comprehend the new machines Winter invented, and often bungled things up worse than they were.

But he knew better than to argue.

After dinner, Winter led his uncle to the work room. His mother pulled him to the side while his uncle went to work.

"I know you want to do this alone, but everyone needs a hand sometimes. Let go and let others contribute, too."

His uncle toyed with a metal bracket. "You know this is crooked?"

Winter rolled his eyes. Of course, he knew the bracket was crooked. That had nothing to do with his problem. Straightening the bracket would be a waste of time.

His uncle hammered at it. Bang. Bang. Bang.

Each smash with the hammer dug into Winter's spirit. Wasted time. Wasted energy. For what? Aesthetics? The bracket didn't need to be straight to function.

"Winter, come here while I hammer at this."

Winter looked to his mother: get me out of this.

She pushed him forward. "Let others help you."

Bang. Bang. Bang.

Winter shook his head.

Bang. Bang. Bang.

His mother put her hands on his shoulders. "Let others help you, son."

Bang. Bang. Bang.

Bang. Bang. Bang.

The girls were firing the boom weapons, both Candlestick and Violin, aiming their weapons up to the ceiling where multiple monsters tore into the roof.

Winter groaned and sat up.

Violin's weapon clicked. She put her arm down, examining it. "It's broken," she shouted.

Winter struggled to stand, dizzy and disoriented. "Stop."

Candlestick ignored him, firing blindly toward the ceiling. The claw marks were larger now and giant, sharp hands were digging in.

"Stop booming!" Winter shouted.

Both girls turned to him.

"Come here."

They listened, but as they moved toward him, they kept their attention on the claws reaching in.

Winter grabbed Candlestick's hand. "You. It has to be you."

"What?" She said.

"What do you mean?" Violin asked.

"Candlestick. You have to save us."

CHAPTER 25

The Traveler

Chucky nearly dropped his glass of water. Good thing he didn't. Who knew how sensitive the hearing was on those things? There were two of them, as far as Chucky could see, giant, lanky fuckers with claws and sharp teeth, like straight out of one of his horror movies. The things moved their heads back and forth, scanning the environment with their flashlight faces.

What. The. Fuck.

Chucky suppressed a laugh, something he tended to do at inappropriate times. A nervous thing, he called it. He laughed at his mother's calling hours because the anxiety of hosting so many people freaked him out, especially with the basement being what it was.

The day he woke up and found humanity non-existent, he must have laughed a hundred times. It took him three days to come to terms with it. When his wife was gone, he wasn't surprised. They had a happy marriage and all, but he didn't have illusions about his value in the relationship, looking how he did. When he had driven down empty roads littered with abandoned cars, he assumed something happened, but not that everyone disappeared from the planet. Maybe an emergency broadcast told everyone to get to a shelter because a nuke was headed their way or something like that. When he got home, fired up the generator and got the electricity running, he scanned all the channels on the radio, but only got static. Maybe an attack already happened?

He ran to his computer to check the internet, but shit, everything was down. He thought about his security cameras, but if they lost power, the digital cameras would have just shut down before catching anything, and even so, it all uploaded to a website which, clearly, wouldn't be functioning. *Fuck.*

Well, it was a good thing he had a bunker. So, he went down there and hung out for a while, just in case a nuke had landed in New York or somewhere. Chucky didn't want any of the fallout turning him into Godzilla. Or, maybe he did. That thought contributed to one of his many chuckles that day.

As days turned into weeks, Chucky began to see the world for what it was. His. He wasn't a conquering type. Had no interest in taking more than what he had, but he didn't mind not having to deal with people ever again. Except for Lydia, he'd miss her. He didn't cry, but he was sad. She was a nice wife and he loved her in the ways he knew how. He had to survive, though. He couldn't let emotions bring him down.

Last man standing. He always assumed that would happen, but he thought it would be because he was prepared for some disaster, not because he slept through the damned disappearance of humanity. What the holy hell, right?

He tried to think through what could have caused it. Nothing was destroyed. Buildings were all intact. His house was fine.

But now, standing in the window watching giant fucking monsters trudge through the wintery woods? Well, shit. Years of watching science fiction and horror movies and he never considered them as an explanation. He was too steeped in realism, too egotistical, wanting the reason for his life to continue to be because he outsmarted the world. The same jerks who called him a loon for stocking up on supplies and building a bunker all died while he lived peacefully.

The monsters threatened that, though. Having to quietly

maneuver around a bunch of freaks. *Fuck.* That's what life was already like. He grew up in that world. He thought he had the chance at something different, something he could own.

The creatures marched along, not paying any attention to his house. He worried the smoke from the wood stove would alert them, but he guessed they were more primitive than that. Too stupid to know smoke meant fire, and fire meant people.

He wondered why fear hadn't taken over him. Even when he tried to conjure it, just to feel a rush of adrenaline, none came. All he felt was annoyance, not even shock outside of the initial, quick reaction.

He turned to the couch where a photo of his wife leaned on the arm. He had moved it from the end table yesterday and slept clutching it. He did love her; he just wasn't good at showing it.

"Well, Lydia, is this what did it to you?" He whispered.

No. Wait. The monsters didn't end humanity. There weren't bones lying around, no dead bodies, gnawed or otherwise. Maybe they ate people whole, but there would have been blood, right? Some sign of an attack. This was straight sci-fi shit, though. Maybe they laser beamed folks into oblivion. They did have those glowing faces.

The creatures moved out of his sight, going away from the house, and that was fine by Chucky. Good riddance.

Then, something else moved around the tree line, not far from where the monsters had just been.

A person.

Chucky's heart galloped. He didn't like people. He was a loner. But now that none of them existed, seeing another person brought him joy. When the world was full of humans, he had no use for them. But now, alone in the universe, with giant creatures around, Chucky needed a friend.

He opened the door slowly. A cold breeze struck his face. He waved. He'd give this one chance. If the person saw him, great, but if not, too bad. He sure as fuck wasn't going to yell.

The person hid behind a tree, scoping out where the monsters went, not even looking at Chucky's palace in the woods.

Chucky glanced where the monsters had been, making sure they weren't looking right back at him. When he felt safe, he waved harder, faster, more forcefully.

Finally, he caught the eye of the traveler and the person booked it, running toward him. Chucky smiled as the human came closer. A friend.

"Hurry, shut the door," the man whispered as he entered the threshold.

Chucky closed it fast, but slowed down before it shut, so as not to make noise. The traveler took long, winded breaths.

"What the hell are those things?" Chucky asked.

The traveler shook his head. "I have no fucking clue."

Chucky extended his hand. "I'm Chucky."

The traveler looked up. "Elijah."

CHAPTER 26

Staying Silent

From the moment Winter had knelt down and told Candlestick they'd be leaving their family behind, she stayed silent. Never argued, never grew angry or sad. She knew her father, trusted him to do what was right, and believed in him to make everything okay again.

When they trudged toward an unknown destination, she stayed silent.

When they battled for their home against weird Earth children, she stayed silent.

And now, when monsters screeched and clawed in front of her, and her father and sister argued behind her, she stayed silent, deep in concentration, absorbed in her own being.

Concentrate.

Focus.

"I agree, she is ready. But now is not the time to test it."

"Now is precisely the time to test it. This will bring it out of her. This is what she needs."

What she needs. Candlestick frowned at the words. What she needs had always been decided for her. What she needed was a mother, a grandmother, a stupid uncle. A home, crickets, her toys.

She took a deep breath, inhaling the horrors around her. She fell into her memories. Her father telling her they must leave their home.

"But you can heal them, Dad."

Tears formed in his eyes and Candlestick knew she had struck a nerve, broken something in him, but she didn't understand how.

"I cannot."

"Why? You always can."

"It's not working this time."

Candlestick wanted to say, "It works every time. You're not trying hard enough. You're giving up," but instead, she stayed silent.

"Can I kiss Mom goodbye?" she asked.

Winter shook his head. "If you get close to her, you will get sick, too."

"Okay," she said, and put her head down, staying silent.

Her sister and father continued to debate her worth behind her. A horrific arm with sharp points slashed in front of her.

She inched forward, allowing herself to get so close she could feel a breeze coming from the violent movements.

She put her hands on her chest as her lungs sucked in air.

The monsters had made holes big enough they could shove their heads through. They screamed angrily, wanting to kill. But they wouldn't kill her, she knew. Not her. She didn't know how she knew this, but she did, instinctively.

She reached out a hand, and let her fingers skim the surface of the monster's shoulder, feeling the rough, slimy flesh.

Winter grabbed her, pulling her back, but she yanked herself free from his grip.

"Get away from them!" he shouted.

"I told you," Violin said.

Candlestick focused on the air entering her body, holding it in her stomach, then releasing.

Memories.

. . .

"It is time, girl. You get to pick your name," her mother said, handing her the book.

Candlestick flipped through the pages, but by the time she had reached the end, she hadn't decided yet. None of the pictures stood out to her the way everyone said they would.

Her father put his hands on her shoulders. "Which one do you like best?"

She breezed through the pages again and stopped at one.

Her parents laughed, sheer joy on their faces. Violin put her hands over her face.

"You picked my page," she said.

Candlestick looked to her parents, waiting to see what they would say.

Winter smiled. "This is also what your sister picked. It is called Violin and Candlestick. So, we will call you Candlestick."

She nodded.

"How weird that she picked the same one as me," Violin shook her head, and put her hands on her hips.

"There are hundreds of pictures in there. It does seem to be fate that she selected the same one," her mother said, and they all agreed.

But it wasn't a coincidence, or fate. Candlestick had found the book in her mother's room a few weeks earlier. She carefully studied the markings in it. She couldn't read yet, but she understood letters. Her father had done the alphabet with her, and her grandmother told her the sounds each letter made.

On many of the pictures, Candlestick found a word or two written in the purple ink her Auntie made for them to write with. She studied the words, trying to make sense of them. Eventually, she determined the words were the names of the people who selected each picture. She knew her sister's name. Violin. It starts with a vvvvv sound. Vvvvv. Vee. She flipped the pages frantically, searching for the V.

When she found it, she knew she would pick that picture, too. She decided that on her fifth birthday, she would search the book and see if something stuck out to her, called to her as everyone said it would, but if none did, she would follow in her sister's footsteps.

Sometimes, when nothing feels right, it is better to be someone else.

. . .

She opened her eyes and a heat intensified in her pupils, burning out her vision. She knew if her father or sister saw her face, they'd be looking at a glowing red. For some, it was green, but she knew hers was red. Back to that intrinsic feeling.

Her dad and Violin couldn't see it, though, because they were behind her, arguing.

They'd see her power, nonetheless.

She put her arms up, feeling the air's electricity driving through her body, forging a connection with her. She was one with the gods. Maybe she was even a sibling of Kevin Bacon himself. The idea sent a shiver up her spine and a smile across her face.

She feared no monsters.

Her diaphragm expanded and she released the force of it out of her lungs in a giant scream. Deafening, terrifying, even to her.

She screamed until she collapsed to the floor.

CHAPTER 27
The Good Lord Giveth

Elijah fucking hated Chucky. This dude was a pure, grade A loser. He was worse than Bryce. In fact, he was Bryce in 25 years, after giving up on life ten different times. He considered killing the piece of shit right away, taking over his cabin, and hanging for a while until the monsters gave him enough breathing room to go back out there and get those girls, but he figured he'd deal with the prick long enough to learn if he had any secret stashes of food or something else useful.

Elijah noticed a generator. Maybe good ole Chucky still had gas for it, too. He wasn't using it now, he had a wood fire going, which was nice. This was probably the warmest Elijah felt in weeks.

Chucky pointed Elijah toward the fire while he kept his stupid face in the window, staring at nothing.

The monsters were moving in the other direction, away from the house. They were long out of view now.

Elijah found no use in worrying or freaking out about monsters; nothing shocked him anymore. Nothing scared him. He used to fear everything, he was a little bitch who had anxiety attacks every single day on his way to school. He didn't know it then, but the reason the other kids ignored him, looked away when he walked by, wasn't because they were picking on him. They were terrified of him.

But now, the fucking world had ended. Humanity had just disappeared. It would have been a blessing if the good Lord had left him some women to enjoy. At least the good Lord had left him something, but he had fucking lost them.

"You don't seem very worried about those things," Chucky said, as if reading Elijah's thoughts.

Elijah rubbed his palms together in front of the wood stove. "I'm not."

Chucky finally moved away from the window and sat near him, not uncomfortably close, but getting there. "Why?"

Elijah shrugged, "I woke up one day and the world was over. Everyone had disappeared. I knew there had to be something crazy going on. Aliens, monsters, demons, whatever. Nothing made sense anymore, so everything seemed possible."

Chucky rubbed his chin, "Yeah, I think I understand that."

Elijah doubted it. "Wanna know the truth?"

Chucky nodded.

"I'm fucking happy this shit is happening. I hated the way things were. Fuck people. Now, I get to do whatever the hell I want. If I have to deal with monsters so I don't have to deal with people, it seems like a fucking win."

His heart sped up, a delightful adrenaline. He hoped the man reacted, tried to kick him out or something. Elijah yearned for a reason to hurt this guy.

Chucky stared for a moment, then broke into an obnoxiously loud laugh. "You're a little psycho, huh? Oh, I like you. You know what? I'm gonna show you something I think you'll dig."

He stood up, struggling to his feet thanks to his fat belly. Elijah followed, remembering to touch his gun occasionally, to remind himself of the power he held, and to remind Chucky as well.

Chucky led him down a flight of stairs into a cold basement. Elijah was surprised because the cabin didn't feel like a place that would have a downstairs.

Chucky reached for something in the dark and lit a zippo. The flames carried to a wick, and a torch illuminated an unassuming, rather bare cement square of a room. In one corner, a set of shelves housed a few boxes. The cardboard was unwrinkled, hardly worn. Other than that, the only thing in the room was a metal door, the kind you'd see in a bank.

"What's in the boxes?" Elijah asked.

Chucky darted toward them. Elijah followed, keeping a safe distance, ready to draw when necessary.

Chucky opened a box and pulled out white packets. "Rations. Some of them are true military stuff, and some I got from prepper sites, which are basically just as good. I also have some lighter fluid, antibiotics, all sorts of cool stuff. I even scored some potassium iodide."

"What's that?"

"It protects you if you are exposed to radiation. Keeps the thyroid gland happy."

Elijah nodded. This fucking dude.

"Anyway, that's not what I wanted to show you." Chuck moved to the door and finagled with some mechanics on it. "My wife knew about this place, but we didn't talk about it. She sort of just accepted it was something I needed, but she wanted no part of it."

He opened the door and clicked on a light switch. "Everything down here runs on battery generators right now, totally separate power sources from the rest of the house. I have the gas ones set up for it, too, because those will be handier, but for now, I like running on battery."

He moved out of the way to showcase the room. Elijah nearly fell over. It was goddamned beautiful.

A massive room with a pool table, DVDs, a large screen television, pinball machines, a fucking kitchen. It had everything. "Holy shit, this is cool. How many battery generators are you running in here?"

Chucky laughed. "An absurd amount. The price I pay for being stingy with the gas. Eventually, I will need to switch it over."

"That's a big ass tv."

Chucky waved it off. "Waste of space, honestly. With no cable or

Wi-Fi, it's not like I can stream something. I got the DVDs, but meh, I never have the concentration to watch anything anymore. I do love to play a little pinball here and there, though."

Elijah rubbed his hand over a pinball machine. It was Wizard of Oz themed, and he had to smile. Raised by wilderness folks, forced to appreciate the good ole outdoors, living a minimalist lifestyle, he always salivated to visit family or friends with flashy toys. His cousin had a handheld gaming system, the Nintendo DS. Elijah dreamed of it, days later, while he and his family slept out in the field behind their house.

He remembered the first time he watched the Wizard of Oz at that same cousin's house. From its start, he was absorbed with Dorothy's life. The grey life of a farm girl, how special. She was smoking hot, too. But then the tornado shot her into a colorful hell-hole and Elijah bawled his eyes out. Everyone asked what was wrong, but he couldn't place it, couldn't name what bothered him.

He still wasn't sure. He liked the bland part, and hated the flamboyant vibrancy, but that alone wouldn't upset him to tears. Something else really fucked him up about it, and now, staring at that machine, it was fucking him up again.

Maybe it was time to kill this fat piece of shit.

"This still isn't what I wanted to show you. My wife actually liked the pinball room. You ready for me to reveal my deepest, darkest secret?" Chucky chuckled.

"Go for it." As Elijah followed Chucky to the far wall, he gripped his gun. He needed to kill Chucky, but more than that, something about the dude made Elijah nervous, like he should be ready to defend himself.

Chucky ran his fingers along the wood paneling on the back wall. "Probably not a surprise to you that I wasn't very well liked as a kid. Kind of a goof. But I'll bet this will surprise you. First time I got laid, I was 11."

He knocked on one of the panels, and it popped off, and then took off the two panels next to it. "My whacked-out uncle bought me a hooker as a birthday present, said it would get me off the comic books and help me grow up. Thing is, maybe it would have worked if I had any chance of getting laid like that again. All it did was make me dive even further into fantasy worlds."

He pressed his palm in the center of the bare wall, and with a gentle shake, the whole thing separated from the rest of the wall and swung into a hidden room. It was like something you'd see in one of those DS games.

"Is this a fucking secret room?" Elijah's mouth dropped.

Chucky ignored his question. "I didn't have sex again until I met my wife, fifteen years later. And she wasn't into it, like, at all. I don't mean she didn't dig me and probably went off cheating with one of her coworkers. I mean, she didn't care for sex at all and only let me have it because she knew I wanted it."

Once the wall opened, Chucky moved to the side, revealing a long hallway with yet another door at the end. He walked toward the door. Elijah kept a clean distance. Now it was getting really friggin' creepy. Strip lights shined along the hall, giving him sight at least.

"In other words, even after getting married, I never got anything like I did when I was eleven, and holy shit did I yearn for what I got when I was eleven.

So, I started cheating on my wife, buying prostitutes. We made good money, so I could afford them. Don't know why I never got one before we got married, but I didn't have much for money then, so that's probably it."

At the end of the hall, Chucky pulled out a loose stone in the wall and reached his hand in. He took a set of keys out from the hole. Elijah felt a rush of fear, something even fucking monsters couldn't bring him. Everything about this was fucked. Chucky was going to try to murder him and probably eat him or something. This dude was a Jeffery Dahmer level lunatic.

Chucky slid the key into the door lock. "Anyway, after a little bit, fucking them wasn't enough." He opened the door to reveal a room with a bed, nice and tidy. The sheets tucked in tight, the pillows fluffed. Two sets of chains led from the opposite sides of the frame and met in the center of the mattress.

"I don't know why I'm telling you all of this. Maybe because I felt us meeting the way we did was kismet, like we had a special bond. Or maybe it's because it's the fucking end of the world and the only other person who ever knew what I did was my wife, who refused to discuss it. But this is where I kept women locked up until I was done with them, then they'd go to the lake behind the house. But now the damned world is over and there don't seem to be any women around."

Elijah's hand released the pressure it had built on the handle of the gun. He looked up at Chucky, stared him in the face, and laughed.

"Why is that funny?" Chucky sounded angry.

Elijah put his hand on Chucky's shoulder. "Boy, have I got some news for you."

CHAPTER 28

On Resolve Alone

Winter ran to Candlestick. He lifted her head and cradled her in his arms. The monsters stopped slashing and moved away from the holes they'd created. Streaks of light shone through from the fire disc's ascent.

"It's daytime, that's why the monsters are going," Violin said behind him.

"Yes, but your sister did tap into her power, enough so that it knocked her out."

"She will be okay. Mama said it's what happens your first time using your powers. You played a dangerous game, Dad. Why?"

"Faith in my family is never dangerous. If the sun didn't do it, she would have. Whatever she was tapping into would have worked." He rocked Candlestick's body.

"No. She wasn't ready for so much. That's why she is asleep."

"Shush. Get some water."

Violin rummaged through their belongings and brought him a bottle. He gently tipped it, letting a tiny amount drip onto his daughter's face.

"Should I try to wake her, or let her come back naturally?"

Violin put her hands on her father's shoulders while he rocked Candlestick. "You're scared, aren't you?"

He turned his head to her. "There are giant monsters. Aren't you scared, too?"

She stepped back. "Not that. Of course, I'm scared of that. I mean, you're scared about your powers, aren't you?"

He sighed and put his head down. "Yes."

Lion paced, anxious about the monsters, but at least he stopped yelping.

"You couldn't save them because they had something beyond healing. It wasn't a weakness in your powers. It was a weakness in our people."

Tears formed in Winter's eyes. "You speak too old. You're supposed to be a child."

"There is no time for that anymore. What do we do now?" She pointed toward the destruction, the holes in the ceiling, the overturned boxes, her finger scanning the end of their peace.

Winter lifted Candlestick's head to his and kissed her forehead. "You must wake now, dear. Unfortunately, we don't have the time for you to rest."

Violin sat next to him and crossed her legs. Her fingers picked at the wrinkles in her shirt. Her nervous tic, not much different from her father's. "Should we run? Try to find another shelter like the one we had before?"

Candlestick coughed and opened her eyes. She stared for a moment, her eyes widening. "What happened?"

Winter smiled. "You tapped into your powers. It took a lot out of you."

"What is my power?" Her voice cracked.

"We don't know."

She pushed her head up and sat up straight. "But I made the monsters leave? It worked?"

He nodded. "No. The sunlight did. But you were about to."

"Oh."

They sat in silence for a moment. Winter rubbed her back. Violin held her hand.

"I don't know what to do now. We can't stay here. If we run and don't find some place new to stay, we could get stuck outside at nighttime."

Candlestick reached over Winter and grabbed the bottle of water. She gulped it down.

Violin shrugged. "We could start walking, try to find somewhere, and when the fire disc reaches its highest point, if we haven't found anything, we turn back and run back here. It's not safe shelter, but it's better than being out in the middle of night."

Winter stood up. "Okay. Let us eat very quickly. Fill our bellies and hit the road. It will give Candlestick some time to recover."

They cracked open some cans and wolfed down a meal. Winter fed Lion, too, but hadn't decided what to do with the animal yet. If they needed silence, he was too much of a liability.

After breakfast, Winter refilled his bag with whatever food he could carry. When he lifted it to his shoulder, he winced, and dropped it.

"What's wrong, Dad?" Candlestick asked.

"Nothing. I am fine."

Violin went to him and gently placed her hand on his forearm. They smiled at each other, but then she gripped his wrist and pulled up his sleeve. Red streaks radiated from the site of his bite.

"Oh no, Dad." Violin stepped back.

He shrugged, trying to play it cool, but the bite scared him. It had gotten worse, and he knew this kind of thing could kill him. He refused to die until his children were safe, but he knew he couldn't survive on resolve alone.

She shook her head. "We have to go back. We have to go now."

"We can't." He didn't want to admit he wouldn't even remember the way. "We will die if we do."

She waved her hand at his arm. "You will die if we don't. We need medicine. You know you can't heal yourself."

"No. Let's move. We have to go." He lifted the bag onto his shoulder again, this time on the other side.

"Dad!"

"Enough. We are running out of time. We go now."

He bent down, pulled the handle to the exit sideways, and the door slid open. Fire disc light enveloped them, blinded them. "Here we go again," he said and stepped out onto the cement.

They walked for hours. Violin kept staring at his arm. His feet ached and the back of his boots dug into his Achilles tendons, causing them to bleed. The scenery never changed. Long stretches of cement, destroyed metal wagons, dense woods on each side. Winter's heart kept doing a weird thing where it sped up and thumped harder for a few moments before correcting itself and going back to a steady beat. His arm sent waves of throbbing pain so intense he had to fight against falling over from it.

"So, what do we do, Dad? Tell me that? You know you can't ignore the arm to make it go away, right?"

"I said enough, Violin."

Candlestick stopped. "Dad, you never listen!"

He stopped. "We can't stop to talk about this. Every second we waste is another opportunity for us to die. We have to keep walking."

"So, talk and walk," Violin said.

"I would rather not."

Candlestick stomped her feet and stopped moving. "You want us to keep moving, then speak to us. Otherwise, I won't move from this spot."

Winter turned, biting down hard. He wrapped his arm around Candlestick and lifted her, but a violent, sharp pain drilled up his arm into his skull. He dropped her before he could truly lift her and hollered in pain.

Violin got between them. "Are you done being a child? Talk to us."

"What do you want me to say?"

"I want you to tell us how you plan to get out of this. We need to go back home. It's your only chance. Are you going to find magical medicine up here? Will you know which medicines are which? You can't die, Dad."

Candlestick emerged from behind her sister, tears in her eyes. "We need you."

He tapped on his hip. Pinky, long tap.

"Okay, what? Can we go back home?"

He shook his head. "No. We can't go back home. We can walk and talk."

He turned around and kept moving. He heard them sigh behind him.

"Well, talk then. What are you going to do?"

"I am going to have faith that we will figure it out as we have figured everything out so far. In the other place, I found a shelter filled with food for us. When we were attacked, you figured out a boom weapon and saved us. In the woods, we found our way to this cement place, and we found a new home with tons of food. We survived monsters. We will keep surviving. Something will happen. Something will save us."

"That's the stupidest plan of all time. We survived because we tried, because we fought, because we loved each other, and because we did what we needed to protect each other."

"And we will keep surviving off those things." He cracked his back, which now also ached, thanks to the heavy bag over his shoulder.

"But we are telling you that it is our turn to protect you. You have to listen to us. We have to go back home."

He glanced up at the fire disc. "Do you think it is at its highest? That it will be heading back down soon?"

Violin put her arm above her eyes and looked up. "Yes. We should head back."

Winter dropped his bag and rubbed his eyes. "We have nowhere to go. We can go back there for the night, I suppose, but we can't keep staying there, and if we don't find something in a day's walk, we are trapped."

"You got more worries than that, I'm afraid," a gruff voice said.

Winter turned quickly. A man stood on top of a blue metal wagon with a boom weapon in his hand. Lion barked and ran to the wagon.

Violin moved in front of her father and raised her boom weapon.

Click. A boom weapon pressed against Winter's temple as another man came up to his side. "You're gonna want to tell the little lady to drop her weapon."

Winter kept his head in place, but shifted his eyes to his side, as he reached behind himself to find Candlestick. He swatted but found nothing.

"Don't worry, sir. I got your daughter right here." A third voice said.

CHAPTER 29
The Signal

Winter assessed. There was a boom weapon aimed at them from the top of the metal wagon, another pointed right on his temple, and he assumed the man behind him holding Candlestick had another.

"Violin, lower your weapon."

She listened but took her time lowering it. The man next to Winter reached out a hand while keeping the armed one by Winter's temple. "Good girl, now give that here."

Lion barked and jumped by the blue wagon, ignoring the two men within his reach. Winter felt the bite in his arm and wished his new friend would show the same level of violence toward these villains.

"No," she said.

The man on the top of the wagon pulled something out of a pack he had around his stomach and dangled it in front of Lion. "Come here, pal," he said as he jumped down and opened the door to the wagon. He tossed the object into it, and Lion jumped in after this magical item. Winter shook his head as the man closed the door on the stupid animal.

Wagon Man turned back to them. "Looks like we got off on the wrong foot there, folks, and I suppose that's our fault. You're lucky you only ran into us. We're nice people."

He walked until he was right in front of Violin. "We just want whatever is in your bag there, then we will be on our way, and so will you."

Winter's pulse accelerated as the man knelt in front of Violin, and he hated not hearing from Candlestick. "You can have our bag. We would like to leave now so we can get back to our shelter before the monsters come."

Wagon Man chuckled. "Monsters, you say. You hear that, Doug? Monsters!"

From behind Winter, the man with Candlestick made a spitting noise. "Yeah, yeah. Very fucking funny."

"Tell us about these monsters, mister," Wagon Man said.

Winter wanted out of this. "They come out at night, according to the man who told us about them, and that seems to be true. They attacked us at our shelter, but left in the morning."

Winter almost lunged as Wagon Man gripped Violin's wrist and twisted until she dropped her weapon. Wagon Man picked it up and stood. "Well now, mister, that is one heck of a story. What did these monsters look like?"

Winter darted his eyes all over, planning, or trying to. No solutions came to him. "They had fire for faces."

"Ha! I fucking told you!" Doug said from behind Winter. "Lampposts are real!"

The other two men laughed.

"Alright, I don't have time for this. Grab his bag and let's get moving."

"Good. We are free to leave then?" Winter asked.

The man with the gun to Winter's temple shoved him. Winter caught a deep scar trailing down the man's face from forehead to jaw. "No. You are free to move into the woods that way. You're coming with us for a little bit, then you can leave."

"Why? We have nothing else to give you but what's in that bag."

"We'll decide that, buddy. Now fucking move." He shoved Winter again.

Winter put his head down and walked, but his eyes kept moving. Three men, all with boom weapons. They were going to kill Winter, Violin, and Candlestick. Why else would they bring them into the woods? They were humans; humans liked to kill. He needed a plan, something to get out of this. Avoid death from the humans and get back to the shelter to avoid death from the monsters. The more time he wasted planning, the less likely they'd make it back before dark.

He positioned himself ahead of his daughters. Wagon Man walked in front, leading them. Scar Guy walked directly behind Winter, giving him little breathing room. And somewhere behind them all, Doug trailed with Violin and Candlestick. Winter wished he knew their positioning better.

They hiked down a long stretch of land between thick forest, a layer of white draped over everything. The fire disc crept downward and Winter feared for every second wasted.

He tapped, "Please pay attention."

He made it a point to pause, despite his anxiety to make something happen. If he tapped rapidly, the men would notice he was up to something. They'd have no idea what, but they might try to force him to stop.

"No time. Must act now." He jammed his fingers into his hip with the last word, hoping the girls would see the importance of it.

Three breathes. Enough of a pause. "Candlestick, fall on my signal. I'll cough. Cough equals fall."

He prayed they were seeing this. He had no way to know, and they had no way to respond.

"They will stop. Violin, distract man behind me. Candlestick, stop your man from booming."

His heart slammed against his ribs. This brought about a new level of pain in his arm. He needed to make this happen fast, but there were too many variables, too many problems that could arise. Nothing about this plan was safe, but he had no time to think up another one.

He almost coughed but stopped himself. This plan put his children at risk of death. He couldn't go through with it. He needed something better. His throat turned dry, and that made him almost actually cough.

He wiped sweat from his forehead. Strange, to be so hot in such crisp air. He tilted his head to talk to the man behind him, but also to try and see where his daughters were positioned. "How far until we get to where we are going?"

"Another couple of miles," the man answered.

Winter nodded. He couldn't get a view of them.

They walked and walked, and Winter watched the fire disc fall behind the trees. They'd never make it back before the monsters came out and he only had himself to blame. Too cowardly to make a move, to fight. He couldn't risk his daughter's lives.

But weren't these men going to kill them all anyway? Maybe not. Maybe there was something else happening that Winter couldn't understand. This was Earth after all, none of it made any sense.

That was wishful thinking, he knew, a way to ease himself from the blame of their approaching death, from his lack of action, his fear.

"May I speak to my daughters for a moment?" Winter asked.

"No," Wagon Man said without turning around.

"Can I stop to fix my boot? Something is stuck in there."

"No," the man repeated.

He nodded and kept walking. Monsters or men, something would kill him and his daughters tonight if he didn't make a move. They might as well die trying to live.

So, he coughed.

CHAPTER 30

The Woods are Alive

At first, nothing happened. Everyone kept walking, the white stuff crunching under their feet. Dread filled Winter's lungs and he thought he might suffocate. His daughters hadn't seen his messages.

But then, he heard a loud crunch in the snow and Candlestick shouted, "Ow!" After that, the noises mish-mashed into a chorus of chaos.

Winter couldn't listen enough to figure out how his children fared because he also needed to act. He charged the man in front, who was in mid-turn to see what the racket was about. Winter's shoulder slammed into the man's face and knocked him down. He used the surprise to rip the boom weapon from the man's hands and then boomed it into his chest. A blast of red splattered all over Winter's clothes and the white snow around them. Meanwhile, three more booms went off behind him.

He turned and fell into the snow, hoping the lower angle would provide him with some cover against any wild booms. Candlestick knelt in front of Doug, who lay face down in the snow. Violin stood over Scar Man, who was also down and covered in blood. A coat of red dripped down Violin's face.

"Violin, you killed them both?"

She nodded and said, "Yes," and then she broke down into whimpers and tears.

Winter ran to Violin. "Candlestick, get over here."

The girls wrapped themselves around their father, and he squeezed. "You're all okay? No injuries?"

They both shook their heads. "Oh, my babies. Every time I think it can't get scarier up here."

Violin pulled away, wiping snot from her face, a streak of red painting her sleeve. "I know we are trained for this. I know I'm not supposed to care about humans, but every time I kill one, I feel more like one of those monsters."

Winter shook his head. "No, you can't do that. Humans are evil; it's no worse than killing a cricket. We have to kill them if we want to survive."

"I don't think that's true. I think they are just trying to survive, too, and everyone sees everyone as a threat."

"Nonsense. If they wanted to, they could have taken our stuff and left us. They were dragging us through the woods to murder us. We had no choice but to kill them first."

Violin's hands trembled. "I am metal. I am a wall. I am trained for this."

Candlestick pulled on Winter's shirt. "We have to go." She pointed to the fire disc, which hovered just above the horizon.

"We are out of time. Run. Grab any boom weapons you find." Winter ran to his bag, scooped it up, and grabbed Candlestick's hand to pull her forward. They all dashed through the woods in the direction they had come.

The fire disc's light deteriorated quickly and a grey shadow stole the atmosphere.

They reached the cement, out of breath, the darkness closing in. "We don't have time to get back to where we were. Check for metal wagons that open up."

"We can go in the one with Lion," Candlestick said.

"No. He is too loud. We must separate ourselves from him."

Violin ran to a metal wagon and checked the doors.

Candlestick grabbed Winter by his shirt. "We can't leave Lion. He tried to protect us."

"And he failed, as we will fail him. It's the way life works."

"Dad, please." Candlestick's eyes filled with water.

"Enough," Winter said and moved toward a brown, boxy metal wagon nearby.

"Here," Violin said as she pulled open a door on a tall, grey one. "Lots of room, too."

Winter latched onto Candlestick's arm and pulled her toward the wagon. She didn't fight against him but didn't rush either.

They piled into the back of the wagon and squeezed close together.

"We will have to cuddle for warmth. It's going to only get colder until the fire disc comes back. No matter what, we must remain calm and quiet."

Candlestick stuck her face to the window. "He's right there. I can keep him quiet, but if we aren't with him, he will make his noises and the monsters will eat him."

"I'm sorry. There is nothing we can do for him."

She screwed up her face and her eyes filled with tears. "Dad, I can't just leave him to die. I can't."

Winter pulled her away from the window. "You have no choice. If you save him, you kill us. It's a sad decision, but it's the right one."

He hugged her, but she didn't hug back.

Winter turned toward the wagon Lion was in and saw the animal sticking his nose to the window, and his heart broke.

Lion yipped and scratched at the window, eager to return to his new family. *Family*. The poor soul.

As his yipping intensified, loud rumbles shook the trees on both sides of them.

"They are here," Violin tapped.

Candlestick stared at Lion, pressing her face closer to the window. It startled Winter, and he couldn't help but lean over her to see if she were crying again. Instead of tears, he found glowing, red eyes. Her powers were working. He turned his head, glanced out the window, tried to place what her magic did. Nothing, he saw nothing.

Slowly, Candlestick lifted her finger to her mouth, and said, "Shhhhhhhh."

As soon as she said it, Lion stopped yipping and dropped down out of view.

Candlestick turned back to them. She lifted her hands, which were shaking violently. "He is asleep now."

Winter laughed in a whisper. "Your powers. You can command animals?"

She shrugged. "I guess. I'm not sure."

Violin hugged her. She tapped on her sister's shoulder. "Whatever you did, it saved us."

"I can keep him quiet from now on, so you have to let us keep him, Dad. He's not a problem anymore."

Winter nodded. "Yes. Maybe we can keep him, but for tonight, let him be quiet over there. We need to learn more about your powers first."

"Fine," she said.

They sat in the wagon, trying to sleep, but the bitter coldness kept them awake. Their hugging and cuddling did nothing to stop Candlestick's lips from turning blue. Violin's nose changed to bright red and Winter couldn't keep his limbs from shivering.

They tossed and turned, waking each other up, the cold eating away their precious few hours available for sleep. They couldn't keep living like this.

"I have an idea," Violin said.

She leaned over to her door, and popped it open, slowly and quietly.

"Violin, no. Stay in here."

She turned to him. "I will be right back."

She darted out of the wagon.

"Violin," Winter whispered in as much of a shout as he could make without alerting the monsters.

She went to the wagon next to theirs and cupped her hands above her eyes while pressing her face to the window. After a moment, she went to the wagon behind it, and did the same thing.

Winter understood; she was looking for something to keep them warm.

But as she moved farther from the safety of their space, into a deep darkness potentially filled with monsters, his throat constricted, and his blood traveled through his heart faster than any metal wagon could go. He would chase after her if doing so didn't mean leaving his other daughter behind. She should have told him her plan so he could have gone out into the dangerous territory.

She moved to a third metal wagon, then a fourth.

Farther and farther away.

The anxiety built in his temples, throbbing.

She peeked into the window and turned to them with a smile. When she opened the door, a blasting, horrific sound came from the wagon and a set of lights in the front of it blinked on and off. Violin froze in place.

The woods came alive with rumbles and screeches.

CHAPTER 31

A Creature Crawling in the Skull

"Stay here," Winter said to Candlestick. He ran out of the car, closing the door on his way out to give her extra protection.

The rumbling came from both sides, getting louder by the second. Violin stood in shock, not moving an inch. "Go. Go. Go," Winter yelled. She stayed in place.

He reached her, out of breath, his heart bouncing into his throat. She still didn't move. He grabbed her hand. "Let's go!"

He pulled her toward the car but was met with resistance. She couldn't move, wouldn't budge, just like when she was a child and getting into trouble. Winter bent low, so her waist was by his shoulder, and hoisted her up. He tried to hold it in but couldn't; he hollered in pain as his bitten arm warned his brain against the activity. He'd never felt pain like it, a blast of ache from his arm to his skull.

He almost dropped her, so shocked by the intensity, but he held on and marched forward. He walked fast, too exhausted to run, but trying his hardest to build up speed.

A tree crashed behind him, and a screech told him the monsters were on the cement path now.

The sounds of metal crashing into metal, glass shattering, and pounding feet surrounded him. He moved away from them as fast as he could while trying not to make noise.

In front of him, a few feet from the wagon in which Candlestick sat, a lamppost stomped by. It stood between him and his destination: his daughter, safety. He dipped behind another wagon, the one just behind his. He put Violin down and tapped, "I need you to wake up." She didn't respond, as if she had turned to glass.

He crept down, assessing in all directions. Multiple monsters tore into Violin's noise-making wagon, he guessed at least seven of them. The one monster between him and Candlestick was moving toward the loud wagon. Soon it would be out of his way. Two more monsters came through the tree line, from opposite sides of the cement. If the timing worked, the monster in his way would pass him, allowing him to run to Candlestick before the new one from the woods got too close and spotted him. If the timing didn't, he'd be dead in seconds.

He stood a little, and a whoosh of blood shot to his head, creating speckles in his vision. For a moment, he thought he might pass out.

He tapped again, "Violin. Wake up. Now."

Nothing. The monster in his way moved past him, focused solely on the loud car. He re-hoisted his daughter over his shoulder, and again his arm shot waves of sharp pain into his skull.

He crept toward Candlestick. Five feet. Four. Closer. Closer. The monsters all focused on the loud wagon. He was in the clear.

Then Violin screamed. *"NO! MAMA! NO! MAMA! MAMA!"* She flailed, kicking and punching Winter.

The monsters all turned and screeched, one unified voice of horror.

Winter ran, jumped in the car, and slammed the door.

"Shush. Please, shush."

Violin continued to scream, flail, and fight. She whacked Winter and Candlestick. Winter shoved his hand over her mouth. "Please, be quiet. I need you to be quiet."

She didn't. Couldn't. Something had broken in her and wouldn't stop hollering.

Candlestick rocked back and forth, gripping her forehead where her sister had struck her. She started shouting, too. *"GO AWAY! GO AWAY! GO AWAY!"*

"MAMA!"

"GO AWAY!"

Winter couldn't control them. The monsters marched toward the wagon, coming from all sides. Their giant steps shook the ground under them.

"MAMA."

"GO AWAY."

Violin stopped her violent strikes and her screaming turned into heaving, as if something blocked her from breathing. She convulsed, shaking and twitching.

"Violin, baby, what's wrong?"

He stroked her hair. "Baby, what is it? What is happening?"

"Help her, Dad. Help her."

He shook his head and placed his hand on her forehead, pressing tightly.

The door opened on his side.

"Candlestick!"

She turned to him. "Just fix her."

"Get back here."

The monsters charged. Violin heaved and convulsed, flopping all over the back seat. Winter reached for Candlestick. "Get in here, now."

Candlestick yelled, "Shut up and fix her! I will fix them."

"Get back in here." He let go of Violin and grabbed Candlestick. He yanked her, pulling her back in, but she fought against him. The monsters were there now, hovering over her.

She looked up and screamed into the sky. *"GO AWAY!"*

And they did. Their long claws and melting faces evaporated, streaming up to the cloudy night sky.

Winter made an audible gasp. "What just happened?"

Candlestick turned to him. "Just fix her."

Violin's body floundered and fell off the seat to the ground.

Winter struggled to lift her, her rigid body fighting against him. He pushed her up to the seat, ignoring the searing pain in his arm.

"Help me hold her in place," Winter said to Candlestick. She got back in the car and held Violin's legs, but she was too small to control her older sister.

Winter rubbed his hand on her forehead. "Shhhhhh." He pressed firmly, allowing his fingertips to dig in. A deep breath, ignoring the trauma around him. Concentrate. His vision snuck away, giving way to the green glow.

He absorbed the pain inside of her. It was different than any he'd experienced before, more visceral, more alive. It came from the brain, he knew, not a physical ailment. As it left her body and entered his, it weakened, broke apart into bits, but still, he felt the overwhelming sadness of it. Violin's grief had turned into an entity, a creature crawling in her skull, and it almost killed her.

He backed away, tears pouring down his cheeks. His daughter lay sleeping on the back seat, calm and temporarily peaceful. He knew his fix wouldn't be permanent. He could heal the immediate reaction but couldn't extract the deep hurt inside her.

Candlestick rubbed his shoulder. "She's okay now."

Winter leaned his back against the back of the front seat. "No, no she is not. Neither are you." He looked at her, revelation washing over him.

"What do you mean, Dad?"

"Those monsters. They are yours, aren't they?"

CHAPTER 32

A Checklist for Dying Peacefully

Candlestick grimaced. "What do you mean?"

"Are you making those monsters?" Winter stepped toward her but looked back to check on Violin. She slept heavily, her chest moving up and down with her breath.

Candlestick shook her head, tears filling the corners of her eyes. "No. I mean, I don't know."

Winter put his hand out. "You're not in trouble. You're not doing it on purpose. But you know, don't you? They are yours."

The tears escaped, rolling down her cheeks. "I don't want to. I hate them. But I know they belong to me. Why is this happening? How did you know?"

He knelt, opening his arms to her. "Because I felt them inside your sister's head. She is making them, too, but hers aren't leaving her brain. None of that matters. You made them go away. Can you control them?"

She quivered. "I don't think so. I mean, I did, but I don't know how. I just knew I could right then, but normally I don't feel that way. I think I could if I learned how."

Winter nodded. "Yes. And do you think you could learn how? Do you think you could figure it out?"

She nodded again and finally let herself fall into his hug. He rubbed her hair and squeezed tight.

"You're a good girl." Her tears dripped onto his neck.

"No. I am making monsters. They're killing everything."

"They haven't killed us yet, but they have probably killed some humans. Seems like a good thing to me."

"But they will kill you. I know they want to. They won't hurt me, but they want to kill you and Violin. I don't know how I know that, but I do."

He let her go, grabbed her upper arms, and stared directly into her eyes. "But we won't let them. I will keep fighting for us. Violin will keep fighting for us. And you will keep fighting for us."

"I will. I think they are gone for the night. I made them go away for a while, but I don't think it's going to stay that way. They're stronger than I am, here." She pointed to her temple.

As Winter thought, Lion began to yip again. "Let's check on your sister and get Lion out from his wagon. What do you say?"

She smiled. "Yes, please."

"When Violin is ready to go, we will start walking. I trust you when you say you think the monsters are gone for the night. If that's so, it gives us more time to walk and find somewhere more permanent to stay."

"Okay." Her leg tapped, anxious to unlock the animal.

"I am tired of just surviving. We need to find somewhere to fight for. Somewhere to live forever."

"Yes." She leaned forward.

He rubbed her shoulder. "Now, go get your friend."

He leaned on their metal wagon, monitoring her as she ran to Lion. She let him out, and he jumped on her, excited to be reunited.

The sight made Winter smile. He leaned down and slipped into the backseat. Violin slept soundly. Candlestick leaned in, and Lion stuffed his face below the seat, sniffing and licking the air.

Winter planned to let Violin sleep until she woke up naturally, but within moments, Lion had squirmed his way onto the floor by the seat and woke Violin by tickling her face with his whiskers.

She woke with a start and her eyes darted all over. "What happened?"

Winter explained everything. Violin denied it, having no recollection of anything after they killed the men in the woods. He chose not to press her. Candlestick almost chimed in, but Winter stopped her. There was no use trying to convince Violin of anything. She knew they weren't lying, but her mind couldn't properly accept it yet.

He gave her some time to fully wake, let her bearings adjust, while he prepared their bag and planned what they should do. Following the cement made the most sense, because what was the point of them if they didn't lead to something, but he also worried the cement would attract more violent humans than the woods.

The monsters, however, always seemed to come from the woods. While he trusted Candlestick when she said they wouldn't be back for a bit, he didn't want to tempt them, either.

Violin stepped out. "Are you sure we are safe from the monsters?"

Winter nodded.

"So, what now?"

He tapped, "We follow the cement path, but stay to the side, near the trees, still hugging close, so we can use metal wagons as cover if we need it. We must be more vigilant than last time. There are clearly more humans than we expected. We must always be prepared for them."

Violin rummaged through Winter's bag and dug out the jug of water. She gulped some down, rubbed her eyes, and stood up. "Let's go, then."

"Okay." He pulled the bag over his shoulder, hiding his reaction to the pain it caused.

As they walked down the road, Winter thought about dying. He could never find a cure for his arm. He would die sooner than expected, so he needed to find a home for the girls. They could easily defend themselves, but they couldn't set up a functioning place to live. He had to do that for them before he died.

Find a place.

Get electricity running.

Plant seeds for food.

Kiss his children goodbye.

Then, maybe, he could die peacefully.

His heart whispered to him, telling him he might not have time for all of it. Up here, he might not accomplish any of it.

As he walked along a line of metal wagons, something touched his fingers. He looked down, Candlestick, wrapping her small hand around his. Violin placed her arm around his waist from the other side.

"My favorites," he said.

They smiled.

"Another story, then?" he asked.

Candlestick jumped. "Yes, what did Kevin Bacon find in the woods?"

Winter put his finger up. "Actually, I think it's time to check in on Dance and her battle with the woodland creatures."

CHAPTER 33

Fistful of Dirt

Dance cracked her knuckles and stuck her tongue out as she played with some buttons on her newest machine. She'd created an army of tiny metal wagons that she could control with her mind and sent them through the forest carrying even smaller little machines. The smaller machines were the real prizes. When someone stepped near them, it sent an electrical relay through multiple ports, which in turn sent them all into one tiny container inside the machine, forcing the electricity out in a big ole bolt, frying anyone nearby.

She hated having to kill tiny forest animals, but the war was inevitable, and she wasn't going to take threats from raccoons.

Something caught her attention deep in the forest, loud crashes and yelling. It was far enough away, but something bad had happened, and she feared how it related to her.

Deep in the woods, a giant man with a beard and a top hat hovered over the treetops, and with his monstrous hands splayed the greenery to see inside the dense forest.

Her heart sputtered. "Do you see that?" She asked her crops.

They waved their tall bodies in affirmation.

More action happened, but Dance could not see it; she only

heard the banging and crashing, the shouting and arguing. Maybe this event had nothing to do with her after all. Seems that everyone was at war these days. She guessed they always had been. No one notices war until it's on their doorstep. Then, they see it everywhere.

Blick Blick, the corn stalk, let out a low whistle. The woodland creatures were here.

The woods surrounding her came alive with crinkling leaves and rustling bushes. From all sides, the animals came. Squirrels, blobbers, big horned things, sniffling fangers, red fangers, the whole lot of forest creatures, lined in rows, stretched back beyond Dance's vision. They were ready for war, and even with all her machinery, she knew she stood no chance.

"Crops, are you ready?" She shouted.

"Wait," Rapture scooted from behind a line of raccoons. "Wait."

He waltzed toward her, sucking on a cigar. "Settle down."

She stood straight up. "Doesn't look like you're ready to settle down," she said and moved her finger into a circle where all the animals waited for war.

"Precautionary," he said. "I told ya we were gonna talk to the council, and you seemed to agree with that decision, but the next thing ya know, we are finding mechanical weapons all over our forest. Sounds to me like you're the one ready for war. All we wanna do is create a peaceful solution to our problems." He took a big drag on his cigar and raised his eyebrows, satisfied to place all the blame on Dance.

"Well, then, I guess this was all a big misunderstanding. You can send your friends home and we can all go about our business."

He chuckled. "We still need a solution, right?"

She rubbed her thumbs over her fingernails, a way to steady the shakiness building in them. She refused to show them her fear. "What do you propose?"

Rapture threw his cigar to the dirt and stomped on it. "We have two options. I think you'll find both agreeable." He smiled, showing the razor-sharp teeth he hid behind his cute face.

"Let's hear them then." She waved one hand, but with the other, she slowly pulled a machine from her pocket. A small thing, no bigger than a peapod. In its center, a small button, visually unassuming, but would, if pressed, shred the lining of the forest to dust, taking a large portion of the animals with it. If Rapture tried anything, his friends would die quickly.

Rapture hopped forward. "The first is you give up your crops, and we take them from here on out. We, of course, show you the same kindness you showed us, and we allow you to hop in and nibble occasionally." With that, he gave a snarl.

She chuckled. "So, you came here to mock me? You know I'll never separate myself from them. Besides, only I can heal them. They will just die in your hands."

Rapture sighed. "No, I am not mocking you. I am giving you very viable options. Maybe you ain't the only one who can keep them alive."

Her fingers trembled on the button, so close to pushing. "What's option number two?"

"I rip your throat out right in front of the crops and while they weep over your dead body, my friends can feast on them."

She pressed.

Nothing happened. She pressed again. Nothing. She held the device up, clicking.

Rapture laughed heartily, tears forming in his eyes. "Look at her, she keeps trying to press it."

The woodland creatures surrounded her and burst into a chorus of mocking laughter.

"What's happening?"

From behind her, a man swept in, the same one she had seen at Rapture's last meeting. He slid his hand down her arm, grabbed the device from her, and swooped in front of her. It all happened so fast. She crumbled into her seat, defeated, shocked.

"What is happening?"

The man knelt to her and brushed a strand of hair from her eyes. "Hush, hush, little girl." He tilted his head and smiled. "Quite beautiful, you are. I'm sorry for what is about to happen. I'd like to kill you quickly, but Rapture thought it best you see your crops die first. He's cruel, I know, but every once in a while, I like to give him what he wants."

Dance slowly lifted her head, looking over the man's face. Her eyelids sunk, defeat creating a river down her cheeks. "Blick Blick, kill them all."

The giant corn crop roared and bent backward. Then, he shot himself forward, coming down forcefully. If he had hit the ground with that speed, he could have annihilated half the woodland creatures. Maybe Dance would have died in the blast, too. It would have been worth it. But Blick Blick never hit the ground. Instead, the man raised his hand and froze Blick Blick in mid-swing.

"It's really unfair that you're going to die knowing everything you love will go with you. I don't like it. You should at least get a few kills in on your way out," the man whispered, as he handed the device back to her. "It'll work now, I promise."

She took it, weeping and panicked. She knew the war could lead to her death, but now that it was imminent, her entire body froze in fear. Well, all but her finger. She pressed the button, and as the man promised, it worked.

Instead of blasting the woodland creatures to smithereens, it blasted in the center of the crops, evaporating her friends to dust.

Pieces of her pals scraped her face like tossed gravel.

She fell to her knees. "Noooooooooooooooooooooo!"

Rapture also fell to the ground, rubbing his belly, laughing hysterically. "She killed her own army."

The man grabbed her chin and lifted her head so they were seeing each other eye-to-eye. "All of your beautiful machines, such nice work. But they are nothing against my mind. I moved them while you and your crops slept. All I had to do was think about it. Just, poof," he flicked his fingers on both hands, and pushed his arms outward. "They went wherever I wanted them to be."

He shook his head and wiped a tear from her cheek. "You see, you thought you were building an arsenal against me, but just like everyone else, you've always been working *for* me."

He stood up and she flopped down, letting her head press to the dirt. She no longer feared death, no longer cared. All she had ever loved just evaporated to dust.

"The animals relied on those crops. Why would you let me destroy them?" She asked.

The man snickered. "Because we are petty fuckers."

Rapture cleared his throat and walked away. "Well, let's not make this gratuitous. Just kill her and be done with it."

The animals charged. The ground shook under her cheek until they were on her. Searing pain came from everywhere as they scratched and bit her body.

She did nothing, made no attempt to free herself. Blood dripped from her neck, back, arms, and legs, mixing with the gravel, swirling in front of her eyes. She bit her lips, holding in screams of pain.

Something took a giant chunk of flesh from her arm and in doing so, it shook her body wildly in its mouth until it flung her to where her crops had grown.

This violent movement sparked a change in attitude within Dance. As the animals piled on her again, she slowly moved her gnawed arm and splayed her fingers on the soft earth where her friends once grew. As the creatures dug deeper into her flesh, she pressed firmly, cupping a fistful of dirt. "Come back to me," she said as a creature ripped into her throat and ended her life.

CHAPTER 34

Everything in Its Right Place

Candlestick let go of Winter's hand. "I don't understand." Winter stopped, plopped his bag to the ground, and breathed in relief as the heftiness left his back and shoulder. "I must take a break."

Violin wrapped the bag's handle around her hand and hoisted it onto her shoulder. "I will carry it. We must keep going."

Winter sat, leaning his back against a green metal wagon. "Just one minute, please."

The girls sat next to him, one on each side.

"So, explain the story, Dad."

He shrugged. "What don't you understand?"

Candlestick leaned her head against his shoulder. "You said all the stories would connect somewhere. But it only connected because she saw Abe Lincoln over the trees. The blinking thing Kevin Bacon saw was probably her machine, but that's not a real connection. That's just a strand."

"I have to admit, it was pretty flimsy, Dad," Violin said.

Winter laughed. "You must have patience."

"Patience for what? She's dead. How can she connect to Kevin Bacon now that she's dead? I assumed she was one of his siblings, but she's dead. Dead. Dead." Candlestick stood up. "The more I think about it, the more I don't like it. Why did she have to die?"

Winter stood too, his back cracking, knees ready to give. He let out a low grumble as he straightened himself. "Everything will connect in time. I don't know how many times I must tell you that. Everything. Trust me."

"Whatever you say."

They marched on until the fire disc rose behind the tree line, streaks of pink painting the sky. Eventually, Violin shouted, "Look!" and ran forward.

Standing on the side of the cement path, cut through the forest, was a long house with multiple doors. They ran to it with hope overriding their battered bodies.

In front of the long building was a cement lot with white lines. One metal wagon razed the setting, and it was a big one, a giant thing with a cylindrical body.

The doors on the building all had numbers on them and when Winter tried to open them, they didn't budge. He almost smashed the windows, but he wanted to stay in there and found it unwise to take away any sealing from the cold.

In the front portion of the long house, there was a room with glass walls and a glass door. This door opened. Winter tapped to tell Violin to drop the bag. He sifted through it and found a boom weapon but wasn't sure if it was the one that broke on Candlestick. He had no way to test it without making a lot of noise, so he searched for a second one, and tucked them both into his pants. He crept in the glass room and searched. It had a desk, a couple long chairs, like the ones in the houses, and one of those weird Sony boxes. He opened a door behind the desk and found a small, cramped room with a chair, a table, and another large rectangular box. This one didn't say Sony, but it looked the same. On the table, a well-thumbed book lay opened, spine up. He grabbed it, stupidly curious. "The Wonderful Wizard of Oz."

He left the smaller room, back into the one with the glass walls. Behind the desk, he found a wooden board with hooks holding small metal pieces. The pieces had numbers on them, matching the numbers on the doors outside. Winter stood up and waved the girls in.

They ran to him, Lion staying right next to Candlestick.

"Look," he tapped, holding up a small metal piece.

"What is it?" Violin tapped.

He shrugged. "I hoped you could tell me. They are numbered like the doors. They must go to them somehow."

"Maybe the metal pieces open the doors?" Candlestick said.

He flipped the piece in his hand. "That's what I was thinking, but how?"

"Let's go find out." Violin snatched the piece from his hand.

As she walked out of the room, Winter grabbed the other metal pieces and filled his pocket with them. The girls led him toward the door marked, "10." Their bodies shivered. When they were in the glass room, he had seen the red on their cheeks, the dry cracks on their lips. A purplish tint had grown under their eyes. He would die soon, he knew, but not while the girls looked like that.

Violin examined the metal piece and waved it in front of the door. Nothing happened. She waved again, adding some extra oomph. Still nothing.

"Let me try." Winter grabbed the piece and shook his good arm wildly. Nothing. He slapped the metal piece against the door. Nothing.

"Dad, look." Candlestick tapped as she rubbed her other hand's fingers on a small opening in the door handle.

"Of course." He jingled the metal piece, trying it one way, and then another, until it fit into the opening. He twisted it, and the door popped open.

A wave of excitement built within him as the entrance slowly widened. He gripped his boom weapon tighter, too.

The opening revealed a giant bedroom with a huge sized bed. Another Sony box stood on a thick table with drawers. What were those boxes? They must be important, because humans had them in every damned room.

He put his arm out to stop the girls from entering. Raising his boom weapon, he crept in and checked behind the bed. He entered a white room with one of those water bowls, but this bowl had no water in it. Once he felt safe there were no threats, he waved the girls in. They immediately flopped onto the bed, giggling. Lion darted in behind them and sniffed the perimeter.

He asked the girls to go into the white room and take off their wet clothes while he rummaged through their bag for new clothes. The bag did a surprisingly good job of keeping things dry. He pushed aside cans of food and heavy jugs of water and found some outfits. They only had the dresses they had worn when they left their home, and while it was too cold for those, they would serve better than the wet ones they currently wore.

After the girls had changed, he covered them in blankets and told them to cuddle on the bed.

"I'll be right back." He dashed out of the room and walked the entire perimeter of the building, trying to understand the layout, and the surrounding areas, picturing where all potential threats could emerge.

Using the metal pieces, he checked all the rooms on his way around, and they all looked exactly like the one he and his daughters had moved into.

In the back of the building, there was a giant machine. Winter guessed it was a generator, but the technology was brutal and nonsensical to him. He plucked at it, played with it, trying to make sense of it. With a few hours to tinker, he might be able to figure it out. But something better stoked his interest behind a thin layer of trees. A fast-flowing river. If he could find some tools, he could create his own hydro generator, and would probably only need the pieces from the unsophisticated human one.

The human generator looked to be in fine shape, which made him wonder how long humanity had been gone. Besides the crashed metal wagons and the rotten food in the market, most of the human world appeared undamaged.

He decided to give the generator more attention and dug in. He learned its mechanics even quicker than he would have assumed. They made it simple enough. It even had a button that said, "PRESS TO START." However, it didn't start when he pressed. It must be a diesel generator. They didn't use those in the underworld, but his books on electricity talked of them extensively. Unfortunately, this old beast had run out and Winter hadn't a clue where to find fuel, or even what it really looked like.

"Humans, always making things more complicated than necessary." He scoffed.

Winter couldn't shake the feeling this many-roomed house was good luck for him, and that feeling grew only stronger when fortune landed in his lap once again.

As he walked back to the room, he noticed writing on the giant metal wagon in the cement lot:

"TANNER'S SWITCH DIESEL FUEL CO."

"Kevin Bacon, you wonderful god." Winter ran to it, searching all over for a way to remove the fuel. Everything was falling into place for him, but only one piece at a time, and the puzzle only grew with each revelation. Frustrated, he leaned against the giant cylinder, and his hand touched something. A hose.

"It can't be so easy."

He pulled it, yanking it out, and fuel poured out onto the cement. It smelled awful. He quickly reattached the hose, and ran into the glass room, where he found a large bucket. "This is going to be a pain in the ass."

He filled the bucket, plugged the hose back up, and heaved the heavy pail to the back. His arms ached and he sloshed liquid all over the ground on his way. Once he figured out where the fuel went, he poured it in. For each bucket he collected, he would lose more than half as spillage. But for now, it was something. He was accomplishing something. For the first time since he had emerged on Earth, he was acting instead of reacting.

When he finally filled the damned thing, he had spilled enough fuel on his clothes to stink.

He hit the "PRESS TO START" button, fully expecting it not to start, but to his surprise, it chugged, and then made a loud, obscene whirring.

"Too loud," Winter said. It would attract unwanted attention, and it also meant the machine was working too hard, using the diesel too quickly.

He ran around the building to the room with the girls.

When he went in the room, the lights were on, and air was pushing loudly from a metal grate.

Violin tapped, "Candlestick screamed."

"I didn't scream. It was a squeak."

They all laughed.

Winter put his hands on the weird metal grate. "It's pushing air out. I hope it gets hot. I have to do one more thing."

He ran out of the room and opened the other doors, which he had unlocked already. He turned off all the switches, unplugged things from the weird holes in the walls. After he finished, he ran back to the generator to see if it had quieted. It was still too loud for his liking, but it had gone down a few notches.

He went back to the girls and wandered around the room, checking all the switches, seeing what they did. They were mostly lights, and one made four blades on the ceiling spin, creating a cool breeze.

"You stink, Dad," Violin noted.

"It's fuel. It's what's heating the place."

"The box is on!" Candlestick shouted.

Winter followed her line of sight. The Sony box had been lit up, just slightly. It still displayed black in its center, but it was a different black. A glowing black. "So, what does it do?" He asked.

The girls giggled. "I don't know," Violin said.

He found some buttons on the back and pressed them. One turned the glow on and off. Another made letters appear on the screen. HDMI. HDMI 2. But nothing else changed. He shrugged and moved to the bathroom. He turned a knob and yelled with excitement. The girls ran in.

"What is it?" Candlestick asked.

"Water!"

"Can we take a bath?"

"Yes. Let me take one first, to remove this stink."

He turned the knob on the bathtub, but it sprayed water out

from the top, and the water drained out through holes in the bottom.

"This makes no sense." He played with some of the other knobs and found one that made a heavier flow come from a pipe toward the bottom of the tub, but it still drained out through the holes. "I don't know what to do about this. Can we block it with a shirt?"

"What's this do?" Candlestick asked as she reached in and flicked a switch under the pipe.

They all watched as nothing happened.

"Wait. Look." She pointed at the water pooling in the tub.

"Would you look at that. It somehow blocked the holes. But the holes don't look blocked? How does it work?" He looked closer.

The girls left the room. Candlestick danced on the way out. "I figured it out," she sang as they exited.

"This stuff really flows up here, huh?" Winter said to himself.

He gave up on trying to figure out the hole magic, too tired to finagle. He examined some bottles on a sleek shelf. Shampoo. Conditioner. He tossed them to the side. Then he saw an oval shaped object wrapped in paper. SOAP.

"Girls! They have soap here. Humans use soap after all." He ripped it open and smelled it. "It's lovely."

He stopped the bath and sat in it, letting the warm water soothe his achy body. He scrubbed the soap on his stinky hands and the wound on his arm, knowing full well that the infection was already growing inside him. He'd be dead soon, and it was best to accept that now. Kevin Bacon had smiled upon him and granted him his wishes before he died. Winter would have the chance to set the girls up with everything they needed.

When the girls finished their baths, they all ate some canned food, got into the bed, and wrapped themselves in blankets. The heat had kicked in, and the room felt deliciously warm.

"I had been so cold for so long, I forgot what warmth felt like," Winter said.

They all chuckled.

"Can you tell us a story before we go to sleep?" Candlestick asked.

"Too tired tonight, Love. Let's sleep. I'll tell you a good one in the morning."

"Should one of us stay awake and keep watch?" Violin asked.

Winter shook his head. It was stupid to let their guard down, but for tonight, he accepted stupidity, and good luck. He would take it, and absorb it, let it soak the trauma and anxiety from his bloodstream.

He slept deeply, dreaming of circuits and electricity, of hostile animals and melty-faced monsters, of ferocious humans, but none of it startled him awake. Not even the poison running through his veins from his arm wound aroused him. He woke ten hours later, his girls still sleeping next to him. Lion on the floor just below. For once, everything had gone right. When the girls woke, he happily told them a new story.

CHAPTER 35

Kevin Bacon Lives

The blinking machine shot out jolts of electricity in every direction. Kevin Bacon tossed a disc in front of himself which stole the electrical currents and sucked them into the disc's iridescent skin.

"Well, Jeez, that was close." Kevin Bacon cackled.

"Close?" NNNNNOOOO said.

Abraham Lincoln roared a laugh. Kevin turned to see his newfound sibling's hair was sticking straight up. It was a strange sight to see on a blobber.

"Sorry. I tried to get it all in time."

NNNNOOOO shook her body until the fur settled. "Find me that man, now."

Kevin sat down, tapping his hand on his chin.

"What's on your mind, Kevin Bacon?" Abraham asked from above the trees.

"I'm tired of all this running around, playing 'who gets there first.'"

"What do you propose we do?" NNNNOOOO asked. "That man killed my brother. I would like to skip to the part where I eat his throat."

Kevin Bacon put his hand up. "I promise, you'll get there. I'd like to test something out first." He stood up and dusted off his pants. "I can infiltrate people's minds sometimes, talk to them in their heads. But it's always been something I had to be close to the recipient for."

"Are you saying you can speak to people without talking?" Abraham asked.

"Yes," Kevin Bacon replied.

"Prove it."

"I've been talking to you both that way since I started this conversation."

"AAAAHHHHH," Abraham slapped his temples. "You're in my head!"

"Yes, but what I'd like to do is speak to all of our brothers and sisters at once. No more of this running around getting them one by one. Let's get them all at once." Kevin Bacon took the electricity device and fiddled with it.

"How do you plan to get your abilities to stretch far enough for that?" NNNNOOOO asked.

"I'm going to reset this device, and I'm going to electrocute myself."

Now the blobber laughed. "And what makes you think that will work?"

Kevin pressed a button and tossed the machine onto the ground as if it were a dirty pair of underwear. "Don't question me. I've seen everything."

"What does that even mean?" NNNNOOOO asked. When Kevin Bacon didn't immediately respond, she looked up to Abraham for answers. He just shrugged.

"I'd step back if I were you," Kevin said as he jumped toward the machine. It blasted out electricity into Kevin's body. It soared through his bloodstream, jolting his brain, shocking his soul into outer space.

"Brothers and sisters. I am one of you. We are all the products of a horrible god. Have you ever felt different from those around you? Special? Well, you are. You have the blood of the gods in you.

Those gods are awful, though. We, as their offspring, must unite to take over the heavens. Who is with me?"

A chorus of yeses drilled into his mind, a beautiful sound. One of them continued to speak after the rest sang their approval.

"I love the concept, ya see. I think it's a wonderful idea, got it. It's just, I'm going to need more information, if ya please. Does that seem fair? Okay, I do know what you mean, though, ya see. I do feel special, alright. Like, something is just different about me, got it. But I still need more information, if ya please."

"Okay, okay. If you're in, come meet me in the Tanner's Switch Forest. Whoever that was saying they needed more, can you meet us in the forest for said information?"

"Yes, that works, ya see."

Another voice chimed in. "Did you say you were in Tanner's Switch Forest?"

"Yes," Kevin replied.

"That's where I am right now, too. I will find you in about ten seconds."

Kevin fell to the ground. "Ow. That landing sucked."

Abraham Lincoln raised his eyebrows. "I'll say. That electricity nearly shot you all the way up here. You were floating very close to my beard."

"So, what happened?" The blobber asked.

"Oh, sorry. I should have connected you both to the conversation. They are all going to meet us here. One of them is on his way now. I need you both to do me a favor."

"What?" NNNNOOOO asked with a skeptical tone.

"The one who is going to be here in a minute, he's bad news. I could feel it in my bones when he spoke. He's going to attack us. I need you both to let him kill me, but then you can kill him right after. We square?"

Abraham bent over, allowing his head to come closer. "You can't be serious, Mr. Bacon. I wouldn't dream of letting you die. You're my brother."

Kevin waved him off. "Trust me, I'll be fine. All part of the plan."

The sound of crunching twigs and rustling leaves weaved through the shrubbery, coming closer.

"Well, hello there, family. Nice to meet my brothers and sisters." A stubby raccoon came through a bush. He shoved a cigar into his mouth and exhaled a large poof of smoke.

Kevin Bacon clasped his hands together behind his back. "Good to meet you, sir. Rapture, is it?"

"Indeed," the raccoon snarled.

"Well, it is a pleasure to meet you, fellow brother. I look forward to your help on our adventures."

"Just one question," Rapture puffed out more smoke through his nostrils.

"Yes." Kevin noticed NNNNOOOO and Abraham tensing up, so he waved his hand behind his back to tell them to settle down.

"Why do you hate our father?" Rapture asked.

Kevin smiled on one side of his face. "Frankly, because he's an asshole."

Rapture flicked the cigar, a sparkle of ash drizzled toward the forest floor. "How do I know you're not an asshole? Hmmmm? Assholes are always running around calling other people assholes, am I right? People who think themselves the heroes in their own story are often not."

Kevin rocked on the balls of his feet, waiting for the raccoon to make a move, hoping for it. "Well, someone has to be the hero."

"We disagree again. I have long since concluded that there are no heroes, only villains on a sliding scale."

"Bleak outlook, friend."

The bushes behind Rapture rustled. "Now, now, Rapture. Don't be so modest. You're a hero to me." Orelon emerged.

"Dramatic entrance, Dad. Where's the rest of the family? I would love to see our aunts again. Is Azerka reattached to her arm yet?"

Orelon rolled his eyes. "Turns out Mr. Bacon has developed his father's wit. Rapture, end this please."

The raccoon dropped his cigar and lunged toward Kevin's neck. Kevin Bacon lifted his head, giving the raccoon a clear space to kill him. Rapture latched onto Kevin's neck with his sharp teeth and drove them in. Kevin Bacon scrunched his eyebrows. The raccoon dug in, but it wasn't killing him. It hurt quite a bit, but it didn't even knock Kevin down.

Abraham cleared his throat, and with a wisp of bad acting said, "Oh no. The raccoon is killing my brother. Whatever shall I do?"

Kevin glanced up at his brother. "Tone it down there, big fella."

Orelon stepped forward. "What are you doing? What's happening? Why are you letting him kill you?" Orelon eyed the blobber. "Why aren't you jumping in?"

He grabbed Rapture by the back fur. "Something isn't right. Get off him." But when Orelon pulled Rapture away, the raccoon took a chunk of Kevin Bacon's neck with him.

"Ouch," Kevin Bacon said with a smile as the life left his body. "Now, you did it."

He dropped to the forest floor and died.

CHAPTER 36

Fortress

Before Winter turned their new home into a place where his girls could thrive, he wanted to ensure they had the means to protect it.

He made weapons and hid them all over the building, in different bedrooms, in the main room with the front desk, in the ceilings. The girls helped him forge spears and knives, sharp objects that would be easy to obtain on a moment's notice, no matter where the girls were. They hid the weapons enough to keep them out of sight from intruders, but easy enough to access when needed. Fortifying the building became a daily ritual, a fun game played with the family. Violin and Candlestick always beamed with excitement when one of their ideas stuck, and Winter loved to see the glory in their eyes.

He brought back their training. Despite the skills they'd already proven to have, he wanted to keep them sharp, focused on survival.

The girls, as always, proved to be adept learners, and proud of the new skills they were developing.

They turned the generator off as often as they could, trying to preserve the fuel. He didn't know where he'd go to replace fuel when it ran out, and finding a source was on his list of things to quickly learn. He already had to refill it once, after just three days in their new home, but the Tanner's Switch Diesel wagon wouldn't provide him forever. In fact, it probably wouldn't provide him for much longer.

He also didn't know how to grow food in such hostile winter weather, so he'd need to find another place with cans of beans and corn or whatever else he could find. He considered growing a few things in some of the bedrooms, but that would take time, and new bulbs for light. Human bulbs were weak. They had the fire disc, so he supposed they didn't need the level of light Winter and his people made underground.

By the fourth day in their new home, Winter's upper arm had grown fully red. He would be dead very soon. In fact, it was a Baconesque miracle he still lived, let alone walked around and had the strength to keep his family functioning. Maybe his healing abilities did, indeed, have a small effect on him. It wouldn't protect him forever, but somehow, the infection hadn't yet killed him. It moved slowly, and for that he was thankful. He had a mission to complete, and he refused to die before it had concluded.

He took a walk, needing a break from working on their home and wanting to map out the grounds. After an hour of walking, he found a food place. It was smaller than the one he'd found before, but still had some cans of stuff. No beans or corn, but something called Spaghetti Rings. He also found a box of something called cereal which claimed to be made entirely of wheat. In front of the food storage were machines with hoses attached to them. It said "Gas" on it with weird numbers and lots of nonsensical words. Unleaded. Super unleaded. And one word he knew: Diesel. He pulled the hose out and saw a button like the ones on the boom weapons. But when he pressed it, nothing happened.

He tossed the hose. Another puzzle. Another broken piece.

After he gave up on the diesel, he found some bags behind a desk inside and filled them with food stuffs, grabbing as much as he could carry with one arm. He lugged the bags back, feeling the struggle in every muscle. He still hadn't recovered from hobbling along with cans of sloshing diesel fuel, and now he was carrying shelves worth of food.

He dropped the bags off, checked on the girls, and went back for more. He wanted to get it all before someone else did, and the more he could stock up, the more time he had to plan out how to grow their own foods.

After a few trips, he had the girls sit on the bed and he tossed different products on it with them. Before trying anything, he carefully read the descriptions, trying to ensure they were actually eating food and not weird chemicals, or other strange things Earth people needed on shelves. He felt confident about potato chips. They had the word "potato" in them for one thing. Plus, the bag said, "a crunch blast in your mouth." That sounded wholly unappealing to Winter but made him feel comfortable it belonged in the mouth, at least. Humans listed the ingredients on the packaging, which Winter found wonderful, but they also named their ingredients ridiculous words like "monosodium glutamate." What was the point of listing information in gibberish no one could understand? Besides, shouldn't the ingredients on a can of nuts be "nuts?" Why do nuts need things like yellow corn flour and dextrose?

Violin hated the nuts. She coughed and said they made her mouth hot. Winter loved them. Candlestick devoured the potato chips and giggled at each noisy bite. They all struggled with the gum, unsure why anyone enjoyed something so difficult to chew and swallow.

During the past few days, Winter had made sure not to get complacent. They'd seen no monsters, no humans, no big threats, but he had kept a keen eye out, paying attention to the white, icy grounds for footprints. Peace would end, of course it would. But he had tried to make sure the girls enjoyed it while it lasted, even if he remained extra vigilant.

The animals were scaring him, and often sent Lion into a tizzy. The wild ones moved closer to the building with each passing night.

He had first noticed them on their second night as the dark disc came out. A group of creatures like Lion, but bigger and more feral looking, showed up on the cement lot, knocking over barrels filled with rot and junk. The creatures devoured all of it. Lion growled and scratched at the window, which sent the animals into an aggressive display of power, each member of the pack lifting their heads and howling fiercely. As the pack and Lion argued, Winter grabbed Candlestick, telling her to quiet their friend down so as not to attract the monsters. Once Lion was silenced, and the barrels sufficiently emptied, the pack went on their way.

The next night, three of the large, black blobbers showed up. They, too, had no trouble knocking into things, sniffing around for food sources. Winter worried two young girls would be the kind of snack these creatures were looking for, and the dread of his impending death shot through him anew.

After he and the girls finished their dinner of weird foods, Winter decided to tinker in the one area he had given little attention to, the front glass room. In the smaller room within the glass room, behind the desk, he found a small white box. When he opened it, a blast of cold air shot out, along with a horrifying stench. Food stuff had rotted inside, but he understood the cold air was meant to keep the food preserved. Maybe not everything the humans did was stupid.

On top of the white box was a black machine with a glass panel on the front. He hit some buttons, and the inside of the machine lit up. It made a whirring sound as a glass plate spun in the center, under the lights.

"What is the point of this? What are you doing?" He hated not knowing, not understanding.

He turned to the infamous Sony-like box on the wall. The one in this room differed from all the others he had seen, because it had more wires coming in and out of it, wires from everywhere. He hit a button on the bottom of it and the rectangle lit up. As it came to life, little grey boxes appeared. He stared at it. The grey boxes blurred into shapes and his heart danced.

"This can't be real."

At first, he thought they were pictures, but then some tree branches swayed on the outside edges.

"This isn't real. Moving photos?"

Then, something big moved on the screen. The door numbered 10 opened, and Violin stepped out. He watched her walk into the lot toward the glass room.

"Holy mother of Kevin Bacon."

He ran out of the room, into the lot. Sure enough, Violin headed toward him.

"Dad, Candlestick wants to know if you can tell her a story."

"Not now. Get your sister and come here."

He ran back into the room and watched on the black machine as Violin did what her father had told her to. After a moment, she exited the room with Candlestick in tow.

"Amazing." He rubbed his hand on the screen. "Simply amazing. Well done, humans. Well done."

When the girls entered the glass room, Winter called for them. "You have to see this."

They shuffled in. "What is that?" Candlestick asked.

"Is it pictures?" Violin added.

"Better. Stay here and keep your eyes on it. Don't look away. I'll be right back."

He ran out into the cement area and started dancing around, knowing the girls were seeing him in action. He glanced around the building, searching for the magical eyes that showed their vision to the screen. It took a moment of scanning, but he figured it out. A white tube with a black glass front angled downward and toward him. He waved to it and shoveled some white winter stuff into hands. After he balled the frosty stuff into a solid shape, he tossed it at the eye, missing by a few inches.

"I'll bet that looked fun." He laughed.

He ran back to the children.

"How did you do that?" Candlestick asked.

"I didn't do anything. This machine, it sees things through eyes all over the building, and it shows us what is happening."

"So, we can all watch each other from in here?"

He put his hands on her cheeks. "Even better, Candlestick. We can watch out for other people; know they are coming before they know we are here. We have every inch of this place under our eye, and we can do all of that from one room."

Both girls opened their eyes wide, realizing the power of the machine.

He put his arms around both girl's heads and pushed them into his belly. They squeezed into him, and he smiled. "We can make this place safe. We can make this place your home."

They sat on the bed after a hard day of work and ate chocolate bars. "Now, I will tell you a new story. A different kind of story."

"Is Kevin Bacon going to be in this story?"

"No. No. This story is entirely different, but the results of this story will play a big part in what happens next to our friend Kevin Bacon."

"Yay!"

"This story is about something we know all too well. It's about monsters."

CHAPTER 37

Creatures from Below

Dolphi prepared for the march. He slithered to the main drive, checking and rechecking every piece of the mechanics, never confident, never relaxed. So many pieces needed to function properly at the correct time. How could it go right? It would be insane to believe all of it could work as planned.

He met with the marchers, discussed their concerns, made sure they knew their roles and steps.

The black beasts argued with him. They always did, grumbly and loud. "You're not doing enough," they'd tell him, believing negative reinforcement worked best at creating the best possible solutions.

The Black Beasts had the most to lose, of course, if things did not go as planned. This was their march, after all, their introduction to a leadership role.

And on the side of all of this, the Candies watched, giddy for it all to go wrong. Everyone presumed, including Dolphi, that the Candies chose him to organize the march solely because he would fail. Other than selecting Dolphi for the position, the Candies stayed far away from march preparations.

Dolphi waited for it, to catch them sabotaging the event, but it never happened. With all of the preparations needed, it was more than possible they did sabotage it, and he just didn't see it, but the Candies made it a point to showcase themselves far away from where the event would take place, as if they wanted to clear themselves of any wrongdoing before any disaster happened.

If that were the case, it only served to prove how little faith they had in Dolphi making the march go without incident.

The Black Beasts also lacked any faith in Dolphi, and probably would have replaced him by now if tradition didn't get in their way. The losing party always selects the march lead, as their way of handing over the reins peacefully to the newly elected party. Those traditions went back hundreds of years to when the Winter Husks lost their election to the Night Disc Hunters.

But things were different now, the march much more significant.

Dolphi sat with a council, planning out details. They talked through the minutiae, bored and overwhelmed all at once. It didn't help that the council was made up of thousand-year-old slugs.

"Will the blasting fire pipes signal the dancers?" One of them asked.

Dolphi rubbed his eyes, tired of reiterating the same details again and again to a group too feeble to pay attention.

"Yes. That's the plan."

"So, what gets the Rust Warriors out?"

"The water sprays."

"Right. Right." The slug licked his lips in a painfully slow action. "I think it's all set. Nothing to fret about."

Dolphi shrugged. He knew they were wrong, knew everything would fall apart, but they were right that this nonsensical talk was going to get them nowhere. He had been over every detail so many times, it all blurred together. He found nothing, not a single thing, that could possibly go awry, but he knew with every fiber of his slithery skin that it was all going to fail spectacularly.

That night, as he planned to rest before the big day, Piney came to visit him. Piney had a way of making his nerves worse, but somehow this always led Dolphi to see something he missed before, so he welcomed the company.

"Forty years." Piney said as he sat on the edge of Dolphi's sleeping sack, his tall, heavy body bending the thin mattress into a V.

"Forty years?"

"Since the… you know..." Piney raised his spikey arms to the sky. "Boom."

"The Booms, yes. I am aware. Why would you bring that up?"

"Just wanted you to remember how bad it can get tomorrow."

"You think I don't know? Of course, I know! I'm a nervous wreck."

"Phew." Piney exaggeratedly wiped his forehead. "For a minute there, I thought you weren't scared."

"I'm tired, Piney. I need to sleep."

"Oh, I wouldn't do that. Stick to the nervousness. You should be freaking out, completely unable to sleep. It's the only way to make sure nothing gets screwed up. If I were you, I would have pulled myself out of my skin. Don't calm down, Dolphi. That's a mistake."

Piney picked himself up, his tall stick legs bending so his head didn't crash into Dolphi's low bedroom ceiling.

"Good night Dolphi. I hope we don't all die tomorrow."

Dolphi managed a few hours of sleep before waking up for good, about three hours before the march. He slithered obsessively from one corner of the room to the next, trying to pinpoint where the march would collapse. He no longer considered it a paranoid concern, but an all but definite conclusion. Everything would fail. People would die. The Black Beasts would start their term with death on their hands.

He went to the march's start line, where the creatures were already lined up on both sides of the aisles, eager for the transitional celebration. He checked the rooms of his performers, asked how they were holding up, grilled them about their moves and timing.

With nothing left to do but wait, he slithered up to his bench, high above the crowd, to see the march with the leaders of the dark world. The highest level of Black Beasts sat there, waiting. The Candies sat next to them. All eyes landed on Dolphi.

"This better go well," one of the Black Beasts said.

"Yes," said a Candy.

"It will, I assure you," Dolphi lied. If only he knew in which way he was lying.

A series of trumpets set the event into motion. Dolphi slipped down in his seat, his heart beating in his ears.

A group of red-furred animals marched with large staffs, tossing garbage to the onlookers. The crowd cheered. Two of the animals on opposite ends of the group slung their staffs over the shoulder, chopping at a rope. The action pulled the ropes through a tube in the tunnel above. This released a fog from a series of vents, a fine expressive mist.

When the Red Furries marched beyond two holes in the wall, the holes let out a boom and flames blasted out just enough to not hit anyone. The crown wooed and cheered.

After the Red Furries came the Sniffle Snakes, Dolphi's kin. He held his breath as he watched, hoping to the gods that if everything went wrong, it wouldn't be from his own creatures. The Snakes slithered and intertwined with one another, creating images in their movements. Shapes of Candies turned into Black Beasts. The Black Beasts sitting next to Dolphi clapped and whooped at the display. The Candies were more silent.

A snake broke off from the group, hit a bell, and red water drizzled down on the crowd. The audience raised their hands to catch it, laughing and hollering.

"Red drizzles, I love it," one of the Black Beasts said.

"It symbolizes the blood spent to get us here, a symbol of your sacrifice." Dolphi said. He noticed the sideways glance directed at him from the Candies. "All of your sacrifices." He corrected himself.

The next group to appear were the Trunkers. They plodded and swung their noses. One of the council slugs slipped to the upper seats, and whispered to Dolphi, "See, nothing to worry about. It's all going according to plan. The fire worked. The water worked. All smooth sailing from here."

But it was not done yet. They still had to endure the ice chunks, the light displays, the sparks, and the blinking discs. Sure, the fire seemed the most dangerous, mainly because of what happened twenty years ago, but being less than the most dangerous did not take away some of the fangs.

The Trunkers dropped the ice chunks and the heat waves, so pieces of ice fell from the sky and melted into water before landing on the creatures in the audience. Another spectacular display, and another huge crowd pleaser.

The Black Beasts were clapping and patting Dolphi on the back.

"You are impressive, my friend."

"I think someone has earned themselves a place in our government!"

Dolphi imagined the utter astonishment on the faces of the Candies if his march turned into one of the historically great celebrations.

But, he knew not to get ahead of himself.

The next group for the march were the Flunks, giant stalk-like creatures, relatives of Piney. They lumbered, the best way to describe their movements. They were so massive in size, Dolphi hadn't needed to give them a choreographed routine to set off their display. Their heads scraped against the ceiling, and this was enough to activate the...

Oh no.

Not the light display, or the sparks, or the blinking discs. It was the bang shots. He forgot all about the bang shots. The bang shots had to be strapped down or else they would fire willy nilly. Instead of hitting their intended target—a flag representing the old leadership—they would hit, well, everyone. His heart sunk. Fear moved to panic which transformed into dread.

Dolphi slipped from his seat, sliding down to the crowd who were oblivious to imminent death closing in on them. He slithered faster than he'd ever slithered before, praying to escape before it was too late. He would never make it to the bang shots in time to secure them, but he could escape the underworld in time to save himself. And wouldn't that be poetic? One group wished for his failure, for a little blood on his hands to usher in their adversaries, while the successors tormented and shamed him, threatening him to get it all correct. And in the end, they will all die by his hands and he will slither away, free. So many traditions rigidly followed, and for what? For death by habitual structure.

Dolphi found an opening onto the concrete frigidness of the upper world. For a cold second, he took in the awe of the eyes twinkling in the sky, and the night disc glowing above him. He'd always heard stories, but seeing the disc up close made him forget, however briefly, that his entire home world was about to die.

The humans around him screamed in horror at the sight of him. They scattered and ran in different directions.

And then, the booms shot off in rapid fire. Ratatatatatatatata. Now the screaming came from below him. The souls of every creature he'd ever known shot out of the abyss as white cold flakes, blasting into the sky before floating gently to the earth. Soon, the world was covered in the frozen spirits of the underworld. Dolphi slithered through it, forgetting to close the door to the underworld on his way out.

While he snaked his way into hiding, humans found the hole and unleashed the surviving creatures onto the earth. Some of those humans explored the down below, where they found boom shots they would use to kill everything for years to come.

CHAPTER 38

Guns Drawn

Violin and Candlestick sat silently, legs akimbo, eating snacks on the bed.

"That was the weirdest one you've told yet." Candlestick said.

"I think it was the one I liked the most." Violin countered.

"Why?" Winter asked.

"Because it was about us."

Winter put his hand into a bag of chips. "How?"

"Creatures from the underground coming up onto the earth."

Candlestick leaned forward, "But that doesn't make sense, because we didn't introduce people to the boom weapons. They introduced us to them."

Winter pointed at her. "She's right."

Violin leaned back, considering this. "So, what was the point of the story, then? Who were we in it?"

"You don't have to pinpoint yourself into the story to find its point."

"Well, what was it?"

Winter tucked Violin's hair behind her ears. In so many ways, she was better than him, but she was impetuous, unwilling to wait for the answers. "Think on it. Give me the answer when it comes to you."

She huffed.

Something scraped outside the window and they all jumped.

Winter ran to the window, Violin right behind him. At first, he just peeked through the corner of the screen, but once he saw the source of the noise, he pulled it open entirely. A bunch of creatures, those same ones he'd been seeing in packs, were back, digging through the same cans of junk they'd been getting into every night. They must be desperate, he determined, to keep coming back to the same trash hoping to find something they haven't already devoured.

BOOM!

A thunderous sound crashed into the night. Violin and Winter ducked under the window and Candlestick flung herself off the bed and onto the floor.

Winter snuck his head back to the window. The creatures had fled, all but one, which lay dead by the barrel, blood spreading through the white-covered cement.

Two figures approached in the distance. Humans.

"People," Winter tapped.

Violin crawled to her sister. They rummaged through something behind him, He didn't need to look to know Violin was arming them. He kept his eye on the men, heart racing more and more as they grew closer.

Violin tapped him on the back. He turned to her. She held out a boom weapon in her hands, presenting it to him. He took it. She had the other one by her knee.

"Be careful with it. It can kill us too." He wished they had taken the time to practice using them.

The men approached the animal, both holding boom weapons much longer and thinner than the ones Winter had.

"Good Shot, Brian."

The one called Brian crouched down and examined the animal. "Bit of a skinny coyote, but at least we will have some meat for dinner."

Winter tapped, "They're so desperate for food, they are eating animals."

Violin made an exaggerated frown. "Gross." She tapped.

Brian slung the creature over his shoulder and stood up. "Let's head back."

They walked away until the human with Brian stopped and turned back toward the building, staring as if he were looking directly at Winter. Winter's breath quickened.

"Be ready," he said.

Brian turned back toward his partner. "What's up?"

"You hear that?"

"What?"

"Whirring. I think the generator's on."

"No way. It wouldn't still be going."

"Listen, man, I can hear it."

"If it's on, that means there are people in there."

"Shit. We should get out of here."

"Well, what if they are nice people? They might let us stay here."

"You wanna risk it?"

"Hello. Is anyone there?" Brian shouted.

Violin looked up to Winter, waiting to see what he would do. For now, he did nothing.

"They don't seem like the others." She tapped.

"There are no good humans." He responded.

"They could help us, show us how things work, how to survive."

"We are surviving without them."

"For now."

"Forever."

"Where do you get fuel for the generator when it runs out? Where do we get food when we run out? How can we grow our own in this weather?" She was rapid fire tapping against his leg, making sure he understood it all.

"They're eating animals. Animals. You think they know how to do any of those things?"

"Anyone here? Hello." The man dropped the dead animal and

moved a little closer, but keeping a slight distance. "Do you have anywhere we can warm up?"

"Should we just take a room? That generator is definitely on."

"If we are going to do that, we need to check every inch of this place to make sure there aren't any people. Everyone has turned violent. We can't just trust people."

The two men moved onto the cement lining the long path of rooms, about two feet from the window Winter stared out of.

"Come with me," Winter tapped. "First, tell your sister to stay put, and keep her weapon ready." Violin ran around to the other side of the bed and tapped to her sister before coming back and getting behind Winter. He slowly pressed down on the door handle until it opened just a centimeter.

He pushed it open, blasting the winter wind into the room. He ran out, came up right behind Brian, and placed the boom shot behind his head. "I have a weapon on your head. Do not move."

The not Brian one turned in time to see Violin training a weapon on him. "Put your boom weapon down."

"Boom weapon?" The man asked as he raised his hands in the air. His weapon dangled around his shoulder by a strap.

"Your weapon."

"You too," Winter said to Brian.

The men did as they were told.

"What do you want?" Winter said.

"We were just looking for a warm place to stay. We have a cabin, up there in the woods, but we don't have a generator, or to be honest, any idea how to use one, so it's cold. What kind of stupid cabin doesn't have a wood stove?"

"You can't stay here. This is our home."

"I promise you we will stay out of your way. We are good hunters, so we can pay you by sharing our kills."

"Animals? No."

"We can help you protect this place from anyone else. We are good with our guns. We've been attacked already so we understand why you don't trust us, but we aren't bad guys. We just keep to ourselves. Tryin' to survive, just like you."

"The answer remains no."

"Why are you arguing with them, Brian? Let's just get out of here."

"They have power; they have a place to live."

Violin focused on the man, her boom weapon stable, her hands dead still, despite the freezing winter air. "Dad. They dropped their weapons."

"Violin, not now."

"We need help, Dad. If they try anything, we can kill them."

"No."

"Dad, be smart. We have the upper hand. We can kill them."

"Until their friends show up. How many more of you are there?"

"None. It's just us two. Been us two for a long time, before the people disappeared." Brian said.

Winter stayed silent, thinking.

"We can just be on our way," the other one said. "We understand. We will leave."

"No."

"What do you mean no? You said we can't stay."

"And I can't let you leave. If you're lying, if there are more of you, you'll come back with a group."

"Dad. What are you doing?"

"I don't know."

"You're not gonna just kill us, are you?" Brian said. His friend's eyebrows furrowed, fear setting in.

"Dad, you can't just kill them."

"Yes, I can. I will kill anyone to keep us safe."

"They didn't do anything. They didn't threaten us. They didn't attack us."

Winter's finger loosened from the trigger, but not enough where the men could see it. "I need a second to think."

"Please, sir. We promise you, it's just us two. We aren't going to hurt you. We just wanna go on our way and take our dinner."

"I told you we shouldn't have risked it, Brian."

Winter stepped back, taking the gun off Brian's head, but

keeping it trained on the target. "We are going to take your weapons for now. You are going to go into the room with us where you can warm up. You will answer all our questions. If we decide you can stay in one of the rooms, we will hold on to your weapons and give them back to you when necessary. If we decide to let you go, you will never come back around here."

"Okay, and what if you decide against either of those?" Brian said.

"You'll be dead, so it won't matter," Winter said.

His friend nodded. "Just please don't hurt us."

Winter led the two into the room. "Candlestick, come out. Keep your weapon trained."

Candlestick rose from behind the bed, wielding a knife crudely made from wood and scrap metal.

Violin handed her gun to Winter and ran back outside, returning a few seconds later with the men's discarded weapons.

Winter told the men to sit on the bed. Everyone was silent. Everyone looked around, debating what to do next. A room full of people deciding how to kill each other if they had to.

MOTEL

CHAPTER 39

Answers

"Who are you?"

"I'm Brian and this is Corey."

"Where did you come from?"

"We have been staying in a cabin in the woods a few miles south. We were hunting coyotes when we found this place."

Lion arose from his Candlestick-induced sleep. He immediately lunged for the men but Candlestick pulled him back and quelled his nerves with gentle pats. Winter's heart raced, not from the anxiety of the current situation, but from something else. He couldn't place it.

"Where were you from before the cabin?"

"We lived in Tanner's Switch. We had a house over there. We went back to it, but our whole street was gone."

"What do you mean 'gone'?" His mouth felt dry and his body grew sweatier by the second.

Brian looked down and tears formed in his eyes. "It had all been burnt to the ground. Either something caught fire and no one was around to stop it, or someone lit it up on purpose. Neither would surprise me."

Corey touched Brian's arm in the same fashion Candlestick did with Lion. "Nothing surprises us anymore."

Winter noted Corey's sign of affection. "What happened to humans?"

"We don't know."

"Do better than that."

Brian shook his head, working to conjure an answer. "We went on vacation in this revamped underground bunker for a month. I know, it's crazy, we took a whole month off. Completely shut off from technology and society. Well, it had nice accommodations, electricity and heat. But, no TV, no internet, nothing like that. That was the point, a getaway from the hustle and bustle."

"I don't know what those words mean."

"Which words?"

"Doesn't matter. Go on." He hid the pain coursing through him, despite it growing by the minute. He wanted to sleep, needed to. A desperate desire for it as a throbbing, sharp lightning bolt drove from his arm to his heart.

"We lost power two days before our vacation was supposed to end. We left the bunker and no one was around. We kept looking and couldn't find anyone. Then, we were driving around, heading back toward our house, and someone opened fire on our car."

"What's a car?"

At this, Brian and Corey looked at each other, confused.

"What do you mean?"

"What is a car?"

Brian looked from Winter, then to Candlestick, waiting for some kind of joke to reveal itself.

"Answer the question." Winter trained the gun on them.

"Who are you people?"

"I ask the questions. What is a car?"

"Those things on the road, with the wheels."

"The big metal wagons with the different colors?"

Corey looked at Brian and whispered loud enough for everyone to hear. "What the fuck?"

Brian nodded him away. "Were you guys underground, too?"

"Yes. Finish your story. You were in the wagon, and someone did what?"

"How long were you underground?"

Winter pressed the gun against Brian's head. His arm struggled to hold the weapon up, despite it being his good arm. His whole body felt weak, tired, ready to give in. "I said I ask the questions." He said it so loudly, Candlestick flinched, and Corey jolted an inch back.

Brian raised his arms up. "Okay. Okay. Someone shot at us while we were driving back to our house."

"What is driving?"

"I...I...Those machines. They move, help you travel faster than walking. It's called driving. We were moving in the machines."

"That sounds like nonsense."

"I don't know how to answer your questions when they are so bizarre."

"Do your best. What came next?"

"Someone shot our car up."

Corey chimed in. "There must have been a hundred shots in seconds."

"Shots? Boom shots?"

They looked at each other once again. Brian continued to take the lead. "Yes, boom shots." He pointed to Winter's gun. "Anyway, we crashed and just ran. We weren't far from where we lived, so we instinctively headed there. When we got there, it was all destroyed, burnt and gone. Our whole lives. Pictures, memories, our clothes."

"If someone has tried to kill you with boom weapons, why did you call out for people here? Why did you not assume that anyone here would try to kill you on sight as well?"

"I am wondering the same thing," Corey said, glaring at Brian.

Brian returned the look to Corey. "I honestly convinced myself no one was here. That somehow the generator had kicked on when the power went, and just kept going on its own. But I think I was just tired of kill or be killed and hoped, for once, something would work out."

"Where did you get your boom weapons?"

"We found them in the cabin we've been staying in. I'm guessing someone lived there in the fall and lived off the land. It had gardens, too, but everything was dead and we don't know how to grow anything. I'm a good hunter, though, so we've been living off protein. We are starting to run out of ammo, though."

"Ammo?"

Again, Brian looked to Corey. Winter didn't like the way they kept looking at each other. It had an almost mocking feel to it.

"The boom shots. They require ammo. They're called bullets. Basically, pieces of metal that you load into the gun, and it fires them. That's what kills your target."

Winter's face heated up, embarrassed that he thought boom shots released some form of magic onto their victims. Hiding his weakness in knowledge, he said, "I see. I call it metal pieces." He wondered how close they were to running out of this ammo stuff, or even if the weapons he and Violin had aimed at these men right now had any ammo left in them. He could tell by Brian's and Corey's faces that they had the same thought.

Candlestick shifted uneasily on the floor, clearly wishing for this interrogation to end. The men remained calm, but they were trying to communicate through eye contact. Winter didn't know if they were planning to fight, flee, or play nice.

"What do you think happened to people?"

"We've been guessing at this nonstop. At first, I assumed a war happened. Our street was burned to the ground, so maybe a bomb went off. There is destruction if you look around. Cars crashed into one another; planes shattered in the forest."

"What is a plane?"

Brian rolled his eyes. "Basically, a flying car."

Winter shook the gun in front of Brian's face. His heart pounded, slamming into his chest. He wanted to grip where it hurt but refused to show weakness. "Are you playing with me?"

"Stop it. I'm not fucking with you. I'm trying to explain it, if you'd let me, but you keep threatening me every time you don't believe some common knowledge shit. It's bizarre, and I'm fucking scared, and I'm hungry, and I'm fucking trying. Please."

Winter lowered the gun a little. He realized the hard act was only going to slow things down, and a softer approach would be needed with these men. "You're right. I am sorry. Understand, I do not get what is happening around me. I am trying to protect my children."

Brian looked at Candlestick sitting on the floor patting Lion and tried to turn enough to get a view of Violin behind him with a gun trained on his back. "I get it, I do. But this is all scary for us, too. And, and, and, you keep asking questions about common knowledge things, and it scares me even more, because who the hell are you? Where are you from that you don't know what a plane is, or a gun, or a car?"

Winter leaned forward, getting closer to Brian, and while he kept his boom weapon low, he gripped it tight in case they tried to make a move. "I am not ready to tell you that. But just assume I am not from here. I don't know your terms and some of your words are confusing. Now, continue your thoughts on what happened to humans."

Brian rubbed sweat off his forehead. Corey's eyes were pleading and the longer the conversation carried on, the more antsy he appeared. There were nerves firing through him, making him twitchy, and unpredictable.

Brian cleared his throat. "So, I thought humans just went to war. Someone attacked America."

"Sorry, America?" Winter used a calmer voice, hiding his annoyance at his lack of understanding, but he also needed the conversation to move quicker. His body threatened to shut down.

"It's a country. The world is separated by countries, different societies, ways of living, beliefs, leaderships. A lot of times those countries go to war with each other. Many of them don't like America, so we assumed someone came after us, bombed the shit out of us."

Before Winter could ask, Corey chimed in. "A bomb is something that makes a big explosion. Like a gun but much more massive in scale."

Winter nodded and looked back to Brian.

"But the thing is, there isn't that kind of destruction. The streets aren't all blown up. There were definitely a lot of fires, but I wouldn't say bombs. And the big thing?"

Corey again interjected, eager to play this game of conjecture. "No bodies."

Winter shot him a questioning look.

"We've seen a few dead people, sure, mostly from gunshot wounds, but there were 700 million people in America. Where are all the bodies? If there was a war, you'd see people dead everywhere."

Winter straightened. "So, everyone really did just disappear?"

Corey and Brian shrugged at the same time. Brian wiped his face again. "It would appear that way."

"Why are humans so violent?"

"We aren't. Not all of us."

Corey shook his head. "I disagree. Most humans are. Especially the ones left. I know you don't want to hear that, but I think it's true."

Winter liked that Corey told him a truth he knew might upset him.

Brian relented. "I guess that's true. People panic, go into survival mode. They know they don't have the skills to grow their own food, so they know they'll have to kill for what's left. Some people probably hated their previous lives, and their stations in society, and found that through anarchy, they could thrive. This is all philosophical bullshit, I know. I'm just rambling. It's fucking scary out there."

Corey lifted his head, staring at the ceiling. "People are assholes."

Winter rubbed at his beard, still looking to catch them in a lie so he could kill them and get some rest. "Why do you have such a low opinion of humans if you are humans?"

"Well, not all humans. There are good people. I just fear most of them didn't make it to the world we are currently in."

"And I assume you two are the good humans?"

Corey coughed. "We aren't perfect, but we aren't outrageous murderers either."

Brian turned to Violin. "Yeah, and what about you guys? You have a gun to my face and your daughter has one to the back of my head. Are you guys sure *you're* good humans?"

Winter tilted his head back, shocked by the question. "What?" He looked to Violin and Candlestick, both of whom were smirking. "We are not humans at all."

CHAPTER 40

Shot in the Dark

The two men quieted at Winter's revelation about him and his daughters not being human. He knew the men found him strange, unable to understand, but he refused to give them any more answers. They did seem like nicer men than those Winter had previously run into, but humans were tricky creatures, not to be trusted. Their kindness must be a ruse.

Violin pleaded with him through her eyes, begging him to end this interrogation and let them leave.

"I have one more question," he said.

Brian said, "Okay."

"What is that thing that steals the water in that room?" he pointed to the room with the white tiles. An odd question, and an unimportant one, but he knew he'd be dead very soon, and he wanted the answer.

Brian leaned back, examining the room. "Do you mean the toilet?"

"Toy-let? Is that like a small toy?" Something punched at his chest, crashing into his ribs. How stupid to ask such a trivial question. He needed this mess sorted before he could die. Why did he insist on wasting time? Maybe that was it. Maybe he was wasting time, hoping it would keep him alive. He nearly slapped himself at his own stupidity. He couldn't put death on hold by procrastinating on his final missions. Death would take him when it wanted, whether he completed his tasks or not.

"No. It's not a small toy. It's a place to go to the bathroom. You sit on it, and, you know."

He stared, now clutching his chest, unable to hide the hurt. Violin noticed; her eyes grew wide. "You poop?" He wondered if these would be his last words.

"Yes. You poop. And when you flush it with the thing on top, it takes your poop away."

Tears formed in Winter's eyes as the pain rode up to his throat, into his neck and shoulders. "You humans were so capable of making wonderful things. Why did you have to be so horrible?"

Brian and Corey stayed silent, unable to come up with an answer.

He stood up, making a final decision. He would kill the men. He had no choice, really. He wasn't willing to risk trusting anyone, not when the outcome could cause death to his children. Especially when he wouldn't be there to protect them anymore. He needed Violin to see it. She was too trusting, and if he was about to die, he wanted to cement it into her brain that humans can never be friends.

"Stand up. Let's go outside."

Corey and Brian stood, and Winter saw relief wash over their faces. How wrong they were.

"Violin, follow me. Keep your gun on their backs." He ushered the men to the door.

He stepped out of the way, and let them open it, so he and his daughter would both be right behind with guns at the ready.

The cold air blasted into the room as the door opened. A wind picked up the icy cold white stuff, driving it into their faces. Brian and Corey wrapped their arms around their chests and entered the cold darkness where they would meet their deaths. As they crossed the threshold, Violin tapped on Winter's arm. "Are you okay?"

"I'm fine," he tapped back, lying to her.

Winter scanned the lot, ensuring no monsters were out. He hadn't considered the noise the guns would make, and how that might attract the lampposts, but there was no time to alter the plans now. If the monsters came, their new home provided plenty of hiding spots. He just hoped to hang on long enough to get the girls to safety.

He stepped outside, Violin right behind. His knees buckled against the cement. He shook it off, and lifted his arm, but in doing so, sent a wave of pain and dizziness to his brain. His heart rate sped up so much it melded into one solid, long thump.

"Sorry," he said as he pulled the gun to the back of Brian's head.

Bang.

Winter fired as he stumbled sideways.

"No," he thought. "I'm not done." But he was.

The Earth tilted to its side, and the lot flew up to his face, before his skull crashed into the cement.

CHAPTER 41

The Absence of Everything

Kevin Bacon floated through an endless abyss of nothingness. He'd already soared through Everything, Now, he found his way through Nothing, the one thing he needed to complete his transition into a full god. There was nothing demi about him anymore.

He listened to the din of screams from the vast history of human minds breaking at the environment, and he homed in, focusing on the cacophony in search of one soft voice. When he found it, he breast-stroked through the thick emptiness of death until he came close enough for conversation.

"I am here for you."

The voice wept. "I haven't heard a sound in so long."

"It's only been a few minutes since you died," Kevin assured the voice.

"Feels like forever."

Kevin froze, thinking of how it must all feel to a human mind. "I suppose it was forever. You're experiencing eternity."

"Why?" the voice said.

"That's just how it is down here."

"No, I mean, why did you come here for me?"

"Because you are dead and I need you. I'm going to take you back home."

"Why would I get another chance?"

"Because I am going to war with the gods, and your magic is going to bring us to victory."

The voice said nothing, but Kevin thought he heard whimpering. "Reach for me," Kevin Bacon said.

"I don't believe in gods."

Kevin snickered. "You shouldn't. They are fiction. But then again, so are you and I."

"Impossible. I can feel you. I can feel myself."

"That's meaningless. We are all just portions of someone else's story."

"Well, then, wouldn't the storyteller be our god?"

Kevin shook his head. "No. Because he is a storyteller and we are his stories. If he doesn't have us, he doesn't exist. If the identity of the maker is in the making, and he has nothing left to make, he ceases to be. In that sense, we are his gods."

"You're speaking in riddles," the voice said.

"Nonetheless, it is time for us to return. Are you ready for it?"

"Just one question."

"We have an eternity."

"Do I get to kill the raccoon?"

Kevin smiled. "Seems I have a team built on the concept of revenge. You get to make the world however you want it. Freeing it from ole Rapture is just one small piece of a much bigger pie."

Through the darkness, a light reflected, showing the lines and fixtures of a beautiful young face. It smiled. "Then I am ready."

Kevin reached for her hand, but since she no longer existed, he held tightly to unbroken air. "Even though we are not truly here, we are connected. Do you feel it?"

"Yes."

"Then we must move. Follow me." He swam down, where the air grew thicker, the darkness more bleak, the screams louder.

"Wait, we are going the wrong way. We must go up to live again."

"True, but for now, we go down."

"Why?"

"There is someone else to take from the underworld, someone else who needs to live again."

The woman followed. They swam until their ears popped and their hairs stood on end. Until the darkness filled their lungs and crept into their bellies. Until all was truly none. Until the crying and screaming grew so loud it nearly broke them into shattered pieces of sand.

"Where is this person?" Dance asked.

"As dead as dead can be."

"Why are they so much farther down than I was?"

"Because, some deaths weren't meant to be reversed, not ever."

"And you're going to change that?"

"Yes," Kevin said as he narrowed his eyelids. "I am."

CHAPTER 42

Violin Has a Secret

Violin trekked through the muddy woods, her feet splashing in pools of dead snow. *Snow.* A new word learned. She loved the sound. Her back strained against the weight of the bar resting on the back of her neck, two full buckets of water sloshing on each end of the rod.

When she reached the lot, she brought the water to the back of the motel. *Motel.* Another beautiful new word. She lifted the bar over her head, careful to keep it balanced, and placed the buckets down next to her machines.

Corey turned the corner with his hands on his hips. "You need any help?"

Violin brushed hair from her eyes. "I don't think so. I don't really know what I'm doing."

Corey came closer, his eyes on her machines. He tightened his jacket around his torso as a bitter wind swept in. "It looks complicated."

Violin knelt, and pushed on the blades, sending them into a light spin. "It is. Too complicated for me. I watched my father make hundreds of these, but I just don't remember the details."

She stood up and grabbed a lightbulb attached to a wire that traveled to the machine. She handed the lightbulb to Corey. "Can you string this to the fence?"

He took the bulb and spun the wire around the line post of the chain link fence that surrounded the motel's generator.

"Ready?" Violin asked him, unable to hide the nervousness in her eyes.

Corey wiped his hands on his pants, and bobbed on the balls of his feet, as if he were preparing for a fight. "Ready."

She poured a bucket of water into a lip at the front of her machine. As it sloshed into the main box, it hit a series of blades, sending them whirring. The bulb lit up, flickered for about ten seconds, and died.

Corey shot his arms toward the heavens. "Hey, you did it!"

She punched her knee. "No, I didn't. It's supposed to keep going on its own once it starts up."

"How's that possible?" Corey asked.

"Beats me. I'm not the electrician. My dad was."

"But, I mean, if the machines are in the river, won't the water continuously make the machine function?"

She tipped the machine over, staring at the contents in hopes of some spark hitting her, some reminder of what her father did. "Sure. And we will have one functioning light bulb that flickers."

"Maybe we can fill the river with them. Get a machine for everything we need in there."

"Well, one machine won't be enough to heat up the place, and twenty machines won't either. Besides, if we fill the river with these things, we are just going to block it up."

She growled and kicked her makeshift invention.

Corey put his hand on her shoulder. "It's alright. We will figure it out, and in the meantime, Brian can keep stealing diesel trucks from the depot. Just count our blessings he found that place and, even more miraculous, it's fifteen minutes down the road."

"That's finite. It's not a solution. I only have so much time to figure this out." She rubbed her eyes, tired and ready to cry.

"You will get it. You will. And if we run out of fuel in the meantime, we'll build a fireplace or something. It'll be fine."

She pushed away from him. "Nothing will be fine without my father."

He said nothing and his eyes expressed a desire to make her feel better.

"Every day, I watched my father tinker with these machines, making all kinds of miracles. I sat by his side and stared, bored out of my mind while he built. I should know how to do this but the truth is, I never really paid attention. It bored me. I liked the fighting and practicing to defend myself."

Corey shook his head. "We have been here a week now and you guys still won't tell me about where you were raised. You were fighting? As children?"

Violin got back on her knees and turned the machine over, staring at something on its side. "We were trained to fight, yes, because of you. Well, not you personally, but humans. They've attacked us, wanted us dead. So we hid underground and prepared for an invasion from you."

"You're not making sense. I know you said you're not human, which, okay, that's weird, but, even if so, you look human. How would anyone know you're not?"

She tightened a screw. "Why am I doing this? Tightening this isn't going to help make it function. It's not going to fix it, but I still do it." She lifted her head to the skies and sighed. "Humans try to kill us because they are threatened by us. It's instinctual. They don't know why they do it, but they do it."

Corey put his hands out. "Then why haven't I? Why hasn't Brian? I think you were raised to believe things that simply aren't true. Humans don't want to kill you because..." He leaned down and put his eyes level with hers. "Because you are human."

She continued to tinker, knowing full well what she was doing wasn't helping. "When I was around Candlestick's age, I was preparing for my test on guardian training. We had to know, and be able to explain, the entire perimeter of our world down there. We had to know every entry point and exit point. If someone found their way into our home from entrance A, we had to send our people to exit D. You understand?"

Corey nodded. He swayed, a reaction to the cold weather.

"Well, I was roaming the outside areas and I found two things. One, I caught my Aunt Boreas sneaking into a water tunnel where she met a man. A human man. They whispered to one another and giggled. I left, terrified. That's when I saw the second thing. In a tunnel, I witnessed a rat eating a mouse."

Corey stopped rocking on the balls of his feet. "Okay?"

"The point is, you may look at a rat and mouse and think they are not much different, but one has the power to eat the other."

"So, which are you?"

"We are the rats."

"Then why are you afraid of us mice?"

"You outnumber us."

"And the whole thing about your aunt? What's that got to do with anything?"

At this, she stopped her tinkering and stood up again. Her eyes watered and she didn't know if it was from the memories or the bitter bite of evening air hitting her face. "I never told anyone about my aunt, not even my father. In fact, you're the first person I have ever said this to and I don't know why I am saying it. I found her sneaking to meet with a human, the things we feared the most, and that made me curious. Was I wrong about humans? He seemed nice to her. When she came back to the community, she looked so happy, bright eyed, different than normal."

Corey's teeth chattered. He put his hands in his pockets.

"I decided to keep an eye on her from a distance, see when, and if, she would meet him again. The answer was almost once a week, sometimes a little less, sometimes more often. We are good at being sneaky, so I managed to keep this up for a long time and while she wasn't as good at it as I was, she did keep her secret from everyone else. Eventually, she caught me."

Violin cupped her lips into her mouth and squinted, hoping to keep the tears from showing. "I told her what I knew, asked her how she could betray us. She promised me humans were not what we were told, that there were good ones, decent ones. And from every-thing I had seen with her and this man, it seemed true."

Corey smiled. "And it was true. We aren't all evil."

Violin shook her head and moved a step closer to him. "You don't understand. One day, I followed her into the tunnel again. I don't know if she knew I was doing it or not, because I had stopped for a while, but when I listened to them talking, I heard something."

Corey leaned forward, absorbed into her story. "What?"

"He coughed. A lot."

Corey jerked his head back. "He coughed?"

"Yes. A week after that, so did my aunt. Later, so did everyone else. My grandma knew. Right away, she knew. She locked us all in a different area. We stayed in separate sections from the rest of our people for weeks, alone. Eventually, she came to my father and told him they were all dying and he needed to leave. She spoke to him through a door where he wept and begged to see his wife, my mom."

"Oh."

"I said nothing. I never told anyone about my aunt. As we ran to Earth, I didn't think it mattered. Because for all of your speculation, I know the truth."

"What truth?"

She glared at him. "Humanity disappeared because they had a disease."

Corey shook his head and waved his hand. "No, there would be bodies."

"I can't explain it, but I would bet anything, if we went down to my community, there would be no bodies, too. The disease eats them all up. Gone. I had no idea it would have killed off humans so quickly. I assumed we were running from one diseased world to another. But that's not important now. What's important is that, good or bad, it doesn't matter what we think of you humans. In the end, you'll kill us all whether you meant to or not."

"No. No. I'm sorry, but..."

She put her hand up to stop him. "You don't have to feel bad. I held my aunt's secret against my better judgment. I'm responsible for this. I killed them all, too."

He stepped forward and tried to hug her but she brushed him off.

Candlestick came around from the front of the building. She was wearing nothing but her dress despite the cold air, and her pallid face showed true dread.

"Candlestick. What is it?" Violin moved toward her.

"I can't control them without Dad here."

"What?"

Candlestick's words registered in Violin's head just as the woods came alive with volatile crashes. Violin turned to Corey. "Run!"

CHAPTER 43

What is Left?

Violin ran to her sister. She latched her hand around Candlestick's and dragged her to the front of the building. Corey kept close behind.

As they hit the front of the building, Violin saw movement coming from the parking lot. To her surprise, it wasn't lampposts. Instead, the parking lot filled with humanesque creatures. At least, they had the same size and shape as people, but their skin was ashy and gray, and their facial features were nothing but gaping holes. Human husks.

"Shit," Violin said, her heart pounding in her chest. "Come on."

She pulled her sister in the opposite direction, where Corey barreled toward them, confusion and panic streaking across his face.

"Turn around," she yelled, and Corey listened, nearly falling flat on his ass as he spun.

From the woods where the river raged, dozens more of the husks crossed the forest edge. They all whispered something indistinguishable, creating a chorus of wispy words, both horrifying and somewhat beautiful.

Corey screamed at the sight.

Violin stopped and Candlestick banged into her back. "We're stuck. We can't go either way."

Corey turned to her, his eyes begging for direction, for a solution.

Violin glanced all around as the creatures came closer, and the ones from the front made their way around the corner.

They could run into the river, downstream from the husks, but they'd never get far enough away to where these things couldn't catch them.

"The fence. Corey, use the fence and hop onto the roof."

He nodded and wasted no time hopping up onto the chain link. Violin dragged Candlestick. "I'll climb and pull you up. You can do this. In the meantime, focus. Clear your mind and get rid of them."

Candlestick nodded, but her eyes betrayed her. Violin knew her sister didn't have the mental clarity to control these creatures. They were in control of her now. Every day since Winter's body crashed to the cement, Violin worried the monsters inside her own head would devour her, but she forgot to check on Candlestick, forgot to make sure her sister wasn't drowning in grief.

Corey cleared the roof and Violin pulled onto the links. The whispering from the husks grew louder as they cleared the grass leading to the cement path out back.

As Violin planted her feet on the top of the fence, she reached for Candlestick, helping her climb, but her sister was slow, careless, unfocused, and kept slipping down.

She glanced out of the corner of her eye, gauging where the creatures were. "I need you to get it together, Candlestick. Focus."

She pulled her sister up, and while Candlestick's legs flailed as if running in place, Violin managed to lift her high enough to scoop her arms around the top of the fence. Candlestick used the momentum to lift herself entirely.

As the husks moved in, Violin made out words within the whispers and it sent a shiver up her spine. She heard her name. "Vvvvvvviiiiiiooooooooollllllliiiiiiinnnnnnnn."

She jumped to the roof, and Corey pulled her the rest of the way up. She turned to help her sister, but Candlestick wasn't reaching up to her. Instead, she stared down at the husks that now surrounded the fence. They jumped and raised their arms to her. One of them brushed its fingers against her feet.

"Now, Candlestick!"

Candlestick kicked her foot away from the husk's hands. "They aren't going to kill me. Remember, just like the lampposts."

Violin nodded. "You don't know that."

Candlestick crouched down, perched on the top of the fence like a bird. "What are you saying?" She tilted her head to the creatures, trying to get her ear closer.

"Vvvviiiiioooollliiinnnnn."

"Yyyyyoooouuuuuuu mussssssst fffffooooocccccuuussss."

Violin squeaked as the air left her body. "Candlestick, get up here now." She stretched her hand out more.

Candlestick turned to her, smiling. "It's Grandma. It's all of them."

"No, it's not. Get up here now."

"They aren't going to hurt me. It's our family."

There were at least one hundred of the husks crowding around the fence, more than there had been people in the underground community.

"Do they look like your family, Candlestick? They are nightmares."

As if to prove her point, one of the husks snarled, it's lips revealing blackened gums. The whispering continued, but they all spoke different things at once, making it difficult to understand what they said.

Occasionally, Violin pried a word from the wall of sound. It always cut deep, always something personal. "Vvvviiiiooollliiiinnn... Aaaaanngggggrrryyyy.... Wwwwiiiiitttthhhhh. Moooooottttttthhhh-heeeeeerrrr."

One of the creatures latched onto Candlestick's foot and jumped up with an open mouth, chomping down just inches away, and then they were all on her, reaching up to her and pulling her down.

She screamed, and shot her arm up to Violin, stretching her

small limb as far as it would go. Violin grabbed on and Corey reached from her side to help pull. They yanked against the pressure from the husks. One of the things bit into Candlestick's heel. She lost her grip as her body reacted to the bite. She screamed and flailed, but Corey and Violin refused to let go, pulling with all their might.

"Ahhhh!" Candlestick shouted as the things clawed into the bottoms of her feet.

Corey reached down further, gripped Candlestick at her armpits, and yanked her up. Violin and Corey dragged her to safety. The things, enraged, shook the fence. A loud rattling of metal drowned out the whispering chorus.

Violin immediately examined Candlestick's foot, now soaked red with blood. "We need to get you inside. This is bad."

Candlestick cried and wrapped herself in a ball, with her arms clutching her tucked legs. Blood poured from the wounds, creating a small pool under her.

"Corey!" Brian shouted.

"Shit." Corey ran to the front edge of the motel roof and looked down. "Brian, get inside. We're safe up here. Just get inside."

"What the fuck is going on?"

"Just get inside!"

Candlestick rocked on her butt, and now she, too, was whispering something to herself. Violin ran her fingers through Candlestick's hair. "Listen. Did you see how those things were moving really slow at first, and then they got faster. Did you notice their whispers got louder, and they got more violent? You're doing that. Your mind is making them. If you can make them, you can erase them."

She shook her head. "I can't. They're our family."

Violin gripped Candlestick by the cheeks. "They aren't. There are more of them than we had in our whole community. They are creatures, feeding off your pain. Just like the lampposts. Kill them."

"I can't."

"We lost everything. You can't fix that. But you have to fight for what's left."

"What is left?" Candlestick's eyes were glassy and bloodshot.

Violin frowned that the question needed an answer. "Me?"

"We have to go," Corey shouted and pointed to the edge where a trail of blood from Candlestick's foot had painted the surface. Hands latched onto the rooftop. Lots of them.

Violin stood up and pulled her sister up with her. She yanked Candlestick as they ran to the front side of the building, but Candlestick slowed them down with her hobbling.

"Caaaaaannndlesssssssticccckkkk. Yyyyyoooouuuu rrrrruuuiiiinnneeddd the ccccrrrrooooppppsssss."

The husks were halfway up by the time Violin, Corey, and Candlestick reached the roof's edge.

"We have no choice. We have to jump. What the fuck are these things?" Corey asked.

"Candlestick will break her leg if we jump."

Four or five husks were up now, pulling themselves to their feet.

Corey looked to the things, and to the girls. He grabbed Candlestick and wrapped his arms around her, squeezing her into his chest. And he jumped.

He landed on his feet and turned himself around as his body reacted to the impact. He fell on his back, providing Candlestick with a safe landing.

Violin looked back at the husks.

"Vvvvviiiioooollllliiiinnnn."

"Violin, hurry up," Corey said.

One of them listed its head. It was her uncle, she now realized, seeing the thing up close. It broke from the whispers and snarled, letting out a loud barking noise. A cough, maybe. And then with a brassy croak, it said, "Vi-o-lin. You. Have. Weeeee-akened us."

She shook her head, angry at the taunts. "No. I am strong."

"Violin, what are you doing?" Corey asked.

Another husk, one she couldn't identify, a young girl, said, "Where is your power?"

They slowly approached her, spreading out as they did, so they surrounded her.

The one that looked like her uncle rubbed his fingertips with his thumbs. "Weeeee-akened us."

"Where is your power?" Another screamed.

Then, they were all screaming different things, but with the same message: Violin didn't know her power. Violin made her family afraid that through the generations, they were losing their heritage, their strength, their connection.

They were wrong, though, because Candlestick had power. Only Violin didn't know what skills she possessed. Only she couldn't tap into their ancestor's force. Only she failed to live up to the standards of the community.

Just another way she let them all down. Just another failure to add to her slate, a slate she could never clean.

She turned back to Corey, who waited with his arms up, hoping to help her land safely, too. Candlestick stood behind him with her hurt foot off the ground. Her eyes displayed worry for her sister.

"I'm trying to make them go away, Violin," she said.

The husks were close to her now. She could feel them behind her back. Maybe she should give up. Maybe she was the weak link. Maybe Candlestick would be better without her.

"I'm fighting for you, Violin." Candlestick scrunched her face, showing how hard she was trying to concentrate. "Fight for me, too."

As a husk clawed into her arm, she jumped.

CHAPTER 44

A Touch of Adrenaline

Chucky marched behind Elijah and debated on strangling the little shit. The kid was a punk, no doubt about it, but Chucky had believed the scumbag when he told him about the girls. After coming to terms with the fact he'd spend the rest of his life alone, and sexless, he was willing to take the risk at any prospect at all, albeit one that came from a clear carnival huckster because, at the end of the day, that's what Elijah was, a lying, conniving little turd. He'd risk monsters and death to get one more night to touch a female.

If Chucky had to guess, Elijah probably planned to kill him as soon as they found this group of his, so that way he could have the girls to himself, but Chucky would be one step ahead when the time came. *If* the time came. After days of trekking through slush, deeper into the woods, Chucky doubted Elijah had been honest at all. Maybe the kid got so worked up about the bunker, and worried he might get killed, he created this little bit of fiction to save himself. Smart move, really. Chucky had to give him that.

A faint whiff of wood smoke crossed Chucky's nose. At first, he thought nothing of it. Being a man of the woods, it was a scent he'd grown accustomed to, but his mind snapped back to reality and he remembered that wood smoke would mean living people, and living people were not something he wanted to cross today.

"You smell that?" He asked Elijah.

Elijah continued to trudge through the slushy mud. "You smell a fire?"

"Yep."

"Yes, I do." He finally stopped and turned around to face Chucky. He sniffed, making a big show of it. "It's close, isn't it?"

Chucky nodded, a nervous energy building inside him. He had avoided the post-apocalyptic murdering and defending of oneself that happens in all the comics and books thus far, but he also knew when and if they did find this family Elijah talked about, he'd have to do some shooting, so maybe it was best to get the practice in. The idea of seeing a person bleed to death gave him a strange sensation up his back, and he wasn't sure if it was a good one or a bad one. He liked the way it felt, regardless, so he'd take it as a feeling he wanted to lean into.

Elijah waved his index finger, telling Chucky to move behind a tree line. Chucky obliged, trying to be as stealthy as a fat man can.

"I think it's coming from over there." Elijah pointed to the right, which to Chucky, meant deeper into the woods. At this point, he had no idea where they were and he knew Elijah didn't either. They were good and lost, and probably had no hopes of finding the girls, even if they did exist.

"What should we do? Avoid it, or explore? Could be your people, right?" Chucky asked.

"Could be. I'm guessing not, but if I'm wrong, and we were this close, how much would that suck?"

They quietly moved forward toward where Elijah had pointed. As they reached a small clearing, Chucky put his hand up to stop Elijah.

"Look," he pointed toward a mound of clothes, soaked in red, behind some small catmint plants.

Elijah put his chin up, trying to get a better view. "The fuck is that?"

Chucky moved his head left and right, trying to see beyond a few blue spruces and the catmint. There, he noticed a fire pit, snuffed out, but still smoldering.

Before he could mention it to Elijah, something metal pressed against the back of his skull, and a tiny click let him know a bullet was dangerously close to firing his brains all over the woods.

"Don't fucking move. I'm not in the mood for playing around."

Elijah didn't even bother turning toward the action. "You think you're quick enough to blow my friend's head off and then shoot me before I turn around and blast you to bits?"

Chucky kept his head still but looked down to see Elijah's weapon was no longer in its holster.

"How do you know I'm alone, and that one of my friend's isn't aiming at you right now?"

Elijah chuckled, still facing away from the man. "Well for one, you wouldn't ask that question if it were true. You would have made a statement, instead. But also, you had a fire over there and only one sleeping bag next to it. Course, it does look like you weren't alone, but it's hard to see how many dead you got piled up over there."

The metal released from Chucky's head, and he let out a giant gasp of air. The man kept his gun trained as he walked around them, coming into view on their side.

"Follow me," he said. Chucky and Elijah listened.

As they crossed the catmint, Chucky could now see the pile of clothes was two dead men draped on top of each other. Blood drenched their shirts, now dried and just another part of the fabric. They'd been dead for a while, from the looks of it. Despite the winter preserving them somewhat, the rot prevailed. Chucky guessed two weeks at least, maybe a little more.

"What happened?" He asked, probably foolishly.

The man looked him head on, and for the first time, Chucky saw his face well enough. He had a red beard and fiery, long, red hair. He wore a flannel shirt and dirty jeans. The man lifted his shirt to reveal a huge wound in his gut, patched up with ripped fabric and duct tape.

"You taking anything for that?"

"Yeah, I got antibiotics and hydrogen peroxide. Bullet's still in there. Guess it's gonna stay that way." He led them to his fire and waved his hand to tell them to sit. "I don't have the ambition to shoot you anymore. A month ago, me and my boys would have robbed you and killed you, no doubt, but I'm just about ready to give it up, so if you all feel the need to kill me and rob me, I suppose that's what they call Karma. I just don't give a shit."

Chucky assumed that was exactly Elijah's plan, but not yet. Elijah was the type to worm as much information out of a person as he could first. They both sat next to the fire as the man had instructed. Elijah crossed his legs and tucked his knees into his crotch, as if he were doing yoga. Chucky spread his fat legs out, getting his cold, wet feet as close to the fire as he could. Even if it weren't going anymore, it still produced a little warmth.

"What say we get the fire going again and we can all warm up and talk about it?" Elijah asked, and Chucky felt thankful for it.

The man nodded and leaned behind himself to grab a few pieces of firewood he had stacked up. He tossed them into the pit and within a few minutes, the smoldering red flakes took hold and a thin set of flames drizzled up the logs.

Chucky thought about their adventure so far, how frustrating it had been, the days of wandering further from the comforts of his own home, the cold bleakness of the woods in winter, the rationing of food, and how he spent almost every day cursing his decision to follow this kid. Now, sitting by a warm fire, knowing they'd have new food soon, whether it was shared or taken from a dead person, made him feel reinvigorated and excited to continue their hunt.

"Who attacked you?" Elijah asked as he dug through his backpack. He still wore his stupid wilderness scout's uniform. Chucky asked him if he wanted some new clothes, but the kid refused, saying at the end of the world, a uniform, any uniform, inspired fear.

Chucky thought that was bullshit, because the uniform didn't scare him. Instead, he found it laughable. Maybe that was effective too, though, because as he'd been learning from his time with Elijah, the kid was not to be underestimated.

The man stared at his hands and rubbed them close to the fire.

"No one, technically. We attacked them and were bringing them to our camp. Well, not me so much as my brother. We usually just robbed people and killed them, but my brother wanted to keep this group for a while. Probably because they had young kids. Maybe he was thinking up ways to keep them alive. I hate to say it, but maybe he had plans for the little girls."

Elijah looked up. "Little girls? How old?"

The man laughed. "Hate to admit we got fucked up by kids, but it's true. We underestimated them. These kids were trained to fight. Had to be. They knew what they were doing."

"Two girls, right?"

"Yeah, and their father."

Elijah leaned forward, excited. Chucky felt a fluttering in his chest, adrenaline coursing through his veins.

"How old?"

"I dunno. One looked a little less than a teenager, and the other a bunch younger than that. I don't know how to gauge ages for kids."

Elijah stood up. "How long ago was this? How far behind them are we?"

"What, are you guys out hunting for them?"

Elijah's eyes widened.

Chucky rubbed his hands over the fire. "Yup."

"You aren't the only one those pricks fucked with. They killed my entire troop. They look soft, but they are fucking evil," Elijah said.

The man stood up too, Elijah's charm awakening some life in the man. "It was weeks ago, man, and it was way away from here. I dragged my brother and cousin back to the camp. It would be tough to find them now."

"Which way did they go?" Elijah was nearly hopping up and down.

The man pointed behind Chucky. "Toward the road. That's where we found them. They got the jump on us, shot us, and took off back that way."

Elijah tapped Chucky's shoulder. "Come on, dude, let's go."

"Shouldn't we warm up a bit first? We're already weeks behind them."

"No, let's go, now."

Chucky sighed and stood up. His body argued against him by throbbing muscles he didn't even know he had.

"Wait, can I come with you guys?" The man grabbed his bag. "I'll share my supplies. It ain't much, but I got enough to share some food and meds if you all need them. Even got a few bottles of Vodka."

Elijah clapped his hands. "The more the fucking merrier. Let's find these fuckers. Oh, I feel alive again."

Chucky had worn thin of Elijah's charm, but even he found this energetic new sense of purpose a bit rejuvenating. Knowing they were weeks away from their prey felt overwhelming, but since he hadn't known if they were heading in the complete wrong direction just fifteen minutes ago, and wasn't even sure the damned prey existed, the large gap between him and his desires felt possible. It felt palpable, real, close.

As they walked away from the camp, the man jogged to catch up to them. "Hey, one question. Did you see monsters out here? Like, real monsters."

Elijah laughed. "Yeah, my man. Haven't seen them in weeks now, but monsters are fucking real."

Chucky turned his head to the man. "He's not lying, either. Biggest, most fucked up things you'll ever see."

The man looked to his dead family and said, "Told you assholes. I know what I saw."

CHAPTER 45

One Step Ahead

Violin launched herself off the roof as one of the husks reached for her. His bony, sharp fingers scraped her skin as she flew. Her body crashed into Corey, who, to his credit, put himself in place to take a beating so she could land softer.

He let out an, "Oof," as they tumbled to the hard cement. Within seconds, the creatures were hurling themselves off the roof, while others turned the corner from the front of the motel.

"Get inside!" Corey shouted. Violin put her arm around Candlestick's bad side, letting her use Violin as a literal crutch.

They hobbled to the door as Corey pounded on it. Brian opened the door and they all tumbled in, including one of the husks. Brian, seeing the things for the first time, screamed, while Corey and the girls kicked it off them. It flailed on top of them, lying on the floor, wriggling and scratching. As they smashed their feet into its face, it lashed out with sharp teeth but Corey and the girls didn't relent on the foot strikes. Brian grabbed it by its waist and pushed it outside, which caused some of the other husks to trip over it.

He slammed the door as two of the creatures lunged forward, arms extended. Their bodies met nothing but solid wood.

For a moment, the only sound that filled the room was the ragged breaths coming from Corey, Violin, and Candlestick.

Then, the whispering started again.

"Vvvvvviiiiooollllliiiinnnnnn."

Brian stared at the three people in the room. "What the fuck is happening?"

Corey stood up, clutching his knees and drawing out breaths, trying to regulate his heartbeat. "I have no fucking clue. Violin, were you talking to them? Are they calling your name?"

Brian opened the shade. Five husks were pressed against the glass, slapping their hands into it. "Is this what killed humans?"

Violin walked toward the bathroom. "No," she shouted as she exited the bedroom. She grabbed some towels and ran to her sister.

"Do you have any medicine for this?" She asked.

Brian and Corey just stared until, finally, Brian snapped out of it. "Oh, yes. I'm sorry. What happened to her?"

Violin pointed to the window where the husks continued to smack their palms into the glass.

"Jesus, okay," he said as he dug through a backpack. He pulled out a brown bottle. "Here, have her put her foot in the tub and pour this on it. Pour some on a towel, too, and wrap the towel around the wound."

He bent down and turned her leg gently to better see the wounds. "It looks pretty deep. I think she'll be okay, but we gotta make sure we keep it clean so it doesn't get infected."

Violin helped her sister up and brought her to the tub. She did as instructed. Brian watched from the doorway, his hands around his waist. His attention snapped between the girls and the things outside. Corey stayed at the window, staring. Every time a husk made a particularly loud thud, he'd jolt back.

"What are these fucking things and how do you know they aren't what killed people?" Brian asked. "Corey, you should get the guns ready."

Violin wrapped a towel around the cleaned foot and pushed Candlestick's hair behind her ears. She smiled at her. "It's your turn to shine. You can do this. We are protected, temporarily, by the walls, but we don't know for how long. Take your time. Concentrate. Make them go away." Then, she leaned in and tapped against her sister's leg. "We can never tell them you made the monsters. But we can tell them you know how to get rid of them."

Candlestick nodded, but her droopy eyelids showed nothing but worry.

As Violin lifted her sister, and Candlestick winced, Brian said, "Oh, wait," and ran out of the room. He came back with a white circular shaped thing. He tossed it to Violin.

She inspected it. "What's this?"

"It's a bandage. You wrap it around the wound."

She nodded and, again, did as instructed. Things on Earth were sometimes like how they were down below, but always just a little off. They, too, had clothes meant specifically for covering wounds, but they didn't come wrapped in small tubes.

They made their way back into the bedroom and the husks pounded louder and more intensely. Their whispers, once again, turned to growls. "Vvvvviiiooollliiinnnn."

One of them scraped its nails against the window, wiping its hand back and forth, taunting her.

Violin moved past Corey and stood inches in front of the glass. If one of them broke it open, she'd be showered with sharp bits to her face. Two of them looked like people she knew in the underworld but covered in rot. The others she didn't recognize at all.

She wondered why they taunted her, why it was her name constantly on their lips, if it was Candlestick who made them. How did they know her powers—or lack of powers—were such a sore spot to her? How did they know she always worried about being a weakness to her people?

She'd never expressed those feelings to her sister.

She pressed her hands to the glass, so that her palm covered one of the husk's faces. "I'm not afraid of you. I am here and you are not. I made it. You did not. For all of your traditions, all of your training, all of your powers, I am still standing, and you are dead."

She turned back to the group, allowing them to see the tears rolling down her face. Corey and Brian had their arms around each other and their guns on the desk next to them. Their eyes were wide and true terror shined in their pupils.

"These things didn't kill humans, or my people, because they are the dead humans and my dead people. We are being haunted. Luckily, Candlestick can talk to animals, and these things are nothing more than that."

She walked over to Brian and Corey, and as she passed her sister, she brushed Candlestick's shoulder with her fingers. "I know this is scary, and I know you worry about your decision to stay with us, because we are weird, we are different. I know. But trust me, I can make sense of this. Please don't abandon us."

Corey frowned and tears formed in his eyes now, too. "Oh, honey, we won't. The world has gone batshit crazy, but you didn't do that. It'd be that way if we weren't with you."

Candlestick dropped to her knees and screamed. Corey and Brian jolted back, slamming into the wall behind them.

As she continued to scream in one long, solid breath, the creatures snarled and screamed back. Violin blocked her ears, getting shivers every time they screeched her name. The volume grew until she thought her brain might explode. She covered her eyes.

Her sister's shrill voice stopped shouting, and a series of thuds made Violin open her eyes. She gasped. New tears poured down her cheeks, but these ones from overwhelming joy. Candlestick ran past her.

"Dad?"

Winter had risen from his weeks-long slumber. He stepped off the bed with shaky legs, his body gaunt and fragile. The world moved in slow motion, every hope and desperate plea to the gods answered. Violin watched, disbelieving what she was seeing. She froze, stuck in a pile of emotions too large to bear. Succumbing to the fact his recovery was nothing more than a pipe dream, she had grieved, and even now, continued to do so.

As he moved across the room, avoiding Candlestick, who had come in for a hug, Violin grieved. Her eyes filled with water.

Winter flung his weak body forward and flopped on top of Brian, strangling him.

Violin ran to Corey's aide, as he tried to rip her father away from Brian's throat.

"Dad! Dad! Get off him!"

"I will kill you. What is happening here? What did you do to my children?"

They pried Winter off Brian, but he continued to struggle. For someone who hadn't left bed in weeks, unconscious and near death, he somehow had the strength of the gods.

Violin got in front of him, blocking him from attacking again.

"I saved your life, asshole," Brian shouted as he clutched the red ring growing on his throat from the assault. "Way to say thank you."

Corey pushed Brian back. "He just woke up. He's confused. It's okay. You're okay."

Winter fell to the bed, landing on his butt. He rubbed his face, groggy and clearly not as capable of fighting as he thought he was. "What did you do to me? Did you make me weaker? Did you give me some poison?"

Violin kept catching her father's hands as he raised them. She pushed them back down to the bed. "Dad, they saved you. They ran back to their cabin and got medicine. They didn't have to come back, but they did, and they took care of you. Brian is a doctor. He saved you."

Winter scratched his head. His upper body swayed as if bobbing in water. "No. Humans never save, they kill. This is a trick. Somehow, they are tricking us. It was Kevin Bacon who saved me."

"They tricked you back to life? You're being dumb, Dad. They have taken care of us."

They stared at each other for a moment, and finally, Violin wrapped her arms around him. "I love you so much, Dad. I have spent every day worrying you'd never wake up, that you'd just die there. I tried not to get my hopes up because Brian said it would be a miracle if you ever woke up, but you did, and you're here, and I just want to be happy for a minute. Can you just let me be happy for a minute?"

She turned her head to see Brian and Corey staring, so she tapped against her father's back. "Don't worry. I am one step ahead of them."

CHAPTER 46

Repairing the Damage

Everyone calmed a little, but the tension was still thick in the air. The husks were gone, at least, but that did nothing to quell the fear on Corey and Brian's faces. They still had no idea what was going on, and now they had a new threat, albeit a sleepy, half-alive one, sitting on the bed staring at them.

Violin asked Candlestick to sit with Winter and keep him calm while she ushered Brian and Corey outside. The two men were reluctant at first, untrusting of the husks' disappearance. They carried their guns with them and Violin led them to the door. Winter opened his mouth to object to his daughter leaving with them, but Violin raised her hand with one finger up to shush him.

Violin closed the door behind them, and puffs of coldness left their mouths as they breathed.

"I know this is a lot," she said.

Brian rubbed his bare hands together and paced. "It's more than a lot." He glanced toward the woods surrounding the lot, and toward the corners of the motel, still afraid of the husks.

"Listen, my father is a good man, a caring man. But above all else, he cares about me and Candlestick. All we have seen up here, until we met you, are bad humans who wanted to kill us. That is what we were raised to believe. I am young, Candlestick is younger, so we are still learning. But hating people is all he has ever known. And so far, up here, those thoughts have been…"

"…Justified." Corey said.

She nodded. "Yes. But I know it is not true. I know I can trust you both. He will trust me once I talk to him for a while. Please, believe me. We can't live up here without you. Once he is back on his feet, and I have taught him to trust you, he can get his machines running, and we can have all the electricity in the world. And he has seeds; we can grow all sorts of foods. This can be paradise."

"I want to be there for you and Candlestick. I know we've only been here a week, but I've enjoyed being around you, and I think we all make a great team. But, I just don't know." Brian ran his fingers around his throat where bright red finger marks remained.

"You will live a better life here than at your cabin. And we will live a better one with you here. It's good for all of us if you stay."

"You have to tell us more about what those things were."

Violin sighed. The things, of course, were projections created by Candlestick's grief, monsters of her mind come to life, but she knew she couldn't tell them that.

"You guys never saw the lampposts, did you?"

They looked at each other. "You mean streetlights?" Corey asked.

"Monsters." She stared at their widening eyes. "I know it sounds crazy, but maybe less so now that you've seen those things that just attacked us. We have seen a lot of crazy things on Earth. Some, we didn't know if they were normal parts of being on Earth, or new, crazy things. We picked the right time to come up here, when everyone disappeared. It's a bizarre place even to people like you, who have lived here your whole life, so to us, we don't know what is what.

But we saw monsters, and we knew they were not supposed to be here, not part of normal Earth. A man warned us of them shortly before they ate him alive."

Brian and Corey shuddered. Violin hadn't thought of it before, but now that she remembered the man who warned them, she realized he seemed to know all about the monsters. It made her wonder how long Candlestick was creating them, and how long they were terrorizing people, before they closed in on her family.

"These things were huge, taller than those trucks." She pointed to the diesel trucks.

"They attacked us. We were trapped in the back of a big car... A truck? Are the big cars all called trucks? This one had a big back we could stay in, and it had boxes filled with food."

Brian nodded. "Yes, that's a truck."

"We were trapped in there while those things attacked us. We thought we were going to die."

Corey and Brian held hands, showing more belief in her story than they may be willing to admit.

"I know you don't believe us that we aren't human, but it's true. We have powers, all of us. Well, everyone but me, but that is not important right now. Our people start to show their powers around the age of eight. Candlestick's age. So, just as we thought we were about to die, her powers showed up. She screamed and the monsters fled; sort of just disappeared, just like you saw happen in the room." The fire disc (or as Brian called it, the sun) was what actually made the monsters run away, but the full story felt too long to tell.

"It took a few days for us to figure it out, but she can talk to animals. If you don't believe me, test her out with Lion. We can get him out of the other bedroom and I'll show you. You can tell her to make him do anything, and he will do it.

She can even do it with the animals out here. What did you say they were called? Bears? Deers? Coyotes? All those. She can do that. We are still learning, so we stay afraid of those things, but she can do it when she has to. You saw her do it. She made those creatures go away. You know you saw it."

Brian and Corey looked at each, both with eyes pleading for the other to make sense of all of this. Finally, Brian turned to her slowly. "What's Winter's power?"

She smiled. "Don't worry. He can't hurt you. He can heal people who are sick. Like you, right? I guess he's a doctor as well."

Brian gave her the kind of smile adults give to children when they want to soften a bit of harsh news. "If he can heal people, why did I need to pump him full of antibiotics?"

"He can't heal himself. He can a little. It's like his body automatically works on itself, but it's not much. That's probably why he's not dead, though, and why he survived what you said would be a miracle, and how he was able to jump up and fight a little the second he woke up."

They stared, still disbelieving.

She rolled her eyes. "Come on."

She opened the door back to the motel and waved for them to come into the threshold. "How's Candlestick's foot?" She asked.

Candlestick dangled it in the air, off the bed. The wounds were gone and the blood cleared. "It's fine now."

Violin turned to the men, and while their eyes still expressed disbelief, they also couldn't close their jaws.

She shut the door again and waited for them to say something. They didn't.

"Just please do me a favor. Go into one of the other rooms, give me some time to talk to my dad, and relax. Please just give it tonight to think about it and let me work on Winter. I can make all this work. I need you all to trust me. I'm almost twelve, practically an adult."

The men laughed at this, and she wondered why, but was happy to see their nerves settling. Maybe humans had different criteria for what constituted adulthood, but in Violin's world, the children had to prepare, learn, and adapt with rapid speed. Once they hit the age of thirteen, they were off to work all day, just like the rest of the adults. The mark of adulthood was bestowed upon them with a ceremony where their place in the society would be unveiled by Violin's grandmother. She chose their path based on the skills they showed and their powers.

Violin had always wondered what they'd choose for her, considering her powers never revealed themselves. She worked harder than any of the other children, prepping to be a fighter, and the results paid off. She was better with any weapon, stronger, and more adept at hand-to-hand combat, and more vigilant of her surroundings. She hoped for a guard position, prayed for it, but feared without powers she'd be resigned to cleaning duties. Now, she'd never know what they would have chosen.

Corey broke her from her thoughts. "We will stay the night, at least, for sure. If you can calm your father down, we will stick around, but we don't want to be somewhere we aren't wanted, so it's all going to depend on him. In the meantime, we'll be right next door if you need us"

She accepted their answer and went to work on the harder subject: her stubborn father.

Like the husks, she moved slowly at first, but picked up speed the closer to Winter she got, until she was embracing him in a giant hug. She had a lot to talk to him about but needed a few minutes to enjoy the miracle of his return.

"I love you so much, Dad."

"Me too," Candlestick said as she wrapped her arms around him from behind.

Winter stayed still on the edge of the bed. He still looked woozy and out of it. His skin was even whiter than normal and his eyes had sunken with giant pools of black around them.

His fingers were trembling.

Violin ran to the desk and opened a drawer filled with snacks and pulled out some peanuts. She poured him a cup of water from a bottle lying on the floor. Brian had gotten a package of plastic cups from the store Winter had been getting food from. *Store.* So many new words. Humans used cups that could be thrown away when done. *Disposable,* they called it. How fun and stupidly unnecessary.

She brought the cup to her father and rubbed his shoulder while he drank it with his shaky hand. His arm looked better. It was still red and the skin still unhealed, but the wounds were starting to mend, creating fleshy bumps, uneven terrain like a path in the woods.

After he finished the glass of water, he clicked his tongue off the roof of his mouth and spit out an, "Aaahhhh."

Candlestick rubbed his back while Violin stood in front of him with her arms crossed, assessing his ability to discuss anything. After a minute, he decided for her that he, very much, could.

"Tell me what's going on. I was asleep for a week, Candlestick says? A week? And in that time, you befriended humans? We are all buddies now?"

"Stop it, Dad." She tapped her feet, getting angry. "I want to talk to you about this, but not if you talk down to me. I have been fighting to keep us alive while you were out. Treat me with respect, please."

For all of the fragility his body showed, his voice still boomed. "No, I will not. You are a child. You are my child and my responsibility. I will absolutely not treat you with respect when you do foolish things like befriending humans while you were supposed to be protecting your sister."

"Shut up." She paced, anger spewing from her belly into her throat. "I have always listened to you, always, and look where it got us. We have done nothing but fail up here." She loved her father, was so happy to see him return, but in the moment, she wanted to hurt him. "We were happy and things were peaceful until you woke up, so why don't you just go back to sleep."

He leaned forward, almost stood up, but winced in pain and regretted the decision. "Is that right? You wish your father had died?"

She regretted the miscommunication but wouldn't allow it to simmer her rage. "That's not what I meant," she yelled. "I meant just leave me alone and let me take control for once. I am tired of doing and saying nothing. How many times did I save us? You would have been killed by Wilderness Scouts if it weren't for me. And that's right, they are called Wilderness Scouts. I learned that from my new *FRIENDS*!"

Candlestick watched them fight, but as the conversation grew more volatile, she slowly slid back against the bed frame and curled herself in a ball.

"Friends. Humans aren't friends. They never will be. Why did you tap that on my back? What did you mean you're one step ahead?"

She looked to the wall, worried Corey and Brian were listening. Finally, she stepped to her father and whispered in his ear, "It means just because I have let them in, doesn't mean I am not prepared to kill them if they betray me. I have back up plans for everything. I am smarter than you give me credit for."

As she whispered, he rested his head onto her shoulder and by the time she was finished, his hands were wrapped around her, hugging her deeply.

"Why do you insist on this? Why do we need them now that I am healed?"

She pulled away from him, biting back tears. "We need them because they understand this world. I need this because if I am wrong about *this*, then I am wrong about humanity, and I made a terrible mistake that doomed us all."

He scrunched his forehead. "What does that mean?"

She sat down next to him, not wanting to look him in the face. She wanted to tell him about his sister, and how she had met with a human, how Violin heard the man cough, and how it brought disease to their people. But, she knew what he'd say. He'd tell her that the gods were trying to punish humans for being evil and Violin let them bring that punishment to her community. He would never forgive her for it.

She needed to prove her aunt was right, that humans could be good people. Once she did, then she could confess her sins.

She put her hand on top of his and placed her fingers between the gaps in his fingers. "Rest up, Dad. When you are feeling better, I am sending you on a mission with Brian and Corey. If you refuse, I am leaving this motel, and as much as I will miss you all, I will not return."

It was an empty threat, she knew, and she knew he knew it too, but she would try anything at this point. Brian and Corey saved her father. They've done nothing but help. They brought food, showed the girls how to do things Winter would never know, and they genuinely seemed to care. She did not trust humans, but she trusted those two. More than that, she felt compelled to stay with them, as if Kevin Bacon himself called to her and whispered in her ear that this was the right path.

She also knew that she would never go against her father when it came down to it. So, if he refused, she would abandon the humans. A certainty bubbled inside her, telling her that if she failed to make this work, they'd all be doomed.

Winter put his head down. Then, he said, "I want to tell you another story. This is the most important one yet, so listen closely."

CHAPTER 47

Planting a Seed

Dance emerged from the dirt and a rush of cold air surged into her lungs. She coughed up muck and mud and clawed her way out of the underworld, into the frosty forest. Behind her, Kevin Bacon's head pushed out of the moist earth, mud oozing down his face in rivers.

He pushed himself out of the hole, gasping for breath. His arms were wrapped around something tucked into his chest.

"What are you holding? Where is the person you retrieved from the underworld?" Dance asked.

Kevin glanced down at the bundle. "This is them." He removed a piece of blanket, folding it over in a triangle, revealing a chubby, pink infant's face.

"We saved a baby? While I certainly approve, how is that going to help us against these gods you speak of?"

Kevin put his finger to his lip, "Quiet. You'll wake her." He rocked the baby in one arm.

"Do you ever provide answers?"

Kevin smiled. "Not really my style. This baby is the answer to everything, but her mission won't begin for many years. You see, it won't be her who will save us, nor will it be the children she births. No, this little monster will save us many generations from now."

Dance stepped close to him, anger in her eyes. "Are you saying this war is going to go on for longer than I am alive? How do you know that for sure? And if you do, why are we fighting now at all?"

He turned and walked down a long, uneven path in a the forest, with no end in sight. She huffed and followed him. After a few minutes, he spoke.

"The war I have recruited you for won't last very long. Not that it won't be brutal, but it will be short. The problem is one war leads to another. This baby is me planning two steps ahead. It's also my way of planning my retirement, but that is another story for another day."

She rushed forward, trying to catch up. "No. Please. I need more answers than that. So, you can predict the future? You can see what will happen? I assume our enemies can as well. Why do we fight at all, then, if the outcome is known?"

Kevin laughed so loudly he woke the baby, who cried from the startle. Kevin rocked her gently and waved his hand over her face until she fell back asleep. "Well, first, even if we all did see the outcome, it wouldn't change anything. Who wouldn't fight against their own destiny? Hell, knowing your destiny is all the more reason to fight."

He coughed and spat out some dirt. "Yuck. Coming out of the ground like that is a pain in the butt, huh? Anyway, no, I can't predict the future. I have seen the future, but there are many versions of it. Knowing all possible outcomes means I can plan ahead a little, be ahead of the competition, so to speak. Of course, they have the same knowledge and are also planning two steps ahead. This is where it gets tricky. If they make step A and I respond with B, we all die. If they do step A and I do C, we win, until plan D comes into effect, which they know will give them a win, if and only if I respond with R, S, V, or W. But if I respond with F, T, or Y, things are good."

"And the rest of the letters?"

"Everyone dies everywhere."

Dance threw her hands in the air, forfeiting this nonsense. "Oh, that's all. So, what's the baby? What plan is that?"

Kevin turned to her, walking backward to keep moving. "That's the thing. I have seen every single possible outcome in the universe, and in none of those potential outcomes did this baby ever come back to life."

Dance stopped dead in her tracks. "So, what does that mean?"

"I'm not sure." He turned back so he could walk forward again.

"Then, all that stuff about retirements and what not? How do you even know if this baby will have children?"

Kevin pointed toward a cabin tucked behind some oak trees. Dance did a double take. The place looked ready to fall. It leaned to the right and the wood walls were all ripped from their nails, barely hanging together. She followed him as he stepped inside. Dance took careful steps, worried that any forceful movement would knock the roof on top of them.

Kevin placed the baby on a small table, which had an equal level of imbalance to the house. He smiled as he stared at it. "I saw all possibilities when I traveled through everything. That is the sight of the gods, the ability to see and decipher all there is to see. But, when I traveled through the underworld to get you, I also saw nothing. Nothing. It's dreadful to see the absence of all things, but it was important for my true vision, because it's the one thing the gods never saw. You see, they saw everything, they know everything, but they don't know nothing."

"Don't know nothing?"

Kevin shook his head. "Yes, they don't know nothing."

"That's a double negative. It means they know something."

Kevin snapped his fingers. "Exactly. Actually, they know everything."

He opened the baby's cloth and sniffed. "Ah, good. Nothing to change here." He refastened the cloth and put his arms up in victory as the infant continued to sleep soundly.

"I'm tired of trying to understand you, and to be quite frank, coming back from the dead has made my bones and muscles fill with ache. Just tell me what we do now and I will have to trust you. You did bring me back to life, after all."

Kevin leaned down and put his nose to the baby's nose. "In the nothingness, my mind made a story. It was a beautiful tale of a baby who grew to be a woman, and that woman created worlds, and her children expanded those worlds, and her grandchildren..." He paused and lifted his head. "Well, her grandchildren save us all. You see, the gods know everything, or at least they *knew* everything, but it's probably been a while since they've looked. I, in nothingness, created more stuff that never existed in everything. Everything has been updated."

Dance stepped to his side and, for the first time, gave the child more than a passing look. The girl had beautiful black hair, uncanny in length for a baby. "You mean, you created her with your mind?"

Kevin smiled. "I did, but she couldn't be alive. She needed to be a thought buried deep in the abyss, or the gods might sense her coming into being. So, I killed the thought of her as I created her. Then, I saved her." He leaned down and kissed her forehead. "And now, I just gave her the power of the gods."

He turned around, sucked in a whiff of dank cabin air, and marched to the door. "Let's go."

"Go? We can't just leave the baby here. This place isn't safe."

Kevin opened the door, letting the fire disc's light into the shallow darkness of the cabin. "You must believe me. The baby will be fine. What we just did was plant a seed. When we see her again, she will have produced a world of gardens."

Dance felt uneasy about leaving the baby so defenseless, unable to care for itself, but Kevin spoke with such authority, she had to believe him. The fire disc spilled bright white on her eyes as she stepped into the crunchy mud of the woods. "Now what?"

"Now, we waste no more time. We gather our friends and kill the gods."

CHAPTER 48
Cornered Animals

The girls interrogated Winter about his story and what it all meant, but fell asleep disappointed at his aversions to answers. Violin pieced some of it together and understood how the stories related to her and Candlestick, but her mind had more new questions for every answer.

In the morning, Winter's disposition hadn't settled, but his healing had improved. He walked to the bathroom and used the toilet, complaining about humans and mumbling about Violin's stubbornness.

Yet, sitting on a human invention felt like a minor concession.

Violin went to the front room, where she made them all bowls of instant oatmeal in the microwave, something she had learned from their new friends. They told her it was best with milk, but water would have to do because milk would be impossible to find. She thought the oatmeal tasted great with the water, anyway. Cinnamon and sugar, whatever those words meant, represented a delicious, mushy meal.

She brought her father and sister each a bowl after gulping down her own in the front room. Candlestick devoured hers and Winter nibbled on his.

"This is tasty. What is it?"

"It's called oatmeal."

He spit it out into the bowl. "Did those humans teach you about this?"

She grabbed the spoon from his hand and dipped it into the mush. After she spun it around to mix it again, she scooped a heap out and moved it toward his mouth. "Yes, and you will eat it. You need to get your strength back up."

He took the spoon from her and bit into the food. "I can do it myself. I am not a baby."

"You just choose to act like one." Violin walked away, toward the exit.

"Where are you going?"

"I have work to do." She said and slammed the door on her way out.

As she headed toward the back of the building, Corey peeked out of his room, popping his head out. "How'd things go with your father?"

She turned to him, frustration causing her to grind her teeth. "He's a child. It will work out, but he's a stubborn battle. I'm sure he won't try to hurt you again, though. I'm confident about that. You all can do whatever you want. I'm going to survive with or without all of you. That includes my father."

As she stormed away, she regretted the exchange. Corey had done nothing wrong, and actively tried to make it work, but she unleashed her anger on him anyway.

She meant it, though. The world grew teeth and its deadly bite chomped closer to them with each passing day.

Monsters, humans, hunger, cold, all of it, a constant threat. Babying adults and trying to be the voice of reason added too much stress to her mind when she needed to focus on making their modest segment of the world a safe place to live.

She turned the corner and her machine came into view. The first time seeing it each morning sank her heart. A week of working ten hours a day to find materials, shape metal, and build the silly little turbine, and all she had was a dinky box with a small fan inside.

She couldn't fathom how to improve it, especially without more materials. Even with a pile of stuff, she wouldn't know what to do other than make it bigger, which wouldn't help in a shallow stream. Besides, her father's turbines were small and they had provided electricity for their entire community.

Still, she took her rod to the river, filled the buckets, lugged the water back, and poured it into the apparatus. Over and over. Each time, the light bulb came to life, flickering until fizzling out. Again. Walked. Filled the buckets. Heaved them over her shoulder. Carried them back. Poured. Again. Again. Again. The same thing, wishing for a miracle. Hoping that somehow the machine would fix itself, would understand her need for it to work, and would respond in kind. "Here, my dear, enjoy my magic."

Winter came around the corner with Candlestick. He moved with slow, tiny steps, keeping his back straight as if bending it would break him in half.

He stood above her, hands on his waist. "Does this work?"

Violin rolled her eyes. "I know it sucks, Dad. I don't need you lecturing me about it."

He knelt in front of the machine, turning it this way and that, inspecting the parts. "Show me."

"Why?"

"Just do it."

She sighed and poured some water into the turbine. It produced a whirring as the blades spun, and the bulb came to life. A few seconds later, it stopped.

Winter clapped and laughed. Violin jolted back, startled by the reaction.

"You made this?"

She shook her head. "I know, I know. I should have paid more attention to yours."

He stood up, wincing as he rose. "Are you kidding me? This is wonderful."

"Dad, it hardly lights a single bulb."

"Do you know the difference between a reaction turbine and an impulse turbine? Do you know any of these names: Kaplan, Deriaz, Gorlov? What is a Pelton wheel? A cross-flow turbine?"

"No. Stop. I don't need you rubbing it in."

He came to her and put his hand on her shoulder. "Rub it in? No, Violin. You don't know those things because we did not teach you them. My uncle taught me all of this. He gave me books upon books on the subject. I spent years practicing and training to build these because I wanted to. You did nothing but watch your old man tinker. What you have done from that bit of watching is miraculous."

Her cheeks grew warm, and a smile worked its way up her face, but she fought against it. "You're just trying to make me feel better."

"My dear, your very first machine lit a bulb. Do you know what my first turbine did? It broke apart. Literally. I poured water in, and the sides fell off it. I am serious."

She chuckled and Candlestick followed suit.

"Besides, where did you get the parts for this?"

She shrugged. "Brian and Corey went to some place where they found me scraps. I gave them a basic idea of what I needed, and they hunted for it in something they call a scrap yard. Some pieces weren't quite right, but I filed pieces down, or made things work as best I could. It's ugly, but it worked a little. We need better tools, though."

Corey and Brian turned the same corner Winter and Candlestick had come from moments ago, bundled in thick clothes and puffy jackets. They both had their hands stuffed into their pockets and their shoulders scrunched into their necks, fighting the early morning cold.

Violin was cold, too, but had spent years encapsulated in icy cement. Their community had electric heaters, but nothing like the ones on Earth. She had adapted to the cold, her body learning to regulate itself. A few months in the motel and she might lose that adaptability.

Both men eyed Winter and moved a little slower upon seeing him. They walked in an arch to give him a wide berth.

"I'm glad you two are here," Winter said with a smile.

Violin joined Brian and Corey in giving him a skeptical look.

"My daughter insists I work with you, get along with you, trust you. I cannot do that, I just can't. But I will try. I will do what she asks for now, but I am prepared for when you betray us. I promise you, if you do, it will be your end. When I was dying, I almost killed you. Imagine what I can do once healed."

For a moment, no one said anything. Corey broke the growing tension. "Wow. Uh. That was inspiring?"

Brian and Violin held in their laughter until it forced its way out through their noses. They keeled over, tears leaking from their eyes. Candlestick joined in too, although she looked like she didn't know why.

Winter stared in confusion, not understanding the joke. "What? What is happening?"

Violin, hardly able to speak, said, "Dad... You're... An... Idiot..."

He frowned. "Why? What happened? I was nice, like you asked."

The day moved along. Winter spent time with Violin, teaching her some basics of hydroelectric turbines. Most of it went over her head, but she enjoyed the lessons and the quality time with her dad. Winter also hung out with Candlestick, and while they joked and played word games, Violin asked Corey to teach her some cooking skills.

On one side of the motel there was a small room with a few tables. Behind it, a small kitchen with a few stoves. Violin's community cooked food over a fire in a room they called the ventilation room. On both sides of the room, the ceiling opened into another area. Violin had always wished to see what was up there, but the opportunity was gone now. She shook the thoughts from her mind.

The human's stove wasn't much different from the makeshift fireplace in the ventilation room, or the one Winter made in the back of the truck they had stayed in, but it had rings on the top that delivered the fire to the pots and pans. It made for an even distribution of heat. Interesting. Humans liked to convolute simple designs, but sometimes the results were magnificent.

Maybe a complicated life was better. Simplicity breeds comfort, sure, but comfort misses out on magic.

"Here's the thing," Corey said. "I would love to show you some tricks, but honestly, I'm just guessing what to do right now. I need butter, milk, things we don't have and never will again. Man, I'd kill for some rosemary and sage. I make a delicious vegetable medley with cranberries and herbs, but we don't have a dang thing. Canned veggies ain't gonna make us anything special."

"But the dinner you made last week was tasty."

"Well, that was meat and gravy packets. I'm sure it's amazing to someone living off crickets, but it's not exactly fine cuisine."

"Well, what are you planning for tonight?"

"Something vegetarian." He turned a knob on the over and after a series of clicks, a fire burst from the top.

"But you like meat."

Corey grabbed a pan and poured some yellow oil into it. As he tipped the pan back and forth, allowing the oil to coat the inside, he said, "Yes, but your father doesn't and I figure we should do things his way for tonight. I'm trying to be fair to him. Brian is a little angrier, but then again, Brian has fingerprints around his neck and almost had a bullet in his head. Your father scares the shit out of me, but from everything you've told me, I get it."

He plopped the pan on the fire and a few minutes later, the oil crackled and sizzled. Violin smiled at the mystery of it all.

Corey opened cans, and scooped corn, beans, and some other stuff she'd never seen before into the pan. After it all landed in a pile, he opened a few bottles of brown liquid and poured it in.

"I know my father is scary, but more than anything, he is scared."

Corey turned to her as he stirred. "Something you're a little too young to understand, but the people most capable of destruction are the scared ones. If you corner a bear, he's going to fucking eat you."

She put her head down, staring at her feet. "Then why are you still here?"

He went back to the food, tilting the pan, letting the mixture swirl around. "I wish I could explain it, but something in my brain keeps saying, 'Stay,' against my better judgment. Brian said the same thing happened to him. Part of it is you and your sister, and we could have a pleasant life here. But part of it is this weird pull, this feeling."

Winter walked in with Candlestick. "What is that delicious smell?"

"Veggie stir-fry. You're going to love it."

"Okay," Winter said. He stood in the doorway, watching the man work for a minute, suspicion in his glare. "So, I think I will be ready to go find tools with you tomorrow. Violin said she wanted us to do that together. I have some rules, though."

He waited for Corey to respond, but Corey continued to mix and stir, a dancer in mid-routine.

Winter cleared his throat. "I will have my gun, and your guns. I will only give you your guns if we run into trouble. Otherwise, I oversee weapons. I will not allow you to touch them without my permission."

Corey slid the pan off the fire and turned the knob until the fire disappeared. "Of the three of us, you're the only one who tried to shoot one of us. How about this? We keep the weapons and only allow you to have one when necessary."

"No deal."

"I feel the same way."

They stared at each other for an endless amount of time, caught in a game of who would look away first.

What seemed like hours later, Brian walked in. He noticed the stare down and whispered to Violin, "What's happening?"

She leaned toward his ear, "Dinner is ready."

CHAPTER 49

Blood and Hair

Dinner went as expected, mostly uncomfortable. Winter tried to give concessions where he could, but felt so unfamiliar and uncomfortable around humans, he struggled to understand politeness.

His attempts at kindness were for his daughter, but also for himself. While the very sight of a human sent his mind back to his training, the incessant drilling and brutal lessons on killing them on sight, the fear and paranoia built into his teachings, he also yearned to release it all, to erase the painful intrinsic reactions from his aging body. He, like his daughter, needed the humans to be okay, needed to walk away with some sense of peace.

After tasting the stir-fry, he said, "It is tasty, thank you. Did you pour a bucket of salt on it? Is it supposed to be so salty?"

Corey responded with a faux smile and Brian snorted. Winter shrugged, unsure why the men didn't answer his curiosities about their cooking. He ate it all, and didn't hate it, but needed a lot of water to take it all in. By the time he scraped the last bit of brown sauce from his plate, he not only grew to enjoy it, but he also wanted more. However, he'd already heaped more than a fair share onto his plate to begin with and didn't feel polite about asking for more.

"Where is Lion?" He asked.

Violin nibbled on some canned spinach. "He has been staying in room eleven, where Brian and Corey sleep."

Winter bit down on an empty fork. "You know, it might be best to keep him with Candlestick at all times, since only she can make him sleep if he howls at predators."

Violin rolled her eyes, making Winter aware of how much his guidance had turned from a positive attribute to an annoyance.

He slept well that night, falling into a deep sleep with dreams of his old life, his family, and friends. His wife, Sleeping Gypsy. He thought about her touch, the way she rubbed her fingertips against his flesh sent shock waves of lust through his body.

In the morning, with those vivid dreams fresh in his mind, he closed the bathroom door and cried in silence. He'd been so focused on protecting his children, on trying to adapt and stay alert to dangers, that he hadn't taken the time to realize how lonely he was, how much he missed his wife's embrace, her love.

After the children awoke, everyone ate breakfast together in the kitchen, just as they had with dinner. Winter chose not to say anything this time, afraid of offending Violin's friends. Instead, they ate watered oatmeal in silence.

As Winter prepared for the trip with Brian and Corey, a rumbling startled him. He peeked through the window to see a brown metal wagon grumbling outside the door. A car. *Was that it? A car?*

He stepped outside and Brian made the window of the vehicle go down. "Hop in."

"We are going in that?"

Brian nodded. "If we need tools, we have a long distance to clear. If you want to walk, it's gonna take days."

"Not very stealthy, though."

Brian tapped the wheel, and it let out a loud beep. Winter jumped backwards and flailed his hands as if being attacked by a monster.

"What the heck was that?"

Brian and Corey laughed. Corey said, "Just hop in."

Winter put his finger up and ran into his room. He grabbed his gun and tucked it into his pants. Then, he bent low and hugged his daughters, who stood side-by-side, waiting to wish him well.

"Daddy, when you come back, can you tell us a story?" Candlestick asked.

Winter nodded. "Of course."

When he hugged Violin, she latched on tight. "I love you, Dad. Please be careful. I know I've been angry, but I love you, and I need you."

He nodded. "I know, and I understand. I'm worried about you being here alone. Will you stay out of sight for me?"

She smiled. "We're armed, and I will watch the cameras in the front room."

"Cameras?"

"The eyes."

He inhaled a fulfilling gulp of air. "You know this world better than me. I trust you to be safe and to keep your sister that way, but I'll never stop being terrified."

They finished their goodbyes and Winter got in the back seat of the vehicle. Brian rolled out of the parking lot and the experience sent Winter's stomach reeling. He tried to hide his discomfort with the car's motion, but his fingertips clenched the edge of the seat.

They drove in silence, drifting around stationary vehicles on the road.

Brian spoke up. "How about a little music?"

"A little what?"

Corey cracked up. "Come on. You guys didn't even have music down there?"

"What is music?"

"Didn't you guys ever sing or dance?"

Winter furrowed his brow. "Of course, we danced. What do you mean by that?"

"Well, what did you dance to?"

"Nothing. What do you mean? You need anything to dance. You just move your feet."

Brian shook his head and hit some buttons on the front. Corey opened a compartment and flicked through a pack of discs, just like the discs of Kevin Bacon he'd seen at the houses. Corey slid one out and giggled as he handed it to Brian.

Brian turned it over, examining the words on the front. "Oh, okay. This is how we introduce our new friend to the wonders of Earthly music?"

A smile crept up Corey's face. "What better way?"

Brian put the disc into a slot where a bunch of numbers, illuminated in green, told information Winter didn't understand.

Corey cracked his knuckles. "Skip to six."

A noise entered the car, but Brian hit a button, and it stopped. As he continued to hit the button, a number moved on the screen until it said six.

Winter shivered and slid his hand near his shirt, making sure his gun was accessible. A gentle tone seeped in from all directions, as if it were surrounding him, closing in. Gentle. Repetitive. It lulled him, calmed him.

"What is this?"

Corey put his arm around Brian's headrest and twisted himself to get a better view of Winter. "It's music, but just wait."

A soft, gravelly voice carried over him. Shivers danced up Winter's spine and his hairs stood on end. "What is happening? What is this?"

The voice and tone combination weakened him, and he worried music was another human weapon, a device to steal his power. His body shook and that voice, that gorgeous gift of the gods, spoke through his every cell. He wanted to cry, to move, to do something, but he couldn't place what.

Corey said, "You ready for it?" And he lifted his index finger.

Boom. The gentle tone vanished, replaced by bangs and powerful combinations of noise. It created a smooth, yet explosive, wave of what? Sound? It was better than sound; it was something he didn't know and worse, couldn't comprehend. This was too special to live without.

And that damned voice lost all its softness, the woman yelling in unison with the vibrations of sound. The power and beauty of it broke him. He wept.

"Hey, you okay? You want us to turn it off?"

"No, shut up. Do not talk. Can you make it louder?"

Brian twisted a knob and the volume rose, enveloping them all. The music broke into Winter's soul and unleashed a torrent of memories. The woman kept yelling her words, extending them, lowering and heightening her pitch. All the while, conjuring Winter's life, jangling free his imprisoned thoughts and feelings.

He and Sleeping Gypsy, twelve years old. They sat on the floor, cross-legged. Sleeping Gypsy read from a children's book, one much too young for them. She glanced up from the page and smiled at him. "One day, we will see the world," she said.

"She will love you, and you her," Winter's mother had told him, but hadn't believed her. Not until Sleepy Gypsy said those words.

Winter, nineteen years old, knowing Sleeping Gypsy his whole life, his friend, his accomplice in mischief, understood love for the first time, as she drifted her hand from his shoulder to his elbow. "Is this freedom?" Winter wondered. "Loving someone so much that the walls of your cell suddenly feel too far apart?"

Sleepy Gypsy. Twenty-two. She stood naked in front of him, with her dress bunched by her ankles. "One day, we will see the world," she said, smiling at the memory. Winter stood, cupped his hands on her sides, and said, "I already have."

Winter. Twenty-five. They hugged as their bodies swayed. He placed his hand on her belly. "Boy or girl? What do you think?" He asked.

"Doesn't matter," Sleeping Gypsy said.

Sleeping Gypsy. Twenty-five. She screamed in pain, clutching the blankets under her. Pushing and screaming. A weakness washed over Winter at the sight, knowing he couldn't relieve her hurt. A head crowned, blood and hair, forcing itself into the world.

Winter and Sleeping Gypsy. Twenty-five. Winter sat on the edge of the bed as Sleeping Gypsy cradled their new baby girl to her breast. "Which picture do you think she'll choose?" Winter asked.

Sleeping Gypsy shook her head. "I don't know."

Winter shifted in his seat, still reeling from the overflowing emotions. "I'll bet she chooses yours."

Sleeping Gypsy glanced up, her eyes watery. "I hope she doesn't choose at all."

"What do you mean?"

She sat up, keeping the baby tethered to her breast. "I don't want to stay here for another five years. One day, she will see the world."

He sighed. After a lifetime of commitment to his community, he would leave them for his wife's happiness. He had once dreamed of walking on Earth, too. But now that he had Sleeping Gypsy and his beautiful daughter, the walls that caged them also provided him with calm, knowing they kept his loves safe. Still, his job was their happiness and safety meant nothing without joy.

The music tricked him, switching from the booming and yelling to the soft tones again, but it didn't quell the memories flooding in. The singer pressed on, nearly whispering her words, lulling Winter to his past.

Winter and Sleeping Gypsy. Twenty-nine. They'd planned their escape many times, but something always came up. Baby girl got sick. Sleeping Gypsy hurt her leg. Sometimes, fear just fought against them. Now, four years later, the baby girl was just a year from choosing her name and Sleeping Gypsy was pregnant again.

He loved his life, his wife, his daughter, his unborn child. But Sleeping Gypsy would never find happiness in the underground. She'd hated it since childhood. Yet, she feared the change.

Boom. The music blasted again and shook him to his core.

Sleeping Gypsy screamed and released. Blood and hair. Their second child forcing its way into the world.

The music softened before ending. Silence enveloped the car and Winter stared at nothing, hoping the air would fill the void. He yearned for it to play again, to hear all its beauty. Corey turned the knob until the music faded away.

"Well, what did you think?"

"It was the most amazing thing I've heard. Who was that? Are they human?"

Corey chuckled. "Oh yeah, she's human, but maybe a goddess, too. You just experienced 'Wrecking Ball,' by Miley Cyrus."

"Miley Cyrus." He said the name, telling his brain to never forget it. "Miley Cyrus."

The music had ended, but the sounds and voices continued to play in his head.

Winter's mother pushed him into the closed off room at the edges of the community. Behind him and his daughters, a long tunnel leading to a stone slab. Through the thick walls, he could hear coughing from everywhere. He pleaded with his mother to let him see his wife.

She refused, begging him to run.

After days of isolation, Winter's mother relented and brought Sleeping Gypsy to the door, so they could talk through it. Her voice was raspy, harsh, damaged.

"The day is here, Winter. Show them the world."

Winter touched the door and rested his cheek on its cold surface. "Not without you."

"Yes, without me."

Violin and Candlestick held hands, crying. They said nothing.

"Girls. You will see the world," Sleeping Gypsy said.

Winter shook his head. "Will you lie on the floor for me? So, I can see you one last time."

She coughed, hacking. When she finished, she struggled for breath, but eked out, "Okay."

He laid on the cement, his palms picking up pebbles and gravel, and pressed his cheek on the floor. As Sleeping Gypsy did the same, he saw nothing. Too dark, too little space.

She shifted, and he caught sight of her mouth. A deep red trickling from her lips. And her dark brown hair slipped into the crack.

He touched it and cried.

Blood and hair.

He turned towards his girls. "We have to run."

CHAPTER 50

A Sea of Fire

After the Miley song, Corey flicked through the disc collection and popped another into the player. Brian was excited about it being a "mix," whatever that meant.

The first song played. While it had a more peaceful sound than Wrecking Ball, it also sunk into Winter's spirit and jarred loose a lifetime of memories. Brian and Corey knew the song and threw their arms up in excitement as it played. "Oh, you stole a car from someone with good taste," Corey said to Brian.

Three of Hearts by Laura Jane Grace. Winter repeated the words until they etched into his brain. Wrecking Ball. Miley Cyrus. Three of Hearts. Laura Jane Grace.

Brian turned down a road and crept the car forward at a snail's pace. Unlike the other roads, dirt and rough gravel made this path too bouncy, causing Winter's head to bump into the window.

"What are you doing? Are we near a store?"

Brian turned his head left and right, examining each house they passed. "No. We aren't going to a store. Not yet anyway. I was just looking for a neighborhood. Figured we could steal tools from a house."

"What if someone lives in the house? And how do you know they'll have tools?"

"It's too wide open and dangerous to waltz into a Home Depot in some random plaza."

Winter shrugged. "Whatever those things are."

He touched his gun, just to feel safer.

"Windy dirt roads in New England. I call them East Coast 'country.' Lots of land separating the houses around here. I'd guess most of the people who lived here did blue-collar work. We'll find excellent tools, and I'm sure some other stuff we need."

Winter fidgeted with his shirt, unnerved by the shrouded landscape and unfamiliar territory. How stupid to allow humans to lead him into darkness while he recovered from near death. "Then why are we still driving?"

"I figured we should stop somewhere in the middle of the street. It feels less out in the open."

The land rolled long distances, unkempt grass grew thick around the houses. Some yards were littered with junk, tires, or woodpiles. Long stretches set each house back from the main road. Cement paths led to the houses, curved around shrubbery. Many of the houses had trees, wooden barricades, or short stone walls surrounding them.

Brian rolled onto the cement path leading to an enormous house sheltered in darkness by towering oaks. He scanned the area. "The grass grew out. Lights are all off. I think it's safe. What do you guys think?"

Corey nodded. Winter frowned and shrugged.

Brian pointed toward a smaller house next to the main building. "Big garage. I bet it has a lot of tools."

"Garage," Winter said, hoping to etch the word into his mind.

Brian drove closer, until the bumper almost kissed the large door in front of the garage. He turned the car off and exited. Corey followed suit. Winter hesitated. He could steal the tools, kill the men, and tell his daughters a human attacked them. But how would he get home? Driving the car looked complicated. He also worried the men might have a similar plan for him.

As Winter hopped from the car, Corey pulled the garage door open. It roared as it rolled upward and Winter prayed Brian was right about the vacancy. If someone was around, they'd just received an alert about intruders.

Brian was right about one thing; the garage housed more tools than Winter had ever seen before. Some of them were beyond his understanding.

"We should check out the house, see what they have. We can grab the tools on our way out," Corey said.

"Tools. That's the mission. Nothing else." Winter hated veering off course. Simplicity saved lives. Why complicate the mission?

"There might be food in there, clothes, blankets, first aid stuff."

The two men didn't wait for Winter to change his mind. He followed them as they crept around the garage toward a side door.

As they entered, they all pulled out their weapons and scattered.

"I'll check upstairs. Brian, you raid the kitchen. Winter, check the downstairs rooms."

Corey darted up a flight of curvy stairs. Winter headed into a large room with a furry rug. He felt like he walked on clouds. He scanned the area but saw nothing of value.

Brian walked in. "Wanna help me in the kitchen? Lots of food in there. I found bags, too. We can load up the trunk of the car."

Winter nodded, but then something caught Brian's attention.

"Oh, my god." He knelt in front of the rectangle box. A TV? Is that what the men had called it?

Brian grabbed a small box and popped it open. A disc. He tossed it to Winter. The front of the box showed a young Kevin Bacon in a white shirt with his sleeves rolled up.

"Kevin Bacon?" Winter asked.

"You know Kevin Bacon?" Brian laughed.

Winter furrowed his brow. "Of course."

"Have you seen that movie?"

"What's a movie?"

Brian took the box out of Winter's hand, examining it with bright eyes, deep in memory. "How do you know Kevin Bacon without knowing what a movie is?"

Winter just stared, unsure how to answer.

"Anyway, this is Footloose. A classic. It's one of Corey's favorites, so I gotta take it. I'll also have to take the DVD player if we want to watch it." He reached behind the television and ripped some cords from the machine, then pulled a black box from a shelf under it.

"So, what is a movie?" Winter examined the box again, studying the words. *He's a big city kid in a small town. They said he'd never win. He knew he had to. The music is on his side.*

Winter smiled. Damned right, he thought.

"A movie is a story that you watch happen. Kevin Bacon plays the main character in this story. How do you know him?" Brian tucked the black box under his armpit.

"He is the main character in a story I know, too."

Corey appeared at the threshold of the room, carrying a stack of clothes. "They have a ton of nice clothes up there, and blankets, but I can't carry it all."

"Look what else they have," Brian said, holding up his movie bounty.

Corey gasped and dropped the clothes. "You've got to be shitting me." He grabbed the movie out of Brian's hand and hugged it.

"I miss movies."

Brian smiled and rubbed Corey's shoulder. "Me too."

Winter caught movement in his periphery. He ran to the window and saw a shadow dart across the yard and another shadow by their car. "There are people."

He gripped the gun with a little more force. Corey and Brian ran to his side and stared out the window.

The shadow by the car lifted his hand and flicked his fingers. A flame grew from his fist. He dropped the flame and Brian's car drowned in a sea of fire.

CHAPTER 51

Before the Beauty Ends

Violin sat in an office chair, rolling back and forth, staring at the cameras. She and Candlestick had played hide and seek throughout the building, which proved too difficult for the seeker thanks to the overabundance of rooms to hide in. It turned into a tedious experience rather than a fun one, but Violin played to keep Candlestick entertained.

The sun descended, and the motel stayed lit by the faint glow of the night disc. Candlestick drifted to sleep as she waited for her father's return on the lobby couch. Violin worried while the adults searched for tools, so she lasered in on the cameras. Her dream come true: a sentry for her people.

Nothing happened, but she enjoyed watching the subtle changes in the camera until her vision blurred. The occasional white flake fluttered by, leaves skated across the lot, tree branches swayed, the night disc's glow faded behind a sheath of clouds, and a pack of animals gained bravery enough to scour the perimeter for scraps.

On the screen facing the road, a low light appeared, and as it increased in strength, a loud noise came from outside. Violin, gun in hand, ran to the door as the car whizzed by. It passed the motel, but skidded, stopped, reversed, and turned toward the parking lot.

"Oh, no."

She shook Candlestick awake. "Get in the office, now."

Candlestick rubbed her eyes. "What?"

"Now." Violin expressed the severity of the situation with wide eyes.

Candlestick jumped from the couch as a car door clunked open a few feet behind her head. She ran to the office, Violin right behind.

Violin almost clicked the light off but a change in lighting would ensure the driver knew the place was occupied.

"Be ready for anything," she told her sister.

She stared at the cameras, watching a man hop out of the driver's seat and frantically run to the other side. The driver opened the passenger side door and helped a second person exit the vehicle. A woman, who walked with a waddle and a hunched back. The driver put his arm around the lady and aided her in walking.

They headed straight for the office.

The front office door opened, and Violin gripped the trigger on her gun. Brian had trained her with the weapon while her father had recovered from his infection.

She tapped on her hip. "Be as silent as a bean."

"Come on. Lie down," the man said to his woman friend.

"I don't want to do this here," the female said with a shaky tone.

"We don't have much choice, do we?"

Violin wished for a view into the front room. She peeked through the door but couldn't see them. They were on the other side of the counter, crouched down.

The female screamed and huffed. The man shushed and lulled.

Violin debated on what to do. Hiding until they left made the most sense, since the humans were occupied and uninterested in exploring. But she preferred establishing the upper hand, tired of playing defense to constant assaults.

"Stay hidden in here, no matter what," she tapped. After a long inhale, she barged through the door and ran around the counter with the gun raised. "Don't move or I will kill you."

They didn't pay her much attention. The woman was lying on

the floor, screaming with her dress up, exposing herself. The man hovered over her, flailing, unsure what to do.

"Help us. She's having our baby." The man glanced at her with the same pleading, droopy eyes Lion offered when hungry. "Jesus. It's a kid."

"I don't care what she is doing. Leave, or I will kill you." Violin waved the gun, making sure the man noticed.

"I can't do this, Frank. I can't." Tears clouded the woman's eyes.

"You can. You can do this." He looked around. "Do you have water or something? Can you help?"

"Dammit." Violin turned to the back door. "Candlestick, get out here."

Candlestick peeked out, then walked to Violin. Violin handed her sister the gun and posed her arms, aiming it for her at the two people.

"If they do anything suspicious, shoot them." She turned to the man. "She's young, but she's killed people and she will not hesitate to kill you both if you try anything foolish."

Violin ducked behind the counter and grabbed a jug of water. She brought it over to the man, letting him dole it out to his mate. The man drank first, and Violin rolled her eyes at his selfishness.

After Frank fumbled and struggled to assist his suffering woman, Violin rolled her sleeves up. "Get out of the way. I will help her."

"I don't think that's a good idea." The man scratched his head.

"When my cousin was pregnant, my mother made me train to assist in the delivery. I was seven years old. Since then, I have assisted in two other births."

"That sounds insane."

Violin stomped her feet. "Move, and I will help her have the baby. Sit on the couch, or my sister will kill you dead."

The man looked at his mate.

"Let her help," the woman said. "Do we have any better options?"

Violin bent and placed her hand on the woman's forehead. "Take a big breath through your nose and pour the air out through your mouth. I have some critical and upsetting information."

The woman looked at her, worried. Violin held her hand. "Getting a baby out of you is very painful."

The woman combined a scream and a laugh. "I'm aware."

"It will be best if you stand up, lean against the wall. I will hold you and help the baby come out."

"Won't that make the pain worse?"

"Oh, yes. But it will make it quicker." She turned to her sister. "In the backroom, get towels, but keep the gun trained on him."

"What about her?" Candlestick asked.

Violin helped the woman to her feet and leaned her against the wall. "She won't cause any trouble. Couldn't if she wanted to."

"I don't think I can stand. This is a bad idea." The woman's eyes were wide, and she breathed through puckered lips.

"You can and you will. Trust me. You can do whatever you want. You control nature; it doesn't control you." She gripped the woman's hand.

"Who are you? Does your family own this motel?"

"I am not from Earth."

"What?" The woman's breathing grew frantic.

Violin realized her mistake. "Yes, we own this building. I made a joke with you."

The woman's fingers dug into the wall, and she nodded her head. "Oh. That's funny." But no laugh came.

The man stayed seated on the couch, but kept leaning forward, then sitting back, shifting his legs, inhaling like he was preparing to say something, but then letting the air fizzle out of his mouth.

Candlestick exited the bathroom with a stack of towels so high they covered her face. Violin snatched one and placed it underneath the woman. She tossed a second one to the man.

"What's this for?" He held the towel as if it were diseased.

"You'll use it, trust me."

Violin held the women's hands and looked at her, getting up close and personal, eye-to-eye. "This is going to be fun. It's going to be hard, and painful, and annoying, and you'll scream and curse the gods, but it's also the coolest thing that can happen. Ever."

The woman nodded. Sweat bled down her face and her eyes squinted in panic.

"Is it happening now?" The man asked.

"Not yet. It could be a little while." She put her head between the woman's leg, and the woman squirmed.

"I am just seeing if the baby's head is in sight."

"Is it?"

"I don't know. You shut your legs on my face."

"It fucking hurts like it's coming."

Violin laughed. "It hurts now? Just wait."

"Aren't you supposed to be calming her down?" The man stood up and Candlestick raised the gun.

"Sit down," Candlestick said with gnashed teeth.

The man held his arms up in surrender and sat back down. "I just don't think you should talk to her like that."

Violin turned to him. "I apologize. I thought the baby was inside her, but I guess the baby is on the couch. Sorry, but I talk to her, not you. I am sure she can handle the truth. You sit there and whine in silence. Your thoughts live and die in your brain, not mine, please."

The woman nodded and took a large breath before letting out a tremendous scream. Violin panned her surroundings, nervous for the attention this woman could bring upon them. Animals, monsters, men.

"She's right, honey. Shut up, please. This girl is right." The woman gripped Violin's hands tighter and smiled. "It's a miracle we found you. I couldn't have done this alone."

"You wouldn't have been alone," the man mumbled.

"I don't think I can do this standing up, though. People typically lie on a hospital bed."

"People need to learn to embrace that they do things very wrong most of the time, but I admit, you're making it difficult for me to help you when you keep pinching your legs together. We need to go somewhere you can lie down and hold your legs in the air. Do you think you can walk?"

Frank stood, and again Candlestick raised the gun, this time marching to him until the end of her gun pressed against his belly. "Sit down."

"She said we were moving."

"She will tell you when it's time. Until then, sit down."

Violin ran into the office and grabbed her set of keys. "Here is how this works. You on the couch, grab your mate and help her to the room. Candlestick, you stand behind them with the gun. I go first, but everyone stays ten steps behind me. Do not get closer. We are going to room 4. When you reach the door with a 3 on it, you stop and wait until I open door 4. Once it's opened, and I have stepped aside, you all enter ahead of me. Frank, you go right into the corner where you will sit on the floor until I tell you otherwise. Woman with the baby inside her, you will lie down on the bed. Candlestick, gun on him always. Don't worry about the woman. She is in no place to fight."

She didn't wait for everyone to agree or say they understood. Instead, she marched out. Everyone played their part and obeyed her rules with no hiccups. On the way to the room, she observed some dog-like animals gathering on the edges of the parking lot and considered telling Candlestick to fire a warning shot, but the animals were far enough away and she didn't want to alarm the already freaked out woman. But the creatures glared with hungry eyes and Violin knew time ran thin before they'd swarm in packs.

When they entered the room and everyone took their places, Violin grabbed the gun from Candlestick. "I'll watch him for a few. Take my keys, run to the other rooms and get pillows. Get as many as you can grab, but if those animals move closer, come back. Do not risk it. Play it safe. If I must, I'll go out and fire a warning shot and they'll scatter, but I'd rather not make noise for the woman."

Candlestick ran out of the room. A few minutes later, she screamed.

"Stay put." Violin ran out the door. Two animals had Candlestick pinned against a wall. They had sharp teeth exposed by snarled lips, and they closed in on her. Three pillows lay on the concrete floor.

"I didn't see them. I'm so sorry. I didn't see them," she said, staring at the animals, her body squeezed against the wall.

Violin fired into the air. An anger brewed inside her. She wanted to shoot to kill but recognized the moral failings of harming the creatures out of anger. Brian and Corey would have killed them and eaten them, but they'd have removed emotions from the equation. The noise sent the animals running, but Violin noted the animals would, indeed, come after her family when pressed for food.

Violin and Candlestick grabbed the pillows and charged into the room where Frank had moved to the bed, holding the woman's hand.

Candlestick dropped her two pillows on the floor. "Sorry, it's all I could get."

Violin ignored her, raised her gun and marched at the man. "I thought I made myself clear you were not to leave the corner until instructed?"

"She's my fucking wife! I want to be with her."

"Will you just listen to the girl? She's helping," the woman said.

"Is she? Does she know what she's doing?"

"If you don't want my help, he can remove the baby from you."

"No. I don't want his help, I want yours." She turned to the man. "I just want you to stay in the corner. Please. Please. It's nothing against you."

"She's a child!" The man shouted.

"I know, but something about her makes sense."

The man drove his hands through his hair and paced in a circle. "Fine. Fuck it. Fine. I'll be in the corner."

Violin gave the gun to Candlestick, who returned to her sentry post in front of Frank. Violin put the pillows under the woman's legs, propping them up a bit.

"I need to see inside there." She pointed to the woman's legs.

As the woman opened her legs, Violin talked. She understood conversation relaxed people, even when there was nothing to talk about. In fact, the less Violin had to say, the more people loved the conversation.

"I find humans ugly."

"Humans? What are *you*, an alien?" Frank asked, laughing at his own joke.

Violin ignored him. "The only time I could find a person beautiful is in the first moment of birth. It's over so quickly. One minute they are not in this world, the next they are here. Then, they become part of this world, and the beauty ends. But for a moment, before this place ruins them, they are beautiful."

The woman cried. Violin looked at her. "I believe it is almost time. Thank you for gifting me a glimpse of beauty." She smiled.

The woman screamed.

The man pressed the towel to his face and released a yawp of tension.

Candlestick said nothing, just trained the gun.

CHAPTER 52

This Isn't the One

Winter threw himself to the floor as a gun discharged a thunderous roar. Nothing crashed in the house. How did the shadowy figures outside miss such a large target? Brian and Corey crawled next to him, eyes wide, gasping for breath.

"That was a warning shot. You can come out of there with your hands up, or we can shoot until the house looks like Swiss cheese. The choice is yours," a woman shouted from outside.

"What do we do?" Corey asked.

"You two keep them distracted, and I am going to surprise them." Winter crawled away, toward the back of the house.

Brian said something in objection, but his words were lost in the gathering distance between them.

When Winter reached the back door, he crouched and waited to see what the men would do.

Brian crawled to the front door and opened it a crack.

"How do we know you're telling the truth? You just set our car on fire, which isn't exactly a friendly start."

Winter turned the handle, twisting his hand millimeter by millimeter until the doorknob made a gentle click. He pushed the door open and crept into the chilly evening air. *The day vanished fast,* he thought.

The woman threw threats at Brian, telling him she didn't give a shit if he believed her or not. She would blow the house to smithereens if he didn't come out.

Winter ran away from the house. He dove into some shrubs and landed in position to crawl again. He debated on leaving the men stranded, letting the humans kill each other while he searched for a functioning car, but he had promised Violin a better version of himself, and he owed her that.

He crept toward the front, safe behind the thick, overgrown bushes. When he neared the front, he waited to assess how many humans waited outside. Two. All this for two people? Both were women, one much older than the other. The one speaking, making threats, reminded Winter of his mother, strong and proud in her old age.

He continued his trek forward until he was behind them. The women seemed untrained, hence the loud showmanship. Anyone else would have fired to kill. He stood and ran toward the woman, heart racing. Brian opened the door further, helping distract the old lady.

The younger woman caught sight of Winter a fraction too late. "Mom," she shouted as Winter wrapped his arm around her throat and placed his gun against her temple.

"Drop your weapons. Both of you."

"Don't you dare," the older woman said to her daughter. "They'll kill you the second you do."

The old woman kept a firm grip on her weapon, while the younger stood in the open grass, gun dangling at her side, unsure what to do. Brian and Corey pushed the door open further and came out with their guns drawn.

"Shoot them," Winter said.

"I will not kill them," Brian said. "We just want to leave in peace. We need some tools and blankets and stuff. That's all. We have children with us."

The woman leaned her head against Winter's chest and released an enormous sigh. "Paula, run." She lifted her arm and fired. Corey's arm exploded and he flopped to the ground with a furious screech. Brian dropped next to him. "No! Corey. No." She fired again, but Winter pushed her arm up, causing the bullet to disappear into the night.

The woman fought to free herself from his grasp. To end it, he fired into her neck. Blood splashed on his face, and for the first time, his heart sank at the death of a human. Maybe it was her resemblance to his mother, or maybe Brian and Corey had softened him.

No time to think. He ran for the younger woman, who turned to see her mother's body on the ground. Instead of fleeing, she turned back, running for her dead mom. Surprised, Winter raised his weapon. "Stop moving."

The woman brushed past him, dropped to her knees, and cradled her mother's limp carcass.

"What did you do?" Brian shouted.

Everyone screamed different things. Corey yelped in pain, Brian and the young lady hollered at him for murdering the murderer. What had happened? Winter fell backwards at the horrible sights in front of him.

"She was going to kill you."

Brian squeezed Corey's arm, but Corey's flopping and flailing made it difficult. "You could have disarmed her."

The younger woman stood, bloodshot eyes gazing into Winter's soul. "She was keeping us safe. You came onto our land. You were the threats." She raised her gun, arm shaking.

Brian trained his gun on the woman but kept himself focused on Corey. The man would die from bleeding out. Brian didn't know it, but Winter could save Corey.

"Don't shoot him. Let's not make this worse."

"I don't give a fuck if you kill me, too. He killed my mother."

A lump formed in Winter's throat. The anguish pouring through the woman's face broke his heart. Did Miley Cyrus do this? Did she unfold emotions in Winter he'd never experienced before?

"I will save her."

The young woman shook her weapon. "You can't. She's dead."

Winter nodded. He put his head down and walked to the dead woman. "Bring Corey over here."

Brian's eyes darted. "Why? What the fuck are you doing?"

"Just do it." Winter dropped next to the dead lady and placed his palm against her cold forehead. Blood leaked from her neck on both sides, creating a pool in her hair. It soaked into his pants. Brian helped Corey over to them. Even the woman stared in curiosity.

Winter put his other palm on Corey's forehead and breathed. Their pain leached into his body, and he hollered as he felt a million bullets bouncing through every cell.

"What's happening?" the young woman asked.

Brian stood up. "I don't know."

The holes in Corey's arm and the old lady's neck shrunk and the loose flesh reattached itself. Corey grabbed his now-healed arm. "Holy shit."

Paula dropped her weapon, stepped back, and cupped her hands over her mouth. "What is this?"

"Brian, take their weapons," Winter said as he pressed down hard on the dead lady's forehead. Her wounds had healed, but death took longer to overcome.

Brian picked up her weapon and went over to the young lady, a streak of awe in his eyes and his jaws wide apart. Corey sat up on his butt, clutching his healed arm, saying, "Holy fuck," repeatedly.

A gurgle entered the woman's throat, and then she shot up with a horrid gasp as if choking. She coughed and her daughter flung herself around the old lady. "Mom."

Winter stood, giving them room to reunite. After all the killing, here he was, saving a human's life. A violent one at that.

Brian whispered to him. "What do we do now?"

The two women embraced, both confused. "Was I dead? Did he save me?" She touched the wrinkled skin on her neck.

"Yes." Her daughter cried into her mother's shoulder.

"I saw it happen. He took my wounds into his body." She put her hands over her face and wept.

Winter patted Brian on the back. "Now we take them inside for a conversation."

Corey ran to Brian, and they put their arms around each other's shoulders. "I know we saw monsters and whatever, but I believe them now." Corey said. "They aren't human."

The world dissipated.

"Winter, your aunt has a cough. Will you check on her?"

Winter walked into Auntie Menina's room where she lay in bed. Black pools formed under her eyes and her nose was red and raw from rubbing snot from it.

She smiled at the sight of her nephew. "Winter, dear, have you come to make your aunt feel better?"

"Yes, Auntie Menina."

He sat on the edge of the bed and placed his palm on her forehead. She put both her hands around his wrist. "Thank you."

He closed his eyes and sucked in air through his nose. Focused. Ready to inject her pain into his body. He felt something, a sharp tickle on his tongue, but nothing like the aching from when his uncle cut his own finger off, or the gut-punching throb from when his mom stepped on a nail. Maybe the coughing required less and thus offered less in return.

He stood.

"That's it?" Menina asked, sniffling.

"I think."

She coughed, blood droplets dotting her lip.

Winter's mother stepped around him, her brow furrowing in disappointment. "Try a little harder."

Winter sat again and sucked her pain through his palm. Again, nothing more than a bitter pinch on his tongue. What was he doing wrong? He shook his head as his auntie broke into a hacking fit.

He turned to his mother. "What am I doing wrong?"

"Do you feel anything?"

"Yes, I feel her pain entering me, but it's not right. It's not taking hold."

His mother stepped back, her eyes growing in surprise. "We need to separate everyone right now. Grab your daughters and your wife. Now."

He didn't understand what was happening, but listened, and followed his mother out of the room. He ran down the corridor. "Sleeping Gypsy. Candlestick. Violin."

His daughters ran out of their room. "What's wrong, Dad?"

"I don't know."

Winter's mother pushed into him. "You must go to the lockdown room by the forbidden tunnel."

"Wait, I need Sleeping Gypsy."

As he said her name, she turned the corner, her beautiful brown hair showering down her shoulders. Her nose, red.

"There you are," she said. "I think I'm coming down with something. Will you heal me?"

Winter's mother turned to him, pushing him backwards, away from his wife. "Go," she said. "Go."

"Wait. Not without Sleeping Gypsy."

"Yes, without her. You must go."

"Wait. I can heal her."

Violin shook his pants leg. "What's going on?"

"You can't heal her."

Winter shook his head. "I can. I just didn't concentrate enough with Menina."

Sleeping Gypsy stepped back. "Oh, no. Is this the one?"

Winter shook his head harder. "No. I can help you. Just come here."

Winter's mother swatted him back. "Yes, Sleeping Gypsy. This is the one."

Sleeping Gypsy's eyes sunk. "Get out of here. Now."

"Dad, what is going on?"

"Winter, you take my children and get the hell out of here. Listen to your mother."

Winter slammed his fist into the wall. "Damn it! I am not leaving you. This isn't the one. I can save you."

"I love you girls. Make sure you are good for your father. Enjoy the world." Sleeping Gypsy stepped into a room and slammed the door. The bolt clacked into place, locking him out.

Winter pushed his mother out of the way. He slammed his fists into the door. Violin and Candlestick cried behind him. "Mom? Dad? What's happening?"

Winter's mother bent low and hushed the children, using her calm voice to make them feel better. Other members of the community came out to see the fuss. Some of them were coughing.

"Winter, we don't have time. If you don't go now, you might catch it. You already might have." His mother rubbed Candlestick's head.

Winter kicked the door. "Please, Sleeping Gypsy, let me in. I need you. I can fix this. Let me try."

PLEASE! PLEASE! PLEASE!

Corey touched Winter's shoulder, snapping him back to reality. Everyone stared at him, even the two women. He eyed them all, anger, frustration, and hate building in his gut. He took a gun from Brian.

"Everyone, get inside. Now."

CHAPTER 53

Growing up in Danger

Violin guided the woman's breathing while Candlestick sat cross-legged on the floor with the gun trained on Frank. The man bit his nails, glanced around the room but, thankfully, he also kept his mouth shut. Candlestick turned to see her sister smiling at her. She hoped Violin was proud of her, the way she held her stance, steadfast in her position as watchman. She wanted Violin to trust her, to understand she could deliver the baby safely with her sister protecting her for once.

"What are you so nervous about?" Candlestick asked Frank.

"Everything. What if something goes wrong? Those fucking monsters come out at night and we are about to always have a crying baby with us. I don't want it to grow up in danger."

"You've seen the monsters?" Candlestick's voice broke. How many people had her monsters hurt?

"Of course. They almost fucking killed us the first time. After that, we wised up and didn't leave our house at night. But now, with a baby, we can't hide from them anymore. I'm not worried about me, but my wife, and the poor kid." Tears formed in his eyes. "I don't want him growing up in this world."

Violin sighed, moving her hand at the woman as if she were

cupping water and splashing it on herself: *keep going*. "I'm curious. Did the world not have dangers before? Ours did. Death, disease, hunger. All sorts of dangers. My cousin died from drinking dirty water. She was seven."

"Of course it did, but not like this. This world doesn't have any of the nice things in it we used to care about. And reminding me of all the ways someone can die isn't making me feel better."

"I'm not trying to make you feel better. I'm trying to be realistic. Life isn't better or worse for someone who only knows one way. Your child won't have anything to compare it to, so they will love it just fine. You know why?" She didn't wait for an answer. "Because the beauty in life is not knowing what the hell it's doing."

Candlestick cleared her throat as the woman screamed. Lion barked from the other room and Candlestick used her mind to quiet him. She reminded herself to take him for a long walk tomorrow. So much had happened that she hadn't had time for more than quick bathroom breaks with the poor dog.

"It's time," Violin said.

Frank stood, and Candlestick let him, but she also stood and kept the gun level. "If you want to see it happen, you can, but you will have a gun to your head the whole time," she said.

He nodded, stood on his tippy toes, and looked toward his wife. Sweat poured down her face and she released loud bellows of pain. Frank's face turned pale and he fell back into the wall.

"I want to see it but seeing Sheila's pain is hard."

Candlestick smiled, unbothered by the woman's horrific screams. "Why don't you move closer, but sit down, and you can observe while I distract you with a story?"

The man nodded. "Yeah, okay." He wiped his palms on his pants, and a streak of sweat rode down them.

After he sat, Candlestick moved in front of him, but to the side, so he could see the birth. Violin talked the woman through the entire process, using a soothing voice as she explained everything that happened.

Frank watched, but his eyes shifted away every few seconds, unable to keep a steady focus.

"I used to love where I lived," Candlestick said. "I thought it was perfect. When I came here, I hated it. It was always bad, always running, always scared. Now, I don't know. I miss my family, ya know?" She guessed Frank wasn't listening but kept talking anyway. "That's the part of the old world that makes me miss it so much. But I wasn't happy. I'll bet if you think about the world you miss, you could think of a million things you didn't like about it, right?"

To her surprise, he was listening, and he answered. "Yeah, that's true, but it was still better than this."

"No way. This world is about to have your baby in it. The old one didn't. And this one is all broken. That means you can start it over however you want. Were you able to change the entire world before? Would your people let you do that?"

He chuckled. "I could vote, but that doesn't count for much." He bobbed his head, trying to get a better view as Violin said something about crowning.

"See, here, you can fix all those things you didn't like by making the world yours. That's what I'm going to do." She smiled at the thought.

Frank's breathing quickened. His eyebrows rose. After a moment, he turned to her, unable to keep his focus on the intensity behind Candlestick. "Oh yeah, and what would you do to make it yours?"

She frowned. "Don't know. I'm seven. I don't even know who I am yet. How am I supposed to know what I want the entire world to be?"

He laughed, surprising everyone, even his wife. "You're smart for your age. The smartest thing to know is what you don't know."

She chuckled now, too. "Then I'm the smartest person ever, because I know I know nothing."

Sheila released one long scream, and Violin pulled the baby out. Candlestick and Frank stood to watch, and thankfully Frank was so honed in on his new baby, he didn't catch Candlestick had let her guard down.

Violin wrapped the pinkish, purplish thing in a blanket, wiped some sticky stuff off its face, and handed it to the mother. She brought the baby's mouth to Sheila's breast.

"Let her suck on it. It will open her airways."

The baby didn't cry and Candlestick wasn't sure it was breathing. Sheila and Frank had panic all over their faces but Violin looked calm, so Candlestick trusted the situation was okay.

The man moved to his wife's side, sitting on the edge of the bed. The baby suckled, and with it, a normal color flushed across its face.

"I'm sorry," Violin said to Frank.

"Why?" Terror poured into his wide eyes.

"You used the male pronouns for the baby, but it is a female."

"Oh." His body slackened. "I don't give a shit about that. I thought something was wrong."

"Your baby is just fine. Now, my sister and I are going to go outside and give you some space. Enjoy your new child. Also, I helped with the delivery, not the cleanup." She pointed to the sheets under Sheila, now covered in baby goo, blood, and whatever else.

As Candlestick followed her sister outside, the chilly evening air felt glorious after hours in the stuffy birthing room.

Violin leaned into the wall and took a deep breath. "That was crazy."

Candlestick rubbed her arm. "You did amazing."

"Thank you. I exaggerated my abilities. I only helped assist in the minor stuff, like you did. Grab a towel, that kind of thing. I wasn't sure what I would do if something went wrong. I am so glad nothing did."

Candlestick giggled. "Dad's going to kill you for helping bring a human into the world."

Violin chuckled, too. "I don't know what we are going to do when he gets back. He will not be happy with any of this."

Candlestick scanned the lot, making sure no wild animals were around. "I love Dad, but I don't know if I agree with him anymore."

Violin hugged Candlestick. The unexpected show of affection sent a tingle up Candlestick's back. "I don't agree with him anymore, either. Everything our people taught us was wrong. I loved our family, but I don't trust their beliefs anymore. I miss Mom more and more every day, and when I think about her, I think she knew. She always acted like our training was a waste of time, and she talked about humans like they weren't so bad. I mean, she'd never met them, so I just assumed she was being hopeful, but maybe not."

A cold sensation landed on Candlestick's shoulder. "Are you crying?"

She pulled away from her sister. Rivulets ran down her cheeks.

"Yeah."

"Why?"

"Because I don't want to hate them, but I kind of do. My whole life, wasted. Training and learning to fight an enemy I don't think hates us at all. None of them care. They don't even notice we have powers until we tell them. The other people up here were just trying to survive. I killed people, Candlestick, without even thinking twice about it. I killed them."

"Yeah, but they were bad, Violin. Maybe Dad and Grandma were wrong about humans, but some of them are not good. Those people who attacked us were terrible. They were going to kill us, too."

The door shot open, causing Candlestick and Violin to jump in surprise. Frank's hands shook. The baby wailed inside and Candlestick wondered how long she had been oblivious to the sound.

"She won't stop crying. We don't know what to do."

Violin rolled her eyes. "She's a baby, Frank. She's going to cry all the time. You feed her, burp her, rock her to sleep, and clean her poop. If you've done all that, you pray to the gods she stops crying soon."

Frank stared, hoping for more. When he realized nothing more would come, he turned back to his wife.

Violin leaned toward her sister. "Maybe our people were right about some things. Humans sure are stupid."

Candlestick laughed. She and Violin had always been friends, but something new bloomed between them, a more intimate friendship based on mutual respect, and it sent a warm wave into Candlestick's heart.

"I love you, Violin."

Violin squeezed her. "I love you, too."

They hugged for a long time, comfortable in each other's grip.

Violin kissed her sister's temple. "Above all else, I love you. I will protect you, always."

CHAPTER 54

They Screamed

The two women sat on the couch, visibly shaken, the magical wonder of seeing someone return from death now erased thanks to Winter's gun aimed in their direction.

"What are your names?" He asked, back in full inquisition mode.

"Jane," the older woman said. "And this is my daughter, Paula."

Paula smiled and waved, but was unable to disguise the fear in her eyes.

"Where were you when humanity disappeared?"

Brian and Corey stood on each side of Winter with their arms crossed, intently listening to the conversation. They had argued with Winter when he forced everyone back inside for this questioning, but now that he asked the right questions, their desire to learn changed their temperament.

Paula stared off into space, as if traveling back in time to the moment it happened. "We were at work, at the hospital. My mom and I are nurses. We worked at Bacon's Hospital."

"What is a hospital?"

Corey leaned down. "It's a medical place where doctors fix

people. Like how Brian fixed you. It's a place just for sick people or hurt people."

"They named a healing place after Kevin Bacon?"

Every face in the room shifted into one of confusion.

"What? No. It's named after Bacon Street, which is named after Francis Bacon or some shit. Anyway, we were all on break in the cafeteria when we heard screaming coming from everywhere," Paula said, her mother shaking her head next to her.

Brian covered his mouth. "They screamed? I kind of hoped they just disappeared peacefully."

Jane straightened her back. "Oh no. It was a horrible cry of pain. I'll never shake that noise from my brain. Imagine dozens of people screaming bloody murder all at once. It was as if they saw the devil himself before they went."

Winter pointed to Paula. "You said you went up to see them? Were you downstairs?"

"Yeah, the cafeteria was in the basement."

"What's a basement?"

Corey again translated. "It's underground, if that's what you're getting at."

Winter looked up at him. "You see. Everyone alive was underground."

"I never considered it, but now that you say it, everyone who lived was with us on the bottom floor," Paula said. She and her mother stared at each other from the revelation.

Brian ran his hand over his mouth. "Yeah, but that made sense with just us. We were in a bunker, and you lived in a large bunker yourself, but these two were in a basement. That feels more open. I'll bet millions of people were below ground level. I don't think a million people survived."

Winter shrugged. "Maybe we don't understand it fully, but when I do electricity experiments, I learn something new each time, until a clearer picture arises. There is a trend, no?"

No one said anything, all deep in thought.

"Let's move on. How have you survived this long? How many people have you killed?"

Jane shook her head. "None. First time I ever shot the damn gun was at you guys."

Her daughter sat up. "After the hospital, everyone left kind of freaked out, panicked and took off. We fled back here. Our house is down the road. We wanted to watch the news, see what was going on."

Jane finished her thought, the two feeding off each other. "Of course, it took us two days to get here and by that time, there was no more news, no more television at all. There probably wasn't the second everyone disappeared. The hospital is in the city, so the roads were clogged with cars, most of them smashed into each other, or into buildings, street signs, whatever."

Remembering the details brought an antsy energy to the two women. Paula's toes tapped against the thick carpet. "We ran halfway home. It was insane. We aren't exactly athletes. When we reached the 205, we stole a car, figured at that point it was okay. The 205 has wide lanes and the cars had all veered off road, so it was smooth from that point on. Benefits of living in the country."

Jane chewed on the skin around her fingernail. "We holed up in our house for two days, just waiting for something to change, scared shitless. Nothing changed. None of our neighbors came home from work. We knew this was it. The end of the world."

"Eventually, we raided the houses, found some guns, stole their food. We've been living off that this entire time, trying to balance our resources. We've been too scared to raid the markets. We read a lot of books, so we know what the world would turn into if shit hit the fan. And we knew others survived at the hospital, so there more people out there somewhere. Scared people become killers."

Winter sighed. "People never needed an excuse to become killers."

Jane ignored him. "We decided we would defend this street, make it ours. Luckily, it's off the beaten path so no one has come here until you three. We worried everyone had turned to murder and mayhem. So, we said we would strike first if anyone turned onto this road. Kill or be killed. We don't have a ton of food left, and worried you'd take it all."

Corey waved his hand at her. "I understand."

Winter turned to him, eyes wide. "You understand? She shot your arm off."

"She was protecting her land."

"You fucking humans are crazy." He stood up, angry. "Give us a car to use, and we leave now."

Brian put his hand on Winter's shoulder, and Winter gripped it. "Why are you touching me?"

"Weren't your people trained day in and out to defend your land and kill anyone who entered?"

"They did not train us to kill each other, just you."

Corey and Brian spoke to each other through their eyes. Corey turned to Winter. "They should come with us." Then, to the women, "If you want."

The women didn't answer, but Winter did. "No. That is my motel, not yours. You are guests. You don't have permission to bring friends."

Paula cleared her throat as the tensions between the men grew. "It's okay. Me and my mom are happy here. We will get by."

Brian stepped back, speaking to everyone at once. "Why can't you all understand we will be stronger together? Right now, there are people out there gathering in forces, planning to kill everyone in sight to expand their own resources. We don't need to see that to know it's true. Eventually, one of those groups will find us, and they will kill us all, unless we develop our own group and prepare for it."

Winter touched Brian's shoulder now, giving him the best condescending smile he could muster. "I said no."

Corey jumped to Brian's aid. "Will you stop being so goddamn stubborn and think about this?" He put his hand out to the women. "How many weeks of food do you have left? How long will you live on your own? We have a motel. We have electricity. Winter knows how to grow crops. His children know how to fight and defend. We know how to hunt. Brian's a doctor, you're nurses, and Winter can fucking magically heal wounds. You'll have everything you need."

Winter jumped in. "Exactly. They will have everything they need. What will they provide? They didn't even defend their own home well. She should have shot you in the head, but she's no good at shooting."

Paula and Jane listened to all of this, not chiming in. For all Winter knew, they had already made up their minds and didn't want to join them anyway, but he needed to make it clear to Brian and Corey who was boss.

"They worked at a hospital. Do you know what those places are like? It's non-stop running around. I can guarantee these two are hard workers."

Paula opened her mouth, sighed, and rubbed her eyes. "We have something to offer."

Winter scoffed. "Oh great. Let's hear what the women offer. I can't wait."

Jane stared at her, yelling at her not to say anything with her clenched teeth.

Paula stood, raising her hands over her head to let Winter know she wasn't about to try anything funny. "Follow me. I have something to show you."

CHAPTER 55

Through the Bulkhead

Paula guided the group out of the house, onto the road and toward a house farther from where they had initially entered. Each step forward caused the rhythm of Winter's heart to thrum a beat faster. Brian and Corey showed wisdom by grabbing some mechanical lights called flashlights before taking the woman up on her offer to "show them something."

Winter kept his gun in hand, ready and willing to kill again.

Jane followed her daughter with her head down, grumbling. "This is foolish, Paula. You show them our secret, and they'll kill us for sure."

"Jesus, Mom. If they were going to kill us, they'd have done it already. I mean, for fuck's sake, they *already* killed you, and literally brought you back from the dead. How do we turn down teaming up with them? This one is a walking miracle."

Winter scratched his beard. "I would listen to your mother. I very much want to kill you both."

Brian clicked his tongue on the roof of his mouth. "Stop it, Winter."

Winter threw his hands up in surrender.

They marched up a lawn at the end of the road, leading to a

roughshod wooden house. Paula led them around the house, toward the backyard. Winter nodded to Brian and Corey. "Get your guns ready. This could be an ambush."

"I trust them," Brian said. Still, the two men put their guns at the ready.

Junk littered the lawn behind the house, as if the gods had rained scraps of wood and metal onto it.

Paula pointed to a set of slanted metal doors.

"We're going through the bulkhead?" Brian asked.

Winter noted another new word. Bulkhead.

Paula nodded and bent to open the door. Winter raised his gun, ready for an army to run out.

The bulkhead creaked open. The only army to rush from within was a billion dust motes swarming out into the flashlight beams.

Paula and Jane walked down the cement steps into a thick darkness, vanishing into the abyss. Corey and Brian rushed to keep a light on them, pouncing down the steps. Winter took the back, more than willing to see an ambush kill all his problems in a tiny war down below.

When he reached the bottom step, Brian and Corey stood facing forward, their lights aimed at a wall ahead, their mouths agape.

"Holy shit," Corey said.

"Yeah," Jane responded.

Winter examined the wall. Guns. Lots of them. All different shapes and sizes. He moved in front of the women, awed by the dusty display.

"Jake was always an alarmist but I never would have guessed his basement looked like this," Jane said.

"We found it a few days into our exploring the neighborhood," Paula added.

Brian moved along the wall, casting his light beam on the weapons. "This is insane. Was he going on a killing spree?"

Jane laughed. "Knowing Jake, it wouldn't surprise me."

"That's not all," Paula said and pointed toward a side wall. Brian and Corey both turned their lights toward it. Boxes sat on shelves, covered in a thick layer of dust.

"Grenades, homemade bombs, crazy shit. We're lucky he didn't blow up the neighborhood making some of that shit."

"What is a grenade?" Winter asked.

Brian opened a box and pulled out a blue ball. "Why don't we all go into the yard and show Winter what a grenade is?"

Corey chuckled, and the two women shot each other a nervous glance.

They marched into the yard, one-by-one, Brian leading, Winter taking the rear. When they entered the crisp night air, they lined up along the house.

Brian held the ball in his hands, and twisted his hands, checking it out. "Maybe this isn't a good idea. I've never actually used one of these before. I know how, thanks to movies, but..."

"But you might set the whole damn street on fire?" Jane finished his thought.

"Yeah, that."

Paula smiled. "The Cromleys have an empty swimming pool in their yard."

Winter didn't understand what was happening, but he followed the group toward another house. When they reached the backyard of this other home, they crowded around a large bathtub thing.

"Okay, does anyone know how big of a splash this thing makes?"

Everyone shook their heads.

"No one. Great. Well, let's all step back."

They all did, creating a big arch around one side of the tub, giving it a large berth. Brian held the blue ball high.

"Okay, so, Winter. When you use these, you hold this handle down, pull this ring out, and throw it far away."

"You sure about that?" Corey asked.

"That's how it works in the movies, right?" Brian's question seemed less than rhetorical.

Everyone nodded or shrugged.

"Well, that's reassuring." He sighed, clenched his teeth, and pressed down on the handle.

It took a few seconds before he put his other hand on the ring, and as he did, he squinted his eyes.

He pulled the ring out, and shouted, "Oh fuck." He tossed the blue ball as if it were going to bite his face off. The ball missed the bathtub thing, but it bounced off the cement around it and plopped in. A few seconds later, the ground shook under them, thunder crashed through the air, and a cloud of smoke poured from the tub.

Everyone laughed, the chuckles of people who just avoided death, and instead found victory. Winter clutched his chest, hoping the bangs against his rib would settle.

Corey gripped Winter's shoulder and shook him. "See? Everyone contributes and adds something to the team. Do you know how beneficial it will be to have that arsenal?"

Winter stared at the women. "Yes, but we could just kill them and take their weapons."

"Winter!" Brian shouted. "Stop it. Does everything end in death with you?"

Winter walked away. "Yes. Fine, they can come with us, but we must go. My daughters are alone."

"I don't think we should go either," Jane said. "We're doing perfectly well here."

Paula grabbed her mother's sleeve. "Mom, we'll be dead in six months and you know it. We need people. And they need us. There's so much we can show them. And sorry, but that fucking guy is magic, and I want to be on the same side as the magic person."

After a few minutes of huffing, the women pulled a bulky, rounded car up to the old house at the end of the road. An S-U-V the men had called it. As everyone worked to stockpile the car, Winter reconsidered his decision.

"More people means more mouths to feed. We can't take care of everyone."

Corey continued to shove long guns into the back. "More people means more resources to find food, to work on growing it. It means more people working."

Winter sighed. Adding two more humans to the mix meant outnumbering himself and his kids. This is why he didn't want to invite the men in. He was losing control, and with each move forward, the motel felt less like his own.

The group agreed not to take the homemade bombs, not wanting to explode to bits when the car hit a bump. They filled the back with dozens of guns, a box of grenades, bags of food, and that movie thingy Brian wanted.

They drove to the motel in silence, other than Brian giving directions.

"Put Miley Cyrus back on."

Corey threw his hands up. "Our new friends set the CD on fire, remember?"

Winter slapped his forehead. "You mean there isn't one in every car?"

Corey popped a compartment open in front of his seat, and he tossed some papers out. "Nope. This is a newer car so they probably listened to music from a streaming service."

"What is that?"

"It's something we'll never have again."

Winter punched the side door next to his seat in the back. "You mean to tell me these women killed Wrecking Ball forever?"

Corey and Brian chuckled. "Yeah."

"All the more reason I hate them."

They arrived back at the motel sometime deep into the night, the glowing disc high above their vehicle. Winter's heart skittered. A new car in the parking lot.

He jumped from the vehicle before it finished rolling into a spot, and he dashed to room 4. The door was locked, so he pounded his fist into it, panic building in his chest.

Violin and Candlestick dashed out of room 6 with Lion.

"What's happening?" He asked.

The door to the room he had knocked on opened. A man stood on the threshold with a confused stare on his face.

"Dad, don't freak out."

A baby cried from within the room.

CHAPTER 56

Passing the Torch

The humans sat at two tables set up in the kitchen. Unlike the rest of the group, Brian and Corey remained relaxed, used to Winter's dramatics. Sheila rocked her baby against her chest, eyes darting, feet tapping. Jane and Paula sat forward with their heads resting on their palms.

They all stared at Winter, who paced back and forth, brushing his hands through his hair. Violin read the upset in his features and worried about an incoming explosion. He had lost control of the motel, outnumbered by humans, and it likely fueled a rage inside him.

How could he act mad toward Violin for letting more humans in when he brought two new ones back with him?

He could, and he would.

"This is all too much. I can't take care of all of you. Some of you must go."

Brian stuck his tongue for Violin to see, but only when Winter wasn't looking in his direction. "Winter, settle down."

"I will not." He whispered and yelled at once.

Violin leaned against the back wall and touched Candlestick's hand. Winter had kept his voice down for the baby, despite his anger, and to Violin, that meant he cared.

"This is my motel, and I know how to create a world we can survive in, but I also know when we have reached a tipping point. I can't support a baby."

"Winter, we can't send a couple with a newborn out into the cold. The weather will warm soon, but that baby will die in the meantime." Corey chewed his nail, maybe a little worried about Winter after all.

Violin leaned forward, as if to say something, but thought better of it. Candlestick rubbed Violin's arm and gave her a little scoot forward.

"Dad, may I speak to you?"

He turned to her, surprised. "What is it?"

"Do you trust me?"

The room quieted. One human shifted in their chair, creating a scraping sound on the hard tiled floor.

"Yes, I trust you."

"Good, and I trust them, and I say they stay. You will be in charge of me, and I will oversee them."

He tilted his head. "I know you want to do what's best, but if we are going to survive, we need to focus on us, not them. We can't take care of them."

"Who says you need to take care of us? There's one baby, but the rest of us are adults." Jane crossed her arms around her midsection.

Winter turned to the group. "You are humans. If you could take care of yourself, why is your world a disaster?"

Paula stood up. "Excuse me, but where's your world?"

Winter ran toward her, fury in his eyes. "You don't talk about my world."

Brian stepped between them. "Winter, she doesn't know what happened to you and your people. But we all had families, too, loved ones. We miss people. We cry. But, like you, we all had one thing to keep us going. You have your kids. Paula has her mother. Jane, her daughter. I have Corey, and Corey has me. Those two have a baby, a hope for a future. We all have reason to fight."

Winter scoffed. "Hope? Hope is a snake disguised as a tree branch. You try to hang on to that."

"I believe in them, Dad. They will work hard for us. Except Sheila, because she needs to focus on her baby. But Frank will work hard. He's a bit of a dummy, but he means well."

Frank threw his hands up. "I'm right here."

Violin waved her hand at him. "See. He says obvious things like that all the time." She turned to him. "Hello Frank. We all know you are right there."

Sheila chuckled.

Jane shook her head. "If I may be frank... Wait, before there is any 'who's on first' type comedy sketch building here, frank means blunt. If I may be blunt, Winter, you're the only one fracturing the group right now. The rest of us are ready to work together and make this work. Even your daughters are smart enough to understand strength in numbers. But not a one of us isn't considering leaving, hesitant to stay here, and that's solely because of you."

Winter frowned. "Then, please, leave."

"No!" Violin yelled. Sheila shielded the baby, hoping it wouldn't wake from the shouting.

"They aren't leaving and I'm not having this argument every day. Let's move on. Stop trying to hold us back, Dad. We aren't the same people who came out of the tunnel. Okay? That's not us anymore. You can cling to our family all you want, but they are dead, and so are their ideas. They were wrong. You were wrong. We were wrong. But you don't have to stay that way."

She pushed past her father and stood in front of the group. "I will assign you a bedroom, families together, so we don't have to waste too much electricity on heating the whole place. Tomorrow, meet here for breakfast. I will give each of you a series of jobs that you must complete. I know I am a child to most of you, but my family raised me in a very different world from you. I know how to survive, and how to make a community function. If you can't handle taking orders from a kid, then my father is correct. You should leave. If you listen and work hard, you may find you have a new family."

She spun around, facing her father. "That all goes for you as well, Dad."

Violin stormed toward Candlestick, grabbed her hand, and headed for the door. "Now, everyone get to bed. We have a busy day tomorrow."

She slammed the door on the way out. Winter turned to the group, put his hands on his hips, and sighed. "You heard the girl."

He stormed out after her.

CHAPTER 57

When Plans Fail

Violin waited by the bedroom door. Candlestick sat on the bed, scrubbing Lion's fur. As soon as Winter entered, Violin put her index finger to her mouth. Winter nodded, understanding.

She came to him and whispered, "I meant what I said in there, but you have to know I am always on your side. I just need them to think they have me as a teammate. In case you end up correct, and we can't trust some of them. I will weaken them with false trust." She put her finger to her temple.

A smile crawled up Winter's face. "Very good."

"You said you guys brought back a bunch of weapons?"

He nodded.

"Then, we need to steal some of them from the car tonight while everyone sleeps and keep them hidden from the group. Somewhere only we know."

Winter nodded, and it sent a warm hurricane through her stomach. He was proud of her, happy to see she didn't trust blindly. Violin worried for future fights with her father when he saw how much faith she would put in the humans.

They sat on the bed, waiting. Candlestick cuddled with Lion,

Violin escaped into her mind, thinking of her next plans, and Winter admired his daughters, their growing strength, intelligence, and commitment to a better world than he could foresee.

"While we wait, I'll tell you a story."

KEVIN BACON RETURNED to the woods with Dance following behind. When he arrived, NNNNOOOO, and a host of new folks unfurled the circle they had been hovering in, opening for their leader. Abraham Lincoln towered over the group. He cheered at the sight of Mr. Bacon.

"Thank you all for coming," Kevin Bacon said. "Did you kill the raccoon?"

Abraham shook his head. "Sorry, Mr. Bacon. Our dad took him away.

Kevin Bacon sighed. "Oh well. One of you said you had questions?"

"That was me, ya see." A small man stepped forward. He had a beard, and flower petals for hair. "I just don't like violence, ya see."

Kevin threw his hands up in defeat. "Well, this is a war. Not sure how you'll be able to help if you don't contribute to the violence."

The small man cracked his knuckles, bent low, plucked a few blades of grass, and held up his wares. "Grass, ya see?"

"Uh, huh," Kevin Bacon responded.

The man twisted his hands around, sticking out his tongue as he worked. When he finished, he held up his work. He'd strung the grass into a giant ball. "Not grass no more, got it?"

Kevin Bacon clapped, trying to placate the man, but unimpressed.

"Now, it's a grenade." The small man launched the ball into the air, where it exploded, sending a plume of dirty grey smoke back to earth in a cloud.

Everyone clapped now.

"Okay, that was awesome, but isn't that violence?"

The man shrugged. "Yeah, but I won't be throwing them, ya see? You will. I'm just a tinkerer, got it?"

"That's wonderful. I'm fine with that. Are the rest of you okay with violence? On my way here, I sent you my entire story with these gods with my mind. Did you all receive it?"

Everyone nodded, other than two women leaning against a tree outside the circle. Kevin noticed them and pushed NNNNOOOO and a slender pink woman out of the way to get a better view. "What about you two? Why aren't you joining us?"

The two women leaned backward against the tree, each with one foot planted against the trunk. They wore all black and their eyes were covered with dark glasses. One woman had short, spiky hair, and the other, long brown strands dripping over her shoulders.

The one with the short, spiky hair spoke first. "Not really into the group thing."

"Does that mean you won't join us in war?" Kevin Bacon asked.

The other one crossed her arms. "No, we're down for fighting, just not holding hands and singing each other's praises."

Kevin closed his eyes for a moment. "What're your names?"

"I'm Laura Jane Grace and this is my pal, Miley Cyrus."

"Do you have powers like the rest of us?"

The two women looked at each other and smiled. Miley put her hand out, and Laura Jane Grace leapt up, using Miley's hand as a launchpad. Her feet hit the tree trunk and she ran through the air, her body sideways, as her feet darted from one tree trunk to another. Miley screamed, belting out a song that sent the rest of the group to their knees. Some of them cried while others folded into the fetal position. As Laura Jane Grace ran in circles, she broke tree branches from each oak, and threw them until they stuck into the ground.

After a moment, the two women stopped and reverted to their relaxed stance at the tree. The rest of the group wiped tears and stood up in surprise. The tree branches Laura had thrown caged them in.

Laura Jane Grace smiled at the befuddled faces behind the cage. She sang a few bars, increasing the volume in her voice a little more with each word, until the sticks shattered like glass.

The group, freed from their prison, whistled and clapped.

Once the group stopped their cheering, a solo clap continued. Everyone looked around for where it came from.

Oleron stepped out from behind a tree. "Wonderful performance, my daughters."

Kevin drew two discs from his hands. The rest of the group readied to pounce.

"One of you, a million of you, it doesn't matter. You can't compete with gods. Why not go home and call it a day?"

Kevin spun the discs, powering them up. "For Saria, and every other human you've killed, we will not cede."

Orelon puckered his lips. "How cute. I think many of you will do just that. Ask yourself a question. Why did we stop playing cat and mouse with you over this motley crew? Why did we give up on killing them all before you could reach them?"

"Don't know. Don't care. Maybe you grew a small heart and decided killing wasn't so nice."

Orelon looked up, rage in his eyes. "Oh no, I, very much, still love to kill. In fact, while you were all playing friends in the woods, I was out killing many people." A horrid smile crept up his cheeks.

"What are you talking about?" Kevin Bacon asked.

"Your wives. Your mothers. Your sisters and children. You abandoned them for a fool's errand, and they suffered for it."

Members of the group broke off, stepped backwards. A few ran away at the first words.

"And suffer they did. Long periods of screaming and begging."

"No," Abraham Lincoln fell backwards, causing a mini quake as his butt crashed into the dirt. He stood and ran. "No!" He shouted as his giant frame disappeared in the distance.

Kevin Bacon stared in disbelief. He turned to find only Dance at his side.

She held his hand. "We're the only ones with nothing left for them to hurt."

"That's not true." He pointed to the empty spaces where his crew had just stood. "We had a lot to lose, and we lost them."

Dance wiped a tear from his cheek. "What do we do now?"

Mr. Bacon tossed his discs at Orelon. "We kill him."

Candlestick hopped off the bed. "Finally, we get to the fighting."

Winter glanced out the window. "We can't get the guns. We need keys to open it. They'll know if we break in another way." Behind him, something jingled.

He turned, where Violin held a set of keys in her hand. "I stole them from Jane's bag in the lunchroom. After we unpack some guns, we can toss the keys in the slush in the back somewhere. She'll just assume she dropped them."

Candlestick scrunched her forehead. "But won't they notice the missing weapons anyway?"

Winter scuffled her hair. "Not when you see how many are in there. No one was counting."

He opened the door, and the girls followed him out into the night. They crept around the SUV, walking in slow, steady steps. As they turned to the back of the car, Winter fell at the sight of Jane leaning against the back door.

She lit a cigarette and took a deep inhale. No one said anything. After the smoke left her lungs, she held her hand out. Winter grabbed the keys from Violin and slammed them into the woman's palm.

"See you all nice and early," she said.

CHAPTER 58

Someone is Watching

In the morning, everyone gathered for breakfast, which Corey helped Violin prepare. Oatmeal for all. Violin assigned the humans jobs, but gave Sheila a pass, telling her to take care of the baby and to consider a name for the girl.

"Where I came from, we didn't have names until we were five, when we selected our own. You should give your daughter a name and let her decide if she would like to change it later."

Sheila smiled and agreed, but admitted she struggled to come up with one.

Violin assigned her father to his seeds. "It's about time we planted. The weather is warming. I know it's still cold at night, but I think the seeds will do fine, especially the sister seeds."

Violin and Candlestick spent the day monitoring everyone else, walking through the motel and ensuring everyone kept up on their duties. She put Frank in charge of cleaning, a job he took to heart. She handed him a broom, but after, he showed her the uses of various chemicals in the motel storage room, and how those chemicals cleaned different things. "Sanitization," he chanted.

Because she trusted Brian and Corey the most, she gave them a few weapons and sent them hunting for food. She knew Brian was an excellent shot, and the humans all ate meat, so she wanted them to have what they needed.

Paula played security guard with the cameras, and Jane did laundry. It turned out humans had machines for washing and drying. Miraculous, Violin thought, but also a waste of electricity. Instead, she had Jane hang the clothes up after washing on a line she placed between the motel generator and a tree.

After she set everyone up in their proper places, she brought her sister to visit Winter. They found him hammering wood on the outskirts of the parking lot, near a vast patch of dirt he had already tilled. "What are you doing? I told you to plant seeds, not build things."

Winter wiped his hands on his pants. "It's not like down there. The animals up here will devour our crops. I have to build a barricade."

"Oh." Violin had a lot to learn.

"The sisters will grow well here, good fire disc light. If I can grow them down below with no natural light, I can make them flourish on Earth. We just gotta keep the damn parasites and little Earth creatures away." He pulled his upper lip up, revealing his front teeth, making skittering sounds like a small Earth animal.

Candlestick laughed.

"Why don't you both help me nail some of these boards together, and I will tell you more about the war with Kevin Bacon?"

Abraham Lincoln crashed through the town and climbed the mountain toward his home.

"No," he said as he crossed the land leading to his house. Chunks of ice sprayed all along the lawn. He dipped low, scooping some of it up, feeling it in his hand.

The door crashed open with the power of his foot.

"No."

He fell to the floor, enormous balls of ice flowing from his eyes.

His wife and children, shattered to pieces, spread throughout the cabin.

He slammed his fists into the walls. "Why did I leave you? What was I thinking?"

"I can answer that."

Abraham turned, looked all over. "Who said that? Show yourself."

"I'm not ready for that yet."

"Show yourself so I can squeeze the life out of you. You did this to my family."

The voice laughed. "You think *I* did this? No. Those evil gods did it. I am going to help you kill them."

"Who are you?"

"Let's just say I've got skin in the game."

Abraham kicked the front wall so hard it separated from the rest of the cabin, crashing down on the ground, leaving him exposed to the dewy morning air. "Just leave me to mourn."

"As you wish."

Abraham fell to the floor, lying in a pile of ice chunks. His family. He gripped pieces of them until they melted in his palm, and he wept until his eyes turned black.

The fire disc fell from the sky and the glowing eye of Orelon rose. Abraham never left the floor, never stopped hugging the wet wood, the melted remains of his family.

The trees around the mountain side rustled. Abraham stood up, startled by the sound.

A group of humans made their way forward, brushing past the surrounding shrubbery.

Abraham's eyes narrowed. "How did you get up here?"

One man stepped forward. "We had a little help from a mutual friend."

"Well, you picked the wrong day to start a fight." Abraham made a fist and charged, ready to rip the men to shreds.

All the men raised their arms in defense. "Wait," one said. "Wait, we came here to help."

Abraham stopped dead and unclenched his fists. "Help? What do you mean? You plan to bring my family back to life?"

The man shook his head, nervous. "No, sir. That I can't do. But we saw the gods who did this and we know their evil intents. We want to help you destroy them."

Confusion set in. "But you are my enemies. Why would you help me?"

The men looked at each other, just as confused as Abraham was. "We are your enemies? I did not realize, sir. We were afraid of you, but also thankful. We wanted to tell you many times, but you never spoke to us, always avoided us, and we worried you preferred it that way, that if we tried talking to you, it would sour your favor."

"But some of you tried to climb up here."

"A few, yes. Thom, for one. He always insisted on bringing you bread. Never made it to the top, though. Died trying about two weeks ago."

Another man stepped forward. "We always liked your family, sir. Horrible thing that happened. Those gods terrified us. We know we ain't much in the way of fighting gods, but we will do whatever it takes."

Abraham raised his face to the sky, where Orelon's eye hovered over him. "I fear I have no fight left in me, friends. It was my fight with the gods that brought death to my family. I wouldn't wish that on you and yours."

"If it's all the same sir, maybe you remember the great flood, the fires from the forest, or even the strange winds that killed 37 of our people. The gods have already killed us and will continue to do so unless we destroy them."

Abraham pulled on his beard. "Who is this mutual friend you say we have?"

"Am I free to come out now?" The strange voice returned.

"I suppose so." Abraham looked around, waiting for the voice to appear.

The group of men sundered and a snake broke through the ranks. Abraham laughed.

"It's nice to meet you," the snake said. He stretched his tail forward and placed it in Abraham's hand. Abraham stared at it, holding it in his palm, unsure how to proceed.

"Shake," the snake said.

"Ah." Abraham shook his tail.

The snake made himself into a straight line and still only reached Abraham Lincoln's midsection. Mr. Lincoln dropped to his knees, so the two met face-to-face.

"I'm sorry we're meeting under such unfortunate circumstances, but I must tell you, these circumstances seem to flourish under the weight of the gods. I, too, know the pain of loss, the wiping out of everything I ever loved."

Abraham twisted his head toward his house, the spirits of memory replaying the joys of life. His wife laughing in the bedroom, his children playing on the roof.

"I have something to help you in your quest for revenge. A weapon."

The snake slid back to the men, bit down on a small box, and brought it to Abraham Lincoln. "Do you know what a gun is?"

Abraham lifted the small box, comically tiny in his giant palm. "Of course, I do. Unfortunately, I don't believe a gun can hurt the gods."

He opened the box to reveal a shiny silver gun, too small for him to squeeze the trigger.

"No, a gun won't kill them at all, but the bullet in that gun will. I made it special with ingredients that will evaporate a god."

Abraham brought the gun to his face, squinting. "What ingredients would that be?"

"Proprietary, I'm afraid. There's more bad news."

Mr. Lincoln sighed. "Of course, there is. Spill it."

"Only one bullet. Still, that bullet will eliminate a third of your problems."

"But I can't shoot it."

The snake smiled. "No, you must deliver it to your friend, Mr. Bacon. For you, I have a different present." He nodded toward the side of the cabin.

Abraham turned to see a giant axe. It shined purple and blue. "Does this kill gods, too?"

"It sure can. No propriety ingredients in that one, but it's still special, and can surely kill a god if wielded by the right hands."

"My hands."

"Any hands with enough revenge pumping through their veins."

Abraham smiled, walked to the axe, and lifted it over his shoulder. "This will do just fine. What is your name, kind fellow?"

The snake slid around, heading back toward the group of humans. "The name is Dolphi. Make sure you take these humans with you. They will be the deciding factor in your victory."

"Dolphi's back!" Candlestick said.

Violin touched her father's arm as he explored the blisters formed on his palm from a hard day's work. "Was this story your way of saying you see the value in the humans?"

He shrugged.

"But the humans are helping and Dolphi said they will help win the war."

"Yes, but what is their motive? They only agreed to help because they found something to fear bigger than Abraham."

"No, they said they never wanted to hurt Abraham."

Winter stood, his knees cracking. "Yes, that is what they said. And I bet they believe it themselves."

Brian and Corey came through a clearing in the woods, guns draped on their shoulders.

"Did you find anything?" Violin asked.

Brian shook his head. "Sorry, it was like all the animals disappeared."

Corey bent to examine Winter's work. "We are dangerously close to running into a food problem. I mean, we'll be good for weeks, but our supplies are depleting fast."

"Well, I am growing the three sisters. With the weather turning, we should have corn, beans, and squash in no time."

Corey turned to Brian with worried eyes.

"What is it?" Violin asked.

"There's something else." Corey said.

Winter dropped his hammer and wiped sweat from his forehead. "What is it?"

"We saw footprints around the perimeter. Looks like someone spent a lot of time circling this area." Corey put his head down.

Brian finished his thought. "Like they are watching us."

"How many prints?" Violin put her arm around her sister and scanned the surrounding woods, which felt closer, denser.

"Can't tell, but more than one."

Winter stepped back from the fencing he'd been working on. Violin grabbed his hand.

"Gather the group. All of them. Sheila too," Violin said. "It's time for my father's approach. It's time to show our might."

CHAPTER 59

Not One of Us

Violin lined everyone behind the SUV. Sheila rocked her baby a little too fast, Brian and Corey fidgeted with their shirts, and Frank breathed heavily.

"We have to stop being so cavalier. I am happy we opened our doors to you all, and thankful to have you as a part of our family, but that doesn't mean we can expect the same results from every human we meet. I want Paula, Corey, and my father on the roof during the nights, watching the surrounding area. During the day, Frank, Brian, and my sister. If you see someone in those woods, shoot them dead."

Brian stepped forward. "Whoa. Don't you think we should just scare them off or question them? They deserve a chance, don't they?"

"They lost their chance when they spied on us. Sheila and Frank came right in. You and Corey called out for us. Why are they being so sneaky?"

Jane lit a cigarette. "I'm with the girl. We try playing nice and we end up dead."

Frank closed his eyes and pinched the bridge of his nose. "I can't believe I'm saying this, but I also agree with her." He turned to

Brian. "You can ask my wife. I'm a peaceful guy. I don't like to cause trouble, but I have a baby to protect now. I don't want to take any chances."

All eyes rolled toward Winter. He listed his head. "Don't look at me. I still think we should kill all of you."

Everyone laughed, including Winter. Violin couldn't believe they reached a point where Winter could joke with the humans.

The group took turns bringing weapons to the roof and stocking the rest safely in bedrooms

while Violin and Candlestick stocked cans of food in the kitchen.

Winter came in. "Is that from the SUV?"

The girls nodded. Winter pulled a chair out and sat in it. "I want you both to know I am very proud of you. I know I can be a pain in the ass, but it's because I love you so much and I want to protect you. You girls have done a wonderful job here. I am starting to believe in this place."

"And the people?" Violin asked.

Winter put his head down. "Yes, and the people, a little. I'm not there yet, but I am getting there."

Violin put the cans down and walked to him. "Then I am proud of you, too."

They hugged. After they separated, Winter smiled and raised his hands, pretending to spin something in them. "Kevin Bacon spun his discs."

The girls sat down for a story.

Orelon laughed. As the two discs flew from Kevin's fists, they disintegrated into a dust mote explosion.

"I toyed with you long enough," Orelon said as he charged.

His shoulder slammed into Kevin Bacon's torso, knocking him flat on his back. Dance reached for Orelon, but with a sideswipe, his fist crashed into her temple, taking her down too.

A moan left Kevin Bacon's mouth as the breath reentered his

lungs. He leaned up in time to feel Orelon's boot in his temple, and down again he went.

The two rolled on the forest floor, struggling for the upper hand. Kevin Bacon leveraged his feet against Orelon's stomach and kicked him off. The fight had just begun and, already, he struggled to catch his wind.

Orelon balled his fists. Two poofs popped on the dirt path and his sisters appeared, bringing a twister of dust around them.

"No. Leave. Don't take this from me. They are mine to kill."

"Enough Orelon. It's no longer a game; it needs to end."

Azerka floated toward Dance as the girl stood up. Beelza, with absurd speed, flew into Kevin Bacon, smashing him into a tree. A sharp pain shot up his spine, into his brain, and his body crumbled onto a pile of leaves and twigs.

Before he could right himself, Beelza sat atop him and smashed her fists into his face. Blood splashed into his eyes.

"No. This is my war," Orelon said.

"No, this is your death," something shouted. The ground shook as something bounded across the clearing. A snap and a crack. Kevin wiped the blood from his eyes, and as Beelza continued to punch his face, he saw NNNNOOOO ripping into Orelon, shaking his god body in her mouth.

The pain had ceased. Beelza caused so much of it, it reached a tipping point where it felt like nothing.

NNNNOOOO tossed Orelon into the sky and turned her rage toward Kevin Bacon. "And you? You who can see it all. You knew what they'd do. First my brother, and now they killed my friends. You knew this would happen and still you came to me? Couldn't leave me at peace?"

Kevin talked through the punches, barely getting his words out in more than a whisper. "You don't understand. Seeing everything is the same as seeing nothing." He spit out a tooth and turned his face upward, so Beelza's fists met him head on. "There is infinity to see. You can't know what they'll do."

Beelza smiled as she crashed her knuckles into his cheeks, cracking bone, turning his face to mush. "Now you understand, do you? The sight of the gods is a myth. It's the same as human sight. Worthless."

A gorgeous noise broke through the forest. The birds flew from the trees and the gods froze in place. Orelon dropped to his knees, tears forming in his eyes.

Miley Cyrus and Laura Jane Grace appeared through the shrubbery, knives in their hands, singing memories into the heads of every living creature around them. Laura Jane Grace ripped a branch from a tree and launched it. It drove through the air like a bullet and slipped into Orelon's chest. Meanwhile, Miley dug her knife into Beelza's skull.

Azerka stood up, leaving Dance's bloody heap of a body. "Enough! Orelon, Beelza. Get up now."

Orelon took the branch from his chest and Beelza plucked the knife out of her temple.

Every eye in the forest opened in surprise. The weight of their decision to fight gods hit them, panic pushing them back, stealing their gusto.

"Enough yourself, bitch, ya see?" The man with the flower head turned a corner with a group of Kevin Bacon's other brothers and sisters.

Together, they charged.

Kevin Bacon turned his head toward Dance's lifeless body. He couldn't move, could hardly breathe. He managed to put his hand to his side, closer to his friend. "Dance, I need you to hear me."

Around them, bodies flew, crashed into trees, stepped over them. Blood and gore and violence surrounded them.

"Dance," he said again.

Her head dropped to the side, eyes opening through puffy lids. She breathed with a gurgle, blood in her lungs.

"Dance. You're not one of us."

"What?" she managed.

"You're not one of our siblings. Orelon isn't your father."

"What?" she repeated.

"Your magic is all your own. Let it work."

Blood dripped from her mouth. "In six months."

"Huh?"

"In six months... You'll see my crops growing..."

Kevin Bacon laughed, and it made her laugh, and they both hurt from the laughing. His ribs ached; his face burned. The pain came back. She reached her hand out to her side, and their fingers touched.

"Your magic is bigger than the crops. Tap into it. You own the entire forest."

She shook her head, bringing it a centimeter to each side. "I can't. I can't breathe."

Azerka appeared in view, grabbed Dance by the ankle, and launched her into the sky. Kevin Bacon cried as Dance flew away, where she would surely die on the ride.

"Yikes! Dad!" Violin said.

Winter stared off toward a thin sheath of clouds. "Life is not always pleasant, my dear. You know this better than others."

Candlestick held her dad's hand. "You just have to tell the rest of it. I'll bet it gets better. It always does."

"Sometimes. But sometimes not. As for our friend, we will see. For now, the night disc is rising and we must get ready for our first shift as guardians. Candlestick, get a good night's rest. Our people are trusting you to watch the place during the day."

"Our people?" Violin asked.

Winter waved her away as he walked out of the room. Violin noticed the bend in his back, the slight sliding of his foot as he walked without bending his knees.

"Candlestick, can you put yourself to bed tonight? Maybe cuddle in with Lion. I want to help Dad on watch."

"Violin?"

"Yeah?" She kept her eyes on the door her father just exited.

"Thanks for trusting me to be a guard. I know how important you think that job is."

Violin grabbed her sister and squeezed. "I trust you more than anyone in the world."

"How come you didn't make yourself a guard? It's like your dream."

"You've very astute, aren't you? Because we live in a community now. It can't be about what I want."

Violin said goodnight to her sister and Candlestick ran off to her bedroom. The darkness moved in fast, attacking like a hungry animal.

Violin climbed to the roof where her father, Paula, and Corey camped out, debating over guns.

Paula had two cylinders wrapped around her neck.

"What are those?" Violin asked.

Paula lifted them, giving slack to the cord around her neck. "They're binoculars. You guys really aren't from Earth, are you?"

Violin nodded. "What do they do?"

Paula lifted them over her head and handed them to Violin. "Look through here."

Violin did, to reveal two green, blurry circles.

Paula put her hand on Violin's chin. "Lift."

Violin looked up and through the circles saw the woods as if she were standing in them, but the entire world was green. "Whoa. That's awesome."

"They're night vision, so you can see in the dark."

Violin panned through the forest, noticing the swaying branches, moving animals, all of it. "This is like magic."

A group of animals like Lion dashed through the shrubbery. It reminded her to keep her sister indoors at night. She knew her sister could talk to them, but the last time they surrounded her, Candlestick froze and called for Violin, not adept with her new skills.

Trees. Wind pushing branches.

A Human.

Violin fell back. Her words caught in her throat and she dropped the binoculars.

"Shit," she said as she picked them up.

"What's wrong?" Her father must have noticed the fear in her voice.

She looked again, through the binoculars, but the human was gone. She knew she had seen him, a person creeping through the woods. Fuck. Where did he go? She craned her head back and forth, not quite remembering where she had been aiming.

A human shape crossed between two trees and disappeared out of view.

She yanked the binoculars from her face. "Human."

She pointed. "That way."

CHAPTER 60

Chasing Ghosts

Corey jumped from the roof to the fencing around the generator. Within seconds, he had made his way into the forest, his feet crunching against the slush and slash.

"Fool!" Winter said. "Why would he rush in?"

Violin watched Corey's shadow disappear behind the thick oaks. "I don't know, but we have to protect him."

Winter put his hand on her shoulder. "You stay here. Paula, go to the left of his position, and I'll go right, but stay behind. Keep a distance."

They both hopped down and moved into the woods with their guns at the ready. Violin shook her head. "I thought I was in charge?"

Her stomach turned and she paced, staring off into the woods, waiting for them to return to safety.

BOOM!

A single gunshot, followed by yelling. Violin jumped down and ran into the woods, practicing her stealth, armed with a small handgun.

She found Corey before Paula and her father, and worried why she hadn't crossed them first. "What happened?"

Corey pointed deeper into the forest, toward a lush swath of greenery. "Someone ran that way. Winter shot at him and chased him, but I lost them."

"Just one?"

"That's all I saw."

"Shit. Come on. If my dad is alone, we have to find him before he gets attacked. It might be a setup."

They ran through the forest, sticks and thorny branches ripping at their pants and legs. The deeper they ran, the darker the forest grew, as if the woods were drowning them in brush.

Violin stopped, panting, and Corey took the cue to catch his breath as well. She couldn't see the motel, or much of anything. "If we keep going, we're gonna get lost."

Corey craned his neck. "We might already be."

"Should I call for my father? I can't abandon him, but if I yell, we might get ambushed."

Brush rustled behind them, fierce sounds, something running right for them. Violin lifted her gun, pinched the trigger, getting ready to pull, but not until she knew the approaching runner wasn't her dad.

It wasn't, but it also wasn't a threat. Paula darted toward them, her long dirty blonde hair bouncing with her body. Thankful for Paula's distinguishable hair, Violin lowered her weapon.

"Where's Winter?" She coughed and bent over, hands on knees, heaving.

"We don't know. He chased someone after calling Corey a fool for running in without a plan, then he goes and does the same."

"He called me a fool?"

Violin rolled her eyes. "You were. Don't blame yourself. It's what men do."

"What's the play here?" Paula asked.

"I don't know. We have to find my father." She marched forward, unsure if she was making a smart choice. Maybe she led herself and her friends into danger, but her father came first. She had to save him.

Corey and Paula followed, away from the motel, away from

safety, away from their loved ones. They pressed on for what seemed an eternity, finding nothing.

"Shit," Violin said.

Everyone stopped.

"We are so fucking stupid." She ran past them, back toward the motel.

"What are you doing?" Corey asked.

"What happened?" Paula asked.

As she ran, her heart galloping in her lungs, she explained. "We all just left the motel unguarded. Our families are sleeping unprotected."

"Oh fuck," Corey said. "How fucking stupid are we?"

Violin's legs burned from the intense running and the brambles tearing at her flesh, but she pressed forward, running with all her might. She didn't even know if she ran in the right direction, but she forced herself to keep moving.

When they reached the clearing into the back lot, Winter sat in the middle of the cement on his knees, staring toward the kitchen door, which was open, a light shining on her father.

"Dad?" She ran to him, hugging him.

"Why did you leave?"

She pulled away. "What?"

He pointed toward the kitchen door. "They took everything. The food. It's all gone."

Her eyes widened. "Candlestick."

She ran to the other side of the motel, slammed open the door, and clicked the lights on.

Candlestick slept in the bed with Lion next to her. As Violin's pulse settled, she stared at the dog. "What kind of guard dog are you? You didn't alert everyone when people stole all our food?"

He licked the fur on his back.

Winter walked up behind her. "I already checked on her. Did you not think I would do that when I returned to find no one guarding the place?"

Violin turned to him. Corey and Paula rounded the corner, coming to check on Brian and Jane. "Don't put this on me," Violin shouted. Candlestick shifted in her bed as the bedroom door swung closed.

"You blamed Corey for running in without a plan, and then you did the same thing. Worse, you fired a gun and disappeared. I thought someone shot you. I didn't know what was happening. What was I supposed to do? You're my father. I will always want to protect you. And yes, I want to protect them, too, but when a situation is happening so fast, I have to react without thinking it through. This is your fault for putting me in that position."

She stormed back to the kitchen. Whoever stole from them had toppled the shelves, and they'd taken every piece of food: the cans, the bags, the bottles. All of it. Luckily, the weapons were in the bedrooms with Brian, Jane, and Candlestick. Even more lucky, their families went unharmed.

Winter, Corey, and Paula entered the kitchen, seeing the emptiness. Violin cried, letting out all her frustration and anxiety with a hailstorm of tears.

Winter put his arm around her. "I'm sorry I yelled at you. You're right. This is all my fault."

Corey shook his head, "And mine."

Paula bit back tears of her own. "I should have come back when I lost everyone in the woods. Sometimes I forget you're just a kid."

Violin screamed, an energy explosion evacuating her lungs. Everyone leaned back, startled by the sound. She picked up a chair and flung it across the room, almost hitting Corey on accident.

And then, calm.

"If my screams didn't do it already, wake everyone up."

She sat down at the table. The group stared.

"Now."

CHAPTER 61

Pull, Tug, Snap

Brian, Jane, and Candlestick came into the kitchen, puffy eyed and slouched, but nervous about why their loved ones had woken them. Their faces turned to hardened stone at the turned over kitchen when they finally noticed it.

"What happened?" Brian asked.

Winter slapped his own cheeks. "They outsmarted us. They stole all our food."

Violin stepped in front of her father. She swallowed hard, trying to eat away her nerves. She no longer felt like the powerful leader, but she didn't want to show that to the group. "We will take two cars and look for food stores. My father, Candlestick, and I will go with Frank and his family. Brian and Corey, you will go with Paula and Jane. Paula, you mentioned something about knowing where a food store is, correct?"

Paula nodded.

"Good. We split up the weapons in each car. We leave nothing here."

"I don't understand. Are we abandoning the motel?" Brian asked.

Violin stepped forward. "No. But there could be threats out there and we will be stronger together."

"Shouldn't we leave a few people here in case someone tries to take the motel?"

She puffed her chest, figuring if she made herself appear authoritative to the group, she might even convince herself she was still worthy of it. "No. We don't want to leave anyone vulnerable. If they take the motel, we will come back together in force and we will kill them."

No one seemed thrilled about the plan, but no one argued either. Paula and Brian loaded the SUV and Frank's car with weapons. The depressed mood traveled through the motel like a thickening fog, but the realistic possibility someone could open fire on them at any second also made everyone twitchy and temperamental. Even Brian and Corey snapped at each other over trivial matters. At one point, they bickered over how to stuff the weapons in the trunk.

They piled into the cars and Frank pulled out of the parking lot, Brian driving the SUV in front of them. Violin stared out the back window, watching the motel shrink until it was out of view. An invisible string tied to the motel traveled to her heart, and the distance between them caused the string the pull, then tug, then snap.

Would she lose a third home?

Winter pulled her into him and put his other hand on Candlestick's. "We must get back to our story."

DANCE FLEW, launched by a god, so high the trees turned to thimbles. As her body sailed downward, her stomach lunged into her throat. This was it. The end. She closed her eyes, unable to watch the Earth charging toward her broken body.

She stopped falling, landing softly on something. Impossible, she thought, as she pried her eyes open. A gasp escaped her as she realized where she stood. In front of her, a large, bearded face.

"Caught you," Abraham Lincoln said.

"They're winning," was all she could muster.

Abraham placed her down and slid the tiny box to her. "Not for much longer. Give this to Mr. Bacon."

Dance tried to stand, but her knees failed to sustain her weight. She crumbled to the floor, nothing more than a pile of nuts and bolts with nothing to attach themselves to. "I can't."

Abraham lifted her and once again, she flopped to the Earth. His brow furrowed, and he tried again. But once more, she crumbled. "You must get up now."

She turned her head toward the forest and wept, but as she cried, she noticed a shaking branch on an arrow wood shrub. Blood dripped from her mouth as she smiled. Her hand flopped to her side, and she wiggled her fingers. "Come to me."

The shrub responded with more wiggles, and its neighbors and friends shook too. A wave of activity moved through the forest swell. The branches grew, slithering along the slash and dirt, an army of tendrils coming to Dance. Abraham Lincoln covered his mouth. "By golly, I think something special lives in you, my lady."

"Just go fight. I will meet you there."

"I feel I should wait for you."

The tendrils wrapped themselves around Dance's limbs, and they squeezed so tightly, they melded with her flesh. No pain came as the plants ripped into her skin. Just the opposite, an intense sense of healing, rejuvenation, life, coursed through her veins as she and the forest became one.

She stood and spat the last remnants of blood from her mouth, picked up Abraham's box, and stared at the hulking giant. "Let's go. Now."

"My mother told me to never argue with a tree. Although, I must admit, the sight of you makes me starving."

The two laughed as they marched into battle.

VIOLIN PAID attention to the story, but her mind kept trying to travel away, back to the motel, wondering if it would still be theirs by the time morning broke. The glow disc hovered above the tree line, still working its way up. Their night had been long and she couldn't believe it hadn't even reached its mid-point yet.

"So, is Dance like a tree now?" Candlestick asked.

"Not a tree, a person and the Earth, all rolled into one."

"Well, keep going," she said.

Shiela cradled her baby in her arms. "Frank, go slower. It's not like we have a car seat."

Frank nodded. "Sorry, just nervous, and I need to keep up with them. Winter, can you continue your story? I don't know what the hell is going on in it, but I find it very calming."

Winter giggled. "I don't think this next part will calm you."

KEVIN BACON LAY LIFELESS, covered in blood, dirt, and leaves. Around him, the sounds of war raged. With blurry vision, he witnessed his friends and family falling and screaming, but occasionally, the sounds of pained gods gave him hope.

Azerka mounted him, her knees digging into his ribs. "Your friends are dying. This war is over. I will kill you now, taking the head of this beast from its body. Without you, they will flail and falter."

She smashed her fists into his face, breaking his cheek bones.

"Kevin Bacon!" A voice, a female voice. Dance. She had lived, and with that notion, Kevin Bacon's spirit grew so large it nearly burst from his chest. He changed then, a power he knew he had but didn't understand. His looks, body structure, and features all changed. He turned into himself, only younger, whole, unbroken. Then, he turned into Orelon. His body morphed into a dozen different humans. Each time he turned, the pain of a million stabs tore into his muscles, tendons, and flesh, but each time, his bones healed, his open wounds closed shut. Azerka, unphased, continued pummeling his face. With each heal, she broke his face anew.

He turned his head to see a new version of Dance, one remade in the forest's image. She lashed thin branches from her arms and thwapped Beelza across the face. As she fought, she turned to Kevin, smiled, and slid a box in his direction.

The forest floor shook as Abraham Lincoln returned, rage in his eyes and a giant axe in his hands. "Kevin Bacon! My brother! Open the box and kill the gods!"

Kevin stretched his arm and his fingers finagled with the box, trying to open it. Azerka noticed his attempt and pulled his arm away.

Around him, the motions of war slowed down, allowing Kevin to see the beads of sweat, blood, and dust traveling through the air. Pieces of tree bark, sticks, the guts of the woods, speckled the world. Azerka's punching outpaced Kevin's ability to transform and her force broke through his body and into his soul, as if her strength plucked the magic from his bloodstream. He was dying. Kevin Bacon was dying.

Next to him, a lifeless lump skid across the ground. The flower-headed man. Dead.

NNNNOOOO screamed in pain, the kind that said she would not survive it. The last scream of life.

Kevin reached a little further, using the last bits of might in his limbs. His fingers skimmed the box. Not enough. He turned his head again, but unlike last time, Dance wasn't there. Instead, she was out of view, probably dying again.

Laura Jane Grace appeared in the distance, fighting with Orelon. She held two sharp sticks in her hands. As she prepared to throw one, she glanced in Kevin Bacon's direction and did a double take at the sight of him.

She threw her arm sideways and released one of her sticks. It sailed across the dirt until it hit the box, pushing it into Kevin Bacon's palm.

Azerka punched Kevin Bacon's ribs to smithereens and the bony shards cut into his lungs. He gurgled blood as he opened the box and felt for the contents. Recognition washed over him as his finger wrapped around the trigger.

He laughed.

"Good. Let laughter be your last sound on this Earth," Azerka said.

Kevin lifted his arm, put the barrel to the god's head, and pulled the trigger.

The blast sent his ears ringing and the violence hushed around him. Azerka stood, shocked. She touched the gaping hole in the side of her skull and examined the blood on her fingers. Every cell in her body separated and a cloud of tiny beads swarmed until the wind pushed each dot further apart. Azerka dissipated, her body nothing more than ash blowing in the breeze.

One.

God.

Dead.

THE SUV PULLED into a parking lot. A giant food store loomed in front of them, completely dark. The lot itself was shrouded in darkness, only illuminated by the faint shimmer of the glow disc. Frank pulled in next to the SUV at the far end of the parking lot, away from the building. The group gathered at the backs of the cars. Winter took over the leadership role, and for the first time in a while, Violin welcomed it.

"Everyone, grab two guns. A long weapon, and one you can tuck into your pants. Brian, Corey, and I will move toward the front doors. Paula and Jane stay far to the left, guns ready to protect us. Frank, you take the right, doing the same thing. Sheila, Violin, and Candlestick, you stay at the car, but you should also arm yourselves. Just in case. If guns start firing, Sheila, drive my children away from here."

Violin almost argued, but her self-doubt got the better of her and thought it might be best if she stayed out of the way.

As Paula popped the trunk on the SUV, footsteps clunked behind them.

"I'm going to have to ask you all to step away from those vehicles, nice and slow."

The group turned in unison to see a lanky man in clean blue clothes smiling at them. He had his arms crossed, but the fifteen or so men and women behind him had their hands on large guns, aimed at Violin's new family.

CHAPTER 62

Strength in Numbers

Violin's ears rang. She didn't know what caused it. No one had made a loud noise, nothing hit her in the ears. They just rang at such absurd volumes; she couldn't hear anything around her.

The man in blue shouted while the people with guns surrounded Violin's family and friends. They pushed the group forward by butting the muzzles on their weapons against Brian and Winter's back. The man in blue pointed to the building, shouting repeatedly. Violin heard nothing but understood. "Go."

She pushed herself in front of her father and sister. Everyone had their hands raised by their heads, so Violin followed suit. It would offer a better view for her father to see the message she needed to send.

She tapped on the side of her head. "When the door opens, turn and fight."

But as she finished tapping the last words, her father gripped her wrist and nodded. "No."

Violin's hands shook. She clenched her teeth. Instead of tapping, she slapped her palms against her temples. Hopefully, the message was obvious.

When they reached the supermarket, one gunman swerved in front of the group and pushed the doors apart. When one door shifted away, the other moved in the opposite direction. It would have awed Violin, if not for her increasing rage.

She expected an offensive odor inside the market, a warning she'd received from Brian, Corey, and her father, but the store sent an aroma so wonderful it made her mouth salivate. She couldn't place most of it. Cooked meat she recognized from Corey's time in the kitchen, but the rest was a pleasurable mix of newness.

When Winter was unconscious at the motel, Brian had taught Violin the basics of fishing for food. One day, he spent hours teaching different knot types. The strongest, he said, was the Palomar knot. She never learned how to make it. No matter how hard she tried, she couldn't get the proper force on the string to tighten it. But now, a Palomar grew in her belly the closer her group moved toward the back of the store with an army of gunmen behind them. It squeezed her stomach with a combination of anxiety and dread.

The man in blue swung around the group and pushed open a set of double doors with a sign on them that read, "Employees Only."

To Violin's surprise, about twenty more people moved about in this back room. Most of them appeared unbothered by the events unfolding in front of them. They continued sitting and talking to one another, eating, hanging out. One man stood in front of a black oven thing, fire shooting through a grate onto some kind of food. Whatever it was, the smell broke the Palomar knot free from Violin's belly and replaced it with an insatiable hunger. She envisioned shooting the room clean of humans, ripping the brown discs from the fire, and devouring them.

The ringing still played in her ears, but it diminished, and she heard the cacophony of voices around her. Joking. Laughing.

Maybe it was stupid to ask the aggressors a question, but she had to know. "How do you have so many people?"

The man in blue laughed. "This? This is just the night crew. Now, everyone sit."

He signaled to some of the other men and women in the room, and they jumped from their current tasks, grabbing chairs wherever they could find them and sliding them into position for the group to sit in one long line.

"Now, I'm real sorry for the overly aggressive introduction, but that's the way we have to do things in this new world." He spoke with an accent Violin hadn't noticed before. Humans all spoke differently from one another, some even had different words unused by others. This man's accent stuck out to her even more than normal.

"Hopefully, from this point forward, we can all be friends. Does that sound good to you?"

No one in the group said anything, but Frank nodded in agreement. His baby woke up and cried. Sheila brought the child to her breast and popped her nipple out. The baby went for dinner, and the man in blue watched in a way that made Violin squirm.

"I'll take that as a yes." He paused and waved the gunmen away. They scattered, keeping their weapons in hand, but their posture loosened, and they intermingled with the others, forgetting their targets.

"Jake and Mariana, why don't you both go back on watch?" Two of the gunmen nodded and left the room.

"Billy?"

The man cooking food glanced up, and the man in blue gave him a signal, twirling his hand in a loop before bringing it in front of Violin's group.

"I'm assuming you all came to this market for food, and I can give you some as a parting gift. In fact, my friend Billy over there is gonna bring you some tasty burgers right now. Just like how you remember them from before the world went to shit."

He sat down on a table in front of the group, scooted his butt until he was comfortable, and then clapped his hands. "Now, I'm trying to be friendly, because friendly is what we do around here. But we also do war pretty dang well, when necessary, too." He smiled, his teeth revealing both charm and poison.

Violin balanced listening with learning, hearing his words as she scanned the environment, counting the enemies, planning exits, preparing to fight.

"As big of a group as we are, we try to keep this place a secret from outsiders. Now, don't get me wrong, we love to invite new people in, but we usually vet them first. Thing is, they don't know they're being vetted, and they certainly don't know about this here home base of ours. This is our little secret until we let you in. Now, y'all haven't been vetted, and y'all know about our little secret. That's a problem."

Winter cleared his throat, uncharacteristically subdued. "How do we resolve this problem?"

The man in blue showed those fiery teeth again. "That's gonna be wholly up to you. Look, we base out of a supermarket. I'm aware people are gonna show up here from time to time looking for food. Most of those folks come in packs of two or three, at the most. We can easily persuade them to turn the fuck around. Pardon my French. But you, well, you've come with an impressive sized crew. That scares me a little. But I also see a woman with a baby and two small children. Scared eyes." He sighed and scratched the hair above his ear.

"Yeah, I don't feel like y'all will be much trouble. The bad folks, the ones who enjoy the killing, they don't move around with babies and children. But, then again, desperation makes folks do some crazy things."

Violin realized the man was openly deciding if he would kill them, and while the rest of her group seemed content letting the scenario play out, she wanted to end it before he reached his conclusion.

Billy came around with plates and handed them off to each person. Bread covered the brown discs, and a small pile of potato chips surrounded it. Billy handed off plates, went back to the oven, grabbed more, and brought those until everyone had a plate full of food.

Frank and Jane went right to work on their food. Brian and Corey were a little slower to decide if they should, but eventually the hunger won them over. Winter placed his plate on his lap, not eating it, but not dismissing it either. Candlestick mimicked her father. Violin waited.

"See there. Right now, you are telling me a lot. You're hungry, but you ain't starving. You aren't savages. Some of you..." He pointed to Winter. "... are cautious. Nothing wrong with that."

He leaned forward. "Do me a favor, rip that burger right in half for me, and hand me whichever half you want."

Winter stared at him for a moment, then did as he asked. The man took the half burger and shoved it into his mouth. He exaggerated an exhale as he crewed and said, "Mmm, mmm."

After he swallowed, he unleashed the teeth again. "See, now, that is a tasty burger. Trust me, my friend, if I wanted to kill you, we'd kill ya with a bullet, not poison. I'm not sadistic. If I must kill, I like it to happen..." He snapped his fingers.

Winter put his head down and ate his burger. Candlestick, excited by her father's actions, took a huge bite from her own.

"You know that's meat, Dad?" Violin said as she put her plate on the floor by her side.

The man smiled. "Oh, we got veggie burgers too, if that's more your style?"

Winter waved the man's comment away and took another bite. Each chew, a betrayal to Violin.

"Here's what I'm thinking. We got an entire city's worth of folks with us, not all here at the market, but around. We got doctors and nurses, electricians and plumbers. We have teachers for the children, and just about everything else you can imagine. That's how we are functioning. Electricity is a powerful tool in the new world. We can freeze our food, heat our bodies. Whatever we need. We have farmers and butchers taking care of bringing in new, fresh supplies. It's a little utopia, all things considered. And we also have soldiers, warriors, strong folks.

"Now, looking at y'all, I think I see a lot of potential. Y'all look like you weren't doing so bad out there, and I'm gonna guess when you were about to open them trunks, you had some nice weapons, too. We could use folks like you around here, but we'd have to keep you under surveillance for a while, to make sure you ain't one of the troublemakers. We don't do so well with those. Ya see, we also got prisons and guards."

Violin opened her mouth to speak, but the man went on, nearly read her mind.

"Of course, none of y'all have to stay, if you were happier where you were. But I need to make sure that anyone who walks out that door knows it's not smart to come back here, no matter how much artillery you're packing."

He picked up a small green box and clicked a button. It came to life with a series of flashing red dots and a squawk. He held down another button and spoke into it. "Everyone, give me an update."

He put the machine down and held out his palm as if showing it off to everyone. After a few seconds, various voices came from the machine, speaking back to him.

"All clear on 9."

"We got some coyotes by 7."

"All Clear on 32."

He turned the machine off, interrupting the constant influx of fresh voices. "You get the point. I have eyes everywhere and guns up the wazoo. So, if you want to stay, you're more than welcome. If you want to leave, we will give you a nice parting gift of food, but you must never return here. Ever."

He stood up and came to Violin, bending down to look her in the eyes. "This little lady asked an excellent question. How did we get to have so many of us? The answer is kindness, but also a hell of a lot of searching. We have parties always protecting this place, but we also have groups who go out and keep vigilant for other humans. If we find some, we watch 'em for a while, see if they look like a good fit. Then, we invite them in. We've stretched as far as New Hampshire to the north and Virginia to the south. Strength in numbers. Ya understand? It's our philosophy. More doesn't spread us thin; it makes us durable, Teflon tough."

Frank raised his hand. The man snapped a finger at him. "Speak now, my friend, or forever hold your peace."

"We would like to stay. My wife and I." He pointed to Sheila, who still fed the baby.

"Us too." Jane said.

Paula shook her head. "What? No. I want to stay with them." She pointed at Winter.

"Are you crazy? We just had our home ransacked. This place is safe."

Paula and Jane continued to argue as a new rage boiled in Violin's blood. Cowards, all of them.

Frank turned to Winter. "I'm sorry. I hope you understand, but we have a baby, and this place is safe. They have doctors, people who can keep our daughter healthy."

Paula heard this and put a finger up to stop her mom from talking. She turned her attention to Frank. "But Winter can..."

Before she could finish, Winter put his hand over her mouth. "No. He doesn't know about that. No one does. And they wouldn't believe you if you told them."

The man stood up and waved to his group. "We are going to give y'all some space for a few and let you figure this out on your own."

The entire crew walked single file out of the room. Billy turned the over burners off and shut the lid. Silence.

Winter broke it. He placed his hand on Frank's knee. "I understand your decision, and I think it's the best one for your family."

"You can't be serious," Violin shouted. "Your baby wouldn't even be here if it weren't for me."

Sheila cried, still rocking her baby against her breast. She used her other arm to wipe tears from her cheeks. "I know, and I love you for that, but Frank's right. It's not about what we owe and to who, it's about making the best choice for our child."

Winter walked to Violin and put his arm around her. "They're right. You didn't help them deliver their baby so they would owe you something. And these people are opening their arms to help them now too. They need to do what's best for their child."

Violin pushed his arm off her shoulder. "What, do you want to stay here, too?"

"I'd be lying if I didn't say I'm considering it. I want what is best for you. You could be safe here. But I am also concerned about the place. It scares me a little. I would rather we put our destinies in our own hands."

"Amen," Brian said. "This place creeps me the fuck out. Besides, Corey and I decided a long time ago, we are sticking with Violin and Candlestick no matter what happens."

A piece of the growing mountain of rage crumbled. At least Brian and Corey understood the value of family.

The arguments continued for another ten minutes before the man in blue returned. "How's it going in here?"

Winter stood. "Thank you for your offer, but my daughters and I will be leaving. As will these two men." He pointed to Brian and Corey. "The rest would like to stay with you."

The man in blue gave a thumbs up. "Fair enough. Those staying can hang back here. Some of our crew will be in to introduce themselves and hopefully y'all make some quick friends. The rest of you, follow me."

As Brian, Corey, Winter, Violin and Candlestick followed the man toward the front doors, a thought came into Violin's head. What if this was a trick and they were going to kill them? They'd be afraid, wouldn't they? No matter how many guns and men they had, they'd worry Winter and the gang might return. A secret was out. No one wants that. She worried because she would do the same thing.

Panic set in. She moved to her father's side and tapped. "They're going to kill us."

CHAPTER 63

A Dead Light at the End of the World

Winter responded without tapping. "No. You're wrong. You've let my influence misguide you."

She held in a scream, but a small angsty grunt escaped her lungs. "You're a fool."

Winter's judgement served true, though. Instead of bullets and death, the market folks offered baskets filled with food, cleaning supplies, and other junk she didn't recognize.

"We don't need your shit. We have our own," Violin said.

Winter put his hand on her arm. "Violin, they are being kind."

The man in blue laughed. "I'll tell ya, I'm sad to see you go. That kind of scrap does well in the new world, and we sure would be better off with ya."

A woman ran down the aisle from the back room toward the group. She gave the man in blue a look, as if asking permission to make a statement. He nodded his approval.

The woman got on her knees and held out an object to Violin. A yellow box with a wire coming off it. In the middle of the wire, it split in two, extending toward two round circles. "This was mine when I was a kid. When everyone disappeared, I went to my parent's house to see if they were alive, but they weren't. I took a bunch of stuff with me and traveled for a while before finding these people. I don't know why I took this. I'd never need it, but it just meant something to me."

The woman wrapped the cord and pushed it forward toward Violin's hand. "I hope it can mean something to you, too. A girl your age might find comfort in it the way I did."

Violin wanted to smash it to bits, but her desire to get out of this place and head home superseded her hate, so she took it, and smiled. "Thanks."

They left the building, got into the car, and everyone took a big breath. Brian rubbed his eyes before starting the car.

"What is this thing she gave me?" Violin asked.

Corey turned from the passenger seat. "It's called a Walkman. Very old school. I'll be shocked if it still works. Anyway, you put those circles on your ears, and hit that big button and it will play music."

"Miley Cyrus?" Winter asked.

Corey put his hand out and Violin handed it to him. He pressed something and a small door opened. Corey slid a smaller box from the big one. The one inside was clear, with a brown strand running through it. "It says *Mix Tape Summer of 92*, so it won't have any Miley on it. Sorry."

He handed it back to Violin.

"Damn it," Winter said.

They drove out of the lot and onto the main road. "I have to say, I like their idea of searching for other humans," Brian said.

Winter nodded. "Me too. If I hadn't been so stubborn, who knows how much of a community we could have built."

"Don't be stupid. Most of the people we have run into were shooting at us," Violin said. She hated everyone for the moment. Even Brian and Corey, who had stuck by her side. They were humans and humans betrayed, just as Winter said they would. Their attachment to Violin was based solely on what they received from the transaction. *Oh, a nice motel with electricity? We will be friends. But wait, the motel is unsafe thanks to other humans. Sorry, see you later.*

Winter put his arms around his daughters. "Anyway, we should get back to our friend Kevin Bacon."

Corey turned again. "What about Kevin Bacon?"

"I demand you shut up and face forward," Winter said.

Violin wanted to shut Winter out, ignore his story, but she feared these tales were ending, and she knew she'd hate herself for missing the finale.

KEVIN BACON STARED at the clouds, the world covered in a sheath of red from the blood in his eyes. His fingers trembled against the stony earth. War raged around him and he needed to get back into the battle. Straining, he forced his cells to change, to transform him into a younger version of himself, one not so close to death.

He grunted and groaned, bit down hard, and pushed through the pain until a wave of relief washed over him, and his skin and body took on a new form. Without the strength to guide, Kevin's body took a form of its own choosing.

He stood and saw the surrounding horror. NNNNOOOO trembled in a pool of her own blood against a thick oak. Miley Cyrus and Laura Jane Grace clutched their ribs and labored for breath. Even the giant Abraham Lincoln oozed war from open wounds in his skull. Most of the other brothers and sisters were dead heaps melding with the dirt.

Dance clenched her vines into fists and turned to see her friend up and ready to fight, but she did a double take at the sight of him. "Kevin Bacon, what happened? You're a small child, a little girl."

Kevin Bacon glanced down at his tiny frame, the red dress, the white shoes, and knew exactly who he was. "I am Saria."

He swallowed hard, made a fist, and glared at the gods. "I am Saria. Revenge is mine."

He grew two discs and shot them toward Orelon and Beelza, who hadn't yet noticed their sister had died.

One disc blazed by Beelza's cheek, cutting into it. The other disc drove right into Orelon's chest. He shouted, a combination of anger and pain. Beelza ran toward Kevin Bacon, fists out, jaw clenched. Before she could reach him, Dance extended her viny arms and wrapped them around the god. Beelza struggled, fighting to release herself. The vines clenched, but they were no match for Beelza's power, and one by one, they snapped. Dance used her other arm and wrapped the god anew.

Kevin Bacon tossed disc after disc, slicing Beelza's face to mush. Orelon ran to her rescue, pulling at the vines.

A giant roar shook the earth, sending birds scattering and gravel bouncing. Everyone looked up in time to see Abraham Lincoln dropping his axe on Beelza. Orelon dodged in time, but the blade sliced Beelza in two.

Like her sister, her cells separated. Before fully falling apart, her eyes went wide, and her jaw dropped, a horrifying sight amidst the gashes and blood surrounding her facial features. Kevin Bacon smiled as the woman vanished into a cloud of dust motes.

"Just one left," he said as he turned to Orelon.

Orelon stood, wheezing. "So, you're a little girl now, Kevin? Fitting. And both of my sisters?"

"Dead," Kevin Bacon stepped forward.

Orelon laughed through his labored breathing. "For years, I slaved for those two, always toying with the idea of killing them and having this world as my plaything. Never took the shot, though."

He bowed. "So, thank you for doing the work for me. I suppose I can kill you all now and go nap for a century."

He stepped on NNNNOOOO's head and crushed it. It crackled as his foot ground it into the dirt.

As everyone charged him, he grabbed Dance and ripped her in half, tossing both sides in opposite directions.

"No!" Kevin Bacon shouted as he jumped and kicked Orelon in the face. As the god stumbled backwards, Laura Jane Grace dug two sticks through his back. They ripped out of his chest, pieces of gore and ribs dripping from their tips. Miley Cyrus bit into his cheek and tore off a hunk of flesh. The top half of Dance wrapped her vines around his throat.

Still, he laughed.

"You can hurt me all you like." The wounds in his face healed, and the sticks in his body pushed themselves out, dropping to the forest floor. Those wounds, too, healed.

"You can't hurt me. Whatever you did to my sisters to end their lives, I assure you won't work on me."

Abraham Lincoln swung his axe, chopping through trees, sending them colliding all around. Kevin Bacon and his team had to jump, roll, and maneuver around the collection of bouncing trunks. When the axe reached its destination, it cut Orelon across the torso, sending his top soaring away from his feet.

He landed upright in a pile of leaves and rolled his eyes. "Seriously, give it up guys. Your magic axe must have run out of juice."

His legs walked toward his upper body, and when they reach it, Orelon climbed up them and reattached himself.

"Now!" Abraham Lincoln shouted.

A crowd of humans charged through the forest armed with weapons ranging from knives to frying pans.

They piled on top of Orelon and cut into him, smashing him, ripping his limbs from his body. He screamed in pain. Each one of the humans shouted the name of a lost loved one.

"For Beth."

"For John."

"For Bob."

Kevin walked forward, patting Miley and Laura Jane Grace on the shoulders as they clutched their wounds and watched the unfolding events.

Abraham Lincoln bent down and whispered to Kevin Bacon, "The strongest weapon against the gods is revenge in your blood."

Orelon fought back, snapping humans in two, ripping them apart, tossing them through the air. But there were too many, and for every person he killed, ten more shredded his body.

Kevin moved through the crowd, easing men and women back, until he reached a nearly dead Orelon. They'd removed his skin, leaving him nothing more than a series of a blood red muscles, and those too had been separated from their bones.

He gasped and reached for Kevin Bacon at the sight of him.

Kevin Bacon grew a disc in his palm. "For Saria," he whispered as he sliced the disc through Orelon's neck.

He lifted the head for all to see and shouted, "For Saria."

Orelon's face wept and giggled at the same time.

"What do you laugh at now, you pathetic god?" Kevin Bacon asked.

Behind him, Orelon's body dissipated into dust.

Blood dripped from Orelon's mouth as he spoke. "In the beginning, twelve Gods watched the earth. They were malicious, horrifying monsters. Three Gods, two sisters and a brother, malicious themselves, watched in horror as the other nine descended into madness, creating humans for no other purpose than to torture them. The unspeakable acts committed by the nine made the other three blush with shame.

"So, the three planned on how to stop it. One night, while the nine slept, the two sisters snuck into their rooms, removed their hearts, and hid them where they could never be released." Orelon's head spun around in Kevin Bacon's hand, facing the ash cloud his body left floating in the air.

Within the mist, a series of white glowing chunks fluttered toward the sky.

"They hid the hearts of the nine inside their brother's belly."

Kevin dropped Orelon's head, and a snake slithered from behind a tree.

Abraham Lincoln bent low. "Dolphi?"

"Enough talking from you." Dolphi bit into Orelon's head.

"If you thought we were bad. Wait until you see what you just released. You do not know what you've done." Orelon shouted his warnings as Dolphi chewed on his face until it joined his body as a cloud of dust.

"What is happening?" Kevin Bacon asked.

Dolphi looked up at him and smiled. "You won. You killed the gods."

"Why do I feel like that's not the end of it?"

"It's not. You just unleashed the end of everything. The nine are free. Which you'll soon find out is wonderful news for me, and dreadful news for you."

The snake slid into the woods, leaving the group dumbfounded and terrified.

Laura Jane Grace punched Kevin Bacon in the face. "What did we just do?"

"I've seen all plausible scenarios and I've never heard of the nine before."

"What does that mean?"

"It means Orelon blocked them from existing. He hid them from existence."

Dance put her leafy hand on Kevin Bacon's arm. "Is this like what you did with the baby?"

"What baby?" Miley asked.

"It's exactly like that, but instead of creating something outside the realm of everything, they morphed everything, making it so the nine existed but didn't show up in the colorful blobs."

"The colorful what?" Laura Jane Grace asked.

"Imagine a room filled with brightly lit bulbs, hundreds of them, all so bright they could blind you. Now, imagine you put one somewhere in the middle that didn't turn on. Could you find it? Even though it was there, right out in the open, you'd never see it, because the surrounding lights were too bright. That's what I think happened here. They hid the nine from me. They knew I'd travel through the colorful blobs and they turned the lights off."

"What does any of this mean?" Miley pushed him.

"It means we're all going to die. Everyone is going to die. The world is ending. Now."

CHAPTER 64

They'll Be Okay

Brian parked down the road from the motel. They all exited the car and grabbed guns from the trunk.

Candlestick said, "Let's hurry and get back there. I want to make sure Lion is okay."

"We creep, and we check the perimeter before closing in. Then, we check all the rooms. Everyone understand?" Winter asked.

The group nodded. Violin stayed behind, uninterested in the action. Of course, she still wanted to protect her family, but the motel felt antiquated now, a weakness more than a strength. Something they clung to that no longer held value. Just like her family's old values, it failed to stand the test of time. If the bad guys wanted the motel, let them have it. Maybe her family was better at wandering.

When they reached the back of the motel, they walked as a group, those in the back (Violin and Candlestick), walking backwards to keep guns ready from all directions. Nothing moved in the woods and nothing showed signs of trespass.

When they cleared the back, they did the same in the front, checking each of the rooms. Candlestick grabbed Lion and Winter and Brian checked the woods by the front lot. Violin noticed her father giving some attention to the three sister seeds. A fragile little garden, ripe with opportunity for disappointment and destruction. Everything at the motel felt weak, ready to crumble, wall by wall.

The building cleared with no signs of intruders. Brian and Winter confirmed they saw no new footprints in the woods. Still, Violin doubted sleep would come for any of them for some time.

Brian and Corey left to get the car and Winter turned to his daughters. "Are you both okay?"

They stood in the parking lot in front of room 4, wisps of mist leaving their mouths as they spoke.

"I'm okay, Dad," Candlestick said.

"I'm not."

"What's bothering you, Violin?"

"You let the humans leave. You didn't even fight for them."

Winter threw his arms up. "What was I supposed to do, dear? Force them to live with us?"

"No. Fight for them. Remind them we were supposed to be a family. But this is what you wanted, anyway. You argued against them joining us in the first place, and you got your wish."

He reached a hand to her, and she pushed it away. "Violin, you know my opinion of the humans has changed. I wished they would stay too, but they were right to consider their families. They made the best choice for themselves. It wasn't against us. It made them sad to leave us, I'm sure. But they made the choice they had to make."

"I don't want to talk to you." She reached over and grabbed the motel keys clipped to his hips, and unlocked room four. After dropping the keys on the cement, she slammed the door.

She hopped on the bed and lay down, staring at the ceiling. After a minute, she took the circles from the Walkman and put them to her ears. Then she hit the button Corey showed her. She jolted upright as the noise penetrated her ears. Her father had discussed the music he heard with Corey and Brian, but she couldn't picture it, couldn't fathom the sounds he tried to describe.

It snuck into her soul, nearly paralyzing her. A combination of noises created a beautiful, haunting mixture of tones vibrating in her eardrums. A voice kicked in; a slow, melancholy feminine voice.

She found a dial and turned it, increasing the volume. Then, she sunk back into her pillows and allowed the fragments of memory and regret to form a stalactite in her throat.

Keeping her aunt's secret when she rendezvoused with a human.

Not saying goodbye to her mother.

Her family's coughing and pained moans.

Killing humans.

Allowing herself to love them, to care about people.

She turned the dial up louder until the music frazzled her brain, screaming sharp tones into her ears, and she cried.

Candlestick rubbed her dad's arm. "It's okay. She will be okay."

Winter huffed. "She is torn between a lot of teachers, all of them wrong. Myself included."

They stared at each other for a moment. "Why don't you take Lion around the lot and let him go to the bathroom?"

The dog wagged his tail and licked Winter's hand as he extended it to the animal.

Candlestick nodded.

"But you stay right in this lot. I want to see you the whole time."

Candlestick nodded again. She walked with the dog toward the front of the building and along the entrance of the lot. Winter walked to where he planted the seeds. He dug his hand into the dirt, away from where the plants would grow.

"Good dirt," he said to himself. He glanced up at the glow disc. "Good light."

He smiled. "They'll be good. They'll be okay."

Candlestick walked by and Lion stopped for a pee right near Winter's crops.

"Watch your urine, dog. That's our dinner."

Candlestick giggled and kept the dog moving. Winter stood tall and put his hands on his hips.

A few seconds later, Lion went crazy. His fur stood up, and he growled and yelped toward the woods.

Winter's eyes grew wide. "Get inside now."

He drew his gun, aiming it into the dark depths of forest.

Boom.

He dropped his weapon and placed his hands on the small hole going through his gut. Blood soaked his hands.

Candlestick screamed.

She ran to him as he fell to the ground. His head landed where he had planted the sister seeds.

Lion ran into the forest, chasing after the predators. Candlestick wrapped herself around her father and pressed her palm against his wound, trying to stop the blood, but it was too late. Winter knew this was it.

The trees shook and an incredible, violent screech filled the air.

"Get this fucking thing off me," a voice shouted. He came into the clearing, out from the woods, Lion ripping at his leg. Winter recognized him. It was the man who had kidnapped Winter and his daughters on the road.

As Lion dug his teeth into the man's flesh, the man tried to beat Lion away with the butt of his gun, but the animal proved resilient and steeled by the need for revenge.

"Good dog," Winter said as a red rivulet dripped from his lip to the soft earth. Another man broke through the clearing, and this one Winter didn't know. A fat man. Horrible eyes. Cold. Dead.

He kicked at Lion, trying to help his friend. "Where'd the fucking kid go? I knew that shit was up to something."

As he kicked at Lion, a giant claw came from behind a tree and sliced into the man's fat belly, ripping upward until his guts poured from his body. A lamppost stomped into view, crushing the rest of the fat man between its toes. It picked up the second man, Lion still attached to the guy's leg, and bit his head off. His body flopped to the forest floor, singeing from the molten heat dribbling out of the lamppost's face.

Candlestick continued to scream and the monsters went crazy, knocking down trees, slamming their fists, breaking the world in two.

Brian and Corey ran around the corner. "There's monsters at the car," Corey shouted.

Then they saw the blood, and Winter, and the monsters around in the woods. They froze. Candlestick craned her head toward them, gnashing her teeth. Fire in her eyes.

A monster screeched and charged toward them. Five more followed behind.

CHAPTER 65

The Mouse and the Wolf

Violin stared at the ceiling, the music on full blast, pounding into her brain. It hurt and she loved it. She saw the door opening from the corner of her eye, and sighed, not wanting to talk it out with her father yet. Annoyed by the disruption, she tossed the circles off her ears, and horror set in. Volatile sounds surrounded the room. Screaming, banging, monster growls.

None of that gripped her with terror as much as the face in her doorway. His red hair, sideways smile, strange uniform with badges.

"I've waited so long for this moment." He closed the door and leaned his back against it. "It's fucking insanity out there. Those monsters came back."

He laughed an insane cackle.

Violin shifted off the bed on the side away from him. Her heart slammed into her ribs, and her mouth turned to parchment.

"This was so not how I thought shit would go," he said. "Gotta give it to Chucky. He came up with the food plan. You know we didn't even steal it? We just stashed it by the river. I mean, we ate some things, but most of it is still there. We just needed you to think it was gone."

He rubbed his eyes and laughed again. "I just assumed you'd

send a few people out to get more. Then we'd have you separated and could kill whoever was left. Except you, of course. You were never gonna die. If Chucky had it his way, you'd have belonged to all of us. But fuck that. You're mine."

He leaned his head back now, too. Sighed. Tapped his fingers against the door like a man tasting heaven for the first time.

Violin stepped back, just a small step, almost unnoticeable. She placed her hand behind her back and rubbed her fingers down a floppy leaf on the ugly, potted plant. Tears built in her eyes, and a dizzy spell came over her. She reminded herself to breathe.

"When you all left together, I thought we fucked it up. I figured we lost you again." He smiled, showing his square, beady teeth. "Not that I would ever give up on you. Even so, it would have been a pain in the ass to find you again. Then you came back! And there were less of you. I waited a bit to see if the others were just coming back late, but nope. You lost them out there, didn't you? My plan was to kill Chucky and that other fucking weirdo so I could have you all to myself, but luckily, those monsters did it for me."

He stretched his smile further.

Violin pushed her hand into the soil under the plant. Her heart steadied with her breathing but her fingers continued to tremble.

He clicked the bolt lock. "Now, it's just us. No one is coming in and you aren't going out."

She laughed, a hard, loud, mocking laugh. It was for show, but she knew it would work. The terror stayed rooted deep in her bones but she refused to show it to him.

"What are you laughing at?" He stopped smiling.

"Imagine a mouse bragging that he locked himself in a room with a wolf." She plucked a knife from within the soil and in one swoop of her arm, the blade left her hand and soared through the air, landing in the boy's upper arm.

She realized her fatal mistake and ran while the boy hollered in pain and worked to pull the blade from his arm. Yes, she'd hurt him, but she'd just gifted him a weapon. Not that he didn't already have a gun tucked into his pants, but now she left herself unarmed.

As she ran toward the television, he grabbed her, wrapping his bloody arm around her neck and pulling her into him. "Where are you going?"

He threw her onto the bed and lunged. Her chest tightened, as if her ribs were caving in, trying to embrace her spine. She fought for breath.

He pinned her arms against the mattress, holding the knife in one hand. It pressed into her flesh as he tightened his grip on her forearm.

She squirmed, but he outweighed her. His beady teeth reflected both sick pleasure and crazy rage.

"I love you," he said.

The words traveled into her head and shook her brain. As the words drove through her veins, it poisoned her heart, sent acid into her gut, and prickled her skin. What kind of monster could use those words?

She freed a leg from the weight of his knee, and drove it up, kicking him square in the groin. He winced and groaned but held his grip. She kicked repeatedly, smashing her knee into him. He flopped over and she rolled with him. Even after he covered his area with his hands, she continued to slam her knee into it, unrelenting. Every ounce of rage in her body found an outlet through her blows. It felt so good to hurt him. She couldn't stop. Kick after kick, taking weight from her shoulders. She growled, snarled, fierce moans.

He pushed her off and she fell to the floor, snapping her back to reality. Even after all those kicks, he forced himself up, grabbed her by the hair and crashed her face into the television.

Her ears rang again and blood gushed from her forehead. It took a few seconds to regain her understanding of the world around her, as if the head crashing sent her reeling to another planet. Unfortunately, seconds were all it took for him to do it again. Adrenaline coursed through her, the boiling rage returning, fighting against the intense pain. Her fingers slid to the drawer under where the television once sat. She slid it open and fumbled for the gun she had stashed in it.

Bang. Another blow. Skull meeting wall.

She found the weapon, bent her arm backwards, and pulled the trigger.

The pressure on her hair loosened.

She turned, nearly falling over. She wiped the blood from her face and saw the boy falling to the floor with a hole in his gut. His mouth opened, and she regretted not hearing his pained cries, but her ears rang too intensely for her to hear anything.

She needed to check on her family, but her confused mind only allowed to focus on one thing.

Kill.

She grabbed the knife the boy had dropped on the bed and fell on top of him. He clutched his stomach where his blood soaked through his clothes. She stabbed his chest, dug the knife out, and stabbed again. Same place. Why not? On the third stab, she went for the neck. The fourth, his face. After that, she lost focus and just let the knife land wherever it wanted, over and over.

She watched his mouth stretch and his Adam's apple bounce, and she nearly cried, longing to hear his pain.

But the fucking ringing.

Still, she stabbed. Blood squirt all over the room, her face, her clothes. She wore it proudly. With one hand, she wiped it on her face like it was cleansing bath water.

And she stabbed and stabbed and stabbed. His neck and head turned to mush, unrecognizable. His nostrils twitched, the last breath leaving his body.

When all the energy left her body, she took one last stab to his eye and fell over, lying next to his corpse. She lay there, staring at the ceiling, imagining the music still playing in her ears, catching her breath.

The real world howled back into her brain like a tremendous wind, knocking sense into her limbs. She jolted up.

"Candlestick. Dad."

She struggled to stand, almost toppling over as soon as she hit her feet. After a deep breath, and a little help from the bed's edge, she righted herself and stumbled to the door. Before she opened it, she reconsidered, stepped back, and picked up her gun.

On her way out, she fired into the boy's face.

The door opened, cold wind blasting into Violin's face. The horror outside was incomprehensible. Blood and gore soaked the trees. Monsters ran around the lot, screaming with rage. Candlestick lay on top of Winter, screaming with the monsters. Dozens of Husks lined the lot, wailing, flailing their arms at nothing. A pool of blood trailed away from Winter's body, branched rivulets draining into the cement lot.

"Candlestick?"

She fell over, landing on her knees.

"Candlestick?"

CHAPTER 66

Last Words

Violin ran to Candlestick, but as she moved, the lampposts leaned forward and growled, hot liquid dribbling from their toothy maws. She paused. Her sister clutched their father, screaming, crying, wailing.

"Candlestick."

Candlestick ignored her or couldn't hear her over her own bellows.

Violin stepped forward, hands out as if to say, "I mean you no harm."

The lampposts didn't care. They snarled and stepped toward her. The husks were mimicking Candlestick's screams, causing a chorus of painful howls, like a forceful wind blasting through a thick wood.

Violin wiped more blood from her forehead, streaking it across her shirt sleeve. "I don't have time for this game. Get out of my way."

She stepped forward and the monsters matched her, moving closer, blocking her from her family.

It was her turn to scream, one of frustration and rage. It did nothing to sway the lampposts, but Candlestick finally looked up.

"Make them move," Violin said to her sister.

Candlestick stood and ran to Violin. "He's dying," she shouted on the way.

They latched hands and Candlestick guided her through the monsters.

Winter lay on the cold dirt, blood pouring from his stomach. He clutched the wound with his pale fingers. His lips shook and his breath left him in shaky, raspy gasps.

Violin dropped to her knees. Candlestick bawled.

"Dad. What happened?"

He moved his hand to her arm in a slow, trembling motion. "They shot me."

His mouth opened wide, and he brushed his hand across the crusted blood on her chin. "What happened to you? Oh no, my poor girl."

"I'm fine. Look at me. I'm strong. You don't need to worry about me. Worry about you. Hold your wound tight."

He looked at her, but it didn't feel that way. It was as if he stared beyond her to something in the sky.

The monsters dashed around the lot, smashing into things, screeching, howling. The husks did the same. A frenzy of confused emotions.

Violin grabbed her sister's head, pressing tightly above the ears. "I need you to hear me. Focus and make them leave. Make the monsters leave. Where did Brian and Corey go?"

"The monsters attacked them."

Violin closed her eyes. She hated Corey and Brian right now, hated all humans, but she also needed them. "Focus. Close your eyes. Make the monsters leave."

Candlestick closed her eyes. Tears trekked down her cheeks and she squeezed her lips shut tight. She mumbled something and Violin almost asked her what it was, but realized her sister was speaking to the monsters, not her. Something new washed over Candlestick. Power.

The monsters roared, all of them, the lampposts and the husks, and then they stormed off.

Candlestick opened her eyes and smiled for a brief second before clicking back to the horror in front of her, her dying father.

Violin brushed her hand through Candlestick's hair. "I need you to hurry and find Corey and Brian. Bring them back here. Please, go."

Candlestick stood, and with her new confidence and power, her appearance changed. Older, wiser, stronger.

"You look so beautiful right now," Violin said.

Candlestick ran toward the front of the building, across the road, and into the woods.

BRIAN DASHED THROUGH THE WOODS. He had lost Corey as they ran from the creatures. Fuck.

"Corey!" he shouted.

The rumbling of giant feet flanked him. His heart blasted in his chest. He worried about Winter. He worried about Corey.

Then, the monsters stopped. Their foot pounding ended as if they vanished into thin air. He should keep quiet, but strategy failed him to the fear of loss.

"Corey!"

He fell to his knees. "Please, God. Bring me Corey."

A light wind shook the surrounding branches.

"Please God."

CANDLESTICK RAN into the woods where Corey and Brian had gone and tripped down a ravine into a cold branch of the river. The water was low here, barely skimming past the rocks within it. She still soaked herself in the low stream, and the coldness shocked her.

Fear wormed into her brain, eating away at her newfound confidence, eroding her strength. She scanned the world around her, dark, bleak, thick with foliage.

She was so small.

❄

"DAD, HOLD MY HAND."

Winter listened and Violin clutched.

"Breathe deep."

His eyelids drooped. "Oh, honey. I will not survive this one."

She shook her head. "I know, but I need to keep trying. Will you let me keep trying?"

She fought back the wave of tears building behind her eyes, not wanting to cry in front of him.

"Of course. I need to talk to you before I go, though. I need you to listen."

She gripped his hand a little tighter and tapped. Pinky, long tap.

"Your mom," He groaned. "She said something to me once while she slept."

He coughed and a spattering of blood shot from his mouth. "She tossed and turned, and with her eyes still closed, she grabbed me and said, 'Let her see the world. Tell her to find out what happened.'"

Violin furrowed her brow. "Dad, please just rest. This isn't making sense."

He shook his head. "It didn't make sense to me, either. But it does now. You need to find out what happened to the humans."

"What? Why? Why does that matter? Please, Dad, just stop talking and take deep breaths."

He tapped on her hand. "Just listen."

Then he spoke. "It matters. It's everything. It's your destiny."

"No. My destiny is not tied to humanity. I want nothing more to do with them. They abandoned us. They shot you."

He shook his head frantically, as if this point were the most pressing in the world. "No. You're wrong. I was wrong. Brian and Corey are our beacon. They haven't abandoned us. They are proof we were wrong. Your mother was always right. We need the humans and the humans need us."

"No. Dad. No."

358

BRIAN SQUEEZED his hands together in supplication and gasped in frustration. Some shrubbery to his side rustled and he stood up, raising a fist.

Corey came through the other side, winded, eyes wide in terror and relief. "Oh, thank God," he said as he ran to Brian. They hugged and kissed, squeezing tight, and letting the world melt away for a moment.

"I love you so much," Brian said.

"I love you, too. Where the fuck are we?"

They laughed.

"I don't know, but we need to find Winter."

"I know. Let's go."

CANDLESTICK DUG DEEP WITHIN HERSELF, huffing in a mouthful of air. "Be strong," she told herself and trekked forward, deeper into the woods.

VIOLIN HUGGED HER FATHER, laying down next to him, placing her head onto his shoulder. He stared straight up toward a series of thin branches that created an illusion of cracks in the glow disc.

"Now, it is my turn to tell you a story," Violin said.

Winter smiled. "Yes, please."

KEVIN BACON's team looked to him for answers, to which he had none. For the first time in his war with the gods, true terror infiltrated his psyche.

A strange color oozed through the sky, turning the once blue and purple dome into a deep blood red. Loud booms rocked the world, shaking everyone and everything. Somewhere far away, Kevin Bacon felt the entire village surrounding Abe Lincoln's mountain collapse to rubble.

"I need you all to hide. There's a place, untouched by the gods, barely visible within their omniscient sight. I will deliver directions to it to your mind."

Miley wrapped her arm around her sister and hugged her tight. Abraham Lincoln loaded the humans onto his shoulders. Dance cried.

"I will meet you all there shortly."

Dance stepped forward. "Where are you going?"

"Hopefully, to save us."

COREY AND BRIAN darted through thick shrubs, holding hands, unwilling to let go of one another again.

DARKNESS SURROUNDED CANDLESTICK, growing thicker with each step she took. Silence everywhere. She couldn't breathe. As she turned back, a new fear washed over her. She couldn't remember which way she had come from. She was lost.

VIOLIN'S HEAD shook as Winter's breathing quickened, deepened. He was struggling to cling to life. She needed to finish the story.

KEVIN BACON RAN with power and speed he didn't know he possessed. Time was running out.

BRIAN'S MUSCLES screamed for a break, needing to relax, but he pressed forward.

CANDLESTICK SHIVERED, crossing her arms and clutching her shoulders.

As VIOLIN FINISHED HER STORY, she pressed her pinky and thumb together and tapped against her father's arm three times. She repeated this over and over as she finished the story.

KEVIN BACON SEARCHED for the one person who could save them all, the only one who had the strength to defeat the gods.

BRIAN STUMBLED, causing Corey to stumble too, but they righted themselves and pushed forward, ignoring the pain coursing through their bodies.

CANDLESTICK LEANED against a tree and sunk to the ground. The bark of the trunk ripped into her back.

VIOLIN, pinky and thumb pressed together. Three taps. Three taps. Three taps. Winter smiled.

KEVIN BACON RAN AND YELLED…

BRIAN AND COREY ran and yelled…

CANDLESTICK RAN AND YELLED…

"WINTER!"

WINTER TOUCHED Violin's arm and tapped as the last breath left his body. Pinky and thumb pressed together. Three taps.

Also by Gage Greenwood

Short Stories:

Through Flickering Lights, A Silhouette

Grackles on the Feeder

Coming in 2023:

Winter's Legacy

Bunker Dogs

On a Clear Day, You Can See Block Island

About the Author

Gage Greenwood is a proud member of the Horror Writers Association and the Science Fiction and Fantasy Writers Association. He's the author of four hit serials on Kindle Vella, and the host of Gage Greenwood Writes on YouTube.

He's been an actor, comedian, podcaster, and even the Vice President of an escape room company. Since childhood, he's been a big fan of comic books, horror movies, and depressing music that fills him with existential dread.

He lives in New England with his girlfriend and son, and he spends his time writing, hiking, and decorating for various holidays.

facebook.com/gagegreenwoodauthor

twitter.com/gage_greenwood

instagram.com/gagegreenwood

amazon.com/author/gagegreenwood

tiktok.com/@gagegreenwoodauthor

youtube.com/gagegreenwoodwrites

Acknowledgments

First, I need to thank Becky and Nolan. They often had to test their patience, and lose their precious time so I could write this, but they never expressed anything but love and support. In fact, they pushed me forward when I was wallowing in self-doubt, urging me to write and publish.

My aunt Barbara, who always rooted for me and supported the making of this book in many ways.

My father, Gail, and Jenny, who read everything, liked, faved, cheered, and celebrated.

Jason, who did all of the above, but also spent hours talking me through survival techniques, and teaching me the basics needed for this story.

This book certainly wouldn't be possible without Callie Chase and Michael Lee from Book Genie. They've been mentors, tutors, helpers, and most importantly, friends.

Sophie Davis was always there to answer my barrage of daily questions. Without her, I'd be a fish flopping on land, asking strangers how to breathe.

Mary Danner, for making me look like a better writer than I am, and for showing no mercy to my many, many commas.

Cheryl Latos, for providing me with the time to write all of this by being the best grandma in the world, but also for reading it each week as it published in serial format, and always rooting me on.

Winter would never have opened the stone slab and seen the light of day without Jaxon Lee Rose. Her Dead Wolf Diaries led me to Kindle Vella, where Winter thrived and came to life. I'm forever in your debt, Jaxon, and I will always consider you a catalyst to my writing career.

My new writer family, a group of super talents artists anyone reading this should check out. Jae Mazer, Megan Stockton, Joshua MacMillan, and Peter Marsh. They came into my life after this book was written, but their inspiration and skill inspired me to press forward and get this published as its currently written. In other words, it would be a different story without them.

Luke Spooner, whose art compliments my writing in the best of ways.

To all the Gagents of Chaos out there, any of you who have supported me in whatever way you have. Without you this book wouldn't exist. This was never my story. It was always ours.

Which brings me to the original Gagents of Chaos, those who were always with me, who supported me and inspired me, who were there to celebrate any of my victories. Catie McGuinness, Emily Morash, Justine Manzano, Jason Danowski, Frank Ryan, and many more who I am currently not thinking of, but I love you all.

And all of the friends I've made in the BoH Facebook page. I've never met such an outstanding group of people, and I am thankful every day for finding that special place on the internet where acceptance and kindness are intrinsic, and a love for horror is a powerful force for goodness.